Born in Peru and rais... e author of eight novels, inclu... Fortune and *Portrait in Sepia*. She has also written a collection of stories, four memoirs and a trilogy of children's novels. Her books have been translated into thirty languages and have sold more than fifty-seven million copies. In 2004 she was inducted into the American Academy of Arts and Letters. Isabel Allende lives in California.

From the reviews of *Island Beneath the Sea*:

'*Island Beneath the Sea* is a seductive, intoxicating saga. It starts with slavery, forbidden relationships and rebellion in Haiti, and expands to include struggles over secret children, racial castes and family heirs in Louisiana. Isabel Allende's latest novel is sweeping, provocative and impossible to put down'
Lawrence Hill, author of *The Book of Negroes*

'A complex and involving saga of human passions and cruelties . . . Allende's message is that ideas and ideals – freedom, dignity, compassion – are as fundamental to survival as the sheer animal will to live' *TLS*

'Alive with spell-binding imagery and laced with intriguing folklore. . . . This is a satisfying and powerful saga, lending insight and understanding to a deeply troubled land' *Irish Times*

By the same author

The House of the Spirits
Of Love and Shadows
Eva Luna
The Stories of Eva Luna
The Infinite Plan
Paula
Aphrodite: A Memoir of the Senses
Daughter of Fortune
Portrait in Sepia
My Invented Country
Zorro
Inés of My Soul
The Sum of Our Days

For Young Adults
City of the Beasts
Kingdom of the Golden Dragon
Forest of the Pygmies

ISABEL ALLENDE

Island Beneath the Sea

Translated from the Spanish by
Margaret Sayers Peden

FOURTH ESTATE · *London*

Fourth Estate
An imprint of HarperCollins*Publishers*
77–85 Fulham Palace Road
Hammersmith
London W6 8JB

This Fourth Estate paperback edition published 2011
5

First published in Great Britain by Fourth Estate in 2010
Simultaneously published in the United States by Harper
Originally published as *La Isla Bajo el Mar* in Spain in 2009 by Random House Mondadori

Copyright © Isabel Allende 2009
Translation copyright © 2010 HarperCollins*Publishers*

PS section © HarperCollins*Publishers*, except 'A conversation with Isabel Allende' used with the
permission of Dow Jones. PS™ is a trademark of HarperCollins*Publishers* Ltd

Isabel Allende asserts the moral right to be identified as the author of this work

A catalogue record for this book is available from the British Library

ISBN 978-0-00-734865-7

Typeset in Fournier MT by Palimpsest Book Production Limited,
Falkirk, Stirlingshire

Printed and bound in Great Britain by Clays Ltd, St Ives plc

Mixed Sources
Product group from well-managed
forests and other controlled sources
www.fsc.org Cert no. SW-COC-001806
© 1996 Forest Stewardship Council

FSC is a non-profit international organisation established
to promote the responsible management of the world's forests.
Products carrying the FSC label are independently certified
to assure consumers that they come from forests that are managed
to meet the social, economic and ecological needs
of present and future generations.

Find out more about HarperCollins and the environment at
www.harpercollins.co.uk/green

To my children, Nicolás and Lori

Zarité

In my forty years I, Zarité Sedella, have had better luck than other slaves. I am going to have a long life and my old age will be a time of contentment because my star—mi z'étoile—also shines when the night is cloudy. I know the pleasure of being with the man my heart has chosen. His large hands awaken my skin. I have had four children and a grandson, and those who are living are free. My first memory of happiness, when I was just a bony, runny-nosed, tangle-haired little girl, is moving to the sound of the drums, and that is also my most recent happiness, because last night I was in the place Congo dancing and dancing, without a thought in my head, and today my body is warm and weary. Music is a wind that blows away the years, memories, and fear, that crouching animal I carry inside me. With the drums the everyday Zarité disappears, and I am again the little girl who danced when she barely knew how to walk. I strike the ground with the soles of my feet and life rises up my legs, spreads up my skeleton, takes possession of me, drives away distress and sweetens my memory. The world trembles. Rhythm is born on the island beneath the sea; it shakes the earth, it cuts through me like a lightning bolt and rises toward the sky, carrying with it my sorrows so that Papa Bondye can chew them, swallow them, and leave me clean and happy. The drums conquer fear. The drums are the heritage of my mother, the strength of Guinea that is in my blood. No one can harm me when I am with the drums, I become as overpowering as Erzulie, loa of love, and swifter than the bullwhip. The shells on my wrists and ankles click in time, the gourds ask questions, the djembe *drums answer in the voice of the jungle and the timbales, with their tin tones. The* djun djuns *that know how to speak make the invitation, and the big* maman *roars when they beat her to summon the* loas. *The drums are sacred, the* loas *speak through them.*

In the house where I spent my earliest years, the drums were silent in the room we shared with Honoré, the other slave, but they were often taken out. Madame Delphine, my mistress then, did not want to hear the blacks' noise, only the melancholy laments of her clavichord. Mondays and Tuesdays she gave classes to girls of color, and the rest of the week she taught in the mansions of the grands blancs, *where the mademoiselles had their own instruments because they could not use the ones the mulatta girls touched. I learned to clean the keys with lemon juice, but I could not make music because Madame Delphine forbade us to go near her clavichord. We didn't need it. Honoré could draw music from a cookpot; anything in his hands had beat, melody, rhythm, and voice. He carried sounds inside his body; he had brought them from Dahomey. My toy was a hollowed gourd we made to rattle; later he taught me to caress his drums, slowly. And from the beginning, when he was still carrying me around in his arms, he took me to dances and voodoo services, where he marked the rhythm with his drum, the principal drum, for others to follow. This is how I remember it. Honoré seemed very old to me because his bones had frozen stiff, even though at the time he was no older than I am now. He drank* taffia *in order to endure the pain of moving, but more than that harsh rum, music was the best remedy. His moans turned to laughter with the sound of the drums. Honoré barely could peel sweet potatoes for the mistress's meal, his hands were so deformed, but playing the drum he never got tired, and when it came to dancing no one lifted his knees higher, or swung his head with more force, or shook his behind with more pleasure. Before I knew how to walk, he had me dance sitting down, and when I could just balance myself on two legs he invited me to lose myself in the music, the way you do in a dream. "Dance, dance, Zarité, the slave who dances is free . . . while he is dancing," he told me. I have always danced.*

Part

One

SAINT-DOMINGUE

(1770–1793)

The Spanish Illness

Toulouse Valmorain arrived in Saint-Domingue in 1770, the same year the dauphin of France married the Austrian archduchess, Marie Antoinette. Before traveling to the colony, when still he had no suspicion that his destiny was going to play a trick on him, or that he would end up in cane fields in the Antilles, he had been invited to Versailles to one of the parties in honor of the new dauphine, a young blonde of fourteen, who yawned openly in the rigid protocol of the French court. All of that was in the past. Saint-Domingue was another world. The young Valmorain had a rather vague idea of the place where his father struggled to earn a livelihood for his family with the ambition of converting it into a fortune. Valmorain had read somewhere that the original inhabitants of the island, the Arawaks, had called it Haïti before the conquistadors changed the name to La Española and killed off the natives. In fewer than fifty years, not a single Arawak remained, nor sign of them; they all perished as victims of slavery, European illnesses, and suicide. They were a red-skinned race, with thick black hair and inalterable dignity, so timid that a single Spaniard could conquer ten of them with his bare hands. They lived in polygamous communities, cultivating the land with care in order not to exhaust it: sweet potatoes, maize, gourds, peanuts, peppers, potatoes, and cassava. The earth, like the sky and water, had no owner until the foreigners, using the forced labor of the Arawaks, took control of it in order to cultivate never-before-seen plants. It was in that time that the custom of killing people with dogs was begun. When they had annihilated the indigenous peoples, the new masters imported slaves, blacks kidnapped in Africa and whites from Europe: convicts, orphans, prostitutes, and rebels. At the end of the 1600s, Spain ceded to France the western part of the island, which they called Saint-Domingue, and which would become the richest colony in the world. At the time Toulouse Valmorain arrived there, a third of the wealth of France, in sugar, coffee, tobacco, cotton, indigo, and cocoa, came from the island. There were no longer white slaves, but the number of blacks had risen to hundreds of thousands. The most intractable crop was sugarcane, the sweet gold of the colony; cutting the cane, crushing it, and reducing it to syrup was labor not for humans, as the planters maintained, but for beasts.

Valmorain had just turned twenty when he was summoned to the colony by an urgent letter from his father's business agent. When the youth disembarked, he was dressed in the latest fashion—lace cuffs, powdered wig, and shoes with high heels—and sure that the books he had read on the subject of exploration made him more than capable of advising his father for a few weeks. He was traveling with a valet nearly as elegant as he, and several trunks holding his wardrobe and his books. He thought of himself as a man of letters, and planned upon his return to France to dedicate himself to science. He admired the philosophers and encyclopedists who had in recent decades made such an impact in Europe, and he agreed with some of their liberal ideas. Rousseau's *Social Contract* had been his bedside book at eighteen. He had barely got off the ship, after a crossing that nearly ended in tragedy when they ran into a hurricane in the Caribbean, when he received his first disagreeable surprise: his progenitor was not waiting for him at the port. He was met by the agent, a courteous Jew dressed in black from head to foot, who informed him of the precautions necessary for moving about the island; he had brought him horses, a pair of mules for luggage, a guide, and militiamen to accompany him to the Habitation Saint-Lazare. The young man had never set foot outside France, and had paid very little attention to the stories—banal, furthermore—his father used to tell during his infrequent visits to the family in Paris. He could not imagine that he would ever visit the plantation; the tacit agreement was that his father would consolidate his fortune on the island while he looked after his mother and sisters and supervised the business in France. The letter he had received alluded to health problems, and he supposed that it concerned a passing fever, but when he reached Saint-Lazare, after a day's march at a killing pace through a gluttonous and hostile nature, he realized that his father was dying. He was not suffering from malaria, as Valmorain had thought, but syphilis, *le mal espagnol*, which was devastating whites, blacks, and mulattoes alike. His father's illness was in the last stages; he was covered with pustules, nearly incapacitated, his teeth were loose and his mind in a fog. The Dantesque treatments of bloodletting, mercury, and cauterizing his penis with red-hot wire had not given him relief, but he continued them as an act of contrition. Just past his fiftieth birthday, he had become an ancient giving nonsensical orders, urinating without control, and passing his time in a hammock with his pets, a pair of young black girls who had barely reached puberty.

While slaves unpacked his luggage under the direction of the valet, a fop who had barely endured the crossing on the ship and was frightened by the primitive conditions of the place, Toulouse Valmorain went out to look over the vast property. He knew nothing about the cultivation of cane, but the tour was sufficient for him to understand that the slaves were starving and the plantation had been saved from ruin only because the world was consuming sugar with increasing voraciousness. In the account books he found the explanation for his father's bad financial condition, which was not maintaining his family at a proper level in Paris. Production was a disaster, and the slaves were dying like insects; Valmorain had no doubt that the overseers were robbing his family, taking advantage of the master's deterioration. He cursed his luck and set about rolling up his sleeves and getting to work, something no young man from his milieu ever considered; work was for a different class of people. He began by obtaining a generous loan, thanks to the support and connections of his father's business agent's bankers. Then he ordered the commandeurs to the cane fields, to work elbow to elbow with the same people they had martyrized, and replaced them with others less depraved. He reduced punishments and hired a veterinarian, who spent two months at Saint-Lazare trying to return the Negroes to some degree of health. The veterinarian could not save Valmorain's valet, who was dispatched by a fulminating diarrhea in fewer than thirty-eight hours. Valmorain realized that his father's slaves lasted an average of eighteen months before they dropped dead of fatigue or escaped, a much shorter period than on other plantations. The women lived longer than the men, but they produced less in the asphyxiating labor of the cane fields, and they also had the bad habit of getting pregnant. As very few children survived, the planters had concluded that fertility among the Negroes was not a good source of income. The young Valmorain carried out the necessary changes in a methodical way, quickly and with no plans, intending to leave very soon, but when his father died a few months later, the son had to confront the inescapable fact that he was trapped. He did not intend to leave his bones in the mosquito-infested colony, but if he went too soon he would lose the plantation, and with it the income and social position his family held in France.

Valmorain did not try to make connections with other colonists. The *grands blancs*, owners of other plantations, considered him a presumptuous youth who would not last long on the island, and for that reason they were amazed to see him sunburned and in muddy boots. The antipathy was mutual. For Valmorain the Frenchmen transplanted to the Antilles were boors, the opposite of the society he had frequented, in which ideas, science, and the arts were exalted and no one spoke of money or of slaves. From the Age of Reason in Paris, he had passed to a primitive and violent world in which the living and the dead walked hand in hand. Neither did he make friends with the *petits blancs*, whose only capital was the color of their skin, a few poor devils poisoned by envy and slander, as he considered them. Many had come from the four corners of the globe and had no way to prove the purity of their blood, or their past; in the best of cases they were merchants, artisans, friars of little virtue, sailors, military men, and minor civil servants, but there were always trouble-makers, pimps, criminals, and buccaneers who used every inlet of the Caribbean for their corrupt operations. He had nothing in common with those people. Among the free mulattoes, the *affranchis*, there were more than sixty classifications set by percentage of white blood, and that deter-mined their social level. Valmorain never learned to distinguish the tones or proper denomination for each possible combination of the two races. The *affranchis* lacked political power, but they managed a lot of money, and poor whites hated them for that. Some earned a living in illicit traf-ficking, from smuggling to prostitution, but others had been educated in France and had fortunes, lands, and slaves. In spite of subtleties of color, the mulattoes were united by their shared aspiration to pass for whites and their visceral scorn for Negroes. The slaves, whose number was ten times greater than that of the whites and *affranchis* combined, counted for nothing, neither in the census of the population nor in the colonists' consciousness.

Since he did not want to isolate himself completely, Toulouse Val-morain occasionally had interchange with some families of *grands blancs* in Le Cap, the city nearest his plantation. On those trips he bought what was needed for supplies and, if he could not avoid it, went by the As-semblée Coloniale to greet his peers, so that they would not forget his name, but he did not participate in the sessions. He also used the occasion to go to plays at the theater, attend parties given by the cocottes—the exuberant French, Spanish, and mixed-race courtesans who dominated nightlife—and to rub elbows with explorers and scientists who stopped by the island on their way toward other more interesting places. Saint-Domingue did not attract visitors, but at times some came to study the nature or economy of the Antilles. Those Valmorain invited to

Saint-Lazare with the intention of regaining, even if briefly, pleasure from the sophisticated conversation that had marked his youthful years in Paris. Three years after his father's death, he could show the property with pride; he had transformed that ruin of sick Negroes and dry cane fields into one of the most prosperous of the eight hundred plantations on the island, had multiplied by five the volume of unrefined sugar for export, and had installed a distillery in which he produced select barrels of a rum as good as the best in Cuba. His visitors spent one or two weeks in his large, rustic wood residence, soaking up country life and appreciating at close range the magic invention of sugar. They rode horseback through the dense growth that whistled threateningly in the wind, protected from the sun by large straw hats and gasping in the boiling humidity of the Caribbean, while slaves thin as shadows cut the cane to ground level without killing the root, so there would be other harvests. From a distance, they resembled insects in fields where the cane was twice their height. The labor of cleaning the hard stalks, chopping them in toothed machines, crushing them in the rollers, and boiling the juice in deep copper cauldrons to obtain a dark syrup was fascinating to these city people, who had seen only the white crystals that sweetened coffee. The visitors brought Valmorain up to date on events in a Europe and America that were more and more remote for him, the new technological and scientific advances, and the philosophical ideas of the vanguard. They opened to him a crack through which he could glimpse the world, and as a gift left him books. Valmorain enjoyed his guests, but he enjoyed more their leaving; he did not like to have witnesses to his life, or to his property. The foreigners observed slavery with a mixture of morbid curiosity and repugnance that was offensive to him because he thought of himself as a just master; if they knew how other planters treated their Negroes, they would agree with him. He knew that more than one would return to civilization converted into an abolitionist and ready to campaign against consumption of sugar. Before he had been forced to live on the island, he too would have been shocked by slavery, had he known the details, but his father never referred to the subject. Now, with his hundreds of slaves, his ideas had changed.

Toulouse Valmorain spent the first years lifting Saint-Lazare from devastation and was unable to travel outside the colony even once. He lost contact with his mother and sisters, except for sporadic, rather formal letters that reported only the banalities of everyday life and health. After his failure with two French managers, he hired a mulatto as head overseer of the plantation, a man named Prosper Cambray, and then found more time to read, to hunt, and travel to Le Cap. There he had met Violette Boisier, the most sought after cocotte of the city, a free young woman with the reputation of being clean and healthy, African by heritage and white in appearance. At least with her he would not end up like his father, his blood watered down by the Spanish illness.

Bird of Night

$\mathcal{V}$iolette Boisier was the daughter of a courtesan, a magnificent mulatta who died at twenty-nine, impaled on the sword of a French officer out of his head with jealousy; he was possibly the father of Violette, although that was never confirmed. Under her mother's tutelage the girl began to exercise her profession when she was eleven; by thirteen, when her mother was murdered, she had mastered the exquisite arts of pleasure, and at fifteen had surpassed all her rivals. Valmorain preferred not to think about whom his *petite amie* frolicked with in his absence, since he was not prepared to buy her exclusivity. He was infatuated with Violette, who was pure movement and laughter, but he had sufficient sangfroid to control his imagination, unlike the military man who had killed her mother, ruining his career and besmirching his name. He limited himself to taking her to the theater and to men's parties no white women attended, events where Violette's radiant beauty attracted all eyes. The envy he provoked in other men as he displayed her on his arm gave him perverse satisfaction; many would sacrifice their honor to spend an entire night with Violette instead of one or two hours, as was her practice, but that privilege belonged only to him. At least, that was what he thought.

The girl had a three-room apartment with a balcony, its iron railing decorated with fleurs-de-lis, on the second floor of a building near the place Clugny, the only thing her mother had left to her aside from some clothing appropriate to the profession. Violette lived there in a certain luxury, accompanied by Loula, a fat, rough African slave who acted as servant and bodyguard. Violette spent the hottest hours of the day resting or tending to her beauty: coconut milk massages, depilation with caramel, oil baths for her hair, herbal teas to clear her voice and eyes. In some moments of inspiration she and Loula prepared ointments for the skin, almond soap, cosmetic salves, and powders she sold among her female friends. Her days went by slowly and idly. At dusk, when the weakened rays of the sun could no longer darken her skin, she would go out for a stroll if the weather permitted, or in a litter carried by two slaves she hired from a neighbor, thus avoiding soiling her feet in horse manure, rotting garbage, or the mud in the streets of Le Cap. She dressed discreetly so as not to insult other women; neither whites nor mulattas tolerated that much competition with civility. She visited the shops to make her purchases and the dock to buy smuggled articles from sailors; she visited her modiste, her hairdresser, and her friends. Using the excuse of having a glass of fruit juice, she would stop by the hotel or some café, where she never lacked for an *homme du monde* to invite her to his table. She knew intimately the most powerful whites in the colony, including the highest ranked military man, the Gouverneur. Afterward she returned home to bedeck herself for the practice of her profession, an intricate task that took a couple of hours. She had clothing of all the colors of the rainbow made of sumptuous fabrics from Europe and the Orient, slippers and matching reticules, plumed hats, shawls with Chinese embroidery, fur capes to drag across the floor, since the climate did not allow wearing them, and a coffer filled with tawdry jewels. Every night, the fortunate friend—she did not call them clients—whose turn it was took her to some spectacle and to dine, then to a party that lasted till dawn; finally he accompanied her to her apartment, where she felt safe, since Loula slept on a cot within range of her voice and, should it be needed, could rid her of any violent "friend." Violette's price was known and never mentioned; the money was left in a lacquered box on the table, and the next meeting depended on the tip.

In a hole between two boards on the wall that only she and Loula knew, Violette hid a chamois pouch of valuable jewels, some given her by Toulouse Valmorain, of whom anything could be said other than that he was a miser, along with gold coins acquired one by one—her savings, her insurance for the future. She preferred paste jewelry that would not tempt thieves or provoke talk, but she wore authentic pieces when she went out with the person who had given them to her. She always wore a modest opal ring of antique design that had been put on her finger as a commitment by Etienne Relais, a French officer. She saw him very seldom because he spent his life riding at the head of his detachment, but if he arrived in Le Cap, she put off other friends to attend him. Relais was the only one with whom she could abandon herself to the enchantment of being cared for by one man. Toulouse Valmorain never suspected that he was sharing with that rude soldier the honor of spending the entire night with Violette. She gave no explanation and had not had to choose between them, since they had never been in the city at the same time.

"What am I going to do with these men who treat me the way they would their bride?" Violette once asked Loula.

"These things resolve themselves," the slave answered, sucking in a deep breath of her strong tobacco.

"Or they are settled with blood. Don't forget my mother."

"That will not happen to you, my angel, because I am here to look out for you."

Loula was right, for time took charge of eliminating one of the suitors. After a few years had gone by, the relationship with Valmorain passed into a loving friendship that lacked the urgency of the first months, when he would wind his mounts galloping at breakneck speed to hold her in his arms. His expensive gifts came less frequently, and he sometimes went to Le Cap without making an attempt to see her. Violette did not reproach him, because the boundaries of that passion had always been clear, but kept the contact, which might be of benefit to both of them.

Capitaine Etienne Relais was known to be incorruptible in an ambience in which vice was the norm, honor for sale, and laws made to be broken, and men operated on the assumption that he who did not abuse power did not deserve to have it. His integrity prevented him from growing rich like others in a similar position, and not even the temptation to accumulate enough to retire to France, as he had promised Violette Boisier, was able to lead him away from what he considered military rectitude. He did not hesitate to sacrifice his men in battle, or to torture a child to obtain information from his mother, but he had never put his hand on money he had not earned cleanly. He was punctilious regarding honor and honesty. He wanted to take Violette to a place where no one knew them, where no one would suspect that she had earned her living in practices of faint virtue, and where her mixed blood was not evident; one would have to have an eye trained in the Antilles to divine the African blood that flowed beneath her light skin. Violette was not overly attracted to the idea of going to France because she feared icy winters more than evil tongues, to which she was immune, but she had agreed to go with him. According to Relais's calculations, if he lived frugally, accepted missions of great risk for the bonus they offered, and rose quickly in his career, he would be able to fulfill his dream. He hoped that by then Violette would have matured and would not attract as much attention with the insolence of her laughter, the mischievous gleam in her black eyes, or the rhythmic sway of her walk. She would always be noticed, but perhaps she would be able to assume the role of wife of a retired military man. Madame Relais. He savored those two words, repeated them like an incantation. His decision to marry her was not the result of a carefully worked out strategy, as was the rest of his life, but of a lightning bolt to his heart so violent that he never questioned it. He was not a sentimental man, but he had learned to trust his instinct, very useful in war.

He had met Violette a couple of years before, one Sunday in the market in the midst of shouting vendors and a crush of people and animals. In a miserable little theater that consisted of a platform covered over with a roof of purple rags, a man with exaggerated mustaches and tattooed arabesques strutted about while a young boy shouted his virtues as the most prodigious magician of Samarkand. That pathetic show would not have caught the capitaine's attention had it not been for the luminous presence of Violette. When the magician asked for a volunteer from the public, she made her way through the lookers on and climbed to the stage with childish enthusiasm, laughing and waving at friends with her fan. She had recently turned fifteen, but she already had the body and attitude of an experienced woman, as often happened in this climate where girls, like fruit, ripened quickly. Obeying the instructions of the illusionist, Violette curled up inside a trunk bedaubed with Egyptian symbols. The hawker, a ten-year-old Negro disguised as a Turk, closed the trunk with two heavy padlocks, and another spectator was chosen to verify they were firm. The man from Samarkand made a few passes with his cape and handed two keys to the volunteer to open the locks. When the lid of the trunk was lifted, one could see that the girl was no longer inside, and moments later, with a roll of drums, the little black announced her miraculous appearance behind the public. Everyone turned to admire, openmouthed, the girl who had materialized out of nothing and was fanning herself with her leg cocked up on a barrel. From the first glance Etienne Relais knew that he could never tear that girl of honey and silk from his soul. He felt that something had exploded inside him; his mouth was parched, and he had lost his sense of direction. It took a great effort to return to reality and realize that he was in the market, surrounded by people. Trying to control himself, he gulped mouthfuls of the humid midday air and the stench of fish and meat spoiling in the sun, ripe fruit, garbage, and animal shit. He did not know the beautiful girl's name, but he supposed it would be easy to find out; he deduced that she was not married because no husband would allow her to expose herself so brazenly. She was so splendid that all eyes were glued on her, and no one, except Relais, trained to observe the least detail, had focused on the illusionist's trick. Under other circumstances he might have revealed the double bottom of the trunk and the trapdoor in the stage out of pure keenness for precision, but he assumed the girl was working as the magician's accomplice and he did not want to cause her trouble. He did not stay to see the tattooed gypsy pull a monkey from a bottle, or decapitate a volunteer, as the young hawker was announcing. He elbowed his way through the crowd and set out after the girl, who was quickly disappearing on the arm of a man in uniform, possibly a soldier from his own regiment. He did not reach her; he was brought up short by a black woman whose muscular arms were covered with cheap bracelets, who stepped in front of him and warned him to get in line, he was not the only one interested in her mistress, Violette Boisier. When she saw how upset the capitaine was, she bent down to whisper into his ear the amount of the tip she would need to put him in first place among the week's clients. That was how he learned that he had been captivated by one of the courtesans who made Le Cap famous.

Stiff in his newly ironed uniform, Relais presented himself for the first time at Violette Boisier's apartment with a bottle of champagne and a modest gift. He left his payment where Loula indicated and prepared to gamble his future in the next two hours. Loula discreetly disappeared, and he was alone, sweating in the warm air of the small room stuffed with furniture, slightly nauseated by the sickly sweet aroma of ripe mangoes on a nearby plate. Violette did not make him wait more than a couple of minutes. She slipped in silently and held out two hands to him as she studied him with half-closed eyes and a slight smile. Relais took those long, fine fingers in his without knowing what the next step was. She dropped his hands, ran her fingers over his face, flattered that he had shaved for her, and indicated he should open the bottle. Relais popped the cork, and the champagne fizzed out before she could catch it in her goblet, wetting her wrist and hand. She stroked her neck with her wet fingers, and Relais had the impulse to lick the drops glittering on that perfect skin, but he was nailed to the floor, mute, stripped of will. She filled the goblet and set it, without tasting it, on a small table beside the divan, then came to him and with expert fingers unbuttoned the heavy uniform jacket. "Take it off, it's hot. And your boots, too," she said, reaching for a Chinese dressing gown painted with herons. It seemed decadent to Relais, but he put it on over his shirt, fighting a tangle of wide sleeves, and then sat down on the divan in anguish. He was accustomed to being in command, but he understood that inside these four walls Violette was in charge. Noise from the street filtered into the room between the slats of the shutters, and also the last rays of sun, which shone in like vertical slices, lighting the small room. The girl was wearing an emerald silk tunic cinched at the waist with a golden cord, Turkish slippers, and a complicated turban embroidered with glass beads. A lock of black wavy hair fell across her face. Violette drank a sip of champagne and offered Relais the same goblet, which he emptied with a desperate gulp, a drowning man. She filled the goblet again and held it by its delicate stem, waiting until he called her to his side on the divan. That was Relais's last initiative; from that moment she took charge of conducting the rendezvous in her own way.

Dove's Egg

*V*iolette had learned to please her friends within the stipulated time without giving them the sensation of being rushed. Such coquetry and teasing submission in an adolescent body completely disarmed Relais. Slowly she unwound the long cloth of the turban, which fell to the floor with a tinkling of glass beads, and shook the dark cascade of her mane across her shoulders and back. Her movements were languid, without affectation, with the freshness of a dance. Her breasts had not as yet reached their definitive size, and her nipples lifted the green silk like little pebbles. She was naked beneath the tunic. Relais marveled at that mulatta body, the firm legs with fine ankles, the voluptuous buttocks and thighs, the indented waist, the elegant fingers that curved backward, free of rings. Her laughter began with a mute purring in her belly and gradually rose, crystalline, pealing, to the thrown back head, the bouncing hair, the long, throbbing neck. With a little silver knife Violette cut a piece of mango, avidly popped it into her mouth, and a thread of juice fell on the neck of her gown, damp with sweat and champagne. With a finger she traced the trail of the fruit, a thick amber drop, and rubbed it on Relais's lips as she swung to straddle his legs with the lightness of a cat. The man's face was between breasts smelling of mango. She bent down, enveloping him in her wild hair, kissed him fully on the mouth, and with her tongue passed him the piece of fruit she had bitten off. Relais took the chewed pulp with a shiver of surprise; he had never experienced anything so intimate, so shocking, so marvelous. She licked his chin, took his head in her hands and covered it with quick kisses like bird pecks, on his eyelids, cheeks, lips, neck . . . playing, laughing. The man clasped her waist and with desperate hands pulled off the tunic, revealing the slim, musk scented girl who yielded, fused, crumbled against the pressed bones and hard muscles of his own body cured by battles and privations. He tried to lift her in his arms to carry her to the bed, which he could see in the next room, but Violette did not give him time; her odalisque's hands opened the heron-painted dressing gown and his trousers; her opulent hips slithered like a knowing snake until she impaled herself upon his rock-hard member with a deep sigh of joy. Etienne Relais felt that he had sunk into a swamp of delectation, without memory or will. He closed his eyes, kissing those succulent lips, savoring the aroma of mango, while his soldier's callused hands stroked the impossible softness of that skin and the abundant wealth of that hair. He thrust into her, abandoning himself to the heat and the savor and the scent of the girl, with the sensation that finally he had found his place in this world after being so long alone and drifting. In only a few minutes he exploded like a stupefied adolescent, with spasmodic bursts and a yell of frustration for not have given her pleasure, for he wanted more than anything in his life to make her love him. Violette waited for him to finish, motionless, wet, panting, mounted on him with her face buried in the hollow of his shoulder, murmuring incomprehensible words. Relais did not know how long they were embraced like that, until he could again breathe normally and emerge a little from the dense fog that enveloped him, then he became aware that he was still inside her, grasped by elastic muscles that were rhythmically massaging him, pressing, releasing. He managed to wonder how that girl had learned the arts of a practiced courtesan before he was lost in the magma of desire and the confusion of his instantaneous love. When Violette felt he was again firm, she wrapped her legs around his waist, crossed her feet behind his back, and gestured toward the other room.

Relais carried her in his arms, still clasped on his penis, and fell with her onto the bed, where they could revel as they wished until long into the night, several hours more than Loula had stipulated. The large woman had come in a couple of times, ready to put an end to that overtime, but Violette, moved to see that tough soldier sobbing with love, waved her away without a second thought.

Love, which he had not known before, tossed Etienne Relais about like a tremendous wave, pure energy, salt, and foam. He judged that he could not compete with the girl's other clients, more handsome, powerful, or rich, and so decided at dawn to offer her what few white men would be prepared to give: his name. "Marry me," he said between embraces. Violette sat back on the bed with her legs crossed, her damp hair stuck to her skin, her eyes incandescent, her lips swollen with kisses. Light from remains of the three dying candles that had accompanied their interminable acrobatics fell on her. "I don't have the makings of a wife," she answered, and added that she still had not bled with the cycles of the moon, and according to Loula it was late for that; she would never have children. Relais smiled, because to him children seemed a nuisance.

"If I married you," she said, "I would always be alone, while you fought your campaigns. I have no place among whites, and my friends would reject me because they are afraid of you, they say you are bloodthirsty," she said.

"My work demands it, Violette. The way the physician amputates a gangrenous limb, I fulfill my obligation in order to prevent something worse, but I have never harmed anyone without a good reason."

"I can give you all kinds of good reasons. I do not want to suffer my mother's fate."

"You will never have to fear me, Violette," said Relais, holding her by the shoulders and looking into her eyes for a long moment.

"I hope that is so," she sighed finally.

"We will marry, I promise you."

"Your salary isn't enough to keep me. With you I would lose

everything: clothing, perfumes, theater, and time to waste. I am lazy, Capitaine, this is the only way I can earn my living without ruining my hands, and it will not last much longer."

"How old are you?"

"Young, but this trade is short-lived. Men grow tired of the same faces and same asses. As Loula says, I have to take advantage of the only thing I have."

The capitaine tried to see her as often as his campaigns allowed, and by the end of a few months he had made himself indispensable, caring for her and advising her like an uncle, until she could not imagine life without him and began to contemplate the possibility of marrying him in some poetic future. Relais thought that he could do it in five years. That would give them time to put their love to the test, and for each to save money. He resigned himself to Violette's continuing her usual profession, and he paid for her services like other clients, grateful for spending several entire nights with her. At first they made love until they were bruised and battered, but later vehemence turned into tenderness and they spent precious hours talking, making plans, and resting embraced in the warm shadow of Violette's apartment. Relais learned to know the girl's body and character; he could anticipate her reactions, prevent her rages, which were like tropical storms, sudden and brief, and give her pleasure. He discovered that this sensual girl was trained to give pleasure, not to receive it, and with patience and good humor he strove to satisfy her. The difference in their ages and his authoritarian temperament offset Violette's levity. She let him guide her in some practical matters, to please him, but she maintained her independence and defended her secrets.

Loula administered her money and managed the clients with a cool head. Once Relais found Violette with a black eye, and, furious, wanted to know who had caused it, to make him pay dearly for such insolence. "Loula already collected from him. We arrange things better on our own." She laughed, and there was no way to make her give him the name of the aggressor. The formidable Loula knew that the health and beauty of her mistress was the capital that maintained them both, and that inevitably the moment would come when those virtues would begin to fade. She also had to consider the competition of the new batches of adolescents that assaulted the profession every year. It was a shame the capitaine was poor, Loula thought, because Violette deserved a good life. Love seemed irrelevant to her, since she confused it with passion and she had seen how briefly that lasted, but she did not dare use tricks to get rid of Relais. He was someone to be feared. Besides, Violette showed no signs of being in a hurry to marry, and in the meantime another suitor could come along with a better financial situation. Loula decided to put away some serious savings; it wasn't enough to accumulate jewels in a hole, she had to make more imaginative investments in case the marriage with the officer did not come off. She cut back on expenditures and raised the tariff on her mistress, and the more she charged, the more exclusive her favors were thought to be. Using the stratagem of rumors, Loula puffed up Violette's fame. She spread rumors that her mistress could keep a man inside her all night, and that she could revive the energy of the most enervated man twelve times. She had learned from a Moorish woman and exercised with a dove's egg. She went shopping, to the theater, and to the cock-fights with the egg in her secret place, without breaking or dropping it. There was also no shortage of contenders to fight a duel over the young *poule*, and that contributed enormously to her prestige. The wealthiest and most influential whites docilely put their names on the list and waited their turn. It was Loula who had the idea of investing in gold so that savings would not slip through their fingers like sand. Relais, who was not in a position to contribute much, gave Violette his mother's opal ring, the only thing left of his family.

The Bride from Cuba

In October 1778, the eighth year of his time on the island, Toulouse Valmorain made another of his brief trips to Cuba, where he had commercial affairs he preferred not to divulge. Like all the colonists on Saint-Domingue, he was supposed to do business solely with France, but there were a thousand ingenious ways to dodge the law, and he knew several. It did not seem like a sin to avoid taxes, which, after all was said and done, ended up in the bottomless coffers of the king. The tortuous coast lent itself to discreetly setting sail at night en route to other coves of the Caribbean without anyone's knowing, and the porous border with the Spanish part of the island, less populated and much poorer than the French, permitted a constant antlike traffic behind the backs of the authorities. All manner of contraband, from weapons to miscreants, but most of all sacks of sugar, coffee, and cocoa, passed from the plantations to be shipped to other destinations, avoiding customs. After Valmorain had emerged from beneath his father's debts and begun to accumulate more income than dreamed of, he decided he would keep reserves of money in Cuba, where they would be more secure than in France, and within reach in case of need. He arrived in Havana with the intention of staying just a week to meet with his banker, but the visit was prolonged more than planned because at a ball given by the French consulate he met Eugenia García del Solar. From a corner of the pretentious ballroom he saw in the distance an opulent young girl with translucent skin; her head was crowned with luxuriant chestnut hair and she was dressed in the provincial mode, just the opposite of the elegant Violette Boisier. To his eyes, nevertheless, she was no less beautiful. He had picked her out immediately on the crowded dance floor, and for the first time he felt inadequate. He had acquired what he was wearing several years before in Paris, and it was out of fashion; the sun had tanned his skin to leather, he had the hands of a blacksmith, his wig tickled his head, the lace of his collar was choking him, and his foppish pointy-toed, twisted-heel shoes were too tight, forcing him to walk like a duck. His once refined manners were brusque compared with the ease of the Cubans. The years he had spent on the plantation had hardened him inside and out, and now, when he most needed it, he lacked the courtly arts that had been so natural in his youth. As a crowning blow, the dances in style were a lively tangle of pirouettes, bows, turns, and hops that he was unable to imitate. He found out that the girl was the sister of a Spaniard named Sancho García del Solar, who came from a family of minor nobility that had been impoverished for two generations, no matter the name. The mother had jumped to her death from the bell tower of a church, and the father had died young after throwing the family fortune out the window.

Eugenia had been educated in an icy convent in Madrid, where nuns instilled in her the things necessary to grace the character of a fine lady: modesty, prayers, and embroidery. In the meantime, Sancho had come to Cuba to seek a fortune because in Spain there was no room for an imagination as brazen as his; in contrast, on this Caribbean island where adventurers of every stripe were found, he could lend himself to lucrative, if not always legal, business dealings. He lived the life of a rowdy bachelor, balancing on the tightrope of his debts, which he struggled to pay, always at the last hour, through success at the gaming table and help from his friends. He was handsome, he had a golden tongue for inveigling whoever was near, and he gave himself so many airs that no one suspected how large the hole in his pocket was. Then suddenly, when he least desired it, the nuns sent him his sister, accompanied by a duenna and a brief, straightforward letter explaining that Eugenia did not have the religious calling, and now it was up to him, her only relative and her guardian, to take charge of her. With that virginal young girl under his roof, Sancho's night life came to an end; he was responsible for finding her an adequate husband before she was too old and left to dressing saints for the church—with a vocation or without it. His intention was to marry her to the highest bidder, someone who would lift both of them out of the misery in which their parents' extravagance had left them, but he had not expected as big a fish as Toulouse Valmorain. Sancho knew very well who Valmorain was, and what the Frenchman was worth; he had had in mind proposing some business to him, but he did not introduce him to his sister at the ball because she was at a frank disadvantage compared with the celebrated Cuban beauties. Eugenia was timid; she did not have the proper clothes, and he could not buy them for her, she did not know how to do her hair, although fortunately there was an abundance of it, and she did not have the small figure imposed by current style. He was, then, surprised when the next day Valmorain asked permission to call upon them, with serious intentions, he had said.

"He must be a bandy-legged old man," Eugenia joked when she learned that, tapping her brother with her closed fan.

"He is a true monsieur, cultivated and rich, but even if he were deformed, you would marry him. You will soon be twenty, and you have no dowry."

"But I'm pretty!" she interrupted, laughing.

"Many women in Havana are prettier and slenderer than you."

"You think I'm fat?"

"You cannot play hard to get, especially if it's Valmorain. He is an excellent catch; he has titles and properties in France, but the main part of his fortune is a sugar plantation in Saint-Domingue," Sancho explained.

"Santo Domingo?" she asked, alarmed.

"Saint-Domingue, Eugenia. The French part of the island is very different from the Spanish. I will show you a map so you see that it's very close; you can come visit me any time you want."

"I am not ignorant, Sancho. I know that that colony is a purgatory of fatal illnesses and rebellious Negroes."

"That will only be for a while. The white colonists leave as soon as they can. Within a few years you will be in Paris. Isn't that the dream of all women?"

"I don't speak French."

"You will learn. Starting tomorrow, you will have a tutor," Sancho concluded.

If Eugenia García del Solar was thinking of opposing her brother's designs, she put that idea aside as soon as Toulouse Valmorain came to the house. He was younger and more attractive than she had expected, average height, well built, with broad shoulders, a manly face with harmonious features, skin bronzed by the sun, and gray eyes. His fine lips had a hard expression. Blond hair peeked from beneath his twisted wig, and he seemed uncomfortable in his clothes, which were tight on him. Eugenia liked his way of getting straight to the point and of looking at her as if he was unclothing her, something that provoked a sinful tickling that would have horrified the nuns in the lugubrious convent in Madrid. It was a shame that Valmorain lived in Saint-Domingue, she thought, but if her brother was not deceiving her, it would be for a short time. Sancho invited the suitor to take refreshment in the pergola in the garden, and in less than half an hour the agreement was tacitly concluded. Eugenia was not present for the final details, which were resolved by the men behind a closed door; she was given only the task of a trousseau. That was ordered from France, following the advice of the consul's wife, and her brother financed it with a usurious loan obtained thanks to his irresistible charlatan eloquence. At her morning masses, Eugenia fervently thanked God for the unique good fortune of marrying for money, but to someone she could come to love.

Valmorain stayed in Cuba a couple of months, courting Eugenia with improvised methods because he had lost the custom of dealing with women like her; those he used with Violette Boisier did not serve in this case. He came to his betrothed's house every day from four to six in the afternoon to take refreshment and play cards, always in the presence of a duenna dressed all in black, who kept one eye on her tatting and the other focused on them. Sancho's domicile left much to be desired, and Eugenia had little interest in domestic matters and had done nothing to put things in order. To prevent the grimy furniture from staining the suitor's clothing, Eugenia received him in the garden, where voracious tropical vegetation flourished like a botanical menace. Sometimes they went for a walk, accompanied by Sancho, or glanced at each other in the church, where they could not speak. Valmorain had noted the precarious conditions in which the García del Solars lived, and deduced that if his bride-to-be was comfortable there, she would have greater reason to be so in the Habitation Saint-Lazare. He sent her delicate presents, flowers, and formal notes she kept in a velvet-lined coffer but left unanswered. Until that moment Valmorain had had little exchange with Spaniards—his friends were French—but he soon found that he was comfortable among them. He had no problem communicating, as French was the second language of the cultivated and the upper class in Cuba. He confused the silences of his betrothed with modesty, in his eyes a fine feminine virtue, and it did not occur to him that she scarcely understood him. Eugenia did not have a good ear, and her tutor's efforts were insufficient to instill in her the subtleties of the French language. Eugenia's discretion and her novitiate's ways seemed to Valmorain a guarantee that she would not fall into the debauched conduct of so many women in Saint-Domingue, who used the excuse of the climate to abandon modesty. Once he understood the Spanish character, with its exaggerated sense of honor and absence of irony, he felt comfortable with the girl, and with good nature accepted the idea of being bored with her. That didn't matter. He wanted an honorable wife and dedicated mother who would be an example to her descendants; he had his books and his business to entertain him.

Sancho was the opposite of his sister, and of other Spaniards Valmorain knew: cynical, jovial, immune to melodrama and the alarms of jealousy, a nonbeliever, and skilled in catching on the fly any opportunity floating in the air. Although some aspects of his future brother-in-law shocked Valmorain, he was amused by him and let himself be cheated, prepared to lose money for the pleasure of witty conversation and of laughing a while. As the first step, he made Sancho a partner in smuggling the French wines he intended to bring from Saint-Domingue to Cuba, where they were greatly appreciated. That began a long and solid complicity that would unite them till death.

The Master's House

At the end of November, Toulouse Valmorain returned to Saint-Domingue to prepare for the arrival of his future wife. Like all plantations, Saint-Lazare had a "big house," which in this instance was little more than a rectangular wood and brick building lifted off ground level on three-meter pillars to protect it from slave uprisings and floods in the hurricane season. It had a series of dark bedchambers, several of them with rotted floors, and large drawing and dining rooms that featured opposing windows to facilitate circulation of breezes and a system of canvas fans strung from the ceiling and operated by slaves pulling a cord. With the back-and-forth of the ventilators a thin cloud of dust and dried mosquito wings was loosed to settle like dandruff on the diners' clothing. The windows had no panes, only waxed paper, and the furniture was rough, appropriate for a single man's interim dwelling. Bats nested in the ceiling, and at night one tended to encounter insects in the corners and hear the sound of mice in the bedchambers. A gallery, or roofed terrace, with battered wicker furniture enclosed the house on three sides. Around it were worm-eaten fruit trees, an untended vegetable garden, several patios with pecking hens befuddled by the heat, a stable for fine horses, dog kennels, a coach house, and beyond the roaring ocean of cane fields, as a backdrop, violet mountains profiled against a capricious sky. Perhaps once there had been a garden, but not even a memory remained.

The sugar mills and the slave cabins could not be seen from the house. Toulouse Valmorain went over everything with a critical eye, noticing for the first time its rickety, vulgar appearance. Compared with the place Sancho lived, it was a palace, but measured against the mansions of the other *grands blancs* on the island, and his small family château in France, which he had not visited in eight years, it was embarrassingly ugly. He decided to begin his married life on the right foot and give his wife the surprise of a house worthy of the names Valmorain and García del Solar. He would have to make arrangements.

Violette Boisier received the notice of her client's marriage with philosophical good humor. Loula, who knew everything, told her that Valmorain had a betrothed in Cuba. "He will miss you, my angel, but I assure you he will be back," she said. And he was. Shortly after, Valmorain knocked on the door of Violette's apartment, not in search of her usual services but to ask his old lover to help him receive his wife as she deserved. He did not know where to begin, and he could not think of another person of whom he could ask such a favor.

"Is it true that Spanish women sleep in a nun's nightdress with a hole cut in front for making love?" Violette asked him.

"How should I know that?" The groom-to-be laughed. "I am not married yet, but if that is true, I will rip it apart."

"No! You bring me the gown, and here with Loula we will open another hole in back," she said.

The young cocotte agreed to assist him if he paid her a reasonable commission of 15 percent on monies expended in furnishing the house. For the first time in Violette's dealings with a man no acrobatics in bed were included, and she set about the task with enthusiasm. She and Loula traveled to Saint-Lazare to get an idea of the mission she'd been charged with, and almost as soon as she stepped inside the door, a lizard from the coffered ceiling dropped into her décolletage. Her scream brought in several slaves from the patio, whom she recruited for a top to bottom cleaning. For one week this beautiful courtesan, whom Valmorain had seen only in golden lamplight, bedecked in silk and taffeta, made up and perfumed, directed the squad of barefoot slaves wearing a coarse cloth dressing gown and a rag tied around her head. She seemed in her element, as if she had been doing this rough work all her life. Under her orders the sound floorboards were scrubbed clean and the rotten ones replaced; she changed the mosquito netting and the paper at the windows. She aired the rooms, set out poison for the mice, burned tobacco to drive out insects, sent the broken furniture to the alley of the slaves, and finally the house was clean and bare. Violette had everything painted white inside, and as there was whitewash left over, she used it on the domestic slaves' cabins, which were near the big house, then had purple bougainvillea planted around the gallery. Valmorain promised her that he would keep the house clean. He also set several slaves to laying out a garden inspired by Versailles, though the extreme climate did not lend itself to the geometric art of the landscapes of the French court. Violette returned to Le Cap with a list of purchases. "Don't spend too much, this house is temporary; as soon as I have a manager we will go to France," Valmorain told her, handing her an amount he felt was fair. She ignored his warning, because nothing pleased her as much as shopping.

The bottomless treasure of the colony left from the port of Le Cap, and legal and contraband products came in. A many-colored throng rubbed elbows in the muddy streets, bargaining in many tongues amid carts, mules, horses, and packs of stray dogs that fed from the garbage. Everything from pirates' booty to extravagant Parisian items was sold there, and every day except Sunday slaves were auctioned off to supply demand: between twenty and thirty thousand a year just to keep the number stable, for they did not live very long. Violette spent her allowance but kept purchasing things on credit using the guarantee of Valmorain's name. Despite her youth, she made her selections with great aplomb; her worldly life had set and polished her taste. From the captain of a boat that sailed among the islands she ordered silver tableware, crystal, and a porcelain service for guests. The bride would bring sheets and tablecloths she had undoubtedly embroidered since childhood, so she did not worry about those. She bought furniture from France for the drawing room, a heavy American table with eighteen chairs destined to last generations, Dutch tapestries, lacquered screens, large Spanish chests for clothing, a surfeit of iron candelabra and oil lamps because she maintained that no one should live in the dark, Portuguese pottery for everyday use, a stream of frivolous embellishments, but no rugs because they would rot in the humidity. The *comptoirs* arranged to deliver and hand the bills to Valmorain. Soon carts laden to the top with boxes and baskets began to arrive at the Habitation Saint-Lazare. From the straw packing slaves extracted an interminable series of frills and furbelows: German clocks, birdcages, Chinese boxes, replicas of mutilated Roman statues, Venetian mirrors, engravings and paintings of various styles, chosen by theme, since Violette knew nothing of art, musical instruments that no one knew how to play, and even an incomprehensible collection of heavy glass and brass pipes and little wheels that, when put together by Valmorain like a jigsaw puzzle, turned out to be a telescope for spying on the slaves from the gallery. To Toulouse the furniture seemed ostentatious and the adornments totally useless, but he resigned himself because they could not be returned. Once the orgy of spending was concluded, Violette collected her commission and announced that he needed domestic servants: a good cook, maids for the house, and a lady's maid for Valmorain's future wife. That was the minimum required, according to Madame Delphine Pascal, who knew all the people of high society in Le Cap.

"Except me," Valmorain pointed out.

"Do you want me to help you or not?"

"All right, I will order Prosper Cambray to train some slaves."

"Oh, no, Toulouse! You will not save that way. Field slaves will not do, they're brutalized. I myself will look for your domestics," Violette decided.

Zarité was nearly nine when Violette bought her from Madame

Delphine, a French woman with cottony curls and turkey bosom, along in years but well preserved considering the damages caused by the island's climate. Delphine Pascal was the widow of a minor French civil servant, but she gave herself the airs of a lofty person because of her relationships with the *grands blancs*, even though they came to her only for shady transactions. She knew many secrets, which gave her an advantage at the hour of obtaining favors. It appeared that she lived on the pension from her deceased husband and giving clavichord classes to young mademoiselles, but under cover she resold stolen goods, served as a procuress, and in case of emergency performed abortions. She quietly taught French to cocottes who planned to pass as white and who, although their skin was the appropriate color, were betrayed by their accent. That was how the widow had met Violette Boisier, one of the brightest among her students but one with no pretense of appearing French; to the contrary, the girl openly referred to her Senegalese grandmother. She wanted to speak correct French in order to be respected among her white "friends." Madame Delphine had only two slaves: Honoré, an old man who performed all the chores, including those in the kitchen, whom she had bought very cheaply because his bones were twisted, and Zarité—Tété—a little mulatta who came into her hands when she was only a few weeks old and had cost her nothing. When Violette obtained her for Eugenia García del Solar, the girl was skinny, pure vertical, angular lines, with a mat of very tight curls impossible to comb, but she moved with grace and had noble bones, and beautiful honey-colored eyes shadowed by thick eyelashes. Perhaps she was descended from a Senegalese woman, as was she herself, thought Violette. Tété had learned early on the advantage of silence, and carried out orders with a vacant expression, giving no sign of understanding what was happening around her, but Violette suspected she was much cleverer than could be seen at first glance. Usually Violette did not notice slaves—with the exception of Loula, she thought of them as merchandise—but that little creature evoked her sympathy. They were alike in some ways, although Violette had the advantage of having been spoiled by her mother and desired by every man who crossed her path. She was free, and beautiful. Tété had none of those attributes—she was merely a slave dressed in rags—but Violette intuited her strength of character. At Tété's age, she too had been a bundle of bones, until she filled out in puberty, her angles turned into curves, and the form was determined that would bring her fame. Then her mother began to train her in the profession that had been so beneficial to her, so she had never broken her back as a servant. Violette was a good student, and by the time her mother was murdered she was able to get along on her own, with the help of Loula, who defended her with jealous loyalty. Thanks to the good Loula, Violette had never needed the protection of a pimp and had prospered in an unrewarding profession in which other girls lost their health and sometimes their lives. As soon as the idea of finding a personal maid for the wife of Toulouse Valmorain had come up, she remembered Tété. "Why are you so interested in that runny-nosed little snipe?" Loula, always suspicious, asked when she learned of Violette's intentions. "It's a feeling I have; I think that our paths will cross some day," was the only explanation that occurred to Violette. Loula consulted her cowrie shells without getting a satisfactory answer; that method of divination did not lend itself to clarifying essential matters, only those of little importance.

Madame Delphine received Violette in a tiny room in which the clavichord seemed the size of a pachyderm. They sat down on fragile chairs with curved legs to have coffee in tiny flower-painted cups for dwarfs to talk about everything and nothing, as they had done other times. After a little chatter, Violette laid out the reason for her visit. The widow was surprised that anyone had noticed the insignificant Tété, but she was quick, and immediately smelled the possibility of profit.

"I hadn't thought of selling Tété, but since it's you, such a dear friend—"

"I hope the girl is healthy. She's very thin," Violette interrupted.

"It isn't for lack of food!" the widow exclaimed, offended.

She served more coffee, and soon they spoke of a price that to Violette seemed excessive. The more she paid, the greater her commission would be, but she couldn't swindle Valmorain too brazenly; everyone knew the price of slaves, especially the planters, who were always buying. A bone-thin little girl was not a valuable commodity but rather something given to repay a kindness.

"It is painful for me to let Tété go." Madame Delphine sighed, drying an invisible tear, after they had agreed on the amount. "She's a good child; she doesn't steal, and she speaks French as she should. I have never allowed her to speak to me in the jargon of the Negroes. In my house no one destroys the beautiful tongue of Molière."

"I don't understand what that is going to help," Violette commented, amused.

"What do you mean *what*? A lady's maid who speaks French is very elegant. Téte will serve her well, I assure you. However, Mademoiselle, I must confess that it has cost me some thrashings to rid her of the bad habit of running away."

"That is serious! They say there's no cure for it."

"Yes, that is true of some who were once free, but Tété was born a slave. Free! What pride!" exclaimed the widow, fixing her biddy-sharp eyes on the girl, who was standing by the door. "But do not worry, Mademoiselle, she will not try again. The last time she wandered lost for several days, and when they brought her to me, she had been bitten by a dog and was burning with fever. You can't know the work it took me to heal her . . . but she did not escape punishment!"

"When was that?" asked Violette, taking note of the slave's hostile silence.

"A year ago. Such foolishness would never occur to her now, but keep an eye on her just the same. She has her mother's cursed blood. Do not be easy with her, she needs a harsh hand."

"What did you say about her mother?"

"She was a queen. They all say they were queens back in Africa," the widow mocked. "She arrived pregnant, it's always that way, they're like bitches in heat."

"The *pariade*. The sailors rape them on the ships, as you know. No one escapes that," Violette replied with a shudder, thinking of her own grandmother, who had survived crossing the ocean.

"That woman was at the point of killing her daughter. Imagine! They had to rip the baby from her hands. Monsieur Pascal, my husband—may God hold him in His holy bosom—brought the little thing to me as a gift."

"How old was she then?"

"A couple of months? I don't remember. Honoré, my other slave, gave her that strange name, Zarité, and he gave her jenny's milk; that's why she's so strong and hardworking, though stubborn, too. I've taught her to do all the household chores. She is worth more than what I'm asking for her, Mademoiselle Boisier. I'm selling her to you only because I'm planning to return soon to Marseille; I can still start my life over, don't you think?"

"Of course, madame," Violette replied, examining the woman's powdered face.

She took Tété with her that same day, with nothing more than the rags she was wearing and a crude wooden doll like the ones the slaves used in their voodoo ceremonies. "I don't know where she got that filthy thing," Madame Delphine commented, making a move to take it from her, but the girl clung to her only treasure with such desperation that Violette intervened. Honoré wept as he told Tété good-bye, and promised he would come visit her if he was allowed.

Toulouse Valmorain could not prevent an exclamation of displeasure when Violette showed him whom she had chosen to be his wife's maid. He was expecting someone older, with better appearance and experience, not that frizzy-haired creature covered with bruises, who shrank into herself like a snail when he asked her name, but Violette assured him that his wife was going to be very pleased once she trained her.

"And what is this going to cost me?"

"What we agreed on, once Tété is ready."

Three days later Tété spoke for the first time. She asked if that man was going to be her master; she thought that Violette had bought her for herself. "Do not ask questions and do not think of the future," Loula warned her, "for slaves count only the present day."

The admiration Tété felt for Violette erased her resistance, and soon she willingly fell into the rhythm of the house. She ate with the voracity of someone who has lived with hunger and after a few weeks showed a little meat on her bones. She was avid to learn. She followed Violette like a dog, devouring her with her eyes as she nourished in the secret depths of her heart the impossible desire to be like her, as beautiful and elegant as she, but more than anything, free. Violette taught her to comb the elaborate coiffeurs of the day, to give massages, to starch and iron fine clothing, and all the other things her future mistress could ask of her. According to Loula, it would not be necessary to work too hard because the Spaniards lacked French refinement, they were very coarse. Loula herself cropped Tété's filthy hair and forced her to bathe often, something unknown to the girl because according to Madame Delphine water weakened the system: all she did was pass a wet cloth across her hidden parts and then splash herself with perfume. Loula felt invaded by the little girl; the two of them barely fit in the tiny room they shared at night. She exhausted the child with orders and insults, more from habit than meanness, and she often knocked her about when Violette wasn't there, but she did not skimp on her food. "The sooner you get some flesh, the sooner you'll go," she told her. In contrast, she showered affability on the old man Honoré when he made his timid visits. She installed him in the drawing room in the best chair, she served him quality rum, and she listened, entranced, as he talked about drums and arthritis. "That Honoré is a true monsieur. How we would like it if one of your friends were as nice as he is!" she later commented to Violette.

Zarité

For a while, two or three weeks, I didn't think about escaping. Mademoiselle was entertaining and pretty, she had dresses of many colors, she smelled of flowers and went out at night with her friends, who then came to the house and had their way with her while I covered my ears in Loula's room, although I heard them anyway. When Mademoiselle woke up about midday, I took her light meal to the balcony, as I'd been ordered, and then she told me about her parties and showed me gifts from her admirers. I polished her fingernails with a piece of chamois and made them shine like shells; I brushed her wavy hair and rubbed it with coconut oil. She had skin like crème caramel, that milk and egg yolk dessert Honoré made me a few times behind Madame Delphine's back. I learned quickly. Mademoiselle told me I am clever, and she never beat me. Maybe I wouldn't have run away if she'd been my mistress, but I was being trained to serve a Spanish woman on a plantation far away from Le Cap. Her being Spanish wasn't anything good, according to Loula, who knew everything and was a seer; she saw in my eyes that I was going to flee even before I had decided to do it, and she told Mademoiselle, but she paid no attention. "We lost all that money! What do we do now?" Loula had shouted when I disappeared. "We wait," Mademoiselle replied, and continued calmly to drink her coffee. Instead of hiring a Negro tracker, which is what was always done, she asked for help from her sweetheart, Capitaine Relais, who ordered his guards to find me without any fuss and not to hurt me.

That's what they told me. It was very easy to leave that house. I wrapped up a mango and end of a bread loaf in a kerchief, walked out the main door, and left, not running so I wouldn't draw attention. I also took my doll, which was sacred to me, like Madame Delphine's saints but more powerful, which is what Honoré told me when he carved it for me. Honoré always talked to me about Guinea, about the loas, about voodoo, and he warned me that I should never go to the gods of the blancs because they are our enemies. He explained that in the tongue of his parents, voodoo means divine spirit. My doll represented Erzulie, the loa of love and maternity. Madame Delphine made me pray to the Virgin Mary, a goddess who doesn't dance, just weeps, because they killed her son and she never knew the pleasure of being with a man. Honoré looked after me in my early years, until his bones were knotted like dry branches, and then it was my turn to look after him. What could have happened to Honoré? He must be with his ancestors on the island beneath the sea, because it has been thirty years since the last time I saw him, sitting in Mademoiselle's drawing room on the place Clugny, drinking rum-laced coffee and savoring Loula's little pastries. I hope he survived the revolution with all its atrocities, and that he obtained his freedom in the République Nègre d'Haïti before tranquilly dying of old age. He dreamed of owning a piece of land, of raising a pair of animals and planting his vegetables as his family did in Dahomey. I called him Grandfather, because according to him you do not have to be of the same blood or same tribe to be a member of the same family, but in truth I should have called him Maman. He was the only mother I ever knew.

No one stopped me in the streets when I left Mademoiselle's apartment; I walked several hours and thought I had crossed the whole city. I got lost in the barrio near the port, but I could see the mountains in the distance, and everything was a question of walking in that direction. We slaves knew that there were Maroons in the mountains, but we did not know that beyond the first peaks were many more, so many they can't be counted. Night fell. I ate my bread but saved the mango. I hid in a stable under a pile of straw, although I was afraid of horses, with their hooves like hammers and steaming nostrils. The animals were very near, I could hear them breathing across the straw, a sweet, green breath like the herbs in Mademoiselle's bath. Clinging to my doll Erzulie, mother of Guinea, I slept the whole night without bad dreams, wrapped in the warmth of the horses. At dawn a slave came into the stable and found me snoring with my feet sticking through the straw; he grabbed my ankles and pulled me out with one tug. I don't know what he expected to find, but it must not have been a scrawny little girl, because instead of hitting me, he lifted me up, carried me to the light, and looked me over with mouth agape. "Are you crazy? What made you hide here?" he asked me finally, not raising his voice. "I have to get to the mountains," I explained, also whispering. The punishment for helping a fugitive slave was very well known, and the man hesitated. "Let me go, please, no one will know I was here," I begged him. He thought it over a while, and finally ordered me to stay where I was and be quiet; he made sure there was no one around, and left the stable. He soon returned with a hard biscuit and a gourd of heavily sugared coffee; he waited for me to eat and then pointed to the way out of the city. If he had turned me in, he would have been given a reward, but he didn't. I hope that Papa Bondye has rewarded him. I burst into a run and left behind the last houses in Le Cap. That day I walked without stopping, even though my feet were bleeding and I was sweating, thinking of the Negro hunters of the maréchaussée. The sun was high overhead when I entered the jungle. Green, everything green; I couldn't see the sky, and light barely penetrated past the leaves. I heard the sounds of animals and murmur of spirits. The path was vanishing. I ate the mango but vomited it up almost immediately. Capitaine Relais's guards did not waste time looking for me because I came back alone after spending the night curled among the roots of a living tree; I could hear its heart beating like Honoré's. This is how I remember it.

I spent the day walking, walking, asking and asking, until I reached the place Clugny. I went up to Mademoiselle's apartment so hungry and tired that I scarcely felt it when Loula cuffed me across the room. Mademoiselle, who was getting ready to go out, appeared at that moment, still in her negligee and with her hair down. She lifted me by one arm, pulled me off to her room, and with a push sat me down on her bed; she was much stronger than she *looked. She kept standing, with her arms cocked on her hips, looking at me without speaking, and soon she handed me a handkerchief to wipe off the blood from Loula's blow. "Why did you come back?" she asked me. I didn't have an answer. She handed me a glass of water, and then came my tears, like warm rain, mixing with the blood from my nose. "Be grateful, you stupid brat, that I don't lash you as you deserve. Where were you going? To the mountains? You would never get there. Only a few men do that, the most desperate and courageous. If by some miracle you could get out of the city, cross through the trees and swamps without coming upon a plantation, where dogs would devour you, elude the militiamen, the demons, and poisonous snakes, and reach the mountains, the Maroons would kill you. Why do they want a little thing like you? Do you know how to hunt, fight, use a machete? Do you even know how to please a man?" I had to admit I didn't. She told me that I should be grateful for my luck, that it wasn't at all bad. I begged her to let me stay with her, but she said she didn't need me. She counseled me to behave if I didn't want to end up cutting cane. She was training me to be a lady's maid for Madame Valmorain, an easy task. I would live in the house and eat well, it would be better than being with Madame Delphine. She added that I shouldn't pay attention to Loula, that being Spanish was not an illness, it merely meant speaking differently than we do. She knew my new master, she said, a decent monsieur any slave would be happy to belong to. "I want to be free, like you," I told her, sobbing. Then she told me about her grandmother, caught in Senegal, where you find the most beautiful people in the world. A rich merchant bought her, a Frenchman who had a wife in France but fell in love with her the minute he saw her in the black slave market. She gave him a number of children, and he freed them all. He planned to educate them so they would prosper, like so many people of color in Saint-Domingue, but he died suddenly and left them in penury because his wife claimed his entire estate. The Senegalese grandmother set up a little fried food shop in the port to support the family, but her youngest daughter, twelve years old, did not want to ruin herself gutting fish amid fumes from rancid oil and chose instead to service gentlemen. That girl, who inherited her mother's noble beauty, became the most sought-after courtesan in the city, and she in turn had a daughter, Violette Boisier, to whom she taught everything she knew. This is what she told me. "If it hadn't been for the jealousy of the white man who killed her, my mother would still be the queen of the night in Le Cap. But don't get ideas, Tété, my grandmother's love story happens only rarely. A slave remains a slave. If she escapes, and is lucky, she dies in her flight. If she doesn't, she is caught alive. Tear that idea of freedom from your heart, that is the best thing you can do," she said. Then she took me to Loula to get me something to eat.*

When my master, Valmorain, came to look for me a few weeks later, he didn't recognize me because I'd put on weight; I was clean, my hair was cut, and I was wearing a new dress Loula had sewn for me. He asked my name, and I answered with my firmest voice, not looking up because I knew never to look a white in the face. "Zarité de Saint-Lazare, maître," as Mademoiselle had instructed me. My new master smiled, and before we left he set down a pouch. I did not know how much he paid for me. Another man was waiting in the street with two horses, and he looked me over from head to toe and made me open my mouth to examine my teeth. He was Prosper Cambray, the head overseer. He pulled me up on the croup of his horse, a tall, broad beamed, steaming hot beast that was snorting restlessly. My legs weren't long enough to get a grip, and I had to hold onto the man's waist. I had never ridden on a horse, but I swallowed my fear—no one cared what I felt. Master Valmorain also got on his horse, and we set off. I turned to look at the house. Mademoiselle was on the balcony, waving good-bye, until we turned the corner and I could no longer see her. This is how I remember it.

The Lesson

Sweat and mosquitoes, croaking frogs and whip, days of fatigue and nights of fear for the caravan of slaves, overseers, hired soldiers, and the masters, Toulouse and Eugenia Valmorain. It would take three long days from the plantation to Le Cap, which was still the most important port of the colony, though no longer the capital, which had been moved to Port-au-Prince with the hope of better controlling the territory. The move had little effect; the colonists mocked the law, the pirates sailed up and down the coast, and thousands of slaves fled to the mountains. These Maroons, the always more numerous and bold runaway slaves, fell upon plantations and travelers with justified fury. Capitaine Etienne Relais, "the mastiff of Saint-Domingue," had captured five of their chiefs, a difficult mission because the fugitives knew the terrain, moved like the wind, and hid among peaks inaccessible to horses. Armed only with knives, machetes, and poles, they did not dare confront the soldiers on open ground; theirs was a war of skirmishes, surprise attacks and withdrawals, night forays, stealing, fires, and murders that exhausted the regular forces of the militia—the *maréchaussée*—and the army. The plantation slaves protected them, some because they hoped to join them, others because they were afraid of them. Relais never lost sight of the advantage the Maroons—a desperate people fighting for life and liberty— had over his soldiers, who merely obeyed orders. The capitaine was made of iron, dry, slim, strong, pure muscle and nerves, tenacious and courageous, with cold eyes and deep furrows in a face always exposed to the wind and sun, a man of few words, precise, impatient, and strict. No one was comfortable in his presence, neither the *grands blancs* whose interests he protected, nor the *petits blancs*, whose class he belonged to, nor the *affranchis*, who formed the largest part of his troops. Civilians respected him because he imposed order, and his soldiers, because he did not demand anything of them that he was not himself ready to do. He spent a lot of time trying to hunt down rebels in the mountains, following countless false trails, but he never doubted that he would succeed. He obtained information with methods so brutal that in normal times they were not mentioned in polite society, but since the time of Macandal even fine ladies indulged their taste for cruelty on rebelling slaves; the same *mesdames* who fainted at the sight of a scorpion or the smell of excrement did not shy away from the executions, and afterward commented about them over glasses of lemonade and little cakes.

Le Cap, with its red-roofed houses, noisy, narrow streets, and markets, with its port, where there were always dozens of boats anchored, waiting to take back to Europe their treasure of sugar, tobacco, indigo, and coffee, continued to be considered the Paris of the Antilles, as the French colonials jokingly called it, since the common aspiration was to make a quick fortune and return to Paris and forget the hatred that floated in the island's air like clouds of mosquitoes and April pestilence. Some left their plantations in the hands of managers who to the best of their ability stole and worked the slaves to death, but that was a calculated loss, the price for returning to civilization. That was not the case with Toulouse Valmorain, who had spent several years trapped in his Habitation Saint-Lazare. He had tried a couple of managers brought from France— the Creoles had a reputation of being corrupt—but they were a failure; one died of a snakebite and the other abandoned himself to the temptation of rum and concubines, until his wife arrived to rescue him and take him off without appeal. Now he was trying Prosper Cambray, who like all the free mulattoes in the colony had served the obligatory three years in the militia—the *maréchaussée*—charged with enforcing respect for the law, maintaining order, collecting taxes, and chasing down Maroons. Cambray lacked fortune or patrons and had opted to earn a living at the thankless task of capturing Negroes in that wild geography of hostile jungles and steep mountains where not even mules were surefooted. He had yellow skin pocked with smallpox, frizzy rust colored hair, green, always red-rimmed eyes, a soft, well-modulated voice that contrasted like a joke with his brutal character and killer's physique. He demanded extreme servility from the slaves and at the same time was obsequious with anyone superior to him. At first he tried to win Valmorain's esteem with intrigues, but soon he realized that they were separated by an abyss of race and class. Valmorain offered him a good salary, the opportunity to exercise authority, and the hook of becoming a manager. In the meantime, Cambray chewed on the bit of his ambition and moved with caution, since his employer was suspicious and not an easy prey, as he had at first thought. Even so, he kept alive the hope that Valmorain would not last long in the colony, as he lacked the balls and red blood a plantation required; besides, he was saddled with that Spanish wife with the edgy nerves, whose one desire was to get out of there.

In the dry season, the trip to Le Cap could be made in a single day with good horses, but Toulouse Valmorain was traveling with Eugenia in a hand litter and slaves on foot. He had left women and children on the plantation, along with men who had already lost their will and did not need a lesson. Cambray had chosen to bring the youngest, those who still could imagine freedom. No matter how much the commandeurs lashed the slaves, they could not hurry them beyond human capacity. The route was uncertain, and they were in the middle of the rainy season. Only the instinct of the dogs, and the sure eye of Prosper Cambray, a Creole born in the colony who knew the terrain, prevented them from getting lost in the thick undergrowth, where senses were confused and a person could wander in circles forever. Valmorain feared an attack by Maroons or an uprising of slaves. It would not be the first time that, glimpsing the possibility of flight, the Negroes would face firearms with naked chests, believing their *loas* would protect them from the bullets. While the slaves were afraid of whips and the evil spirits in the jungle, and Eugenia had her own hallucinations, Cambray feared nothing but the living dead, the zombies, and that fear did not consist of encountering them, since they were very few, and timid, but of ending up as one of them. A zombie was the slave of a sorcerer, a *bokor*, and not even death could free him because he was already dead.

The head overseer had often been in that region with the *maréchaussée*, chasing fugitives. He knew how to read the signs of nature, marks invisible to other eyes; he could follow a trail like the best bloodhound, smell the fear and sweat of a prisoner from several hours away, at night see like the wolves, divine a rebellion before it matured and demolish it. He boasted that under his command few slaves had fled from Saint-Lazare; his method consisted of breaking their souls and wills. Only fear and exhaustion could conquer the seduction of freedom. Work, work, work to the last breath, which was not long in coming, because no one's bones grew old there; three or four years, never more than six or seven. "Do not overdo the punishments, Cambray, you are weakening the workers," Valmorain had ordered on more than one occasion, sickened by the purulent sores and amputations that made the slaves useless for work, but he never contradicted Cambray in front of them; in order to maintain discipline, the word of the overseer had to be beyond appeal. That was what Valmorain wanted; it repulsed him to deal with the Negroes, he preferred to have Cambray be the executioner and keep for himself the role of benevolent master, which fit within the humanist ideals of his youth. In Cambray's view, it was more profitable to replace slaves than to treat them with consideration. Once their cost was amortized, it was profitable to work them to their death and then buy others younger and stronger. If someone had doubts about the need to apply an iron hand, the story of François Macandal, the magical Mandingo, dissipated them.

Between 1751 and 1757, when Macandal sowed death among the whites of the colony, Toulouse Valmorain was a spoiled little boy living on the outskirts of Paris in a small château that had belonged to his family for several generations, and had never heard the name Macandal. He didn't know that his father had miraculously escaped the collective poisonings in Saint-Domingue, or that if Macandal had not been captured, the winds of rebellion would have swept the island clean. His execution was postponed in order to give the planters time to reach Le Cap with their slaves; thus the Negroes would be convinced once and for all that Macandal was mortal. "History repeats itself, nothing changes on this damned island," Toulouse commented to his wife as they were going down the same road his father had traveled years before for the same reason, to witness an execution. He explained to her that that was the best way to dishearten the rebels, as the Gouverneur and the Intendant, who for once were in agreement about something, had decided. He hoped that the spectacle would calm Eugenia, but never imagined that the trip was going to turn into a nightmare. Halfway there he was tempted to turn and go back to Saint-Lazare, but he couldn't; the planters had to present a united front against the blacks. He knew that gossip was circulating behind their backs; people were saying that he was married to a half mad Spanish woman, that he was arrogant and took advantage of his social position but did not fulfill his obligations in the Assemblée Coloniale, where the Valmorain chair had not been occupied since the death of his father. The elder Valmorain had been a fanatic monarchist, but his son despised Louis XVI, the irresolute monarch in whose chubby hands the empire rested.

Macandal

The story of Macandal, which her husband told her, stirred Eugenia's dementia but had not caused it—it already ran in her veins. No one had warned Toulouse Valmorain when he sought Eugenia's hand in Cuba that there had been several lunatics in the García del Solar family. Macandal had been brought from Africa, a cultivated Muslim who read and wrote in Arabic, and had knowledge of medicine and plants. He lost his right arm in a horrible accident that would have killed a weaker man, and as he was unable to work in the cane fields, his master sent him to herd cattle. He moved around the region, feeding on milk and fruit, until he learned to use his left hand and his toes to set traps and fashion knots to hunt rodents, reptiles, and birds. In the solitude and silence he recovered the images of his adolescence, when he had trained for war and hunting, as befitted the son of a king. His brow was high, his chest strong, he had swift legs and eagle eyes, and he grasped his lance with a firm hand. The island vegetation was different from that in the enchanted regions of his youth, but he began to experiment with leaves, roots, husks, many kinds of mushrooms, and found that some acted as cures, others provoked dreams and trances, and some killed. He always knew he was going to run away—he would rather leave his hide behind in the worst tortures than stay a slave—but he prepared with care and waited with patience for the right occasion, then finally ran to the mountains and from there initiated the uprising of slaves that was to shake the island like a terrible hurricane. He joined with other Maroons, and soon they saw the effects of his fury and his shrewdness: a surprise attack on the darkest night, the radiance of torches, the thudding of bare feet, cries, metal against chains, fires in the cane fields. The name of the Mandingo traveled from mouth to mouth, repeated by the Negroes as a prayer of hope. Macandal, the prince of Guinea, was transformed into a bird, a lizard, a fly, a fish. A slave bound to a post would see a rabbit race by before the lashing that would sink him into unconsciousness: it was Macandal, witness to his torture. An impassive iguana observed the girl who lay in the dust, raped. "Get up, wash yourself in the river, and do not forget, because soon I will come for revenge," hissed the iguana. Macandal. Decapitated roosters, symbols painted with blood, hatchets in doors, a moonless night, another fire.

First the cattle began to die. The colonists attributed it to a lethal plant that grew hidden in the fields and began, without results, to call on European botanists and local witch doctors to find and eradicate it. Next were the horses in the stables, the mastiffs, and finally entire families were struck down. The victims' bellies swelled, their gums and fingernails turned black, their blood turned to water, their skin peeled off in strips, and they died in the grip of atrocious contortions. The symptoms did not fit with any of the illnesses that ravaged the Antilles, and they were manifest only among whites; at that point there was no doubt it was poison. Macandal, again Macandal. Men dropped dead after drinking a swallow of liquor, women and children after a cup of chocolate, all the guests at a banquet before dessert had been served. The fruit on the trees could not be trusted, nor a sealed bottle of wine; not even a cigarette, because no one knew how the poison was administered. Hundreds of slaves were tortured without telling how death entered their victims' houses, until a girl of fifteen, one of many the Mandingo visited at night in the form of a bat, when threatened with being burned alive revealed the way to find Macandal. She was burned anyway, but her confession led the militiamen to the lair of Macandal, scaling peaks and chasms like goats until they reached the ashen mountains of the ancient Arawak chieftains. They captured Macandal alive. By then six thousand persons had died. It is the end of Macandal, the whites said. We shall see, the Negroes whispered.

The central *place* was small for the public that gathered from the plantations. The *grands blancs* made themselves comfortable under their canopies, stocked with food and drink, the *petits blancs* resigned themselves to sitting on the galleries, and the *affranchis* rented the balconies around the *place* that belonged to other free people of color. The best view was reserved for the slaves herded there by their masters from far away, to witness that Macandal was nothing more than a poor one-armed Negro who would cook like a roasted pig. They crowded the Africans around the bonfire, guarded by dogs tugging on their chains and crazed by the smell of human flesh. The day of the execution dawned with clouds; it was warm, and no air was stirring. The odors of the dense crowd mixed with those of burnt sugar, grease from the fry shops, and the wild flowers that grew tangled in the trees. Several priests were sprinkling holy water and offering a bun for every confession. The slaves had learned to trick the priests with garbled sins, since the shortcomings they admitted went directly to their masters' ears, but on this occasion no one was in the mood for buns. They were jubilantly waiting for Macandal.

The overcast sky threatened rain, and the Gouverneur calculated that they had very little time before the skies opened, but he had to wait for the Intendant, the commissioner who represented the civil government. Finally the Intendant and his wife, an adolescent crushed by the weight of her heavy gown, her plumed headgear, and her vexation, appeared on one of the raised stands reserved for honored guests. She was the only French woman in Le Cap who did not want to be there. Her husband, still young though twice her age, was bowlegged and fat of buttocks and belly, but beneath his elaborate wig he displayed the handsome head of an ancient Roman senator. A roll of the drums announced Macandal's appearance. He was welcomed by a chorus of threats and insults from the whites, mockery from the mulattoes, and shouts of frenetic excitement from the Africans. Defying the dogs, whiplashes, and orders from overseers and soldiers, the slaves rose to their feet, arms raised to the sky in greeting to Macandal. That produced a unanimous reaction; even the Gouverneur and the Intendant got to their feet.

Macandal was tall, very dark, his entire body marked with scars and barely covered by a pair of filthy, bloodstained breeches. He was in chains, but he stood erect, haughty, indifferent. He ignored the whites, the soldiers, priests, and dogs; his eyes passed slowly over the slaves, and each knew that those black pupils saw them, giving to them the unconquerable breath of his spirit. He was not a slave who would be executed but the only truly free man in the throng. That was what everyone intuited, and a profound silence fell over the *place*. Finally the blacks reacted, and in an uncontrollable chorus they howled the name of the hero: Macandal, Macandal, Macandal. The Gouverneur realized that the best course was to end quickly, before the planned circus turned into a bloodbath. He gave the signal, and the soldiers chained the prisoner to the post of the fire. The executioner lighted the straw, and soon the greased logs were blazing, enveloped in dense smoke. Not a sigh was heard as the deep voice of Macandal rose to the sky: I will be back! I will be back!

What happened then? That would be the most asked question on the island for the remainder of its history, as the colonists liked to say. Whites and mulattoes saw Macandal break free of his chains and leap over the blazing logs, but the soldiers fell upon him, clubbed him, and led him back to the pyre, where minutes later he was swallowed up in the flames and smoke. The Negroes saw Macandal break free of his chains and leap over the blazing logs, and when the soldiers fell upon him he turned himself into a mosquito and flew up out of the smoke, made a complete circle of the *place*, so all would be able to bid him farewell, and then was lost in the sky, just before the rainstorm that soaked the bonfire and put out the flames. The whites and *affranchis* saw Macandal's charred body. The Negroes saw nothing but the empty post. The former withdrew, running through the rain, and the latter stayed, singing, washed clean by the storm. Macandal had conquered, and had kept his promise. Macandal would be back. And because it was necessary to demolish that absurd legend forever, Valmorain told his unbalanced wife that that was why they were taking their slaves to witness another execution in Le Cap, twenty-three years later.

The long caravan was policed by four militiamen armed with muskets, Prosper Cambray and Toulouse Valmorain with pistols, and the commandeurs, who being slaves carried only swords and machetes. They were not to be trusted; in case of attack they might join the Maroons. The hungry Negroes moved very slowly, bundles on their backs, linked together with a chain that slowed their march and that to the master seemed excessive, but he could not countermand the head overseer. "No one will attempt to break away; the Negroes fear the jungle demons more than poisonous jungle creatures," Valmorain explained to his wife, but Eugenia did not want to know about blacks, demons, or jungle creatures. Little Tété was unchained, walking beside the litter of her mistress, which was carried by two slaves recruited from among the strongest. The path was lost in the tangle of vegetation and mud, the travelers' procession was a wretched snake dragging itself toward Le Cap in silence. From time to time the dogs barked, a horse neighed, or the whistle of a whip and a scream interrupted the murmur of human breathing and rustling leaves. At first Prosper Cambray tried to keep them singing, to lighten spirits and frighten away snakes, as they did in the cane fields, but Eugenia, stupefied by the swaying and fatigue, could not bear it.

In the jungle, beneath the thick dome of trees, it grew dark early, and the dawn light came late through the dense fog tangled in the ferns. The day was growing short for Valmorain, who was in a hurry, but eternal for the rest. The only food for the slaves was dried meat with a maize or sweet potato soup and a cup of coffee, handed out at night after they camped. The master had ordered a cube of sugar and a jot of *taffia*—the cane liquor of the poor—to be added to the coffee to warm those who were sleeping piled together on the ground and soaked with rain and dew, exposed to the devastation of an attack of fever. That year epidemics had been calamitous on the plantation; they'd had to replace many slaves, and none of the newborn had survived. Cambray warned his employer that the liquor and sugar would corrupt the slaves, and later there would be no way to keep them from sucking the cane. There was a special punishment for that infraction, but Valmorain was not given to complicated torture, except for runaways, in which case he followed the Code Noir to the letter. The execution of Maroons in Le Cap seemed to him a waste of time and money; it would have been enough to hang them without all the fuss.

The militiamen and the commandeurs took turns during the night guarding the campsite and the fires, which held animals at bay and calmed humans. No one felt easy in the darkness. The masters slept in hammocks inside a large waxed canvas tent that also contained their trunks and a few pieces of furniture. Eugenia, once greedy, now had the appetite of a canary, but she sat with ceremony at the table because she still followed the rules of etiquette. That night she sat in a blue upholstered chair, dressed in satin, with her filthy hair caught in a bun, sipping lemonade and rum. Her husband—no waistcoat, shirt open, a growth of beard, his eyes red-rimmed—drank his rum directly from a bottle. The woman could scarcely contain her nausea from the food: lamb cooked with chilies and spices to mask the bad smell of the second day of travel, beans, rice, salted maize cakes, and fruit preserved in syrup. Tété fanned her mistress, unable to avoid the compassion she felt for her. She had grown fond of Doña Eugenia, as she preferred to be called. Her mistress did not beat her, and she confided her worries to her, though in the beginning Tété hadn't understood Doña Eugenia because she was speaking Spanish. She told Tété how her husband had courted her in Cuba with gallantries and gifts, but afterward in Saint-Domingue he had shown his true character; he was corrupted by the bad climate and the Negroes' magic, like all the colonists in the Antilles. She, in contrast, came from the best society of Madrid, from a noble Catholic family. Tété could not imagine what her mistress was like in Spain or Cuba, but she could see that she was deteriorating before her eyes. When she met Eugenia, she'd been a robust young woman ready to adapt to her life as a newlywed, but within a few months she was sick at heart. She was frightened of everything, and wept over nothing.

Zarité

*I*n their tent, the masters ate as they did in the dining room of the big house. A slave swept insects from the ground and waved away mosquitoes, while another two stood behind the masters' chairs, barefoot, their livery dripping sweat and their white wigs stinking, ready to serve them. The master swallowed distractedly, barely chewing, while Doña Eugenia spit out mouthfuls into her napkin because to her it all tasted of sulfur. Her husband repeated over and over that she must be calm and eat, the rebellion had been crushed before it began, and its ineffective leaders were locked up in Le Cap in more iron than they could lift, but she feared the chains would burst, the way the witch doctor Macandal's had done. The master's idea to tell her about Macandal had not been a good one, it had ended up frightening her. Doña Eugenia had heard of heretics being burned at the stake before it occurred in her own country, and she had no desire to witness such a horror. That night she complained that a tourniquet was tightening around her head, she could not bear more; she wanted to go to Cuba to see her brother, she could go alone, it was a short journey. I wanted to dry her face with a kerchief, but she pushed me away. The master told her not even to think of it, it was very dangerous and it would not be appropriate for her to arrive alone in Cuba. "Speak no more of this!" he exclaimed angrily, jumping to his feet before the slave could pull back the chair, and went outside to give the last instructions to Prosper Cambray. She gestured to me, and I picked up her plate, covered it with a rag, *and took it to a corner to eat later what was left, and then I got her ready for the night. She no longer wore the corset, hose, and petticoats she had in her bridal trunks; on the plantation she went around in light shifts, but she always dressed for dinner. I took off her clothes and brought her the chamber pot; I washed her with a wet cloth, I powdered her with camphor to ward off mosquitoes, I bathed her face and hands with milk, I took the pins from her hair and brushed the chestnut hair one hundred times, while she sat there wearing a lost expression. She was transparent. The master said she was very beautiful, but to me her green eyes and pointed teeth did not look human. When I finished tidying her up, she knelt on her prie-dieu and in a loud voice prayed an entire rosary, chorused by me, as was my obligation. I had learned the prayers, though I did not understand what they said. By then I knew several Spanish words and could obey, she did not give orders in French or Creole. It was not her responsibility to make the effort to communicate, it was ours. This is what she said. The mother-of-pearl beads slipped through her white fingers as I calculated how long before I could eat and lie down to sleep. Finally she kissed the cross on the rosary and put it into the leather bag, flat and long as an envelope, she usually wore around her neck. It was her protection, as mine was my doll Erzulie. I served her a goblet of port to help her sleep, which she drank with a grimace of nausea. I helped her into the hammock, covered it over with a mosquito net, and began to rock her, praying she would soon sleep without being distracted by the winging bats, the quiet padding of animals, and the voices that harassed her at that hour. They were not human voices—that she had explained to me—they came from the shadows, the jungle, below the ground, hell, Africa; they did not speak with words but with howls and strident laughter. "They are the specters the Negroes summon," she wept, terrified. "Shhh, Doña Eugenia, close your eyes, pray . . ." I was as frightened as she, though I had never heard the voices or seen a specter. "You were born here, Zarité, that is why your ears are deaf and your eyes blind. If you came from Guinea, you would know that there are ghosts everywhere," I'd been assured by Tante Rose, the healer of Saint-Lazare. They had assigned her to be my* marraine, *my godmother, when I arrived at the plantation; she had to teach me everything and watch that I didn't escape. "Don't even think of it, Zarité, you would be lost in the cane fields, and the mountains are farther than the moon."*

Doña Eugenia fell asleep, and I crawled to my corner; the trembling light of the oil lamps didn't reach there, and I felt blindly for my plate. I picked up a bite of lamb stew and found that ants had beat me to it; I like their spicy flavor. I was reaching for the second mouthful when the master and a slave came in, two long shadows on the canvas of the tent and the men's strong odor of leather, tobacco, and horses. I covered the plate and waited, not breathing, trying with all the strength of my heart not to be noticed by them. "Virgen María, Madre de Dios, pray for us sinners," my mistress murmured in her dreams, and with a cry added, "Devil's whore!" I flew to rock the hammock before she waked.

The master sat in his chair and the slave took off his boots; then he helped him out of his breeches and the rest of his clothes, leaving him clad only in his shirt, which fell to his hips and left his sex exposed, rosy and limp, like hog tripe, in a nest of straw-colored hair. The slave held the chamber pot for the master to urinate, waited to be dismissed, extinguished the oil lamps but left the candles burning, and left. Doña Eugenia again stirred, and this time she woke, terror in her eyes, but I had already served her another goblet of port. I kept rocking her, and soon she was asleep again. The master came over with a candle, and its light fell on his wife. I don't know what he was looking for, perhaps for the girl who had attracted him a year before. He reached out to touch her but thought better, and merely observed her with a strange expression.

"My poor Eugenia. She spends the night tormented by nightmares and the day tormented by reality," he murmured.

"Yes, maître."

"You do not understand anything I am saying, do you, Tété?"

"No, maître."

"Better that way. How old are you?"

"I don't know, maître. Ten, more or less."

"Then you are not yet a woman, are you?"

"*That may be,* maître.*"

His glance went all over me, head to toe. He touched his member and held it as if weighing it. I lowered even farther my burning face. A drop of wax from the candle fell on his hand and he cursed; then he ordered me to sleep with one eye open to look after my mistress. He climbed into his hammock, and I scurried like a lizard to my corner. I waited till my master was sleeping and then ate, very carefully, not making a sound. Outside it began to rain. This is how I remember it.

The Intendant's Ball

The exhausted travelers from Saint-Lazare reached Le Cap the day before the execution of the Maroons, when the city was palpitating with anticipation, and such a crowd had gathered that the air smelled of horse manure and too many people. There was no place to stay. Valmorain had sent a messenger galloping ahead to reserve a barracks for his slaves, but he had arrived late and could rent space only in the belly of a schooner anchored in the port. It was not easy to load the blacks into skiffs and from there to the boat because they threw themselves on the ground yelling with fright, convinced that the deathly voyage that had brought them from Africa was going to be repeated. Prosper Cambray and the commandeurs herded them by force and chained them in the hold to prevent them from jumping into the sea. The hotels for whites were filled; they had arrived a day late, and the owners had nothing available. Valmorain could not take Eugenia to an *affranchi* boardinghouse. Had he been alone, he would not have hesitated to go straight to Violette Boisier, who owed him a few favors. They were not lovers anymore, but their friendship had been strengthened when she decorated the house in Saint-Lazare, as well as by a few donations he'd made to help her with debts. Violette had amused herself buying on credit without adding up the costs, until the reprimands of Loula and Etienne Relais obliged her to live more prudently.

That night the Intendant was offering a dinner for the most select of civil society, while a few blocks away the Gouverneur received the upper echelon of the army to celebrate in advance the end of the Maroons. In view of the urgent circumstances, Valmorain presented himself at the Intendant's mansion to ask for lodging. He arrived three hours before the reception and was met by the scurrying about that precedes a hurricane; slaves were running with bottles of liquor, large vases of flowers, last minute furniture additions, lamps, and candelabras, while the musicians, all of them mulattoes, were setting up their instruments under the orders of a French director, and the majordomo, list in hand, was counting the gold place settings for the table. An unhappy Eugenia arrived half swooning in her litter, followed by Tété with a flask of salts and a chamber pot. Once the Intendant had recovered from the surprise of seeing them at his door so early, he welcomed them though he scarcely knew them, mellowed by Valmorain's prestigious name and the lamentable state of his wife. The Intendant had aged prematurely; he must have been a little over fifty, but fifty years badly lived. He could not see his feet for his belly, he walked on stiff, spraddled legs, his arms were too short to button his waistcoat, he huffed like a bellows, and his aristocratic profile disappeared amid fiery red cheeks and the bulbous nose of a bon vivant; his wife, however, had changed very little from girlhood. She was ready for the reception, attired in the latest mode from Paris, wearing a wig adorned with butterflies and a dress covered with bows and cascades of laces, its deep décolletage hinting at childlike breasts. She was the same insignificant sparrow she'd been at nineteen, when from a box of honor she had watched Macandal burn at the stake. From that time she had witnessed enough torture to feed all the rest of her nights with nightmares. Dragging the weight of her gown, she led her guests to the second floor, showed Eugenia to a room, and gave orders for a bath to be prepared for her, though all her guest wanted was to rest.

A few hours later the guests began to arrive, and soon the mansion was animated with music and voices that reached Eugenia, flat on her bed, as muted sounds. Nausea kept her from moving, and Tété fanned her and applied compresses of cold water to her forehead. Her elaborate iridescent brocade finery awaited on a sofa, along with white silk stockings and high-heeled black taffeta slippers. Down on the first floor the ladies were drinking their champagne while standing, the width of their skirts and their tight bodices making it difficult to sit down, while the gentlemen were commenting on the next day's spectacle in measured tones, since it was not good taste to be overly excited by the torture of some rebellious blacks. After a bit, the musicians interrupted conversation with a blast of cornets, and the Intendant made a toast to the colony's return to normal. Everyone lifted a glass, and as Valmorain drank from his, he wondered what the devil "normal" meant: whites and blacks, free and slaves, all living sick with fear.

The majordomo, in a theatrical admiral's uniform and with the appropriate pomp, struck the floor three times with a gold staff to announce dinner. At the age of twenty-five, the man was too young for a post of such responsibility and dazzle. Neither was he French, as might be expected, but a handsome African slave with perfect teeth; some of the female guests had already cast him a wink. But why would they not notice him, considering that he was six and a half feet tall and bore himself with more grace and authority than the highest of the guests? After the toast, those gathered glided toward the sumptuous dining hall illuminated by hundreds of candles. Outside, the night had grown cooler, but inside the heat was rising. Valmorain, crushed beneath the clinging odor of sweat and perfumes, took in the long tables gleaming with gold and silver, Baccarat crystal and Sèvres porcelain, the liveried slaves, one behind each seat and others lined along the walls to pour wine, pass the platters, and take away the plates, and calculated that it was going to be a very long night indeed; the excessive etiquette caused him as much impatience as the banal conversation. Perhaps it was true that he was turning into a savage man, an accusation his wife frequently made. The guests slowly took their seats in the midst of a confusion of pulled out chairs, crackling silks, conversation, and music. Finally the servants entered in a double row with the first of fifteen dishes announced on a gold lettered menu: tiny quail stuffed with dried plums and presented in the blue flames of blazing brandy. Valmorain had not yet finished digging among the minuscule bones of his bird when the remarkable majordomo came to him and whispered that his wife was indisposed. At the same moment another servant was giving the same message to the hostess, who made a sign to Valmorain from the other side of the table. Both got up without attracting attention amid the hubbub of voices and noise of silver against porcelain, and went up to the second floor.

Eugenia was green, and the room stank of vomit and excrement. The Intendant's wife suggested that Eugenia be examined by Dr. Parmentier, who fortunately was in the dining hall, and immediately the slave at the door ran to look for him. The physician, some forty years old, small, slim, with nearly feminine features, was the *homme de confiance* of the *grands blancs* of Le Cap for his discretion and professional skill, although his methods were not the most orthodox; he preferred the herbarium of the poor in place of the purges, bloodletting, enemas, poultices, and fantasized remedies of European medicine. Parmentier had succeeded in discrediting the elixir of lizard sprinkled with gold dust, which had the reputation of curing the yellow fever of the wealthy—others could not afford it. He had been able to prove that the brew was so toxic that if the patient survived the dread fever, *mal de Siam*, he would die of the poison. He did not have to be begged to go up and see Madame Valmorain, at least he would be able to draw a breath of air that wasn't as thick as that in the dining hall. He found Eugenia weak among the pillows of her bed and proceeded to examine her while Tété removed the basins and rags she had used to cleanse her mistress.

"We have traveled three days to attend tomorrow's event, and look at the state my wife is in," Valmorain commented from the doorway, holding a handkerchief to his nose.

"Madame will not be able to attend the execution, she must rest for one or two weeks," stated Parmentier.

"Is it her nerves again?" her husband asked, irritated.

"She needs to rest in order to avoid complications. She's pregnant," the doctor said, covering Eugenia with the sheet.

"A son!" exclaimed Valmorain, stepping forward to caress his wife's inert hands. "We will stay here as long as you say, Doctor. I will rent a house so we do not impose upon the Intendant and his kind wife."

When she heard that, Eugenia opened her eyes and sat up with unexpected energy.

"We must leave this minute!" she shrieked.

"Impossible, *ma chérie*, you cannot travel under these conditions. After the execution, Cambray will take the slaves to Saint-Lazare, and you and I will stay here and make you well."

"Tété, help me dress!" she cried, throwing off the sheet.

Toulouse tried to hold her, but she gave him a hefty push and with flames in her eyes demanded they flee immediately, Macandal's armies were already on the march to rescue the Maroons from the jail and take vengeance on the whites. Her husband begged her to lower her voice so she not be heard in the rest of the house, but she continued to howl. The Intendant came up to see what was happening and found his guest half naked, struggling with her husband. Dr. Parmentier took a flask from his kit, and among the three men they forced Eugenia to swallow a dose of laudanum that would lay out a buccaneer. Sixteen hours later the scent of scorched flesh blowing in through the window woke Eugenia Valmorain. Her shift and the bed were bloody. So ended the illusion of the first son. And so Tété was saved from seeing the execution of the prisoners, who like Macandal perished in flames.

The Madwoman of the Plantation

Seven years later, in a blazing August battered by hurricanes, Eugenia Valmorain gave birth to her first living child, following a series of miscarriages that had destroyed her health. The long desired child arrived when she was no longer able to love it. By then she was a tangle of nerves, falling into lunatic fits in which she wandered through other worlds for days, sometimes weeks. In those periods of delirium she was sedated with tincture of opium, and the rest of the time calmed by infusions brewed from plants raised by Tante Rose, the wise healer of Saint-Lazare, that changed Eugenia's anguish into perplexity, a state more bearable for those who had to live with her. At first Valmorain had mocked "those Negro herbs," but he had changed his mind once he learned of Dr. Parmentier's deep respect for Tante Rose. The physician came to the plantation when his work allowed—despite the setback to his health the ride caused his frail organism—under the pretext of examining Eugenia when in truth he wanted to study Tante Rose's methods. Afterward he tested them in his hospital, noting the results with fastidious precision. He was planning to write a treatise on the natural remedies of the Antilles limited to the botanicals, knowing that his colleagues would never take seriously the magic that intrigued him as much as the plants. Once Tante Rose became accustomed to this white man's curiosity, she often allowed him to go with her to look for specimens in the jungle.

Valmorain provided them with mules and two pistols, which Parmentier wore crossed at his waist although he did not know how to use them. The healer would not let an armed commandeur accompany them, because in her view that was the best way to attract bandits. If Tante Rose did not find what she needed in her search, and had no opportunity to go to Le Cap, she charged the physician with obtaining what she needed, so that he came to know in detail the port's thousand stalls of herbs and magic, which supplied people of every color. Parmentier spent hours talking with the *docteurs-feuilles*, the "leaf doctors" in the stands along the street and in the cubbyholes hidden behind the shops, where they sold natural medicines, witchcraft potions, voodoo and Christian fetishes, drugs and poisons, charms for good luck and others for curses, angel wing dust, and demon's horn. The physician had seen Tante Rose cure wounds that he would have handled by amputation, perform amputations that would have developed gangrene had he done them, and successfully treat the fevers and diarrheas or dysentery that wreaked devastation among the French soldiers crowded together in barracks. "Do not let them have water. Give them a lot of weak coffee and rice soup," Tante Rose taught him. Parmenier deduced that it was all a question of boiling the water, but he also realized that without the healer's herbal infusions there was no recovery. The blacks were relatively immune to those illnesses, but the whites dropped right and left, and if they did not perish within a few days they were left stupefied for months. Nevertheless, for mental derangements as profound as Eugenia's, Negro doctors had no more resources than the Europeans. Blessed candles, purification with sage incense, and rubdowns with snake oil were as useless as the solutions of mercury and ice water baths recommended by medical texts. In the Charenton asylum, where Parmentier had briefly practiced in his youth, there was no treatment for such hopelessly unhinged patients.

At the age of twenty-eight, Eugenia no longer had the beauty that had captured Toulouse Valmorain's love at the consulate's ball in Cuba; she was consumed with obsessions and debilitated by the climate and miscarriages. Her decline had begun to be noted shortly after she arrived at the plantation, and it was accentuated with each of the pregnancies that did not reach full term. She was horrified by the insects that abounded in such infinite variety in Saint-Domingue; she wore gloves, a wide-brimmed hat with a tightly woven, full length veil, and blouses with long sleeves. Two child slaves took turns fanning her, as well as crushing any insect that came anywhere near. A beetle could provoke a crisis. Her mania reached such extremes that she rarely left the house, especially at dusk, the hour of the mosquitoes. She spent her days wrapped within herself and suffered moments of terror or religious exaltation followed by others of impatience, when she struck at everyone within her reach, though never Tété. She depended on the girl for everything, even her most intimate necessities; Tété was her confidante, the only one who stayed by her side when she was tormented by her demons. Tété fulfilled her wishes before they were formulated; she was always alert to pass her a glass of lemonade as soon as thirst was felt, catch on the fly the plate Eugenia threw to the floor, adjust the hairpins that dug into her head, dry her sweat, or set her on the chamber pot. Eugenia did not notice the presence of her slave, only her absence. In her attacks of fear, when she screamed till she had no voice left, Tété closed herself in with her mistress to sing or pray until the fit dissipated, or until she sank into a deep sleep she emerged from with no memories. During Eugenia's long periods of melancholy, the girl climbed into her bed and caressed her like a lover until the sobbing was exhausted. "What a sad life Doña Eugenia has! She is more a slave than I am because she can't escape her terrors," Tété once commented to Tante Rose. The healer knew all too well Tété's dreams of running away, because she'd had to stop her several times, but for a year or two now the girl had seemed resigned to her fate, and had not again mentioned the idea of escaping.

Tété was the first to realize that her mistress's crises coincided with the summons of the drums on nights of the *kalenda*, when the slaves gathered to dance. Those *kalendas* often evolved into voodoo ceremonies, which were forbidden, but Cambray and the commandeurs did not attempt to prevent them because they were afraid of the supernatural powers of the *mambo*, Tante Rose. To Eugenia the drums announced specters, witchcraft, and curses; all her misfortunes were the fault of the voodoo. Dr. Parmentier had explained in vain that voodoo was not a hair-raising practice, it was a grouping of beliefs and rituals like those of any religion, including Catholicism, and very necessary because it gave a sense of meaning to the miserable existence of the slaves. "Heretic! He must be French, to compare the holy faith of Christ with the superstitions of these savages," Eugenia clamored. For Valmorain, a rationalist and atheist, the blacks' trances were in the same category as his wife's rosaries, and in principle he had no objection to either. He tolerated with the same equanimity voodoo ceremonies and the masses performed by the priests who stopped by the plantation, drawn by the excellent rum of its distillery. Africans were baptized en masse as soon as they disembarked in the port, as demanded by the Code Noir, but their contact with Christianity went no further than that, or than the hasty masses conducted by itinerant priests. It was Toulouse Valmorain's opinion that if voodoo consoled the blacks, there was no reason to prohibit it.

In view of Eugenia's inexorable deterioration, her husband wanted to take her to Cuba, to see if the change of atmosphere would alleviate her condition, but his brother-in-law Sancho explained by letter that the good names of the Valmorains and the García del Solars were at risk. Discretion above all. It would be detrimental to both their businesses if his sister's madness became a topic for comment. In passing he told Valmorain how embarrassed he was that he had let him marry a woman who went berserk. In all honesty he hadn't suspected it, his sister had never showed perturbing symptoms in the convent, and when they sent her to him, she seemed normal, if a little dim. He had not thought of the family antecedents. How could he have imagined that his grandmother's religious melancholy and the delirious hysteria of his mother were hereditary? Toulouse Valmorain ignored his brother-in-law's warning and took the sick woman to Havana, where he left her in the nuns' care for eight months. During that time Eugenia never mentioned her husband, but she often asked after Tété, who had been left at Saint-Lazare. In the peace and silence of the convent she grew calm, and when her husband came to fetch her, he found her much saner and more content. Once she was back in Saint-Domingue, that good health lasted only briefly. Soon she was pregnant again; the drama of losing the child was repeated, and again she was saved from death by the intervention of Tante Rose.

During the brief periods when Eugenia seemed relieved of her confusion, everyone in the big house drew breaths of relief, and even the slaves in the cane fields, who caught a faraway glimpse of her only when, swathed in her mosquito veiling, she came out to take the air, could feel the improvement. "Am I still pretty?" she asked Tété, patting her body, which had lost any trace of voluptuousness. "Yes, very pretty," the girl assured her, but she prevented her from looking in the Venetian mirror in the salon before she bathed her, washed her hair, dressed her in one of her fine, though outmoded, gowns, and rubbed carmine on her cheeks and charcoal on her eyelids. "Close all the house shutters and burn tobacco leaves to kill the insects, I am going to dine with my husband," Eugenia ordered, unusually animated. Thus attired, hesitant, her eyes haunted and hands trembling from opium, she appeared in the dining hall, where she had not set foot in weeks. Valmorain welcomed her with a blend of surprise and suspicion, for he never knew how those sporadic reconciliations would end. After so much marital unhappiness he had opted to ignore her, as if that trapped phantom had no relation to him, but when Eugenia appeared in the flattering light of the candelabra, dressed for a party, his illusions returned for a few moments. He no longer loved Eugenia, but she was his wife and they would be together till death. A few sparks of normality tended to lead them to the bed, where he attacked without preamble, with the urgency of a sailor. Those embraces did not unite them, nor did they lead Eugenia back to the terrain of reason, but at times they did result in another pregnancy, and so the cycle of hope and frustration would be repeated. In June of that year she learned that she was pregnant again, but no one, she least of all, was moved to celebrate the news. By coincidence there was a *kalenda* the same night that Tante Rose confirmed her state, and Eugenia believed that the drums were announcing the gestation of a monster. The creature in her womb was cursed by voodoo, it was a child zombie, a living dead. There was no way to calm her, and her hallucination came to be so vivid that she infected Tété. "And what if it's true?" the girl asked Tante Rose, trembling. The healer assured her that no one had ever engendered a zombie, they had to be created from a fresh cadaver, not at all an easy procedure, and she suggested having a ceremony to cure the imagined sickness her mistress was suffering. They waited till Valmorain was away, and Tante Rose performed a rite she told Eugenia would reverse the supposed black magic of the drums, complex rituals and incantations destined to transform the tiny zombie into a normal baby. "How will we know whether this has had an effect?" Eugenia asked at the end. Tante Rose gave her a tisane to drink, a nauseating infusion, and told her that if her urine turned blue, everything had come out well. The next day Tété took away a chamber pot that held a blue liquid, but that only half calmed Eugenia, who suspected they had put something in the pot. Dr. Parmentier, to whom they had not told a word of Tante Rose's intervention, ordered them to keep Eugenia Valmorain in a constant half-sleep until she delivered the baby. By then he had lost any hope of making her well; he believed that the atmosphere of the island was gradually killing her.

Ceremony Officiant

The drastic measure of keeping Eugenia sedated had a better result than Parmentier himself had hoped. During the following months, her belly swelled normally as she passed her days lying beneath mosquito netting on a divan on the gallery, sleeping or distracted by the passing clouds, completely disconnected from the miracle occurring inside her. "If she was always this tranquil, it would be perfect," Tété heard her master say. Eugenia was fed sugar and a concentrated soup of chicken and vegetables that had been ground in a mortar, a soup invented by the cook, Tante Mathilde, capable of reviving a dead-for-three-days corpse. Tété carried out her tasks in the house and then sat in the gallery to sew the baby's layette and sing in her deep voice the religious hymns Eugenia loved. Sometimes when they were alone, Prosper Cambray would come to visit, using the pretext of asking for a glass of lemonade, which he drank with astonishing slowness, sitting with a leg over the railing and striking his boots with his rolled up whip. The overseer's always red-rimmed eyes would run up and down Tété's body.

"Are you calculating her price, Cambray? She isn't for sale," Toulouse Valmorain said one afternoon when he surprised his overseer by suddenly appearing on the gallery.

"What did you say, monsieur?" the mulatto answered in a defiant tone, not changing his position.

Valmorain motioned to him, and the head overseer unwillingly followed him to the office. Tété did not know what they talked about; her master told her only that he did not want anyone wandering through the house without his authorization, not even the overseer. Cambray's insolence did not change after that run-in with his employer, and his only precaution before coming to the gallery to ask for a drink and unclothe Tété with his eyes was to make sure Valmorain wasn't nearby. He had lost respect for him some time ago, but he didn't dare push too hard because he was still nursing the ambition to become manager.

When December arrived, Valmorain summoned Dr. Parmentier to stay at the plantation for as long as necessary, until Eugenia gave birth; he did not want to leave the matter in Tante Rose's hands. "She knows more about these things than I do," the physician argued, but he accepted the invitation because it would give him time to rest, read, and annotate the healer's new remedies for his book. Tante Rose was often consulted by people from other plantations, and she treated both slaves and animals, fighting infections, stitching wounds, relieving fevers and injuries, helping at births, and trying to save the lives of punished blacks. She was permitted to travel over large areas while searching for her plants, and she was often taken to buy ingredients in Le Cap, where she was left with money, then picked up in a couple of days to return to the plantation. She was the *mambo*, officiating at the *kalendas* attended by Negroes from other plantations, something Valmorain did not object to even though his head overseer had warned him they ended in sexual orgies or with dozens of possessed writhing on the ground with their eyes rolled back in their heads. "Do not be so strict, Cambray. Let them unwind, it makes them more docile at work," the master had replied with good humor. Tante Rose would disappear for days, and when the head overseer was proclaiming that the woman had run away to the Maroons, or crossed the river into Spanish territory, she would return, limping, exhausted, with her herbal pouch filled. Tante Rose and Tété escaped Cambray's authority because he believed that the healer would turn him into a zombie, and Tété was the personal slave of the mistress, indispensable in the big house. "No one watches you, *marraine*," Tété commented one day. "Why don't you run away?" "How would I run with my bad leg? And what would become of the people who need my care? Besides, it doesn't mean anything for me to be free and everyone else slaves," the healer answered. Tété hadn't thought of that, and it kept buzzing around her brain like a bottlefly. She talked about it with her godmother many times, but she was never able to accept the idea that her freedom was irreparably bound to that of the other slaves. If she could escape she would do it without a thought for those left behind, she was sure of that. After her searches, Tante Rose would call her to her cabin, and they would close the door and make the remedies that required precise preparation, proper rituals, and nature's fresh greenery. Witchcraft, Cambray said, that's what those two women are up to; nothing he couldn't resolve with a good lashing. But he didn't dare touch them.

One day Dr. Parmentier spent the hottest hours of the afternoon sunk in the lethargy of the siesta, and then went to visit Tante Rose to find out if she had a cure for a centipede bite. As Eugenia was tranquil and watched by another slave, he asked Tété to go with him. They found the healer sitting in a wicker chair before the door of her cabin, which had been slightly damaged by recent storms, singing in some African tongue as she removed the leaves from a dried branch and placed them on a cloth, so absorbed in the task that she did not see them until they were right before her. She started to get up, but Parmentier stopped her. As he wiped the sweat from his forehead and neck with a handkerchief the healer offered him water he would find inside. Her cabin was larger than it looked from outside, very orderly, everything in a specific place, dark and cool. The furniture was splendid compared with that of other slaves: a board table, a badly chipped Dutch armoire, a rusted tin trunk, several boxes Valmorain had provided her to keep remedies in, and a collection of little clay pots for preparing her brews. A pile of dried leaves and straw covered with a checked cloth and thin coverlet, served her as bed. From the palm ceiling hung branches, bunches of herbs, dried reptiles, feathers, strings of beads, seeds, shells, and other things needed for her science. The doctor swallowed two long drinks from a gourd, waited a couple of minutes to catch his breath, and when he felt better went to take a closer look at the altar, where there were offerings for the *loas*: paper flowers, slices of sweet potato, a thimble of water, and tobacco. He knew that the cross was not Christian, it represented crossroads, but he had no doubt that the painted plaster statue was the Virgin Mary. Tété explained to him that she herself had given it to her godmother, it was a gift from the mistress. "But I like Erzulie best, and my Tante Rose does too," she added. The physician started to pick up the sacred voodoo *asson*, a gourd painted with symbols, mounted on a stick, decorated with beads and filled with the little bones of a newborn child, but he stopped in time. No one should touch it without its owner's permission. "This confirms what I have heard. Tante Rose is a priestess, a *mambo*," he commented. The *asson* is usually in the power of the *houngan*, but in Saint-Lazare there was no *houngan*, and it was Tante Rose who conducted the ceremonies. The physician drank more water and dampened his handkerchief and tied it around his neck before he stepped back out into the heat. Tante Rose did not look up from her meticulous labors, and neither did she offer them a seat, because she had only the one chair. It was difficult to calculate her age; her face was young but her body was mangled. Her arms were slim and strong, her breasts hung like papayas beneath her shift, her skin was very dark, her nose straight and broad at the base, her lips well delineated, and her gaze intense. The kerchief around her head covered an abundant mass of hair that had never been cut and was divided into hard, crimped curls like sisal rope. A cart had run over one of her legs when she was fourteen, breaking several bones that healed badly; that was what caused her to walk with such difficulty, supporting herself on the walking stick a grateful slave had carved for her. Tante Rose considered the accident a stroke of luck, for it freed her from the cane fields. Another injured slave would have ended up stirring boiling molasses or washing clothes in the river, she was the exception, for from the time she was very young the *loas* had chosen her to be a *mambo*. Parmentier had never seen her in a ceremony, but he could imagine her in a trance, transformed. In voodoo all were officiants and could experience the divinity of being mounted by the *loas*; the role of the *houngan* or the *mambo* consisted solely of preparing the *hounfor* for the ceremony. Valmorain had expressed to Parmentier his worry that Tante Rose was a charlatan who took advantage of her patients' ignorance. "What's important are the results. She is more successful with her methods than I am with mine," the physician responded.

Voices of slaves cutting cane came drifting to them from across the fields, all following the same beat. Work began before dawn, as they had to look for forage for the animals and wood for the fires. Then they labored from sunrise to sunset, with a pause of two hours at midday when the sun turned white and the earth sweated. Cambray had attempted to eliminate that rest, which was stipulated by the Code Noir and ignored by most of the planters, but Valmorain thought it necessary. He also gave the slaves one free day a week to tend their vegetables; there was never enough to eat, but they had more than on some plantations, where survival was based on what the slaves grew in their gardens. Tété had heard about a reform of the Code Noir—three free days a week and abolition of the whip—but she had also heard that no colonial would adopt that law in the hypothetical case the king approved it. Who was going to work for another person without a whip? The doctor could not make out the words of the slaves' song. He had spent many years on the island and had become accustomed to hearing the Creole spoken in the city, a language derived from French, jerky and marked by an African rhythm, but the Creole of the plantations was incomprehensible to him; the slaves had changed it into a tongue in a code that excluded whites, and for that reason he needed Tété to translate. He leaned down to examine one of the leaves Tante Rose was pulling from the branch. "What are these good for?" Parmentier asked her. She explained that *koulant* is for a drumming in the chest, for sounds in the head, for weariness that comes at dusk, and for despair. "Would it help me? My heart is failing," he said. "Yes, it will help you, because *koulant* also prevents farts," she replied, and all three burst out laughing. Just at that moment they heard the sound of a horse approaching at a gallop. It was one of the commandeurs, and he was looking for Tante Rose because there had been an accident at the cane press. "Séraphine put her hand where she shouldn't have," he yelled from atop his horse and left immediately, without offering to take the healer. She delicately wrapped the leaves in the cloth and asked Tété to take them inside her cabin. She picked up the pouch she always had ready and set out walking as fast as she could, followed by Tété and the physician.

Along the way they passed several carts that were moving at the slow pace of the oxen, laden to the top with a mound of recently cut cane that could not wait more than a day or two to be processed. As they neared the crude wood, reed-roofed buildings, the thick smell of molasses clung to their skin. On both sides of the road slaves were working with knives and machetes, watched over by commandeurs. If those men showed the least sign of compassion, Cambray sent them back to cutting cane and replaced them. To supplement his slaves, Valmorain had hired two crews from his neighbor, Lacroix, and they were treated even worse, for Prosper Cambray had no interest in how long they would last. Several children were running up and down the rows with pails and a large ladle to hand out water. Many blacks were nothing but bones, the men wearing only rough flax cloth breeches and straw hats, the women in long shifts with kerchiefs tied around their heads. Mothers tied their infants to their backs and cut cane all day, bent over from the waist. During the first two months they were given time to nurse, but after that they had to leave their infants in a shed under the care of an old woman and the older children, who looked after them as best they could. Many died of tetanus, paralyzed, their jaws frozen; that was one of the island's mysteries, because whites did not suffer from that disease. The masters did not suspect that those symptoms could be provoked, undetected, by sticking a fine needle into a soft part of the baby's head before the cranial bones hardened. In that way the baby went happily to the island beneath the sea without ever experiencing slavery. It was rare to see Negroes with gray hair, like Tante Mathilde, the cook at Saint-Lazare, who had never worked in the fields. When Violette Boisier bought her for Valmorain, she was already along in years, but in her case that didn't matter, only her experience, and she had served in the kitchen of one of the richest *affranchis* in Le Cap, a mulatto educated in France who controlled the exportation of indigo.

In the mill they found a girl on the ground amid a cloud of flies and the deafening noise of machines being pulled by mules. The process was delicate and it was entrusted to the most skillful slaves, who had to determine exactly how much lime to use and how long to boil the syrup to obtain quality sugar. The mill was where the worst accidents occurred, and on this occasion the victim, Séraphine, had bled so much that at first sight Parmentier thought something had exploded in her chest, but then he saw that the blood was flowing from the stump of one arm she was pressing against her round stomach. In one quick move Tante Rose pulled the cloth from her head and tied it above the girl's elbow, murmuring a prayer. Séraphine's head fell backward onto the doctor's knees, and Tante Rose moved to take her into her own lap. She pried open the girl's mouth with one hand and with the other poured in a dark stream from a flask she took from her pouch. "It's just molasses, to revive her," she said, although he had not asked. A slave explained that the girl, pushing cane into the crusher, had been distracted for a moment, and the toothed rollers had caught her hand. Her screams alerted him, and he had been able to stop the mules before the suction of the machine pulled her arm in to the shoulder. To free her, he'd had to cut off her hand with the hatchet that always hung on a hook for precisely that purpose. "We have to stop the bleeding. If she is not infected, she will live," the doctor pronounced, and ordered a slave to go to the big house and bring him his bag. The man hesitated because he took orders only from commandeurs, but at a word from Tante Rose he went running. Séraphine had opened her eyes slightly and was mumbling something the doctor could scarcely capture. Tante Rose bent down to hear. "I can't, *p'tite*, the white man is here, I can't," she answered in a whisper. Two slaves came and lifted Séraphine to take her to a nearby shed, the slaves' hospital, where they laid her on a bench of raw wood. Tété shooed away hens and a pig nosing through the garbage on the ground, while the men held Séraphine and the healer washed her stump with a rag and water from a pail. "I can't, *p'tite*, I can't," she repeated every once in a while into the girl's ear. Another slave brought hot coals from the mill. Luckily Séraphine had lost consciousness by the time Tante Rose cauterized the stump. The doctor noticed that the girl was some six or seven months pregnant and thought that with the loss of blood she would surely abort.

At that moment the figure of a horseman appeared at the threshold of the shed; one of the slaves ran to take the bridle and the man jumped to the ground. It was Prosper Cambray, with a pistol at his waist and whip in his hand, dressed in dark trousers and a shirt of common cloth, but also wearing leather boots and an American hat of good quality, identical to Valmorain's. Blinded from the light outside, he did not recognize Dr. Parmentier. "What is all this uproar?" he asked in the soft voice that could sound so threatening, striking his boots with the whip, as he always did. Everyone stood back so he could see for himself; with that he saw the doctor, and his tone changed.

"Don't bother yourself with this foolishness, Doctor. Tante Rose will take care of it. Allow me to accompany you back to the big house. Where is your horse?" he asked amiably.

"Have this girl taken to Tante Rose's cabin so she can care for her. She is pregnant," Parmentier replied.

"That is not news to me," Cambray replied with a laugh.

"If the wound becomes infected with gangrene, the arm will have to be cut off," Parmentier insisted, red with indignation. "I am telling you that she must be taken to Tante Rose's cabin, immediately."

"That is what the hospital is for, Doctor," Cambray replied.

"This is not a hospital, it's a filthy stable!"

The head overseer looked around the shed with a curious expression, as if seeing it for the first time.

"It isn't worth your time to worry about this woman, Doctor; she cannot work the cane anymore and will have to be used for a different—"

"You have not understood me, Cambray," the physician interrupted, defiant. "Do you want me to speak directly with Monsieur Valmorain to resolve this?"

Tété did not dare take a peek at the overseer's expression; she had never heard anyone speak to Cambray in that tone, not even the master, and she was afraid that Cambray was going to lift his hand against the white man, but when he answered his voice was humble, like that of a servant.

"You are right, Doctor. If Tante Rose saves her, we will at least have her offspring," he decided, touching Séraphine's bloody belly with the handle of his whip.

A Being Not Human

The garden of Saint-Lazare, which emerged as an impulse that struck Valmorain shortly after he wed, had over the years become his favorite project. He designed it by copying drawings from a book on the palaces of Louis XIV, but European flowers did not thrive in the Antilles, and he had to hire a botanist from Cuba, one of Sancho García del Solar's friends, to give him advice. The garden was colorful, with luxuriant blooms, but it had to be defended against the voraciousness of the tropics by three indefatigable slaves, who also cared for the orchids that grew in the shade. Tête went out every day before the worst heat to cut flowers for house bouquets. That morning Valmorain was walking with Dr. Parmentier along the narrow garden path that divided the geometric sections of shrubs and flowers, explaining how after the hurricane of the previous year he'd had to plant everything anew, but the physician's mind was wandering elsewhere. Parmentier lacked an artistic eye for appreciating decorative plants; he considered them an extravagance of nature, being much more interested in the ugly clumps and clusters in Tante Rose's gardens that had the power to cure or to kill. He was similarly intrigued by the healer's sorcery because he had verified its benefits among the slaves. He confessed to Valmorain that more than once he had felt tempted to treat a patient by using the black healer's methods, but his French pragmatism and fear of ridicule had stopped him.

"Those superstitions do not deserve the attention of a scientist like yourself, Doctor," Valmorain bantered.

"I have seen miraculous cures, *mon ami*, just as I have seen people die from no cause at all, only because they believe themselves victims of black magic."

"Africans are very suggestible."

"And also whites. Your wife, without going any—"

"There is a fundamental difference between my wife and an African," Valmorain interrupted, "no matter how addlepated she may be, Doctor! Surely you do not believe that the blacks are like us?"

"From the biological point of view, there is evidence that they are."

"It is obvious that you have had very few dealings with them. Blacks have the constitution for heavy work, they feel less pain and fatigue, their brain power is limited, they do not know how to make choices, they are violent, disorderly, lazy, and they lack ambition and noble sentiments."

"The same could be said of a white brutalized by slavery, monsieur."

"What an absurd argument!" The other smiled disdainfully. "Blacks require a firm hand. And you may be sure that I am referring to firmness, not brutality."

"In that matter there is no median. Once you accept the notion of slavery, how you treat them makes little difference," the physician rebutted.

"I do not agree. Slavery is a necessary evil, the only way to manage a plantation, but it can be done in a humanitarian way."

"It can never be humanitarian to own and exploit another human," Parmentier rejoined.

"And have you never had a slave, Doctor?"

"No. And neither shall I in the future."

"I congratulate you. You have the good fortune not to be a planter. I do not like slavery, I assure you, and I like less living here, but someone must manage the colonies if you are to put sugar in your coffee and smoke a cigar. In France they avail themselves of our products, but no one wants to know how they are obtained. I prefer the honesty of the English and Americans, who approach slavery from a practical point of view," Valmorain concluded.

"In England and the United States there are also those who seriously question slavery, and who refuse to indulge in the products of the islands, especially sugar," Parmentier reminded him.

"They are an insignificant number, Doctor. And I have just read in a scientific journal that Negroes belong to a specimen different from ours."

"How does the author explain how the two different species can have offspring?" the physician asked.

"When you cross a horse with a donkey you get a mule, which is neither one nor the other. Mulattoes are born from the combination of white and black," said Valmorain.

"Mules cannot reproduce, monsieur, mulattoes can. Tell me, if you had a child with a slave woman, would it be human? Would it have an immortal soul?"

Irritated, Toulouse Valmorain turned his back and went to the house, and they did not see each other again till that night. Parmentier dressed for dinner and appeared in the dining hall experiencing the tenacious headache that had tormented him since his arrival at the plantation thirteen days before. He suffered migraines and fainting spells; he said his organism could not endure the island's climate, yet he had never contracted any of the illnesses that decimated other whites. The atmosphere of Saint-Lazare depressed him, and the discussion with Valmorain had left him in a foul humor. He wanted to return to Le Cap, where other patients were waiting for him, as well as the discreet consolation of his sweet Adèle, but he had promised to attend Eugenia and he intended to keep his word. He had examined her that morning and calculated that the birth would occur very soon. His host was waiting for him and welcomed him with a smile, as if the unpleasant disagreement at midday had never happened. During the meal they talked about books and European politics, every day more incomprehensible, and they were in agreement that the American Revolution of 1776 had had enormous influence in France, where some groups attacked the monarchy in terms as devastating as the Americans had used in declaring their independence. Parmentier did not hide his admiration for the United States, and Valmorain shared it, though he also wagered that England would regain control of her American colony with blood and gunpowder, as any empire with plans to survive would do. And if Saint-Domingue should declare independence from France, the way the Americans had broken away from England? Valmorain speculated, immediately clarifying that his was a rhetorical question and in no way a call to sedition. The subject of the accident at the mill also came up, and the physician suggested that perhaps there would be fewer if the shifts were shorter, because the brutal work of the shredders and the heat from the boiling cauldrons clouded reason. He reported that Séraphine's hemorrhage had been stopped and that it was too early to detect signs of infection, but that she had lost a lot of blood, was in shock, and so weak that she did not respond, though he refrained from adding that he was sure Tante Rose was keeping her asleep with her potions. He did not mean to return to the theme of slavery that had so annoyed his host, but after dinner, when they were settled in the gallery, enjoying the cool night air, the cognac and cigars, it was Valmorain himself who mentioned it.

"Forgive my abruptness this morning, Doctor. I am afraid that in these solitudes I have lost the good habit of intellectual conversation. I did not mean to offend."

"You did not offend me, monsieur."

"You will not believe me, Doctor, but before coming here I admired Voltaire, Diderot, and Rousseau," Valmorain told him.

"And not now?"

"Now I must doubt the speculations of the humanists. Life on this island has hardened me, or let's say that it has made me more realistic. I cannot accept that Negroes are as human as we, even though they have intelligence and soul. The white race has created our civilization. Africa is a dark and primitive continent."

"Have you been there, *mon ami*?"

"No."

"I have. I spent two years in Africa, traveling from one side to the other," the physician said. "In Europe very little is known of that enormous and diverse territory. In Africa a complex civilization already existed when we Europeans were wearing skins and living in caves. I concede that the white race is superior in one aspect: we are more aggressive and greedy. That explains our power and the extent of our empires."

"Long before the Europeans arrived in Africa, the blacks were enslaving each other. They still do," said Valmorain.

"Just as whites are enslaving each other, monsieur," the physician countered. "Not all Negroes are slaves, nor all slaves black. Africa is a continent of free people. Millions of Africans are subjected to slavery but many more are free. Slavery is not their destiny, just as is also the case with thousands of whites who are slaves."

"I understand the repugnance you feel for slavery, Doctor," said Valmorain. "I, too, am attracted by the idea of replacing it with a different labor system, but I am afraid that in certain cases, like that of the plantations, there is no other. The world economy rests upon it, it cannot be abolished."

"Perhaps not overnight, but it could be done in some gradual form. In Saint-Domingue the opposite occurs, the number of slaves goes up every year. Can you imagine what will happen when they rebel?" asked Parmentier.

"You are a pessimist," his dinner companion commented, draining the dregs of his glass.

"How could I not be? I have been in Saint-Domingue a long time, monsieur, and to be frank, I have had enough of it. I have seen horrors. To go no further, only a short time ago I was at the Habitation Lacroix, where in the last two months several slaves have killed themselves. Two leaped into a cauldron of boiling molasses—how desperate they must have been."

"There is nothing keeping you here, Doctor. With your royal license you can practice your science wherever you please."

"I suppose I will go someday," the physician replied, thinking that he could not mention his one reason for staying on the island: Adèle and the children.

"I would like to take my family to Paris myself," Valmorain added, but he knew that was a remote possibility.

France was in crisis. That year the director general of finances had called an *assemblée des notables* to force the nobility and the clergy to pay taxes and share the economic burden, but their initiative had fallen on deaf ears. From afar, Valmorain could see how the empire was crumbling. It was not the moment to go back to France, and neither could he leave the plantation in the hands of Prosper Cambray. He did not trust him, but neither could he dismiss him; Cambray had been in his service for many years, and changing him would be worse than putting up with him. The truth of the matter, something he would never have admitted, was that he was afraid of him.

The doctor drank the last of his cognac, savoring the tingle on his palate and the illusion of well-being that invaded him for brief instants. His temples were throbbing, and the pain had concentrated in his eye sockets. He thought of Séraphine's words, which he had barely overheard in the mill, asking Tante Rose to help her and her unborn child to go to the place of Les Morts et Les Mystères, back to Guinea. "I can't, *p'tite.*" He asked himself what the woman would have done had he not been present. Perhaps she would have helped the girl, even at the risk of being caught and having to pay dearly. There are discreet ways to accomplish it, the doctor concluded, feeling very weary.

"Forgive me for pursuing the conversation of the morning, monsieur. Your wife believes she is the victim of voodoo; she says that the slaves have bewitched her. I think we can use that obsession to her benefit."

"I don't understand," said Valmorain.

"We could convince her that Tante Rose can countermand the black magic. We will lose nothing by trying."

"I will think about it, Doctor. After Eugenia gives birth, we will occupy ourselves with her nerves," Valmorain answered with a sigh.

At that moment the silhouette of Tété passed across the patio, illuminated by the moonlight and the torches that were kept lighted at night as a safeguard. The men's eyes followed her. Valmorain called her with a whistle, and an instant later she appeared in the gallery, as silent and light-footed as a cat. She was wearing a skirt discarded by her mistress, faded and mended but nicely made, and an ingenious turban knotted several times that added a hand's width to her height. She was a slim young woman with prominent cheekbones and elongated eyes with sleepy eyelids and golden irises; she had a natural grace, and precise and fluid movements. She radiated a powerful energy, which the doctor felt on his skin. He divined that beneath her austere appearance was hidden the contained energy of a feline at rest. Valmorain pointed to the glass, and she went to the sideboard in the dining hall, returned with a bottle of cognac, and poured some for both.

"How is madame?" Valmorain asked.

"Tranquil, *maître*," she replied, and stepped back to leave.

"Wait, Tété. Let's see if you can help us resolve a doubt. Dr. Parmentier maintains that blacks are as human as whites, and I say the contrary. What do you believe?" Valmorain asked in a tone that to the doctor sounded more paternal than sarcastic.

She said nothing, her eyes on the floor and her hands clasped.

"Come, Tété, answer, don't be afraid. I'm waiting . . ."

"The *maître* is always right," she murmured finally.

"Or, that is, you believe that Negroes are not completely human."

"A being who is not human has no opinions, *maître*."

Dr. Parmentier could not contain a spontaneous guffaw, and Toulouse Valmorain, after a moment's hesitation, laughed too. With a wave he dismissed the slave, who faded into the shadow.

Zarité

The next day in the middle of the afternoon Doña Eugenia gave birth. It was quick, although she did nothing to help up to the last moment. The doctor was at her side, watching from a chair, because catching babies is not a thing for a man to do, as he himself told us. Maître *Valmorain believed that a doctor's license with a royal seal was worth more than experience, and he did not want to call Tante Rose, the best midwife in the north part of the island; even white women called on her when their time came. I held my* maîtresse, *I kept her cool, I prayed with her in Spanish, and I gave her the miraculous water she'd been sent from Cuba. The doctor could clearly hear the baby's heartbeats, it was ready to be born, but Doña Eugenia refused to help. I explained that my* maîtresse *was going to give birth to a zombie and that Baron Samedi had come to take it away with him, and the doctor burst out laughing with such gusto that tears ran down his cheeks. That white man had been studying voodoo for years. He knew that Baron Samedi is the servant and associate of Ghede,* loa *of the world of the dead. I don't know what he found so amusing. "What a grotesque idea! I do not see any baron!" The baron does not show himself to those who do not respect him. Soon he understood that the matter was not amusing, because Doña Eugenia was so agitated. He sent me to look for Tante Rose. I found my master in a chair in the drawing room, fallen asleep after several glasses of cognac; he authorized me to call my godmother, and I flew out to look for her. She was waiting for me, all ready, wearing her white ceremonial gown and her necklaces, and carrying her pouch and the asson. She went to the big house without a question, up to the gallery, and entered through the door for the slaves. To reach Doña Eugenia's room she had to pass through the drawing room, and the thudding of her walking stick on the floorboards woke the master. "Be careful what you do to madame," he warned her in a hoarse voice, but she paid no attention and continued onward, feeling her way down the corridor till she came to the room where she had often come to attend Doña Eugenia. This time she had not come as a healer, but as a mambo; she had come to confront the associate of Death.*

From the doorway Tante Rose saw Baron Samedi, and a shudder ran down her spine, but she did not retreat. She greeted him with a bow, shaking the asson with its clinking of little bones, and asked permission to go to the bed. The loa of cemeteries and crossroads, with his white skull face and black hat, moved aside, inviting her to approach Doña Eugenia, who was gasping like a fish, wet with sweat, her eyes red with terror, fighting against her body, which was struggling to cast out the baby while she was using all her strength to hold it in. Tante Rose placed one of her seed and shell necklaces around my mistress's neck and spoke a few words of consolation to her, which I repeated in Spanish. Then she turned toward the baron.

Dr. Parmentier was watching with fascination, although he saw only Tante Rose's part, while I saw everything. My godmother lighted a cigar and waved it around, filling the air with a smoke that made it difficult to breathe because the window was always closed to prevent mosquitoes from coming in. Then she drew a chalk circle around the bed and whirled in a few dance steps, pointing to the four corners of the room with the asson. Once her greeting to the spirits was concluded, she made an altar out of several sacred objects she took from her pouch and then placed offerings of rum and little stones on it. Lastly she sat at the foot of the bed, ready to negotiate with the baron. The two of them became immersed in a long exchange in Creole so fast and incomprehensible that I understood little of it, though several times I heard

Séraphine's name. They argued, they grew angry, they laughed, she smoked the cigar and blew out smoke that he swallowed in big mouthfuls. That continued for quite a while, and Dr. Parmentier began to lose patience. He tried to open the window, but it had been shut for so long it was stuck. Coughing and teary from the smoke, he took Doña Eugenia's pulse as if he didn't know that babies emerge far below the pulse in the wrist.

Finally Tante Rose and the baron reached an agreement. She went to the door and with a profound bow showed the loa *out, who left making his little froglike hops. Then Tante Rose explained the situation to my mistress: what she had in her womb was not cemetery meat but a normal baby that Baron Samedi would not take away. Doña Eugenia stopped arguing and concentrated on pushing with all her might, and soon a gush of yellow liquid and blood stained the sheets. When the head of the baby appeared, my godmother took it gently and helped the body out. She handed me the newborn child and announced that it was a little boy, but the mother did not even want to look at it; she turned her face to the wall and closed her eyes, exhausted. I pressed the baby to my chest, holding it tight because it was covered with something lardy and slippery. I was absolutely sure that it would be up to me to love this child as if it were my own, and now, after all these years and all that love, I know that I was not mistaken. I wept.*

Tante Rose waited until my mistress expelled what was left inside her and cleaned her up; then with one swallow she drank the rum offering on the altar, put her belongings back into her pouch, and left the room, clutching her walking stick as all the while the doctor was rapidly writing in his notebook. I kept weeping as I washed the baby, who was as light as a kitten. I wrapped him in the little blanket I had knitted during my afternoons in the gallery and carried him to his father so he would know him, but my master had so much cognac in his body I couldn't wake him. In the corridor a slave with swollen breasts was waiting, recently bathed, her head shaved for lice; she would give her milk to the son of the masters in the big house, while her baby was given rice water in the Negro quarters. No white woman nursed her children; that's what I thought then. The woman sat down on the floor, legs crossed, opened her blouse, and took the little one, who fastened himself to her breast. I felt that my skin was burning and my nipples hardened; my body was ready for that baby boy.

At that same hour, in Tante Rose's cabin, Séraphine died alone, unaware because she was sleeping. This is how it was.

The Concubine

They named the boy Maurice. His father was shaken to his boots by that unexpected gift from heaven, which had come to combat his loneliness and stir his ambition. That child was going to carry on the Valmorain dynasty. The master declared a feast day; no one on the plantation worked. He had a number of animals roasted, and assigned three helpers to Tante Mathilde so there would be no shortage of spicy corn dishes and vegetables and cakes for everyone. He gave permission to have a *kalenda* in the main patio in front of the big house, which soon filled with a noisy crowd. The slaves adorned themselves with what little they had—a colored rag, a necklace of shells, a flower. They brought their drums and other improvised instruments, and after a bit there was music and people were dancing under the mocking gaze of Cambray. The master had two barrels of *taffia* distributed, and every slave received a generous dose in his gourd for a toast. Tété appeared in the gallery with the baby wrapped in a mantilla, and the father took him and lifted him over his head to show to the slaves. "This is my heir! He will be called Maurice Valmorain, that is my father's name!" he exclaimed, hoarse with emotion and still hungover from his drunkenness the night before. A silence like the depths of the sea greeted his words. Even Cambray was startled. This ignorant white man had committed the incredible blunder of giving his son the name of a deceased grandfather, who on being summoned could rise from his grave and kidnap his grandson and take him back with him to the world of the dead. Valmorain believed that the silence was respect, and ordered a second round of *taffia* and a continuation of the rejoicing. Tété took back the newborn and rushed away with him, sprinkling his face with a rain of saliva to protect him from the disgrace invoked by his father's rashness.

The next day, when the domestic slaves had cleaned the refuse from the patio and the others had gone back to the cane fields, Dr. Parmentier quickly prepared to go back to the city. Little Maurice was suckling like a calf at his wet nurse's breast, and Eugenia was showing no symptoms of fatal womb fever. Tété had rubbed her breasts with a mixture of honey and butter and bandaged them with a red cloth, Tante Rose's method for drying up milk before it began to flow. On Eugenia's night table she lined up the vials of drops for sleep, the cachets for pain, and syrups for enduring fear, not to heal her, as the doctor himself admitted, but to ease her existence. The Spanish woman was a shadow of ashen skin and ravaged face, more from tincture of opium than from her deranged mind. Maurice had suffered the effects of the drug in his mother's womb, the physician explained to Valmorain, which was why he had been born so small and frail; he would be sickly and needed air, sun, and good nourishment. He ordered them to give three raw eggs a day to the wet nurse to fortify her milk. "Now your mistress and the baby are both in your care, Tété. They could not be in better hands," he added. Toulouse Valmorain paid the doctor generously for his services and bade him farewell with regret, for he truly esteemed the cultivated, good-natured man with whom he had enjoyed countless card games in the long evenings of Saint-Lazare. He would miss the conversations with him, especially those in which they were not in agreement, because that forced him to exercise the forgotten art of arguing for pleasure. He chose two armed commandeurs to accompany the physician to Le Cap.

Parmentier was packing, a task he did not delegate to slaves, being very meticulous about his possessions, when Tété rapped discreetly at his door and asked in a thread of a voice if she might have a word with him in private. Parmentier had been with her often; he used her to communicate with Eugenia, who seemed to have forgotten her French, and with the slaves, especially Tante Rose. "You are a very good nurse, Tété, but do not treat your mistress like an invalid, she has to learn to take care of herself," he advised her when he saw her spooning pap into Eugenia's mouth and learned that Tété set her on the chamber pot and wiped her nether regions so she would not soil herself when she stood up. The girl always answered his questions with precision, in correct French, but she never initiated a dialogue or looked him in the eye, which had allowed him to observe her at his pleasure. She must be about seventeen, he thought, though her body was more like that of a woman than an adolescent. Valmorain had told him Tété's story on one of the hunting trips they made together. He knew that the slave's mother had been pregnant when she arrived at the island and was bought by an *affranchi*, a man who had a horse trade in Le Cap. The woman attempted to provoke a miscarriage, but what she got were more lashes than anyone else in her state could have borne; the little one in her womb, however, was tenacious and in due time was born healthy. As soon as the mother could stand, she tried to smash the baby's head against the floor, but she was grabbed from her in time. Another slave took care of the newborn child for several weeks, until their owner decided to use her to pay a gambling debt to a French official named Pascal, but the mother never learned of it because she had thrown herself into the ocean from a cliff. Valmorain told Parmentier that he had bought Tété to be a personal maid for his wife and had come out well rewarded, as the girl had become both nurse and housekeeper. Apparently now she would also be Maurice's nursemaid.

"What is it, Tété?" the doctor asked, as he carefully placed his valuable silver and bronze instruments into a polished wood case.

She closed the door, and with a minimum of words and no expression on her face, told him she had a son a little more than a year old, whom she had seen for an instant when he was born. Parmentier thought her voice was breaking, but when she continued, explaining that she had the baby while her mistress was resting in a convent in Cuba, she spoke in the same neutral tone as before.

"My *maître* has forbidden me to mention the child. Doña Eugenia knows nothing about it," Tété concluded.

"Monsieur Valmorain did the right thing. His wife had not been able to have children and was very upset when she saw them. Does anyone know about your baby?"

"Only Tante Rose. I think the head overseer, Monsieur Cambray, suspects but has not been able to confirm it."

"Now that madame has her own baby, the situation has changed. Surely your master will want you to get your child back, Tété. After all, it is his property, no?" Parmentier commented.

"Yes, it is his property. It is also his son."

Why hadn't the most obvious thing occurred to me? the doctor thought. He had not glimpsed the least sign of intimacy between Valmorain and the slave girl, but it was easy to conjecture that with a wife like his, a man would console himself with any woman within reach. Tété was very attractive, there was something enigmatic and sensual about her. Such women were gems that only a trained eye would pick from among the stones, he thought, closed boxes that the lover must open little by little to reveal their mysteries. Any man could feel very fortunate to have their affection, but he doubted that Valmorain knew how to appreciate this girl. He thought of his Adèle with nostalgia. She too had been a diamond in the rough. She had given him three children and many years of companionship, so discreetly that he never had to give explanations to the mean-minded society in which he practiced his science. If it had been known that he had a concubine and children of color, whites would have repudiated him; instead they had accepted without question the rumors that he was a sodomite, and that was why he remained a bachelor and frequently disappeared into the barrios of the *affranchis*, where pimps offered young boys for every taste. Because of his love for Adèle and the children, he could not go back to France, however desperate he was on the island. "So little Maurice has a brother. . . . In my profession you learn everything," Parmentier muttered to himself. Valmorain had sent his wife to Cuba not to recover her health, as had been announced at the time, but to hide from her what was happening in her own house. Why so fastidious? It was a common, and accepted, situation; the island was filled with bastards of mixed blood, and he thought he had noticed a couple of little mulattoes among the Saint-Lazare slaves. The only explanation was that Eugenia could not have endured the knowledge that her husband had bedded Tété, her one anchor in the profound confusion of her madness. Valmorain must have divined that Tété's pregnancy would have been the nail in his wife's coffin, and he was not cynical enough to accept that his wife would be better off dead. Finally, the physician decided, it wasn't his concern. Valmorain must have had his reasons and it was not up to him to inquire what they were, but he was intrigued to know whether he had sold Tété's baby or was just raising it away from the plantation for a prudent period of time.

"What can I do, Tété?" asked Parmentier.

"Please, Doctor, can you ask Monsieur Valmorain? I have to know whether my son is alive, whether he sold him, to whom . . ."

"It isn't appropriate for me to do that, it would be discourteous. If I were you, I would not think about the baby any more."

"Yes, Doctor," she replied, her voice nearly inaudible.

"Don't worry, I am sure that he is in good hands," Parmentier added, pained.

Tété left the room, noiselessly closing the door.

With the birth of Maurice the household routines changed. If Eugenia was calm when she woke, Tété dressed her, took her out for a few steps around the patio, and then installed her in the gallery, with Maurice in his cradle. At a distance, Eugenia seemed a normal mother watching over her baby's sleep—except for the mosquito netting that covered them both—but that illusion faded on closer view, when the woman's absent expression became visible. A few weeks after the birth, Eugenia suffered another of her crises and did not want to go outside, convinced that the slaves were watching and waiting to kill her. She spent the day in her room, slipping between the befuddlement of laudanum and delirium of her dementia, so lost that she remembered very little of her son. She never asked how he was being fed, and no one told her that Maurice's nourishment came from the bosom of an African, or she would have concluded that he was suckling poison milk. Valmorain hoped that the unwavering instinct of maternity would make his wife sane again, like a gust of wind blowing over her bones and heart, leaving her clean inside, but one day when he saw her shake Maurice like a stuffed doll to quiet him, with the risk of breaking his neck, he realized that the most serious threat to the baby was its own mother. He grabbed Maurice from her and, unable to contain himself, slapped her so hard that she toppled backward to the floor. He had never struck Eugenia, and he himself was surprised at his violence. Tété helped up her mistress, who was crying without understanding what had happened, tucked her into bed, and went to prepare an infusion for her nerves. Toulouse stopped her on the way and put the child in her arms.

"From this minute on you are in charge of my son. You will pay dearly for anything that happens to him. Do not allow Eugenia to touch him ever again!" he bawled.

"And what do I do when my *maîtresse* asks for her son?" Tété asked, clutching the tiny Maurice to her breast.

"I don't care what you do! Maurice is my only son, and I will not allow that imbecile to harm him."

Tété partially carried out his instructions. She took the infant to Eugenia for brief moments, and let her hold him while she was watching. The mother would sit motionless with the little bundle on her knees, looking at him with an expression of amazement that soon gave way to impatience. After a few minutes she would hand him back to Tété as her attention wandered off in another direction. Tante Rose had the idea of wrapping a rag doll in Maurice's blanket and they found that the mother did not notice the difference; in that way they could space the visits until eventually they were no longer necessary. They moved Maurice to another room, where he slept with his wet nurse, and during the day Tété carried him on her back, tied in a cloth the way African women carried theirs. If Valmorain was in the house, she put the baby in his cradle in the drawing room or in the gallery, so he could see his son. Tété's smell was the only one Maurice identified during the first months of his life; the wet nurse had to put on one of her blouses before the baby accepted her breast.

The second week of July, Eugenia went outside before dawn, barefoot and in her night shift, and tottered off in the direction of the river along the lane of coconut palms that was the entrance to the big house. Tété sounded the alarm, and crews formed and immediately joined with the plantation guards to look for her. The hounds led them to the river, where they discovered her in water up to her neck, her feet stuck in the thick mud of the bottom. No one could understand how she had come so far since she was afraid of the dark. At night her fiendish howls often reached as far as the slaves' huts, giving them gooseflesh. Valmorain believed that Tété was not giving his wife enough drops from the blue vial, since had she been sufficiently sedated, she could not have escaped, and for the first time he threatened to have Tété flogged. She spent several terrifying days anticipating the punishment, but her master never gave the order.

Soon Eugenia was completely disconnected from the world. The only person she tolerated was Tété, who slept by her side at night, curled up on the floor, ready to rescue her from her dreams. When Valmorain wanted the slave, he let her know with a gesture at dinner. She would wait until the sick woman was asleep, then stealthily cross through the house to the main room on the opposite side. It was one such time that Eugenia had waked alone in her room and escaped to the river, and that may have been why her husband did not make Tété pay for that breach of her mistress's care. These behind-a-closed-door, nocturnal embraces between master and slave in the large bed chosen years before by Violette Boisier were never mentioned in the light of day, they existed only on the plane of dreams. At Eugenia's second attempt at suicide, this time a fire that nearly destroyed the house, the situation became clear, and after that no one tried to maintain appearances. It was known in the colony that Madame Valmorain was demented, and few were surprised, since rumors had circulated for years that the Spanish woman came from a long line of hopeless madwomen. Besides, it was not a rare thing for white women who had come from outside the island to become deranged in the colony. Their husbands sent them to recover in a different climate and consoled themselves with the stream of young girls of every shade and tone the island offered. Creoles, on the other hand, flourished in that decadent ambience, where they could succumb to temptations without paying the consequences. In the case of Eugenia, it was already too late to send her anywhere except an asylum, an option Valmorain's sense of responsibility and pride would never allow him to contemplate: dirty linen was washed at home. His house had many rooms, a drawing room and a dining hall, an office and two large storage rooms, so he could spend weeks without seeing his wife. He had entrusted her to Tété, and he focused his attention on his son. He had never imagined that it was possible to love another being so deeply, more than the sum of all his previous affections, more than he loved himself. There was no emotion that resembled what Maurice evoked in him. He could spend hours just watching him; he constantly surprised himself thinking about his son, and once he turned when he was on the way to Le Cap and raced back at a full gallop with the presentiment that something horrible had happened to him. His relief when he found that was not the case was so overwhelming that he burst into tears. He would sit in his easy chair holding his son in his arms, feeling the sweet weight of his head against his shoulder and his warm breath on his neck, breathing in the odor of sour milk and childish sweat. He trembled thinking of the accidents or plagues that could take Maurice from him; half the children in Saint-Domingue died before they reached five. They were the first victims in an epidemic, and that was not even counting intangible dangers like curses, which he insincerely jeered and mocked to others, or an uprising of slaves in which the last white would perish, as Eugenia had prophesied for years.

Slave to Every Need

The mental illness of his wife gave Valmorain a good excuse to avoid social life, which he abhorred, and by three years after the birth of his son he had turned into a recluse. His business obliged him to go to Le Cap, and from time to time to Cuba, but it was dangerous to move about because of the bands of Negroes who descended from the mountains to lay siege to the roads. The ceremonial burning of the Maroons in 1780, and others after that, had not discouraged slaves from running away or the Maroons from attacking plantations and travelers. He preferred to stay at Saint-Lazare. I need nothing, he told himself with the cunning pride of those with a calling for solitude. As the years passed he became less fond of people; everyone, except Dr. Parmentier, seemed stupid or venial. He had only commercial relations, like his Jewish manager in Le Cap or his banker in Cuba. The other exception, aside from Parmentier, was his brother-in-law, Sancho García del Solar; though Valmorain seldom saw him they had a rather regular correspondence. Sancho amused him, and the businesses they undertook together had turned out to be beneficial for both. Sancho often good-humoredly confessed that that was a true miracle, because he had never done well before he met Valmorain. "Prepare yourself, brother-in-law, because any day now I will sink you," he would joke, but he continued to ask for loans that after a while were returned many times over.

Tété managed the domestic slaves with geniality and firmness, minimizing problems in order to prevent the master's intervention. Her slim figure, in a dark skirt and percale blouse, a starched *tignon* on her head, keys clinking at her waist and Maurice riding her hip or clinging to her skirts as he learned to walk, seemed to be everywhere at once. Nothing escaped her attention, neither instructions for the kitchen or bleaching the clothing, not the stitches of the seamstresses or the urgent needs of the master or child. She knew how to delegate and was able to train a female slave who no longer worked in the cane fields to help her with Eugenia and free her from sleeping in the ill woman's room. The slave stayed with Eugenia, but Tété administered the remedies and washed her mistress, because Eugenia would not let herself be touched by anyone else. The one thing Tété did not delegate was Maurice's care. She adored with a mother's jealousy that capricious, delicate, and emotional child. By then the wet nurse had returned to the alley of the slaves and Tété shared a room with the boy. She slept on a light mattress in the corner, and Maurice, who refused to stay in his cradle, curled up beside her, pressed against her warm body and generous breasts. Sometimes, waked by the boy's snores she would caress him in the dark, moved to tears by the smell of him, his unruly curls, his limp little hands, his body sprawled in sleep, thinking of her own son and wondering if another woman somewhere was lavishing the same affection on him. She gave Maurice everything Eugenia could not: stories, songs, laughs, kisses, and from time to time a swat to make him obey. On the rare occasions when she scolded him, the boy would throw himself on the ground, kicking and threatening to complain to his father, but he never did, somehow sensing that the consequences would be grave for the woman who was his universe.

Prosper Cambray had not managed to impose his law of terror among the household servants; a tacit frontier had been established between Tété's small territory and the rest of the plantation. Her domain was run like a school, and his like a prison. In the house, precise chores were assigned to each slave, who carried them out smoothly and calmly.

In the fields people marched in rows under the always ready whips of the commandeurs; they obeyed without a word and lived in a state of alert, for any carelessness was paid for with blood. Cambray charged himself personally with discipline. Valmorain did not lift a hand against the slaves, he considered it degrading, but he attended punishments to establish his authority and to make sure that the overseer did not overstep himself. He never reproached Cambray in public, but his presence at the place of torture imposed a certain restraint. The house and fields were worlds apart, but nonetheless Tété and the overseer did occasionally meet, and then the air was charged with the threatening energy of a storm. Cambray looked for her, excited by the young woman's obvious scorn, and she avoided him, made uneasy by his brazen lust. "If Cambray goes too far with you I want to know it immediately, do you understand me?" Valmorain warned her more than once, but she never went to him; it was not good to provoke the overseer's wrath.

By order of her *maître*, who did not tolerate hearing Maurice *parler nèg*, speak like the blacks, Tété always spoke French in the house. She spoke Creole with all the others on the plantation, and with Eugenia the Spanish that was becoming reduced to a few indispensable words. The ill woman had sunk into a melancholy so persistent, and an emotional indifference so complete, that if Tété hadn't fed and washed her she would have died of hunger, filthy as a pig, and if she hadn't moved her and changed her position, her bones would have frozen in place, and if she hadn't urged her to speak, she would have been mute. She no longer suffered panic attacks but spent her days half awake, half asleep in a large chair, eyes staring ahead, like a huge doll. She still recited the rosary, which she always wore in a small leather bag she hung around her neck, even though she could no longer say the words. "When I die you will have my rosary—do not let anyone take it from you, because it is blessed by the pope," she had told Tété. In rare moments of lucidity she prayed for God to take her away. According to Tante Rose, her *ti-bon-ange* was stuck in this world and needed a special service to liberate it, nothing painful or complicated, but Tété had not decided to take such an irrevocable step. She wanted to help her hapless mistress, but responsibility for her death would be a crushing burden, even shared with Tante Rose. Perhaps Doña Eugenia's *ti-bon-ange* still needed to do something in her body; they would have to give it time to get free by itself.

Toulouse Valmorain imposed his embraces on Tété frequently, more out of habit than affection or desire, without the urgency of the period when she entered puberty and he was overcome by a sudden passion. Only Eugenia's dementia explained why she had not realized what was happening right before her eyes. "The *maîtresse* suspects, but what is she going to do? She can't stop him," was the opinion of Tante Rose, the one person Tété dared confide in when she became pregnant. She had feared the reaction of her mistress when she began to notice, but before that happened, Valmorain took his wife to Cuba, where he would gladly have left her forever if the convent nuns had agreed to take care of her. When he brought her back to the plantation, Tété's baby had disappeared, and Eugenia never asked why her slave's tears were falling like little pebbles. Valmorain's sensuality was gluttonous and hurried. In bed as at the table he did not like to waste time in preliminaries—just as he was bored by the ritual of long tablecloth and silver candelabra that Eugenia had always used at dinner he found the amorous game equally useless. For Tété it was one further chore, which was fulfilled in a few minutes except on those occasions when the devil possessed her master; that did not often happen, though she always anticipated it with fear. She was grateful for her luck; Lacroix, the owner of the plantation neighboring Saint-Lazare, kept a seraglio of girls chained in a barracks to satisfy his fantasies, in which guests and a few blacks he called "my studs" participated. Valmorain had attended those cruel evenings only once, and was so profoundly affected that he never returned. He was not excessively scrupulous but he believed that sooner or later a man paid for fundamental crimes, and he did not want to be near Lacroix when it was time for him to pay his. He was Lacroix's friend, they had shared interests, from breeding animals to hiring slaves for the cane harvest; he attended his parties, his cattle roundups and cockfights, but he did not want to set foot in that barracks again. Lacroix trusted him completely, with no guarantee but with a simple signed receipt handed Valmorain his savings to deposit in Cuba in a secret account far from the greedy claws of his wife and other relatives. Valmorain had to use great tact to reject Lacroix's repeated invitations to his orgies.

Tété had learned to let herself be used with the passivity of a sheep, her body loose, not offering any resistance, while her mind and soul flew elsewhere; that way her master finished quickly and then fell into the sleep of death. She knew that alcohol was her ally if she poured it in exact measure. With one or two goblets her *maître* became excited, with the third she had to be careful because he became violent, but with the fourth he was enveloped in a fog of intoxication, and if she delicately eluded him he fell asleep before he touched her. Valmorain never wondered what she felt in those encounters, just as it would never have occurred to him to ask what his horse felt when he rode it. He was used to her and rarely looked for other women. At times he awoke with faint distress in the empty bed that still held the nearly imperceptible mark of Tété's warm body; then he would remember his long-past nights with Violette Boisier or the love affairs of his youth in France that seemed to have happened to another man, one whose imagination was sent flying at the sight of a female ankle and who was capable of romping with renewed brio. Now that was impossible. Tété did not excite him as she once had, but it did not occur to him to replace her; he was comfortable with her, and he was a man of deeply rooted habits.

Sometimes he trapped a young slave on the fly, but that did not yield much beyond a rape as fast, and not as pleasureful, as reading a page of his current book. He attributed his lack of enthusiasm to an attack of malaria that had nearly dispatched him to the other world, leaving him weakened. Dr. Parmentier warned him about the effects of alcohol, as pernicious in the tropics as fever, but he did not drink too much, he was certain of that, only what was indispensable to palliate boredom and loneliness. He paid no account to Tété's persistence in filling his goblet. Before, when he was still traveling frequently to Le Cap, he used the occasion to divert himself with a fashionable courtesan, one of the beautiful *poules* who fired his passion but left him feeling empty. On the road he would anticipate pleasures that once consummated he could not remember, in part because during those trips he drank very heavily. He paid those girls to do the same thing he did with Tété—the same rough embrace, the same haste—and in the end he would stumble out with an impression of having been swindled. With Violette it would have been different, but once she started living with Relais, she had left the profession. Valmorain returned to Saint-Lazare earlier than planned, thinking of Maurice and eager to regain the security of his routine. "I am getting old," he muttered, studying himself in the mirror as his slave shaved him, seeing the web of fine wrinkles around his eyes and the beginning of a double chin. He was forty years old, the same age as Prosper Cambray, but he lacked his energy and was putting on weight. "That's the fault of this accursed climate," he added. He felt that his life was passing aimlessly, drifting like a ship without a rudder or compass, waiting for something he did not know how to name.

He detested the island. During the day he was kept busy around the plantation, but evenings and nights were endless. The sun set, darkness fell, and the hours began to drag by with their load of memories, fears, regrets, and ghosts. He tricked time by reading and playing cards with Tété. Those were the only moments she lowered her defenses and abandoned herself to relish of the game. When he first taught her to play, he always won, but he guessed that she was losing on purpose, afraid she would anger him. "There is no pleasure in that for me. Try to beat me," he demanded, and then began to lose consistently. He wondered with amazement how that mulatta girl could compete head to head with him in a game of logic, cleverness, and calculation. No one had taught Tété arithmetic, but she kept count of the cards by instinct, just as she did the household expenses. The possibility that she was as skilled as he perturbed and confused him.

Valmorain dined early in the dining hall, three simple but filling dishes, his main meal of the day served by two silent slaves. He drank a few goblets of good wine, the same he smuggled to his brother-in-law Sancho and sold in Cuba for twice what it cost in Saint-Domingue. After dessert Tété brought him a bottle of cognac and caught him up on domestic matters. The young woman slipped along on her bare feet as if she were floating, but he perceived the delicate tinkling of keys, the swishing of skirts, and the warmth of her presence before she entered. "Sit down, I don't like for you to talk above my head," he would say every night. She would wait for that order before taking a seat a short distance away, sitting very straight in the chair, hands in her lap, eyes lowered. In the light of the candles her harmonious face and long neck seemed carved in wood. Her elongated, sleepy-lidded eyes shone with golden reflections. She answered his questions without emphasis, except when he talked about Maurice; then she became animated, celebrating every bit of the boy's mischief as if it were a feat. "All little boys chase hens, Tété," he would say, in his heart sharing her belief that they were raising a genius. It was for that, more than anything, that Valmorain appreciated her; his son could not be in better hands. Despite himself, because he was not given to excessive pampering, he was moved when he saw them together in that complicity of caresses and secrets mothers share with their children.

Maurice returned Tété's affection with a loyalty so exclusive that his father often felt jealous. Valmorain had forbidden him to call her Maman, but Maurice disobeyed. "Maman, promise me that we will never, never be apart," he had heard his son whisper to her behind his back. "I promise, little one." Lacking anyone else to talk to, Valmorain was used to confiding his business worries, the management of the plantation and slaves, to Tété. These were not conversations, since he did not expect an answer, but monologues in which he could unburden his thoughts and hear the sound of a human voice, even if his own. At times they exchanged ideas, and to him it seemed that she did not add anything because he did not realize how she manipulated him in a few sentences.

"Did you see the merchandise Cambray brought in yesterday?"

"Yes, *maître*. I helped Tante Rose look them over."

"And?"

"They do not look good."

"They just got here, they lose a lot of weight on the trip. Cambray bought them in a quick lot, all for the one price. That's a bad method, you can't examine them and they give you a cat for a hare; those slave traders are expert in deceitful trading. But after all, I suppose that the head overseer knows what he's doing. What does Tante Rose say?"

"Two have the runs, they can't stand on their feet. She says to leave them with her a week so she can cure them."

"A week!"

"That is better than losing them, *maître*. That's what Tante Rose says."

"Is there a woman in the bunch? We need another woman in the kitchen."

"No, but there's a fourteen-year-old boy—"

"Is that the one Cambray flogged on the way back? He told me the boy tried to escape, and he had to teach him a lesson right there."

"That is what Monsieur Cambray says, *maître*."

"And you, Tété, what do you think happened?"

"I do not know, *maître*, but I think that the boy will do better in the kitchen than in the fields."

"Here in the house he will try to run away again, there isn't much oversight."

"No house slave has run away yet, *maître*."

The dialogue was inconclusive, but later, when Valmorain was looking over his new acquisitions, he picked out the boy and made a decision.

When dinner was over, Tété would leave to see that Eugenia was clean and calm in her bed, and to be with Maurice until he went to sleep. Valmorain would settle on the gallery, if the weather permitted, or in the dark drawing room, caressing his third cognac, reading a book or a newspaper by the bad light of an oil lamp. The news arrived weeks late, but that didn't matter to him; all the events occurred in a different universe. He would dismiss the domestic servants, because at the end of the day he was already bored by their divining his thought, and sit reading alone. Later, when the sky was an impenetrable black cloak and all he could hear was the eternal whistling of the cane, the whispers of the shadows inside the house, and, sometimes, the secret vibration of distant drums, he would go to his room and take off his clothes by the light of a single candle. Tété would come soon.

Zarité

This is how I remember it. Outside, crickets and the hooting of an owl, inside, the moon illuminating with precise stripes the sleeping body. So young! Watch over him for me, Erzulie, loa of deepest waters, I would ask, rubbing my doll, the one my grandfather Honoré gave me and that was still my companion. Come, Erzulie, mother, beloved, with your necklaces of pure gold, your cape of toucan feathers, your crown of flowers, and your three rings, one for each husband. Help us, loa of dreams and hopes. Protect him from Cambray, make him invisible to the master's eyes, make him cautious before others but proud in my arms, quiet his African heart in the light of day so that he may survive, and instill courage in him by night so that he not lose his wish for freedom. Look upon us with benevolence, Erzulie, loa of jealousy. Do not envy us, because this happiness is as fragile as the wings of a fly. He will go. If he does not, he will die, you know that, but do not take him from me quite yet, let me stroke the slim boy's back before it becomes a man's.

He was a warrior, this love of mine, like the name his father gave him: Gambo, which means warrior. I whispered his forbidden name when we were alone. Gambo . . . and that word resonated through my veins. It cost him many beatings to answer to the name they gave him here, and to hide his true name. Gambo, he said to me, touching his chest the first time we made love. Gambo, Gambo, he repeated until I dared say it to him. Then he spoke to me in his language, and I answered in mine. It took a while for him to learn Creole and to teach me something of his tongue, the one my mother was not able to give me, but from the beginning we did not need to talk. Love has mute words, more transparent than the river. Then Gambo had just arrived, he looked like a child, he was nothing but bones, frightened. Other larger and stronger captives had been left floating in the bitter sea, looking for the current that flowed toward Guinea. How did he endure the crossing? He came with his flesh raw from lashings, Cambray's method for breaking in new slaves, the same he used with dogs and horses. On his chest, over his heart, was a red burn bearing the initials of the slave trade company put on him in Africa before embarking and still had not healed. Tante Rose told me to wash the wounds with water, a lot of water, and to cover them with poultices of a Moorish herb, aloe, and lard. They had to close from inside out. On the burn, no water, only fat. No one knew how to cure like she did, even Dr. Parmentier wanted to know her secrets and she gave them to him, though they were used to help other whites, because knowledge comes from Papa Bondye and it belongs to everyone, and if not shared it is lost. And that is so. Those days she was occupied with the slaves who arrived sick, so it fell to me to treat Gambo.

The first time I saw him he was lying facedown in the slave hospital, covered with flies. With difficulty I helped him sit up and gave him a sip of taffia and a small spoonful of the maîtresse's drops I had stolen from her blue vial. Then I began the unpleasant task of cleaning him up. The wounds were not too badly inflamed, for Cambray had not been able to douse them with salt and vinegar, but the pain must have been terrible. Gambo bit his lips, not complaining. After he was clean, I sat down beside him to sing to him, since I didn't know any words of consolation in his language. I wanted to explain to him how to behave in order not to provoke the hand that held the whip, how he should work and obey while his vengeance was growing, that fire that smolders inside. My godmother convinced Cambray that the boy had the plague and that it was best to leave him alone so he wouldn't give it to the rest of the crew. The overseer gave her permission to take him to her cabin because he never lost hope that Tante Rose would contract some fatal fever; she was immune, however, she had a deal with Legba, the loa of sorcery. In the *meantime I began to put in my* maître's *head the idea of assigning Gambo to the kitchen. He would never last in the cane fields because the overseer had had his eye on him from the beginning. Tante Rose left us alone in her cabin during treatments. She guessed. And the fourth day it happened. Gambo was so foggy from pain, and from everything he'd lost—his land, his family, his freedom—that I wanted to put my arms around him as his mother would have done. Affection is good for healing. One touching led to another, and I found myself sliding down, not touching his shoulders, so he could rest his head on my breast. His body was burning, he still had a lot of fever, I don't think he knew what we were doing. I didn't know love. What the master did with me was dark and shameful, that is what I told Gambo, but he didn't believe me. With my* maître, *my soul, my ti-bon-ange, let go and went flying elsewhere and only my* corps-cadavre *lay in that bed. Gambo. His light body on mine, his hands at my waist, his breath on my lips, his eyes looking at me from the other side of the sea, from Guinea, that was love. Erzulie,* loa *of love, save him from all things bad, protect him. That was my supplication.*

Turbulent Times

ore than thirty years had gone by since Macandal, that legendary sorcerer, planted the seed of insurrection, and since then his spirit had traveled with the wind from one end of the island to the other, infiltrating slave quarters, cabins, *ajoupas*, mills, and tempting slaves with the promise of freedom. He adopted the form of a serpent, a beetle, a monkey, a macaw, he blended with the whisper of the rain, he clamored with the thunder, he incited rebellion with the howl of the storm. Whites sensed him too. Every slave was an enemy, and there were already more than half a million of them, two-thirds of whom came directly from Africa bearing their enormous load of resentment and living only to burst their chains and reap revenge. Thousands of slaves arrived in Saint-Domingue, but never enough to fill the insatiable demands of the planters. Whip, hunger, work. Neither vigilance nor the most brutal repression kept many from escaping; some managed to do that in the port, as soon as they were unloaded and their chains removed to be baptized. They ran off naked and sick, with one thought: get away from the whites. They crossed plains, crawling through pasturelands, they plunged into jungle and climbed the mountains of that unfamiliar territory. If they succeeded in joining a band of Maroons, they were saved from slavery. War, freedom. The *bozales*, born free in Africa and ready to die to be free once again, infected those born on the island with courage, the ones who had never known freedom and who knew Guinea as a hazy kingdom at the bottom of the sea. The planters lived armed, waiting. The Régiment Le Cap had been reinforced with four thousand French soldiers who barely touched terra firma before they dropped, struck by cholera, malaria, and dysentery. The slaves believed that mosquitoes, the cause of that death toll, were Macandal's armies battling against the whites. Macandal had freed himself from the fire of the stake and metamorphosed into a mosquito. Macandal had returned, as he promised. In Saint-Lazare fewer slaves had fled than in other places, and Valmorain attributed it to the fact that he did not vent his cruelty on his Negroes, none of that coating them with molasses and exposing them to red ants, as Lacroix did. In his strange nightly monologues he would comment to Tété that no one could accuse him of cruelty, but if the situation continued to grow worse he would have to give Cambray carte blanche. She was careful not to mention the word *insurgency* in his presence. Tante Rose had assured her that a general uprising of slaves was only a question of time, and that Saint-Lazare, like all the other plantations on the island, was going to disappear in flames.

Prosper Cambray had commented on that improbable rumor with his employer. Ever since he was able to remember the talk had been the same, and never came to anything. What could miserable slaves do against the militia and men like him, resolute in all things? How would they organize and arm themselves? Who was going to lead them? Impossible. He spent the day on horseback and slept with two pistols within reach of his hand, one eye open, always on guard. The whip was an extension of his fist, the language most known and feared by all; nothing pleased him as much as the fear he inspired. Only his employer's scruples had kept him from using more imaginative methods of repression, but that was about to change, the bursts of insurrection had multiplied. The opportunity had come for him to demonstrate that he could manage the plantation under the worst conditions. He had been waiting too many years to be given the position of manager. He couldn't complain, because in the meantime he'd amassed a not inconsequential amount of money through bribes, petty thievery, and smuggling. Valmorain never suspected how much disappeared from his storage rooms. Cambray boasted of being a bull with the slave girls; none escaped serving him in his hammock and no one interfered. As long as he did not molest Tété he could fornicate at will, but because she was out of his reach she was the only one who fired him with lust and rage. He watched her from a distance, spied on her from nearby, trapped her at some careless moment, but she always wriggled away. "Be careful, Monsieur Cambray. If you touch me, I will tell the master," Tété would warn him, trying to control the tremble in her voice. "*You* be careful, whore, because when I get my hands on you, you are going to pay. Who do you think you are, wretch? You are already twenty; soon now your master is going to replace you with another, younger girl and then it will be my turn. I am going to buy you. Your master will be happy to sell you," he threatened, playing with his braided leather whip.

Meanwhile, the French Revolution had hit the colony like the slash of a dragon's tail, shaking it to its foundation. The *grands blancs*, conservatives and monarchists, looked upon the changes with horror, but the *petits blancs* supported the republic, which had done away with differences among classes: *liberté, égalité, fraternité* for whites. As for the *affranchis*, they had sent delegations to Paris to negotiate their right to citizenship before the Assemblée Nationale, because in Saint-Domingue no white, rich or poor, was disposed to give that to them. Valmorain indefinitely postponed his return to France because he realized that there was now nothing that tied him to his country. Once he had raged about the monarchy's profligate ways, and now he complained about the disarray of the republic. After so many years of not fitting into the colony, he had ended by accepting that his place was in the New World. Sancho García del Solar wrote him with his usual candor to propose that he forget about Europe in general and France in particular; there was no place there for enterprising men, the future lay in Louisiana. He had good connections in New Orleans, and all he lacked was capital to launch a project several people were already interested in; he wanted, however, to give preference to Valmorain because of family ties and because when they both put their fingers on something gold burst from it. He explained to Valmorain that in its beginnings Louisiana had been a French colony and for some twenty years had belonged to Spain, but the population was obstinately loyal to its origins. The government was Spanish, but the culture and language continued to be French. The climate was similar to that in the Antilles, and the crops were the same, with the advantage that there was much more space and land was cheap; they could acquire a large plantation and exploit it without political problems or rebelling slaves. They would make a fortune in only a few years, he promised.

After losing her first child, Tété had wanted to be as sterile as the mules in the mill. For her to love and suffer as a mother, Maurice was enough, that delicate child capable of weeping with emotion over music or wetting himself in anguish when he witnessed cruelty. He was afraid of Cambray; he had only to hear the click of his boot heels in the gallery to run and hide. Tété relied on Tante Rose's remedies to keep from getting pregnant again, as other slaves did, but they were not always effective. The healer said that some children insisted on coming into the world because they could not suspect what was waiting for them. That was how it was with Tété's second pregnancy. The handfuls of fiber soaked in vinegar did nothing to prevent it, nor the infusions of pine needles, the burning mustard, or the rooster sacrificed to the *loas* to abort it. After the third moon without menstruating, she went to beg her godmother to end her problem with a sharp stick, but she refused; the risk of infection was enormous, and if they were caught attempting anything against the master's property, Cambray would have the perfect motive to flay them with his whip.

"I suppose this one is the master's too," commented Tante Rose.

"I'm not sure, *marraine*. It might be Gambo's," Tété murmured, alarmed.

"Whose?"

"The helper in the kitchen. His real name is Gambo."

"He's a young boy, but I see that he already knows how to do as men do. He must be five or six years younger than you."

"What does that matter? What matters is that if the baby comes out black, my *maître* will kill both of us!"

"Children with mixed blood often come out dark as their grandparents," Tante Rose assured her.

Terrified at the possible consequences of her pregnancy, Tété thought of it as a tumor, but at the fourth month she felt the flutter of a dove's wing, an obstinate breath, the first unmistakable manifestation of life, and she could not avoid the affection and compassion she felt for the being curled in her womb. At night, lying beside Maurice, she asked forgiveness in whispers for the terrible offense of bringing a child into the world as a slave. This time it was not necessary to hide her belly, nor did her master shoot off with his wife to Cuba, because the poor woman no longer noticed anything. It had been a long time since Eugenia had contact with her husband, and the few times she glimpsed him in the hazy atmosphere of her madness she asked who that man was. Neither did she recognize Maurice. In her good moments she returned to her adolescence; she was fourteen, and while waiting at breakfast for her thick hot chocolate was playing with other noisy schoolgirls in the nuns' convent in Madrid. The rest of the time she wandered in a misty landscape that had no precise outlines, a place where she no longer suffered as she once had. Tété decided on her own to suppress her opium, and there was no change in Eugenia's behavior. According to Tante Rose, her mistress had fulfilled her mission when she gave birth to Maurice, and there was nothing left for her to do in this world.

Valmorain knew Tété's body better than he had come to know Eugenia's, or any of his transitory lovers', and soon he noticed that she was getting larger around the waist and that her breasts were swelling. He asked her when they were in bed, after one of those mountings she bore with resignation and that were for him merely a nostalgic unburdening, and Tété burst into tears. That surprised him because he had not seen her spill a tear since the time they took her first son from her. He had heard that Negroes have more capacity for suffering; the proof was that no white could bear what the blacks endured, and just as they take pups from bitches, or calves from cows, they were able to separate the slaves from their children; in a short while they recovered from the loss and later did not even remember. He had never thought about Tété's sentiments; he assumed they were very limited. In her absence she dissolved, she was erased, she was suspended in nothingness until he needed her, then she materialized again. She existed only to serve him. She wasn't a girl anymore, but it seemed to him she hadn't changed. He vaguely remembered the skinny little girl he had picked up from Violette Boisier years before, the blossoming adolescent who emerged from such an unpromising chrysalis, the one he deflowered in one burst in the same room where Eugenia slept sedated, the young girl who gave birth without a single moan, biting on a piece of wood, the sixteen-year-old mother who with a kiss on the forehead said good-bye to a baby she would never see again, the woman who rocked Maurice with infinite tenderness, the one who closed her eyes and bit her lips when he penetrated her, the one who sometimes slept at his side, exhausted by the fatigues of the day, but sprang awake with Maurice's name on her lips and ran to see to him. All these images of Tété fused into one, as if time had not passed for her. That night when he felt the changes in her body, he ordered her to light the lamp, so he could look at her. He liked what he saw, that body with long firm lines, the bronze skin, the generous hips and sensual lips, and concluded that Tété was his most valuable possession. With a finger he wiped a tear that was sliding down beside her nose and without thinking touched it to his lips. It was salty, like those of Maurice.

"What's the matter?" he asked her.

"Nothing, *maître*."

"Don't cry. This time you will be able to keep your baby, it won't matter now to Eugenia."

"If that is so, *maître*, why not bring back my son?"

"That would be very troublesome."

"Tell me if he is alive. . . ."

"Of course he's alive, woman! Your duty is to take care of Maurice. Do not mention that boy to me again, and be happy that I will allow you to bring up the one you are carrying."

Zarité

Gambo preferred cutting cane to the humiliating work in the kitchen. "If my father saw me he would rise up from the dead to spit on my feet and abhor me, his eldest son, for doing women's work. My father died fighting against men who attacked our village, the natural way for men to die." That is what he told me. The slave hunters were from another tribe, they came from far away, from the west, with horses and muskets like the ones the overseer has. Other villages had burned to the ground, the young had been taken away; they killed the elders and children, but his father believed that they were safe, protected by distance and the jungle. The hunters sold their captives to beings who had crocodile claws and teeth like hyenas and fed on human flesh. No one ever returned. Gambo was the only one of his family they caught alive, good fortune for me and disaster for him. He struggled through the first part of the journey, which lasted two complete cycles of the moon, keeping on his feet, tied to the others with rope and with a wood yoke around his neck, herded with poles, with almost no food or water. When he could not take one step more the sea rose up before his eyes, something no one in the long line of captives knew, and also an imposing castle on the sand. They had no time to marvel at the expanse and color of the water, which they confused with the sky on the horizon, because they were immediately locked in. Then Gambo saw whites for the first time and thought they were demons; later he learned they were people, but he never believed that they were humans like us. They were dressed in sweaty rags, with metal breastplates and leather boots, yelling and flogging their captives for no reason. No fangs or claws, but they had hair on their faces, weapons and whips, and their smell was so repugnant that they sickened the birds in the sky. That is how he told it. They separated him from the women and children; they put him in a corral, hot by day and cold at night, with hundreds of men who did not speak his language. He did not know how long he was there because he forgot to follow the moon's passings, or how many died because no one had a name and no one kept count. At first they were pressed so tight that they could not lie down, but as bodies were dragged away there was more space. Then came the worst, what he did not want to remember but lived over and over in his dreams: the ship. They were laid one beside the next, like firewood, on shelves of wood planking, with chains, and iron at their necks, not knowing where they were being taken or why that enormous gourd was bouncing and reeling as it was, all of them moaning, vomiting, shitting, dying. The stench was so bad that it reached the world of the dead, and his father smelled it. Neither could Gambo calculate time there, even though he was under the sun and the stars several times when they took them in groups to the deck to slosh them with pails of sea water and force them to dance around so they would not forget the use of their arms and legs. The sailors threw the sick and the dead overboard, then picked out a few captives and flogged them for entertainment. The most combative were hung by the wrists and slowly lowered into water boiling with sharks, and when they pulled them up there was nothing left but arms. Gambo also witnessed what they did with the women. He watched for a chance to jump overboard, thinking that after the feast of the sharks that followed the ship from Africa to the Antilles his soul would swim on to the island beneath the sea to rejoin his father and the rest of his family. "If my father knew that I was planning to die without fighting, he would again spit on my feet." This is how he told it.

The only reason Gambo stayed in Tante Mathilde's kitchen was that he was preparing to escape. He knew the risks. In Saint-Lazare there were slaves without a nose or ears or with shackles welded around their ankles that they could not take off; no one would ever run wearing those shackles. I think that he put off his flight for me, for the way we looked at each other, the messages of little stones in the henhouse, the treats he stole for me in the kitchen, the anticipation of embracing each other that was like the prickling of pepper over all our bodies, and for those rare moments when we were alone and could touch. "We will be free, Zarité, and we will be together forever. I love you more than anyone, more than my father and his five wives, who were my mothers, more than my brothers and my sisters, more than all of them together, but not more than my honor." *A warrior does what he has to do, that is more important than love, I understand that. We women love more and for longer, too. I also know that. Gambo was prideful, and there is no greater danger for a slave than pride. I begged him to stay in the kitchen if he wanted to stay alive, to be invisible to avoid Cambray, but that was asking too much, it was asking him to live the life of a coward.* "Life is written in our z'étoile, and we cannot change it. You will come with me, Zarité?" *I could not go with him; I was very heavy, and together we would not have got far.*

The Lovers

several years earlier, Violette Boisier had given up Le Cap's night life, not because she had faded—she could still compete with any of her rivals—but for Etienne Relais. Their relationship had evolved into a loving friendship seasoned with his passion and her good humor. They had been together nearly a decade, which to them seemed a very short time. The first years they spent apart, able to see each other only during Relais's brief visits between military campaigns. For a while she had continued her trade, offering her magnificent services to only a handful of clients, the most generous. She became so selective that Loula had to take the most impetuous, the irremediably ugly, and those with bad breath off the list; she gave preference to older men because they were grateful. A few years after he met Violette, Relais was promoted to major in the army, charged with security in the north, and with that he traveled for shorter periods. As soon as he was established in Le Cap, he stopped sleeping in the barracks and married Violette. He did that defiantly, with pomp and ceremony in the church and an announcement in the newspaper, just like the weddings of the *grands blancs*, scandalizing his fellow military, who were unable to comprehend his reasons for marrying a woman of color and, further, one of questionable reputation, when he could have kept her as a lover. No one, however, asked questions to his face, and he offered no explanation. He was counting on the fact that no one would dare denigrate his wife. Violette notified her "friends" that she was no longer available and shared among other cocottes the party dresses she could not transform into more discreet gowns; she sold her apartment, and went to live in a house Relais bought in a barrio of *petits blancs* and *affranchis*. Their new friends were mulattoes, some rather well-to-do, owners of land and slaves, Catholics, although in secret they often reverted to voodoo. They had descended from the same whites who scorned them; they were their children and grandchildren, and they imitated them in all things and denied when they could the African blood of their mothers. Relais was not a friendly man—he felt comfortable only in the rude camaraderie of the barracks—but from time to time he accompanied his wife to social gatherings. "Smile, Etienne, so my friends will lose their fear of the mastiff of Saint-Domingue," she would ask of him. Violette commented to Loula that she missed the glitter of the parties and spectacles that had filled her nights. "You had money then and you had a good time, my angel, now you are poor and bored. What have you gained with your soldier?" They lived on the major's modest salary, but without his knowledge the two women had dealings with petty smugglers and lent money at interest, and were increasing the capital Violette had earned and Loula knew how to invest.

Etienne Relais had not forgotten his plans to return to France, especially now that the republic had given power to ordinary citizens like himself. He was fatigued with life in the colony, but he did not have enough money saved to retire from the army. He was not repelled by war—he was a centaur of many battles, accustomed to suffering and making others suffer, but he was tired of the uproar. He did not understand the situation in Saint-Domingue; alliances were made and broken in a matter of hours, the whites fought among themselves and against the *affranchis*, and no one gave much weight to the growing insurrection among the blacks, which he considered the most serious matter of all. Despite the anarchy and violence, the pair found a peaceful happiness they had never known. They avoided speaking of children, she could

not conceive and he was not interested in them, but when one unforgettable evening Toulouse Valmorain had appeared at their house with a
new baby wrapped in a mantilla, they welcomed it as a pet that would
fill Violette and Loula's hours, never suspecting it would become the
son they had not dared dream of. Valmorain had brought the infant to
Violette because he could not think of another way to make it disappear
before Eugenia's return from Cuba; he had to prevent her from learning
that Tété's baby was his as well. It could not be anyone else's because
he was the only white at Saint-Lazare. He hadn't known that Violette
had married a military man. He didn't find her in the apartment on place
Clugny, which now had a different occupant, but it was easy to trace her
to the new address, and there he arrived with the baby and a wet nurse he
had obtained at his neighbor Lacroix's. He put the matter to the couple
as a temporary arrangement, having no idea how he was going to resolve
it later, and was relieved when Violette and her husband accepted the
infant without asking more than its name. "He has not been baptized,
you can call him whatever you want," he told them at the time.

Etienne Relais was as fierce, vigorous, and healthy as he'd been in his
youth, the same bundle of muscles and fiber, with a thatch of gray hair
and the iron character that caused him to rise in the army and earned him
several medals. First he had served the king, and now he would serve the
republic with equal loyalty. He still, frequently, wanted to make love to
Violette, and she happily accompanied him in the playful cavortings that
according to Loula were inappropriate for a mature husband and wife.
The contrast was marked between his reputation as a merciless soldier
and the hidden softness he lavished on his wife and the baby, who rapidly
won his heart, the organ that in the barracks it was maintained he did
not have. "That little fellow could be my grandson," he often said, and
in truth he doted on him like a grandfather. Violette and the boy were
the only two people he had loved in his life, though if pushed slightly he
admitted he also loved Loula, the bossy African woman who had given
him such a battle at first, when she was trying to get Violette to choose a

more suitable groom. Relais offered to emancipate her, and Loula's reaction was to throw herself to the floor, wailing that they meant to get rid of her, as happened to so many slaves that age or illness rendered useless and whose masters abandoned them in the street to keep from having to support them. She had spent her life caring for Violette, and now that they no longer needed her they were going to condemn her to begging or dying of hunger, and on and on at the top of her lungs. Finally Relais was able to get her to listen, and assured her she could be a slave to her last breath, if that is what she wanted. After that promise, the woman's attitude changed, and instead of putting dolls stuck with pins under his bed, she outdid herself to prepare him his favorite meals.

Violette had matured, slowly, like mangoes. With the years she had not lost her freshness, her haughty bearing or soft, purring laughter; she had only grown a little plump, which her husband found enchanting. She had the confidence of those who enjoy love. With time, and the strategy of Loula's rumors, she had become a legend, and wherever she went people looked at her and whispered, including the same people who would not receive her in their houses. "They must be wondering about the dove egg," Violette said, laughing. Arrogant men doffed their hats when she went by and they were alone, many remembering passionate nights in the apartment on the place Clugny, but women of any color looked away out of envy. Violette dressed in cheerful colors, and her only adornments were the opal ring that was her husband's gift and the heavy earrings of gold that flickered over her magnificent features and the ivory skin owed to a lifetime of never being exposed to a ray of sun. She had no other jewels; they had all been sold to augment the capital indispensable for their dealings as moneylenders. She and Loula had through the years buried their savings, in solid gold coins, in a hole in the patio, without raising her husband's suspicions, waiting for the moment they would leave.

Violette and Relais were in bed one Sunday at the hour of siesta, not touching because it was so hot, when she announced that if in fact he wanted to return to France, as he had been saying for an eternity, they had the means to do so. That same night, sheltered by the darkness, she and Loula dug up their treasure. Once the major weighed the bag of coins, recovered from his astonishment, and set aside the objections of a macho humiliated by women's cleverness, he decided to present his resignation to the army. He had more than paid his duty to France. Then the couple began to plan the voyage, and Loula had to resign herself to the idea of being free, for in France slavery had been abolished.

The Master's Children

That evening, as Violette explained to Loula, she and Relais were waiting for the most important visit of their lives. The couple's house was somewhat larger than the three-room apartment on the place Clugny, comfortable but not luxurious. The simplicity Violette had adopted in her clothing extended to her home, decorated with the furniture of local artisans with none of the chinoiserie she had formerly fancied so greatly. The house was welcoming: trays of fruits, flowers, cages of birds, and several cats. The first to show up that evening was the notary with his young scribe and a large book with blue binding. Violette showed them to an adjacent room that Relais used as an office, and offered them coffee and delicate beignets made by the nuns; according to Loula the pastries were nothing but fried dough and she could make better. Shortly after, Toulouse Valmorain knocked at the door. He had gained weight, and looked broader and more worn than Violette remembered, but with his *grand blanc* arrogance intact. That attitude had always seemed comic to her since she had been trained to undress a man with one look, and naked neither titles, power, fortune, nor race had value; all that counted were physical condition and intentions. Valmorain greeted her and bowed to kiss her hand, but did not touch it to his lips; that would have been discourteous in front of Relais. He took a seat and the glass of fruit juice he was offered.

"A number of years have gone by since the last time we saw each other, monsieur," she said, with a formality that was new between them, trying to veil the anxiety squeezing her chest.

"Time has stopped for you, madame—you look the same."

"Do not offend me, I look better." She smiled, amazed that the man blushed; perhaps he was as nervous as she was.

"As you know by my letter, Monsieur Valmorain," began Etienne Relais, dressed in his uniform, stiff as a post in his chair, "we are planning to go to France fairly soon."

"Yes, yes," Valmorain interrupted. "First of all, it is fitting for me to thank both of you for having taken care of the boy all these years. What is his name?"

"Jean-Martin," said Relais.

"I suppose he is quite a little man by now. I would like to see him, if that is possible."

"In a minute. He is out for a walk with Loula and will soon be back."

Violette tugged at the skirt of her sober green crêpe dress with purple trim and served more juice in their glasses. Her hands were trembling. For a pair of eternal minutes no one spoke. One of the canaries began to sing in its cage, breaking the heavy silence. Valmorain watched Violette out of the corner of his eye, taking note of the changes in that body that once he had made love to so persistently, although he could no longer remember very well what they did in bed. He wondered how old she might be, and whether she used mysterious balms to preserve her beauty, as he had read somewhere the ancient Egyptian queens did, the ones that ended up as mummies. He was envious as he imagined Relais's happiness with her.

"We cannot take Jean-Martin with us under the present conditions, Toulouse," Violette said finally in the familiar tone she had used when they were lovers, putting a hand on his shoulder.

"He does not belong to us," added the major, stiff-lipped, his eyes fixed on his former rival.

"We love this boy very much, and he thinks we are his parents. I always wanted to have children, Toulouse, but God did not give them to me. For that reason we want to buy Jean-Martin, emancipate him, and take him to France using the name Relais, as our legitimate son," said Violette and immediately burst into tears, shaking with sobs.

Neither of the two men made a move to console her. They stood looking at the canaries, uncomfortable, until she was able to calm herself, just as Loula came in holding a little boy's hand. He was handsome. He ran to Relais to show him something clutched in his fist, speaking excitedly, his cheeks bright red. Relais pointed toward the visitor, and the boy went to him, held out a plump hand, and timidly greeted him. Valmorain studied him, pleased, and saw that he did not resemble either him or his son Maurice in any way.

"What is it you have here?" he asked.

"A snail."

"Are you giving it to me?"

"No, I can't, it is for my papa," Jean-Martin replied, returning to Relais to climb up on his knees.

"Go along with Loula, son," the major ordered. The boy obeyed immediately, caught the woman's skirts, and both disappeared.

"If you are in agreement . . . well, we have summoned a notary in case you accept our proposition, Toulouse. After that it will have to go to a judge," babbled Violette, on the verge of crying again.

Valmorain had come to the interview without a plan. He knew what they were going to ask, because Relais had explained it in his letter, but he had not made a decision; he wanted to see the boy first. Jean-Martin had left a very favorable impression, he was good-looking and apparently did not lack character; the boy was worth a lot of money, but it would be a nuisance for Valmorain to have him. The couple had pampered him from the time he brought the infant to them, that was obvious, and he had no idea of his true position in society. What would he do with that little mixed blood bastard? He would have to keep him at home for the first few years. He could not imagine how Tété would react; surely she would turn all her attention to her son, and Maurice, whom she had until that moment brought up as her only child, would feel abandoned. The delicate balance of his home could come tumbling down. He also thought of Violette Boisier, of the hazy memory of the love he had had for her, of the services they had rendered each other through the years, and also about the simple truth that she was much more Jean-Martin's mother than Tété was. The Relais were offering the boy what he could not think to give him: freedom, education, a name, and a respectable situation.

"Please, monsieur, sell Jean-Martin to us. We will pay what you ask, even though, as you can see, we are not wealthy people," Etienne Relais pleaded, crisp and stiff, as Violette trembled, leaning against the jamb of the door that separated them from the notary.

"Tell me, Major, how much have you spent on keeping him through these years?" Valmorain asked.

"I have never added that up," Relais replied, surprised.

"Well, that is what the boy is worth. We are even. You have your son."

Tété's pregnancy went by without any changes; she kept working from sunrise to sunset as always, and went to her master's bed every time he wished, to do it like dogs once her belly became an obstacle. Tété cursed him in her heart, but she also was afraid he would replace her with another slave and sell her to Cambray, the worst fate imaginable.

"Don't worry, Zarité, if that moment comes I will take care of the overseer," Tante Rose promised.

"Why don't you do it now, Marraine?" the girl asked.

"Because one must not kill without a very good reason."

That evening Tété sat sewing in a corner a few steps from Valmorain, who was reading and smoking in his easy chair. She was swollen and had the sensation she was carrying a watermelon inside. The sharp fragrance of the tobacco, which in normal times she found pleasing, now turned her stomach. It had been months since anyone had visited Saint-Lazare. Even the most frequent guest, Dr. Parmentier, was afraid of the road; now no one could travel through the north of the island without heavy protection. Valmorain had established the habit of having Tété keep him company after dinner, a further obligation added to the many he imposed on her. At that hour all she wanted was to lie down, curled up beside Maurice, and sleep. She could barely endure her always hot, exhausted, sweating body, with the pressure of the creature on her bones, the pain in her back, the hard breasts with burning nipples. That day had been the worst; there seemed to be little breathable air. It was still early, but a storm had brought on the darkness and forced her to close the shutters; the house was as oppressive as a prison. Eugenia had been sleeping a half hour, attended by the slave who cared for her, and Maurice was waiting for Tété, though he had learned not to call her because that annoyed his father.

The storm ended as suddenly as it had begun; the pounding of rain and blasts of wind gave way to a chorus of frogs. She went to one of the windows and opened the shutters, taking a deep breath of the dampness and coolness that swept through the room. The day had seemed very long. She had stopped by the kitchen a couple of times, using the excuse of talking with Tante Mathilde, but hadn't seen Gambo. Where had the boy gone? She was trembling with fear for him. Rumors had reached Saint-Lazare from the rest of the island, passed from mouth to mouth by the blacks and openly discussed by the whites, who never guarded what they said before their slaves. The latest news was the *Déclaration des droits de l'Homme et du citoyen* proclaimed in France. The whites were on edge, and the *affranchis*, who had always been marginalized, at last saw the possibility of achieving equality with whites. The rights of man did not include the Negroes, as Tante Rose explained to the slaves who had gathered for a *kalenda*; freedom was not free, you had to fight for it. They all knew that hundreds of slaves had disappeared from nearby plantations and joined the bands of rebels. In Saint-Lazare twenty had escaped, but Prosper Cambray and his men had gone after them and returned with fourteen. The other six had been shot and killed, according to the overseer, but no one had seen their bodies, and Tante Rose believed they had succeeded in escaping to the mountains. That fortified Gambo's determination to flee. Tété could no longer hold him back and had begun the calvary of saying good-bye and tearing him from her heart. There is no worse suffering than to love with fear, said Tante Rose.

Valmorain looked away from the page to take another sip of cognac, and his eyes lighted on his slave, who had been standing a good while beside the open window. In the weak light of the lamps he saw her, panting, sweaty, hands joined over her belly. Suddenly Tété choked back a moan and pulled her skirt up above her knees, looking with dismay at the pool spreading across the floor and wetting her bare feet. "It is time," she murmured and left, steadying herself on pieces of furniture, in the direction of the gallery. Two minutes later another slave hurried in to wipe up the floor.

"Call Tante Rose," Valmorain ordered.

"They have already gone to get her, *maître*."

"Tell me when it is born. And bring me more cognac."

Zarité

Rosette was born the same day that Gambo disappeared. That is how it was. Rosette helped me through the worry that they would take him alive and with the emptiness he left in my heart. I was absorbed in my daughter. That Gambo was running through the jungle pursued by Cambray's dogs occupied only a part of my thoughts. Erzulie, mother loa, *look after this baby. I had never known that kind of love because I had not put my firstborn to my breast. The* maître *had warned Tante Rose that I was not to see him, for that would make the separation easier, but she let me hold him one moment before he carried him away. Then she told me, while she was cleaning me up, that the baby was a healthy, strong boy. With Rosette, I understood better what I had lost. If they also took this baby from me I would go mad, like Doña Eugenia. I tried not to think about it because that could make it happen, but a slave always lives with uncertainty. We cannot protect our children, or promise them that we will be with them when they need us. All too soon we lose them, and that is why it is better not to bring them to life. At last I forgave my mother, who did not want to go through that torment.*

I always knew that Gambo would leave without me. In our heads, we had accepted that, but not in our hearts. Alone, Gambo could save himself, if it was signaled by his z'étoile *and if the* loas *allowed it, but not all the* loas *together could keep him from being caught if he took me with him. Gambo would put his hand on my belly and feel the child move, sure that it was his and that he would name it Honoré in memory of the slave who brought me up in Madame Delphine's house. He could not name it for his own father, who was with Les Morts et Les Mystères, but Honoré was not my blood relative, and that was why it was not imprudent to use his name. Honoré is a proper name for someone who puts honor above all else, including love. "Without freedom there is no honor for a warrior. Come with me, Zarité." I would not make it with my swollen belly, neither could I leave Doña Eugenia, who now was nothing but a tame rabbit in her bed, and much less Maurice, my little boy, to whom I had promised we would never be apart.*

Gambo did not learn that I had given birth because while I was pushing in Tante Rose's cabin he was running like the wind. He had planned well. He left at dusk, before the guards went out with the dogs. Tante Mathilde did not give the alarm until the next day at noon, even though she noticed his absence at dawn, and that gave him several hours' advantage. She was Gambo's god-mother. In Saint-Lazare, as on other plantations, the African born bozales were assigned another slave to teach them to obey, a godfather, but as they had put Gambo in the kitchen they gave him Tante Mathilde, who was getting along in years; she had lost her children and became fond of Gambo, happy to help him. Prosper Cambray was out with a group of the maréchaussées, chasing slaves who had run away earlier. He had told everyone that he had killed them, so no one understood his tenacity in continuing to look for them. Gambo started in the opposite direction, and it took the overseer some time to shift course to include him in the hunt. Gambo had left that night because that was what the loas had indicated; it also coincided with Cambray's being away and with the full moon—no one can run on a night without moon. So I believe.

My daughter was born with open, elongated eyes, the same color as mine. She was slow to take a breath, but when she did her bellows made the candle flame tremble. Before she washed her, Tante Rose placed her on my breast, still joined to me with a thick cord. I named her Rosette for Tante Rose, whom I asked to be her grandmother since we had no other family. The next day the master baptized her by dripping water on her forehead and murmuring a few

Christian words, but the next Sunday, Tante Rose held a true Rada service for Rosette. The maître *gave his permission for a* kalenda *and added a pair of goats to roast. So it was. It was an honor, because the birth of slaves was not celebrated on the plantation. The women prepared food and the men built bonfires, lighted torches, and played the drums in Tante Rose's* hounfor, *the healing center and sanctuary. With a thin line of corn flour my godmother drew the sacred writing of the symbolic* vévé *around a central post, the* poteau-mitan; *that was how the* loas *descended and mounted several servitors, but not me. Tante Rose sacrificed a hen. First she broke its wings and then tore off its head with her teeth, as it is supposed to be done. I offered my daughter to Erzulie. I danced and danced, breasts heavy, arms lifted high, hips crazed, legs independent of my thought, responding to the drums.*

At first the master was not interested in Rosette at all. It bothered him when she cried, and when I tended to her. Neither did he let me carry her on my back, as I had done with Maurice; I had to leave her in a drawer while I worked. Very soon he summoned me to his room again; he was excited by my breasts, which had grown to twice their size, and his just looking at them caused my milk to flow. Later he began to notice Rosette because Maurice clung to her. When Maurice was born he was a pale, silent little mouse I could hold in one hand, very different from my daughter, large and very loud. It had been good for Maurice to spend his first months pressed close to my body, like African children who, I've been told, do not touch the ground until it's time to learn to walk; they are always in arms. With the heat of my body and his good appetite he grew healthy and shook off the illnesses that kill so many children. He was clever, he understood everything, and from the age of two asked questions not even his father could answer. No one had taught him Creole, but he spoke it as well as French. The maître *did not allow him to mix with the slaves, but he would slip away to play with the few little blacks on the plantation, and I could not scold him for it because there is nothing as sad as a solitary child. From the beginning, he was Rosette's guardian. He never left her side, except when his father took him to ride around the property to show him his possessions. The master always put emphasis on Maurice's inheritance, which was why he suffered many years later at his son's betrayal. Maurice sat for hours playing with his blocks and his little wood horse near Rosette's drawer; he cried if she cried, he made faces at her and died laughing if she responded. The master forbade me to say that Rosette was his daughter, something that had never occurred to me to do, but Maurice guessed or invented it, because he called her* ma soeurette, *my little sister. His father scrubbed his mouth with soap, but he could not stop that habit the way he had cured him of calling me Maman. He was afraid of his real mother; he didn't want to see her, and called her "the ill lady." Maurice learned to call me Tété, like everyone else, except the few who know me inside and out and call me Zarité.*

The Warrior

At the end of a few days of chasing Gambo, Prosper Cambray was livid with rage. There was no trace of the boy, and he had a pack of crazed dogs on his hands, half blind and with raw, sore muzzles. He blamed Tété. It was the first time he had accused her directly, and he knew that at that moment something fundamental was defined between him and his employer. Until then one word from him had been enough to condemn a slave without hope of appeal, and with immediate punishment, but with Tété he had never dared.

"The house is not run the same way the plantation is, Cambray," Valmorain explained.

"She is responsible for the domestics," the overseer insisted. "If we don't make this a lesson, others will disappear."

"I will take care of this my own way," Valmorain replied, little inclined to raise his hand against Tété, who had just had a baby and had always been an impeccable housekeeper. The house functioned smoothly, and the servants carried out their tasks well. Besides, there was Maurice, of course, and the affection the boy had for the woman. To flog her, as Cambray intended, would be like flogging Maurice.

"I warned you some time ago that that young black was a troublemaker. I should have broken him as soon as I bought him, I wasn't hard enough."

"It's fine, Cambray. When you capture him you can do what you think best," Valmorain said, while Tété, who was standing listening in a corner like a prisoner, tried to conceal her anguish.

Valmorain was too preoccupied with his business and the state of the colony to be concerned about one slave here or there. He didn't remember Gambo at all, it was impossible to distinguish one among hundreds. On one or two occasions Tété had mentioned the "boy in the kitchen," and Valmorain had the idea he was a runny-nosed child, but that could not be the case if he was that daring; it took balls to run away. He was sure that Cambray would not be long in catching up with him, he had more than enough experience in hunting down blacks. The overseer was right; they should beef up discipline, there were enough problems among the free blacks on the island without allowing insolence from the slaves. The Assemblée Nationale in France had taken from the colony what little autonomous power it had enjoyed; that is, some bureaucrats in Paris who had never set foot in the Antilles and who scarcely knew enough to wipe their asses, he would say with emphasis, were now deciding matters of enormous gravity. No *grand blanc* was willing to accept the absurd decrees being made for them. Who could believe such ignorance! The result was pure noise and disorder, like what had happened to one Vincent Ogé, a wealthy mulatto who'd gone to Paris to demand equal rights for the *affranchis* and come back with his tail between his legs, as might be expected: where would things be if the natural distinctions between classes and races were erased! Ogé and his crony Chavannes, with the help of some abolitionists—there were always some of them around— had incited a rebellion in the north, very close to Saint-Lazare. Three hundred well armed mulattoes! It took all the effort of the Régiment Le Cap to defeat them, Valmorain told Tété during one of his evening monologues. He added that the hero of the day had been an acquaintance of his, Major Etienne Relais, a man of experience and courage, but one with Republican leanings. The survivors were captured in a swift maneuver, and over several days hundreds of scaffolds were raised in the center of the city, a forest of hanged men gradually decomposing in the heat, a feast for the buzzards. The two leaders were slowly tortured in the public plaza without the mercy of a coup de grâce. And it was not, Valmorain said, that he was party to cruel punishment, but sometimes it was instructive for the populace. Tété listened without a word, thinking of Major Relais, whom she scarcely remembered and would not recognize if she saw him; she had been with him only once or twice in the apartment on the place Clugny, many years before. If the man still loved Violette, it must not be easy for him to fight the *affranchis*. Ogé could have been her friend or relative.

Gambo had been assigned the task of tending the men captured by Cambray, who were in the filthy barn that served as a hospital. The women on the plantation fed them corn, sweet potato, okra, yucca, and bananas from their own provisions, but Tante Rose went to see the master to make a plea—one that Cambray would certainly have refused—for the lives of these men who would not survive without a soup she would make of bones, herbs, and the livers of the animals that were eaten in the big house. Valmorain looked up from his book on the gardens of the Sun King, annoyed by the interruption, but that strange woman intimidated him and he listened. "Those Negroes have had their lesson by now. Give them your soup, woman, and if you save them I will gain by not having lost so much," he answered. Gambo fed them during the first days because they could not feed themselves, and distributed among them a paste of leaves and quinoa ash that Tante Rose said they were to keep rolling like a ball in their mouths to endure pain and furnish energy. It was a secret of the Arawak chieftains that somehow had survived three hundred years and that only a few healers knew. The plant was very rare; it was not sold in the magic markets and Tante Rose had not been able to grow it in her garden, which was why it was kept for the worst cases.

Gambo took advantage of those moments alone with the punished slaves to find out how they had escaped, why they had been caught, and what happened to the six who were missing. Those who could talk told him that they had separated when they left the plantation; some had headed to the river with the idea of swimming upstream, but could fight the current only a while; in the end, it always won. They heard shots and were not sure if the others had been killed, but whatever their fate, no doubt it was preferable to that of the captured. He questioned them about the jungle, the trees, the vines, the mud, the stones, and the strength of the wind, the temperature and the light. Cambray and other hunters of blacks knew the region by heart, but there were places they avoided, like the swamps and crossroads of the dead, where escapees never went however desperate they might be, and places inaccessible by mule and horseback. They depended completely on their animals and their firearms, which at times became a hindrance. The horses fractured their pasterns and had to be put down. Loading a musket required several seconds; they tended to get clogged, or the powder got damp, and in the meantime a naked man with a knife for cutting cane seized his advantage. Gambo understood that the most immediate danger were the dogs, able to catch the scent of a man from a kilometer away. Nothing was as terrifying as a chorus of barking coming nearer and nearer.

In Saint-Lazare the dog kennels were behind the stables, on one of the patios of the big house. The hunting and guard dogs were kept locked up by day so they would not get to know people, and taken out by night to make the rounds. The two Jamaica mastiffs, covered with scars and trained to kill, belonged to Prosper Cambray. He had acquired them for dog fights, which had the dual merit of satisfying his taste for both cruelty and gambling; that sport had taken the place of the slave tourneys he'd had to give up when Valmorain forbade them. A good African champion able to kill an opponent with his bare hands could be very lucrative for his owner. Cambray had his tricks; he fed his fighters raw meat, maddened them with a mixture of *taffia*, gunpowder, and hot chili before every tourney, rewarded them with women after a victory, and made them pay dearly for a defeat. With his champions, a Congo and a Mandingo, he had plumped up his pay when he'd been a Negro hunter, but then he sold them and bought the mastiffs, whose fame had reached as far as Le Cap. He kept them hungry and thirsty, tied so they did not tear each other to shreds. Gambo needed to get rid of them, but if he poisoned them Cambray would torture five slaves for every dog until someone confessed.

At the hour of siesta, when Cambray went to refresh himself at the river, the boy went to the head overseer's cabin, which was located at the end of the avenue of coconut palms, separated from the big house and the quarters for domestic slaves. He had found out the names of the two concubines the overseer had chosen for that week, girls who had just entered puberty and already were as skittish as beaten dogs. They were startled to see him, but he calmed them with slices of cake he had stolen from the kitchen and asked them to get coffee. They began to poke at the fire while he slipped into the house. It was small but comfortable, oriented to catch the breeze and built on an earthen elevation, like the big house, to escape damage in floods. The furnishings, spare and simple, were some Valmorain had discarded when he married. Gambo saw it all in less than a minute. He thought about stealing a blanket, but in a corner he saw a basket of dirty clothing and quickly pulled out one of the overseer's shirts, rolled it into a ball, and threw it out the window into some brush; then he took his time drinking his coffee and told the girls good-bye with the promise of bringing them more cake as soon as he could. As night fell, he returned to look for the shirt. In the pantry, the keys for which were always hanging at Tété's waist, there was a sack of hot chili, a toxic powder used to combat scorpions and rodents; after they smelled it the dawn found them dead and dried up. If Tété realized that too much chili was being used, she said nothing.

On the day indicated by the *loas* the boy left at dusk, with the last memory of light. He had to pass through the slave quarters, which reminded him of the village where he had lived the first years of his life and which had been blazing like a bonfire the last time he saw it. Workers had not yet returned from the fields, and the quarters were nearly empty. One woman, who was carrying two large pails of water, was not surprised to see an unfamiliar face; there were many slaves, and new ones were always arriving. For Gambo those first hours would make the difference between freedom and death. Tante Rose, who could go at night where others did not dare venture by day, had described the terrain with the pretext of telling him about medicinal plants and also those that were necessary to avoid: lethal mushrooms, trees whose leaves rip off skin, anemones that hide toads whose spit is blinding. She explained to him how to survive in the jungle on fruit, nuts, roots, and stems as succulent as a slice of roast goat, and how to be guided by fireflies, stars, and the whistling of the wind. Gambo had never left Saint-Lazare before, but thanks to Tante Rose he could locate in his head the region of the mangrove swamps, where all the snakes were venomous, and the sites of crossroads between two worlds, where Les Invisibles waited. "I have been there and have seen Baron Kalfour and Ghede with my own eyes, and was not afraid. You have to greet them with respect, request their permission to pass, and ask them which road to follow. If it is not your hour to die, they will help you. They decide," the healer told him. The boy asked her about zombies, whom he had heard mentioned for the first time on the island; in Africa no one suspected they existed. She clarified that they can be recognized by their cadaverous appearance, their rotten odor, and their way of walking with stiff arms and legs. "More than a zombie, you need to fear some of the living, like Cambray," she added. The message did not escape Gambo.

When the moon came out, the boy started to run, following a zigzag course. Every so often he left a piece of the overseer's shirt in the vegetation to confuse the two mastiffs, which since no one else came near them knew only Cambray's smell, and to disorient the other hounds. Two hours later he reached the river. He sank into cool water up to his neck with a moan of relief, but kept his bundle dry on top of his head. He washed away sweat and blood from being scratched by branches and cut by rocks, and used the opportunity to drink and urinate. He moved forward in the water without nearing the shore, although he knew that would not throw off the dogs; they would nose and sniff in wider and wider circles until they picked up the scent, but it would slow them down. He did not intend to cross to the other side. The current was implacable and there were few places where even a good swimmer could risk it, but he did not know them and did not know how to swim. From the position of the moon he guessed that it was about midnight, and calculated the distance he'd come; then he left the water and began to sprinkle the chili powder. He felt no fatigue; he was drunk with freedom.

He kept moving for three days and nights, his only food Tante Rose's magic leaves. The black ball in his mouth numbed his gums and kept him awake and free of hunger. From cane fields he passed to woods, jungle, swamps, skirting the plain in the direction of the mountains. He did not hear dogs barking, and that encouraged him. He drank water from puddles, when he could find them, but he had to make it through the third day with no water and with a fiery sun that painted the world an incandescent white. When he could not take another step, a brief, cool cloudburst fell and revived him. At that time he was in open country, a route only someone demented would dare undertake, which was why Cambray ignored it. Gambo could not waste time looking for food, and if he rested he would not be able to get back on his feet. His legs were moving on their own, pushed by the delirium of hope and the ball of leaves in his mouth. He no longer was thinking, he felt no pain, he had forgotten fear and everything he had left behind, including Zarité's body. All he remembered was his name: warrior. He walked some stretches with long strides, not running, overcoming obstacles of terrain with calm, so as not to wear himself out or lose his way, as Tante Rose had instructed. It seemed to him that at some moment he wept copiously, but he wasn't sure, it could have been a memory of dew or rain on his skin. He saw a bleating nanny goat with a broken foot standing between two sharp boulders and resisted the temptation to slit its throat and drink the blood, just as he resisted hiding in the hills, which looked only a short distance away, or lying down to sleep a moment in the peace of the night. He knew where he had to go. Every step, every minute counted.

Finally he came to the foot of the mountains, and began the difficult climb, stone by stone, never looking down, to avoid succumbing to vertigo, or up to escape despair. He spit out the last wad of leaves and was again assaulted by thirst. His lips were swollen and split. The air was boiling, he was confused, dizzied, he could barely remember Tante Rose's instructions and he cried out for shade and water, but he kept climbing, clinging to rocks and roots. Suddenly he found himself near his village, on infinite plains, tending long-horned cattle and getting ready for the meal his mothers would serve in his father's hut at the center of the family compound. Only he, Gambo, the eldest son, ate with the father, side by side, like equals. He had been readying himself since his birth to take his place. He tripped, and the sharp pain of striking rock brought him back to Saint-Domingue; the cattle disappeared, his village, his family, and his *ti-bon-ange* was again trapped in the bad dream of slavery, which had now lasted a year. He ascended sheer mountainsides for hours and hours, until it was no longer he who was moving but another: his father. His father's voice repeated his name: Gambo. And it was his father who held at bay the black bird with the slick featherless neck flying in circles over his head.

He reached a very high area with a narrow path that bordered a precipice, snaking among peaks and crevasses. At one turn he saw the suggestion of steps carved into solid rock, one of the hidden paths of the Arawak chieftains who, according to Tante Rose, had not disappeared when the whites killed them because they were immortal. Shortly before nightfall, he came to one of the feared crossroads. Signs of it warned him before he saw it: a cross formed of two poles, a human skull, bones, a handful of feathers and hair, another cross. The wind carried an echoing of wolves among the rocks and two black vultures had lighted on the first, observing him from above. The fear he had kept behind him for three long days attacked head-on, but he could not retreat. His teeth chattered, and his sweat froze. The fragile path of the caciques suddenly disappeared before a lance driven into the ground and held by a pile of stones: the *poteau-mitan*, the intersection between the sky and the place lower down, between the world of the *loas* and that of humans. And then he saw them. First, two shadows, then the gleam of metal: knives or machetes. He did not look up. He said a humble "Greetings," repeating the password Tante Rose had given him. There was no answer, but he could feel the warmth of those beings so near him, as if by putting out a hand he could touch them. They did not smell of rottenness or the cemetery, but emitted the same odor as the people in the cane fields. He asked permission of Baron Kalfour and Ghede to continue, and again there was no answer. Finally, with what little voice he could drag through the rough sand that closed his throat, he asked which path he should follow. He felt something take his arms.

Gambo awaked much later in darkness. He tried to sit up, but every fiber in his body hurt and he could not move. A moan escaped his lips; he closed his eyes again and sank into the world of Les Mystères, one that is entered and left unwillingly, at times shrunken with suffering, at others floating in a dark, deep space like the firmament of a moonless night. Slowly he recovered consciousness, wrapped in fog, stiff. He lay quiet and in silence as his eyes adjusted to the darkness. No moon or stars, no murmuring breezes, only silence, cold. All he could remember was the lance at the crossroad. He perceived a vacillating light moving a short distance away, and soon after, a figure with a small lamp bent down beside him; a woman's voice said something he could not understand, an arm helped him sit up, and a hand put a gourd filled with water to his lips. He drank all it held, desperately. That was how he knew he had reached his destination; he was in one of the sacred caves of the Arawaks that served the Maroons as a guard post.

During the days, weeks, and months that followed, Gambo would be discovering the world of the runaways, which existed on the same island and in the same time but in a different dimension, a world like that of Africa, although much more primitive and miserable. He would hear familiar tongues and known stories, he would eat the *fufu* his mothers made, he would again sit beside a fire to sharpen his weapons of war, as he had done with his father, but beneath other stars. The camps were scattered about the most impenetrable parts of the mountains, true little villages, thousands and thousands of men and women who had escaped slavery, and their children, born free. They lived on the defensive and did not trust the slaves who had escaped from the plantations because they could betray them, but Tante Rose had communicated to them through mysterious channels that Gambo was on his way. Of the twenty runaways from Saint-Lazare, only six had reached the crossroads, and two of them were so badly wounded they did not survive. Then Gambo confirmed his suspicion that Tante Rose acted as contact between the slaves and the bands of Maroons. No torture could tear the name of Tante Rose from the men Cambray had captured.

The Conspiracy

Eight months later, in the big house of the Habitation Saint-Lazare, Eugenia García del Solar died without either agitation or anguish. She was thirty-one years old; she had passed seven years out of her mind and four in the wake-sleep of opium. That early morning the slave caring for her overslept, and it fell to Tété, who came in as always to give her mistress her breakfast pap and clean her up for the day, to find her drawn up like a newborn babe among her pillows. Her mistress was smiling, and in the contentment of dying she had regained a certain touch of beauty and youth. Tété was the only person who lamented her death; after taking care of her for so long, she had ended by truly loving her. She washed her, dressed her, combed her hair for the last time, and placed her missal between Eugenia's hands, crossed over her breast. Tété took the blessed rosary in its chamois pouch, her mistress's bequest to her, hung it around her neck, and tucked it beneath her bodice. Before making her final farewell, she removed a small gold medallion graced with the image of the Virgin, one Eugenia always wore, to give to Maurice. Then she went to call Valmorain.

Little Maurice was not aware of his mother's death because for months "the ill lady" had been secluded, and now they did not let him see the corpse. As they took the silver-studded walnut coffin from the house, the one Valmorain had bought as contraband from an American during the time she tried to kill herself, Maurice was in the patio with Rosette, improvising a funeral for a dead cat. He had never witnessed rites of that kind, but he had a lively imagination, and he buried the animal with more feeling and solemnity than his mother received.

Rosette was daring and precocious. She made surprising speed across the floor on her plump knees, followed by Maurice, who never left her from sunrise to dark. Tété locked the chests and other furniture in which she might catch her fingers and used chicken wire to block entries to the gallery to keep her from wandering outside. She gave up on mice and scorpions because her daughter was a curious girl and could have held the hottest chili to her nose, something Maurice, who was much more prudent, would never think of doing. She was a pretty child. Her mother admitted it unhappily, because for a slave beauty was no favor, invisibility was much more desirable. Tété, who at the age of ten had wished so strongly to be like Violette Boisier, saw with wonder that through some trick of destiny's sleight of hand Rosette, with her wavy hair and captivating, dimpled smile, resembled that beautiful woman. In the island's complex racial classification she was a quadroon, the daughter of a white man and a mulatta, and in color she had come out looking more like the father than the mother. At her early age Rosette was mumbling a jargon that sounded like a language of renegades, and Maurice translated with difficulty. The boy put up with her whims with the patience of a grandfather, which later was transformed into an unflagging affection that would mark their lives. He would be her only friend, he would console her in her sorrows and teach her what was indispensable for her to know, from staying away from fierce dogs to learning her ABCs, but that would be later. The essential thing he imparted to her from the beginning was the direct path to her father's heart. Maurice did what Tété did not dare to; he kept the girl near Toulouse in ways that could not be challenged. Her master stopped thinking of her as one of his properties and began to search for something of himself in her features. He did not find it, but at any rate he gave her the tolerant affection pets inspire and allowed her to live in the big house instead of sending her to the slave quarters. Unlike her mother, in whom seriousness was nearly a defect, Rosette was talkative and seductive, a whirlwind of activity that brightened the house, the best antidote against the uncertainty prevalent in those years.

When France dissolved the Assemblée Coloniale in Saint-Domingue, the Patriots, as the monarchist colonists called themselves, refused to submit to authorities in Paris. After having spent so much time in the isolation of the plantation, Valmorain now began to plot along with his peers. As he often went to Le Cap, he rented the furnished house of a wealthy Portuguese merchant who had returned for a period to his country. It was near the port and comfortable for him, but he nevertheless planned to acquire a house of his own very soon using the help of the agent who handled his sugar dealings, the same extremely honorable old Jewish man who had served his father. It was Valmorain who initiated the secret conversations with the English. In his youth he had known a sailor who now commanded the British fleet in the Caribbean, whose instructions were to intervene in the French colony the minute there was opportunity. By then the confrontations between whites and mulattoes had reached unimagined violence, and the blacks took advantage of that conflict to rebel, first in the western part of the island and then in the north, in Limbe. The Patriots followed events with close attention, anxiously awaiting the moment to betray the French government.

Valmorain spent a month in Le Cap with Tété, the children, and Eugenia's coffin. He always traveled with his son, and in turn Maurice was not going anywhere without Rosette and Tété. The political situation was too unstable for him to be apart from his son, and neither did he want to leave Tété at the mercy of Prosper Cambray, who had his eye on her, to the point that he had tried to buy her. Valmorain supposed that another man in his situation would sell her to keep his head overseer happy, and in the process get rid of a woman who no longer excited him, but Maurice loved her like a mother. Besides, the matter of Tété had become a silent struggle of wills between him and the overseer. During those weeks in Le Cap he had attended the political meetings of the Patriots, who gathered in his house in an atmosphere of secrecy and conspiracy though in truth no one was watching them. Valmorain planned to look for a tutor for Maurice, who was turning five in a state of total wildness. It was his duty to give him the rudiments of education that would allow him in the future to enter a boarding school in France. Tété prayed that that moment would never come, convinced that Maurice would die if he were far away from her and Rosette. He also had to dispose of Eugenia. The children were used to the coffin lying in corridors and accepted with all naturalness that it contained the mortal remains of "the ill lady." They never asked exactly what the "mortal remains" were, saving Tété the necessity of explaining what would have caused Maurice new nightmares, but when Valmorain caught them trying to open it with a knife from the kitchen, he realized it was time to make a decision. He ordered his agent to send it to the nuns' cemetery in Cuba, where Sancho had bought a mausoleum because Eugenia had made him swear he would not bury her in Saint-Domingue, where her bones could end up in a Negro drum. The agent intended to send the coffin by way of a ship sailing in that direction, and in the meantime left it in a corner of the storeroom, where it stood forgotten until it was consumed in flames two years later.

Uprising in the North

At the plantation, Prosper Cambray waked at dawn to a fire in one of the fields and the yelling of slaves, many of whom did not know what was happening because they had not been included in the secret of the uprising. Cambray used the general confusion to surround the area and to subdue the slaves who'd had time to react. The domestic servants took no part in any of it but clustered together in the big house, expecting the worst. Cambray gave orders for the women and children to be enclosed, and he himself carried out the purge among the men. Not much had been lost: the fire was quickly controlled, only two fields of dry cane burned; it was much worse on other plantations to the north. When the first detachments of the *maréchaussée* arrived with the mission of restoring order to the region, Prosper Cambray limited himself to handing over those he considered guilty. He would have preferred to deal with them personally, but the idea was to coordinate efforts and crush out the rebellion at the roots. The suspects were taken to Le Cap to tear from them the names of the leaders.

The chief overseer did not notice Tante Rose's disappearance until the next day, when those who'd been flogged at the Habitation Saint-Lazare needed to be treated.

In the meantime in Le Cap, Violette Boisier and Loula had finished packing the family's possessions and had stored them in a warehouse in the port to await the ship that would take the family to France. Finally, after nearly ten years of waiting, work, saving, moneylending, and patience, the plan conceived by Etienne Relais in the early days of his relationship with Violette was coming about. They had begun bidding farewell to their friends when the major was summoned to the office of the Gouverneur, Vicomte Blanchelande. The building lacked the refinement of the Intendance; it had the austerity of a barrack and smelled of leather and metal. The vicomte was a mature man with an impressive military career, who had been Maréchal and Gouverneur of Trinidad before being assigned to Saint-Domingue. He had just arrived and only begun to take the pulse of the situation; he did not know a rebellion was brewing outside the city. His authority on the island depended on his mandate from the Assemblée Nationale in Paris, whose capricious delegates could withdraw their support as quickly as they bestowed it. His noble origins and fortune weighed against him among the most radical groups, the Jacobins, who intended to do away with every vestige of the monarchical regime. Etienne Relais was led to the vicomte's office through several nearly bare rooms hung with paintings of multitudinous battles blackened by soot from the lamps. The Gouverneur, dressed in civilian clothes and not wearing a wig, was barely visible behind a rough barracks table battered by many years of use. At his back hung the flag of France, topped by the coat of arms of the Revolution, and to his left, on another wall, was pinned an fanciful unfolded map of the Antilles, illustrated with marine monsters and ancient galleons.

"Major Etienne Relais, from the Régiment Le Cap," Relais presented himself, feeling ridiculous in the dress uniform and decorations that so strongly contrasted with his superior's simplicity.

"Have a seat, Major. I imagine you would like a coffee." The vicomte, who looked as if he'd passed a bad night, sighed.

He stepped from behind the table and led Relais toward two worn leather armchairs. Immediately, from out of nowhere, sprang an orderly followed by three slaves, four people for two little cups: one of the slaves held the tray, another poured the coffee, and the third offered sugar. After serving, the slaves withdrew, backing out of the room, but the orderly stood at attention between the two chairs. The Gouverneur was a man of medium height, slim, with deep wrinkles and sparse gray hair. At close sight he looked much less impressive than he did on horseback in his plumed hat and his medals, with the sash of his charge across his breast. Relais perched uncomfortably on the edge of the chair, clumsily holding the porcelain cup that he could have shattered with a breath. He was accustomed to observing the rigid military etiquette imposed by rank.

"You must be wondering why I have called you here, Major Relais," said Blanchelande, stirring sugar into his coffee. "What is your view of the situation in Saint-Domingue?"

"What is my view?" Relais repeated, disconcerted.

"There are colonials who want to be independent, and we have an English flotilla in sight of the port ready to help them. What would England love more than to annex Saint-Domingue! You must know the ones I am referring to—you can give me the names of the seditionists."

"That list will include some fifteen thousand people, Maréchal, all the property owners and people with money, as many whites as *affranchis*."

"I was afraid of that. I do not have enough troops to defend the colony and to see that the new laws from France are carried out. I will be frank with you, Major, some decrees seem absurd to me, like the one dated May 15, which gives political rights to the mulattoes."

"That affects only the *affranchis*, born of free, property-owning parents, fewer than four hundred men."

"That is not the point!" the vicomte interrupted. "The point is that whites will never accept equality with mulattoes, and I do not blame them for that. It would destabilize the colony. Nothing is straightforward in the politics of France, and we suffer the consequences of that imbalance. The decrees change from day to day, Major. One ship brings me instructions, and the next one brings me the counterorder."

"And there is the problem of the rebellious slaves," Relais added.

"Ah, the blacks . . . I cannot bother about that now. The rebellion in Limbe has been crushed, and soon we will have the leaders."

"None of the prisoners have revealed names, monsieur. They will not speak."

"We shall see. The *maréchaussée* knows how to manage these matters."

"With all respect, Maréchal, I think this deserves your attention," Etienne Relais insisted, setting his cup on a little table. "The situation in Saint-Domingue is different from that in other colonies. Here the slaves have never accepted their fate, they have risen up again and again for almost a century; there are tens of thousands of Maroons in the mountains. And at the present we have half a million slaves. They know that the republic abolished slavery in France, and they are ready to fight to obtain the same here. The *maréchaussée* will not be able to control them."

"Are you suggesting that we use the army against the Negroes, Major?"

"You will have to use the army to impose order, Maréchal."

"How do you intend for us to do that? I am sent a tenth of the soldiers I ask for, and as soon as their feet touch the ground, they fall ill. And this brings us to what I wanted to say: at this moment I cannot accept your retirement."

Etienne Relais rose to his feet, livid. The Gouverneur did the same, and the two measured each other a few seconds.

"Monsieur le Maréchal, I joined the army when I was seventeen years old; I have served for thirty-five years; I have been wounded six times; and I am now fifty-two," said Relais.

"And I am fifty-five, and I would like to retire to my property in Dijon, but France needs me, just as she needs you," the vicomte replied curtly.

"My retirement was signed by your predecessor, le Gouverneur de Peinier. I no longer have a house, monsieur; I am living in a pension with my family, ready to set sail next Thursday on the *Marie Thérèse*."

Blanchelande's blue eyes locked onto those of the Major, who finally clicked his heels and lowered his.

"At your orders, Gouverneur." Relais accepted, defeated.

Blanchelande again sighed and rubbed his eyes, exhausted; then he gestured to the orderly to call his secretary, and went to the table.

"Do not worry, the government will provide you a house, Major Relais. And now come here to the map and show me the most vulnerable points on the island. No one knows the terrain better than you."

Zarité

This is how they told it. This is how it happened at Bois Cayman. This is how it is written in the legend of the place they now call Haïti, the first independent republic of Negroes. I don't know what that means, but it must be important because the blacks say it with applause and praise and the whites say it with rage. Bois Cayman lies to the north, near the great plains on the way to Le Cap, several hours from the Habitation Saint-Lazare. It is an enormous forest, a place of crossroads and sacred trees, where Damballah resides in his serpent form, loa of streams and rivers, guardian of the forest. In Bois Cayman live the spirits of nature and of dead slaves who have not found the way to Guinea. That night other spirits that were well installed among Les Morts et Les Mystères also came to the woods, but they came prepared to fight, because they were called. There was an army of hundreds of thousands of spirits fighting alongside the blacks, and that was why finally the whites were defeated. Everyone is in agreement about that, even the French soldiers, who felt the spirits' fury. Maître Valmorain, who did not believe in anything he did not understand, and as he understood very little believed in nothing, was also convinced that the dead aided the rebels. That explained how they could defeat the best army of Europe, as it was said to be. The meeting of the slaves in Bois Cayman occurred in mid-August, on a hot night wet from the sweat of men and of the earth. How was the news passed? They say that the drums carried the message from kalenda to kalenda, from hounfor to hounfor, from ajoupa *to ajoupa; the sound of the drums travels farther and faster than the roar of a storm, and all the people knew its language. Slaves came from the plantations in the north, even though the masters and the* maréchaussée *had been on the alert since the uprising in Limbe a few days before. Some of the rebels had been taken alive, and it was expected that they would give up information; no one could endure the dungeons in Le Cap without confessing. Within a few hours the Maroons had transferred their camps to the highest peaks in order to elude the horsemen of the* maréchaussée *and had quickly organized the assembly in Bois Cayman. They didn't know that none of the prisoners had spoken, nor would they.*

Thousands of Maroons descended from the mountains. Gambo arrived with the group of Zamba Boukman, a giant who inspired double respect for being a houngan *and a war chief. In the year and a half he had been free, Gambo had grown to man size; he had broad shoulders, untiring legs, and a machete for killing. He had won Boukman's trust. He slipped onto plantations to steal food, tools, weapons, and animals, but he had never come near Saint-Lazare to see me. I got news of him through Tante Rose. My godmother did not tell me how she received the messages, and I came to fear that she made them up to calm me, because during that time my need to be with Gambo had returned and was burning me like hot coals. "Give me a remedy for this love, Tante Rose." But there is no remedy for it. I went to bed exhausted by the day's chores, with a child on either side, but couldn't sleep. For hours I listened to Maurice snorting and Rosette purring, the sounds of the house, the dogs barking, the frogs croaking, the cocks crowing, and when finally I fell asleep it was like sinking into molasses. I tell this with shame: sometimes, when I lay with my master, I imagined I was with Gambo. I bit my lips to hold back his name and in the darkness behind my closed eyes pretended that the white man's smell of alcohol was the green grass breath of Gambo, who had not yet rotted his teeth by eating bad fish, and that the heavy, hairy, panting man atop me was Gambo, slim and agile, his young flesh crisscrossed with scars, his sweet lips, his curious tongue, his whispering voice. Then my body would open and sway, remembering pleasure. Afterward my master would slap my buttocks and laugh smugly, and with that my* ti-bon-ange *would return to that bed and that man and I would open my eyes and realize where I was. I would run to the patio and wash myself in fury before going to lie down with the children.*

People traveled for hours and hours to reach Bois Cayman. Some left their plantations by day, others came along the inlets of the coast; they all arrived in the dark of night. It is said that a band of Maroons traveled from Port-au-Prince, but that is very far and I don't believe it. The forest was filled, men and women stealthily gliding through the trees in total silence, blended with the dead and the shadows, but when they felt the vibration of the first drums on their feet they were energized, they picked up their pace, speaking in whispers, and then shouts; they greeted one another, they gave their names. The forest grew light with torches. Some knew the road and guided others toward the great clearing that Boukman, the houngan, had chosen. A necklace of fires and torches lighted the hounfor. The men had prepared the sacred poteau-mitan, a tall, thick tree trunk, because the road for the loas had to be wide. A long line of girls dressed in white, the hounsis, arrived escorting Tante Rose, also all in white, carrying the asson for the ceremony. People bowed to touch the hem of her skirt or the bracelets that tinkled on her arms. She had grown younger, because Erzulie had been with her since she left the Habitation Saint-Lazare: she had grown able to walk great distances without tiring and without her cane, and had become invisible, so the maréchaussée could not find her. The drums in the semicircle were calling, tam, tam, tam. People gathered in groups and told what had happened in Limbe, and the suffering of the prisoners in Le Cap. Boukman took the word to invoke the supreme god, Papa Bondye, and to ask that he lead them to victory. "Hear the voice of freedom that sings in our hearts!" he shouted, and the slaves answered with a clamor that shook the island. This is how they told it.

The drums began to talk and answer, to set the rhythm for the ceremony. The hounsis danced around the poteau-mitan, moving like flamingos, crouching, rising up, long necks, winged arms, and they sang calling to the loas, first Legba, as is always done, then the rest, one by one. The mambo,

Tante Rose, traced the vévé around the sacred post with a mixture of flour to feed the loas, *and ash to honor the dead. The drums augmented her purpose, the rhythm grew faster, and the whole forest throbbed, from the deepest roots to the most remote stars. Then Ogoun descended with the spirit of war, Ogu-Fer, the virile god of weapons, aggressive, irritable, dangerous, and Erzulie released Tante Rose to make way for Ogoun to mount her. Everyone saw the transformation. Tante Rose rose straight up to double her size, with neither lameness nor years on her back; with her eyes rolled back, she made an astounding leap and landed nearly ten feet away before one of the fires. From Ogoun's mouth came a bellow of thunder and the* loa *danced, rising up from the ground, falling, and bouncing back like a ball, with the strength of the* loas, *accompanied by the roar of the drums. Two men approached, the most courageous, to give him sugar to calm him, but the* loa *picked them up like rag dolls and threw them far from him. He had come to give a message of war and justice and blood. Ogoun picked up a red hot coal, placed it in his mouth, whirled completely about, sucking fire, and then spit it out without burning his lips. Then he took a large knife from the man nearest him, set the* asson *on the ground, went to the sacrificial black pig tied to a tree, and with his warrior's arm cut its throat with a single slash, severing the thick head from the trunk and soaking himself in its blood. By then many followers had been mounted, and the forest had filled with Invisibles, Morts, and Mystères, with* loas *and spirits mixed in with humans, all scrambled together, singing, dancing, leaping, and rolling to the beat of the drums, walking on burning coals, licking red hot knife blades, and eating handfuls of hot chilis. The night air was charged as it is during a terrible storm, but not a breeze stirred. The torches made a light like midday, but the nearby* maréchaussée *saw nothing. This is how they told it.*

Much later, when the huge crowd was shaking like a single person, Ogoun loosed a lion's roar to impose silence. The drums immediately stilled, and all except the mambo *were again themselves as the* loas *retired to the tops of the trees. Ogu-Fer lifted the* asson *toward the sky, and the voice of the most powerful* loa *issued from Tante Rose's mouth to demand the end of slavery,* to call for a total rebellion, and to name the chiefs: Boukman, Jean-François, Jeannot, Boisseau, Célestin, and several others. Toussaint was not named, because at that moment the man who would become the soul of the rebels was at a plantation in Breda, where he served as coachman. He did not join the uprising until several weeks later, after he had put his master's entire family in a safe place. I did not hear Toussaint's name until a year later.

That was the beginning of the revolution. Many years have gone by and blood keeps running, soaking the soil of Haïti, but I am not there to weep.

Revenge

As soon as he learned about the uprising of the slaves and the affair of the prisoners in Limbe, all of whom died without confessing, Toulouse Valmorain ordered Tété to quickly prepare the return to Saint-Lazare, ignoring everyone's warnings, especially those of Dr. Parmentier, about the danger whites were running on the plantations. "Do not exaggerate, Doctor. The blacks have always been rebellious. Prosper Cambray has them under control," Valmorain replied emphatically, although he had doubts. While the echo of the drums was resonating in the north, calling the slaves to the meeting at Bois Cayman, Valmorain's coach, protected by a reinforced guard, headed at a trot for the plantation. They arrived in a cloud of dust, hot, anxious, with the children swooning and Tété jarred by the tossing and bumping of the vehicle. The master leaped from the carriage and closed himself in his office with his head overseer to receive a report of losses, which in fact were minimal, and then look around the property and confront the slaves that according to Cambray had revolted, but not enough to hand them over to the *maréchaussée*, as he had done with others. It was the kind of situation that made Valmorain feel inadequate, and that in recent times had been repeated frequently. The overseer looked after the interests of Saint-Lazare better than the owner; he acted with firmness and few inhibitions, while Valmorain vacillated, little disposed to dirty his hands with blood. Once again he confirmed his own ineptitude. In the twenty-some years he had been in the colony he had not adapted; he continued to have the sensation he was only passing through, and his most disagreeable burden was the slaves. He was not capable of ordering a man to be roasted over a slow fire, though Cambray considered that measure indispensable. His argument with the overseer and the *grands blancs*, since he had had to justify his position on more than one occasion, was that cruelty turned out to be ineffective; the slaves disabled or destroyed what they could, from knife edges to their own health; they committed suicide or ate carrion and wasted away vomiting and shitting, extremes that he attempted to avoid. He wondered whether his considerations served any purpose, or if he was hated as much as Lacroix. Perhaps Parmentier was right, and violence, fear, and hatred were inherent in slavery, but a planter could not allow himself the luxury of scruples. On the rare occasions he went to bed sober he couldn't sleep, tormented by visions. His family's fortune, begun by his father and multiplied several times over by him, was soaked in blood. Unlike other *grands blancs*, he could not ignore the voices rising in Europe and America in denunciation of the hell on Antillean plantations.

By the end of September, the rebellion was widespread in the north; slaves were running away en masse and as they left setting fire to everything. There were not enough workers in the fields, and the planters did not want to keep buying slaves who ran at the first moment of inattention. The slave market in Le Cap was nearly paralyzed. Prosper Cambray doubled the number of commandeurs and carried vigilance and discipline to the extreme, while Valmorain succumbed to his employee's ferocity without intervening. On Saint-Lazare no one slept soundly. Life, which was never undemanding, became pure suffering. *Kalendas* were forbidden and rest hours as well, although in the suffocating heat of midday little work was done. Ever since Tante Rose had disappeared there was no one to act as healer, to give counsel or spiritual aid. The only person happy with the mambo's absence was Prosper Cambray, who gave no sign of pursuing her—the farther away the better when it came to that witch able to turn a human being into a zombie. For what other purpose did she collect dust from graves, the liver of puffer fish, toads, and poisonous plants, if not for those devious purposes? That was why the overseer never took off his boots. The slaves scattered broken glass on the ground, the poison entered through cuts on the soles of the feet, and the night after the funeral they dug up the cadaver, now a zombie, and revived him with a monumental beating. "Surely you don't believe in those tales!" Valmorain said, laughing, once when they were talking on that subject. "I believe nothing, monsieur, but there are zombies, there are," the overseer had replied.

At Saint-Lazare, as on the rest of the island, life was being lived at a rhythm of waiting. Tété heard repeated rumors through her master or from the slaves, but without Tante Rose she no longer knew how to interpret them. The plantation had closed in on itself, like a fist. The days grew long and the nights eternal. Even the madwoman was missed. Eugenia's death had left a void; there were hours and space to spare, the house seemed enormous, and not even the children, with all their racket, could fill it. In the fragility of that time rules were relaxed and distances shortened. Valmorain grew accustomed to Rosette's presence, and ended by tolerating familiarity with her. She did not call him *maître*, but *monsieur*, pronouncing it like the mewing of a cat. "When I grow up, I am going to marry Rosette," Maurice would say. There would be time in the future to set things straight, his father thought. Tété tried to instill in the children the basic difference between them: Maurice had privileges forbidden Rosette, like going into a room without asking permission or sitting on the master's knees without being called. The little boy was at an age to demand explanations, and Tété always answered his questions with absolute truth. "Because you are the master's legitimate son; you are a male child, white, free, and rich, but Rosette isn't." Far from being accepted, that answer provoked attacks of weeping in Maurice. "Why, why?" he would repeat between sobs. "Because that is how twisted and unfair life is, my child," Tété would answer. "Come here and let me wipe your nose." Valmorain thought that his son was more than old enough to sleep by himself, but every time they tried to make him do that Maurice would throw a tantrum and get a fever. He could keep sleeping with Tété and Rosette until the situation became normal, his father told him. However, the tension on the island was far from approaching normality.

One evening several militiamen came to the plantation; they were moving through the north in an attempt to control the anarchy, and among them was Parmentier. The doctor seldom traveled outside Le Cap because of the dangers on the road and his duties with the French soldiers dying in his hospital. There was an outbreak of yellow fever in one of the barracks that he had controlled before it became an epidemic, but malaria, cholera, and dengue fever caused considerable havoc. Parmentier joined the militiamen's party, the one way to travel with some security, not so much to visit Valmorain, whom he saw from time to time in Le Cap, as to consult Tante Rose. He was disappointed when he learned of his teacher's disappearance. Valmorain offered hospitality to his friend and to the militiamen, who were covered with dust, thirsty, and exhausted. For a couple of days the big house was filled with activity, with male voices, and even with music, because several of the men played string instruments. Finally they could use the ones Violette Boisier had bought when she decorated the house thirteen years before; they were out of tune but playable. Valmorain sent for several slaves who had special talent on the drums, and a fiesta was organized. Tante Mathilde emptied the larder of the best it contained and prepared fruit tarts and complicated greasy and spicy creole stews she hadn't made for a long time. Prosper Cambray took charge of roasting a lamb, one of the few remaining, for they mysteriously disappeared. The hogs also vanished, and as it was impossible for the Maroons to steal those heavy animals without the complicity of the slaves on the plantation, when one went missing Cambray chose ten blacks at random and had them lashed; someone had to pay for the loss. In those months the overseer, enjoying more power than ever, was behaving as if he were the true owner of Saint-Lazare, and his insolence with Tété, more and more brazen, was his way of defying his employer, who had drawn into himself since the rebellion broke out. The unexpected visit of the militiamen, all mulattoes like him, fed his arrogance: he distributed Valmorain's liquor without consulting him, gave peremptory orders to the domestic slaves in his presence, and made jokes at his expense. Dr. Parmentier noticed all these things, just as he noticed that Tété and the children trembled when the overseer was around, and he was at the point of commenting on this to his host, but experience made him hold his tongue. Every plantation was a world apart, with its own system of relationships, its secrets and vices. For example, Rosette, the little girl with skin so light she could only be Valmorain's daughter. And what had become of Tété's other child? He would have liked to know, but he never dared asked Valmorain; the relationships of the whites with their female slaves was a forbidden subject in good society.

"I suppose that you have seen the damage caused by the rebellion, Doctor," Valmorain commented. "These bands have devastated the region."

"That is so. As we were coming here, we saw smoke from a fire at the Lacroix plantation," Parmentier told him. "When we got closer, we could see that the cane fields were still burning. There wasn't a soul around. The silence was terrifying."

"I know, Doctor, because I was among the first to reach the Habitation Lacroix after the assault," Valmorain explained. "The entire Lacroix family and their overseers and domestics were massacred; the rest of the slaves disappeared. We dug a grave and buried the bodies temporarily, until the authorities could investigate what had happened. We could not leave them strewn around like carrion. The blacks treated themselves to an orgy of blood."

"Aren't you afraid something like that will happen here?" Parmentier asked.

"We are armed and on guard, and I trust Cambray's ability," Valmorain replied. "But I confess that I am very worried. The blacks vented their rage on Lacroix and his family."

"Your friend Lacroix had a reputation for being cruel," the physician interrupted. "That inflamed the attackers even more, but in this war no one has any consideration for anyone, *mon ami*. You must be prepared for the worst."

"Did you know that for a banner the rebels carry a white infant impaled on a lance, Doctor?"

"Everyone knows it. In France there is a reaction of horror to these events. The slaves can no longer count on any sympathizer in the Assemblée—even the Société des Amis des Noirs is quiet—but these atrocities are the logical response to what we have done to them."

"Do not include us, Doctor!" exclaimed Valmorain. "You and I have never committed such excesses!"

"I am not referring to anyone in particular, only to the norm we have imposed. The Negroes' revenge was inevitable. I am ashamed of being French," Parmentier said sadly.

"If it is a matter of revenge, we have reached the point that it is either them or us. We planters will defend our lands and our investments. We are going to restore the colony as it was. We will not sit here with our arms crossed!"

Their arms were not crossed. The colonists, the *maréchaussée*, and the army went on the hunt, and any black rebel they caught, they flayed alive. They imported fifteen hundred dogs from Jamaica and twice that number of mules from Martinique trained to climb mountains, dragging cannons.

The Terror

One after another, the plantations in the north began to blaze. The fires lasted months, the splendor of the flames could be seen at night in Cuba, and the dense smoke choked Le Cap and, according to the slaves, reached as far as Guinea. Major Etienne Relais, who was in charge of informing the Gouverneur of losses, had by the end of December counted more than two thousand among the whites, and if his calculations were correct, there were ten thousand more among the blacks. In France, opinion changed after people learned of the colonists' suffering in Saint-Domingue, and the Assemblée Nationale annulled the recent decree that granted political rights to the *affranchis*. Just as Relais had told Violette, that decision was completely lacking in logic, since the mulattoes had nothing to do with the uprising; they were the Negroes' worst enemies and the natural allies of the *grands blancs*, with whom they had everything in common except color. Gouverneur Blanchelande, whose sympathy did not lie with the republicans, had to use the army to quash the revolt of the slaves, which was taking on the proportions of catastrophe, and to intervene in the barbarous conflict between whites and mulattoes that had begun in Port-au-Prince. The *petits blancs* carried out a massacre against the *affranchis*, and they answered by committing worse savagery than the blacks and whites combined. No one was safe. The entire island shook from the clash of an age-old hatred that had awaited an excuse to burst into flames. In Le Cap the white rabble, fired up by what had happened in Port-au-Prince, attacked people of color in the streets, broke into and wrecked their houses, ravished their women, slit their children's throats, and hanged the men from their own balconies. The stench of corpses could be smelled on the ships anchored outside the port. In a note Parmentier sent Valmorain, he commented on news of the city: "There is nothing as dangerous as impunity, *mon ami*, that is when people go mad and commit the most hideous bestial acts; it doesn't matter the color of the skin, everyone is the same. If you had seen what I have seen, you would have to question the superiority of the white race, a topic we have so often discussed."

Terrified by the turbulence, the doctor asked for an appointment and presented himself at the spartan office of Etienne Relais, whom he knew from his work in the military hospital. He knew that Relais had married a woman of color and that he went out with her on his arm with no concern for malicious tongues, something he himself had never dared do with Adèle. He calculated that the man would understand his situation better than anyone, and was ready to tell him his secret. The officer offered him a seat in the only available chair.

"Forgive my daring to bother you with a personal matter, Major," Parmentier stammered.

"How may I help you, Doctor?" Relais replied amiably; he owed the doctor the lives of several of his subalterns.

"The truth is that I have a family. My wife's name is Adèle. She is not exactly my wife—you take my meaning, yes? But we have been together many years and have three children. She is an *affranchie.*"

"I already knew that, Doctor," Relais told him.

"How is that?" Parmentier exclaimed, taken aback.

"My position demands that I keep informed, and my wife, Violette Boisier, knows Adèle. She has bought several dresses from her."

"Adèle is an excellent seamstress," the doctor added.

"I suppose you have come to speak to me about the attacks against the *affranchis*. I cannot promise that the situation will improve any time soon, Doctor. We are trying to control the population, but the army does not have sufficient resources. I am very worried. My wife has not put her nose outside the house for two weeks."

"I am afraid for Adèle and the children, Major."

"In regard to what concerns me, I believe that the only way to protect my family is to send them to Cuba until this storm passes. They are leaving on a ship tomorrow. I can offer the same possibility for yours, if you like. They will be uncomfortable, but it is a short voyage."

That night a squad of soldiers escorted the women and children to the ship. Adèle was a dark, heavyset mulatta, unattractive at first view, but she had an inexhaustible sweetness and good humor. No one could help but notice the difference between her, dressed like a servant and intent on staying in the shadow to protect the reputation of her children's father, and the beautiful Violette with her queenly bearing. They were not of the same social class, separated by various degrees of color, which in Saint-Domingue determined one's fate, and by the fact that one was a seamstress and the other a client, but they embraced with sympathy since they would face together the hazards of exile. Loula was weeping, with Jean-Martin clinging to her hand. She had hung Catholic and voodoo fetishes beneath his jacket so that Relais, a resolute agnostic, would not see them. The slave had never been in a dory, much less on a ship, and she was horrified about venturing onto a shark-filled sea in that bundle of badly put together boards with a few sails that looked like petticoats. While Dr. Parmentier made discreet signs of good-bye to his family from a distance, Etienne Relais, in full view of his soldiers, made his farewell to Violette, the only woman he had ever loved in his life, with a desperate kiss and an oath that they would soon be together. He would never see her again.

———

By now no one was going hungry in Zambo Boukman's camp, and people were beginning to get stronger. The men's rib cages were no longer visible, the few children were not skeletons with bloated stomachs and eyes from beyond the tomb, and the women were beginning to hold their pregnancies. Before the uprising, when the Maroons were living hidden in the canyons of the mountains, hunger was eased by sleeping and thirst with drops of rain. Women cultivated scrawny patches of corn, which often had to be abandoned before picking, and defended with their own lives their few goats because there were children who had been born in freedom but destined to a very brief life without milk from those noble animals. Gambo and five other men, the most daring, were in charge of obtaining provisions. One of them carried a musket and could drop a hare on the run from an impossible distance, but their few balls were kept for grander prey. The men crept onto the plantations at night, where slaves shared with them what they had, willingly or not, but that presented a formidable danger of being betrayed or surprised. If they succeeded in getting as far as the kitchens or domestic quarters they could slip out a couple of sacks of flour or a barrel of dried fish, which might not be much but far better than chewing lizards. Gambo, who had a magical hand with animals, sometimes led away an old mule from the mill that would later be used down to the last bone. That maneuver took as much luck as audacity, for if the mule was stubborn there was no way to move it, and if it was docile it had to be hidden until they reached the shadows of the jungle, where they asked its forgiveness for taking its life, as his father had taught him when they went hunting, and then sacrificed it. Among the men they carried the meat up the mountain, erasing tracks to elude pursuers. However, those desperate excursions were different now. No one opposed them any longer at the plantations; they were nearly all abandoned, and they could take anything that had been saved from the fire. Thanks to that there was no shortage in the camp of hogs and hens; there were more than a hundred goats, sacks of corn, cassava, sweet potatoes, and beans, even rum; they had all the coffee they could wish, and sugar, which many slaves had never tasted though they had spent years producing it. The former fugitives were now revolutionaries. It was no longer a matter of squalid bandits but of determined warriors; there was no turning back: a man died fighting, or he was tortured to death. They could only place their bets on victory.

The camp was surrounded with stakes holding skulls and impaled bodies rotting in the sun. They kept the white prisoners in a corral, awaiting their turn to be executed. The women were converted into slaves and concubines, just as black women had been on the plantations. Gambo felt no compassion for the captives—he himself would finish them off if the need to do so arose, but he had not been given that order. As he had swift legs and good judgment, Boukman sent him out to spy and to carry messages to other chiefs. Gambo knew the region, which was dotted with rebel bands, very well. The worst camp for whites was the one headed by Jeannot, where every day several men were selected to be given a slow and macabre death inspired by the atrocities begun by the colonists themselves. Jeannot, like Boukman, was a powerful *houngan* but the war had changed him, and his appetite for cruelty became insatiable. He boasted of drinking the blood of his victims from a human skull. Even his own people were terrified of him. Gambo heard the other chiefs discussing the need to eliminate him before his excesses irritated Papa Bondye, but he did not repeat it, because as a spy he valued discretion.

In one of the camps Gambo met Toussaint, who performed the double role of counselor for the war and doctor; he knew curative plants, and he exercised notable influence over the chiefs, although in that period he kept himself in the background. He was one of the few blacks able to read and write, and thus he learned, though with delays, what was happening on the island and in France. No one knew the mentality of the whites better than he. He had been born and lived as a slave on a plantation in Breda; he educated himself, embraced the Christian religion with fervor, and gained the esteem of his master, who even entrusted his family to him when the moment came to flee. That relationship raised suspicions; many believed that Toussaint subjected himself to whites like a servant, but many times Gambo heard him say that the goal of his life was to end slavery in Saint-Domingue, and nothing or no one would stop him. His personality impressed Gambo from the beginning, and he decided that if Toussaint became a chief, he would change bands without hesitating. Boukman, that giant with the voice of a tempest, the chosen of Ogu-Fer, had been the spark that lighted the fire of rebellion in Bois Cayman, but Gambo sensed that the most brilliant star in the heavens belonged to Toussaint, the ugly little man with a protruding jaw and bowed legs, who spoke like a preacher and prayed to the Jesus of the whites. And he was not mistaken, because a few months later Boukman the invincible, who dodged enemy fire by swatting at bullets with an ox tail as if they were flies, was captured by the army in a skirmish. Etienne Relais gave the order to execute him immediately, to be ahead of the reaction of rebels in other camps. His head was skewered on a lance and planted in the center of the *place* in Le Cap, where no one could fail to see it. Gambo was the only one who escaped death in that ambush, thanks to his awesome speed, and was able to take back the news. Then he joined the camp where Toussaint was, though Jeannot's had more people. He knew that Jeannot's days were numbered. Jeannot's camp was attacked at dawn, and he was hanged without the torture he had imposed on his victims; as there was not enough time preparations were being made to parley with the enemy. Gambo believed that after the death of Jeannot and several of his officers, the time of the white captives had also come, but Toussaint's plan to keep them alive and use them as hostages in negotiations prevailed.

In view of the disaster in the colony, France sent a commission to speak with the black chiefs, who declared themselves ready to return the hostages as a sign of goodwill. They arranged a meeting at a plantation in the north. When the white prisoners, who had survived months of the hell invented by Jeannot, found they were near the house and realized that they were being taken there not to be killed in some horrible manner but to be freed, a stampede followed, and women and children were trampled by the men running to safety. Gambo arranged to stay with Toussaint and the others chosen to confer with the commission. A half dozen *grands blancs*, representing the rest of the colonists, accompanied the authorities just arrived from Paris, who still did not have a clear idea of how things were run in Saint-Domingue. With a start, Gambo recognized among them his former master and stepped back to hide, but quickly realized that Valmorain had not noticed him, and that if he did, he would not recognize him.

The conversations took place outdoors, beneath trees on the patio, and from the first words the tension was palpable. Distrust and rancor reigned among the rebels, and blind pride among the colonists. Stunned, Gambo listened to the terms for peace his chiefs proposed: freedom for themselves and a handful of their followers, in exchange for which the rest of the rebels would quietly return to slavery on the plantations. The commission from Paris accepted immediately—the clause could not be more advantageous—but the *grands blancs* of Saint-Domingue were not ready to grant anything; they wanted the slaves to surrender en masse, without conditions. "What are they thinking! That we are going to make a deal with Negroes? Let them be satisfied with saving their lives!" one of them exclaimed. Valmorain tried to reason with the others, but in the end the voice of the majority prevailed, and they decided not to give anything to the blacks. The rebel leaders withdrew, offended, and Gambo followed, blazing with fury to know that they were ready to betray the people with whom they lived and fought. As soon as I have a chance I will kill them all, one by one, he promised himself. He had lost faith in the revolution. He could not foresee that at that moment the future of the island was being decided; the colonists' intransigence would force the rebels to continue the war for many years, until victory and an end to slavery was achieved.

The members of the commission, impotent before such anarchy, gave up and abandoned Saint-Domingue, and shortly after, another three delegates, led by the French commissioner Sonthonax, a plump young attorney, arrived with six thousand reinforcements and new instructions from Paris. The law had again been changed to grant free mulattoes the rights of every French citizen, the thing they had previously been denied. Several *affranchis* were appointed officers in the army, and many white soldiers refused to serve under their orders and deserted. That stirred up feelings, and the hundred year hatred between whites and *affranchis* reached biblical proportions. The Assemblée Coloniale, which had until then managed the island's internal affairs, was replaced by a commission composed of six whites, five mulattoes, and one free black. In the midst of the growing violence, which now no one could control, Gouverneur Blanchelande was accused of ignoring the mandate of the republican government and favoring the monarchists. He was deported to France with shackles on his legs and shortly after lost his head on the guillotine.

The Taste of Freedom

That is how things were the summer of the following year, when one night Tété suddenly waked with a firm hand over her mouth. She thought it was finally the attack on the plantation they had feared for so long, and prayed that death would be quick, at least for Maurice and Rosette, sleeping beside her. She waited without trying to defend herself to keep from waking the children, and also because of the remote possibility that it was all a nightmare, until she could make out a figure bending over her in the light reflected from the patio torches filtering through the waxed paper at the window. She did not recognize the person because the boy had changed in the year and a half they'd been separated, but then he whispered her name, Zarité, and she felt a flash in her breast, not of terror but of joy. She raised her hands to pull him to her and felt the metal of the knife he held between his teeth. She took it from him, and he, with a moan, dropped down upon the body that shifted to receive him. Gambo's lips sought hers with a thirst stored up during a long absence; his tongue found its way into her mouth, and his hands grasped her breasts through her light shift. She felt him hard between her thighs and opened to him, but she remembered the children she had for a moment forgotten and pushed him away. "Come with me," she whispered.

They got up with care and stepped over Maurice. Gambo recovered his knife and put it in the strip of goat leather at his waist as she closed the mosquito netting to protect the children. Tété made a sign for him to wait and went out to be sure the master was in his room, just as she had left him a couple of hours earlier, then blew out the lamp in the corridor and went back for her lover. Feeling her way, she led him to the madwoman's room on the other side of the house, empty since her death.

Arms around each other, they fell upon the mattress that smelled of moisture and abandon and made love in the darkness, in total silence, choked with unspoken words and shouts of pleasure that evaporated into sighs. During his absence Gambo had found relief with other women in the camps, but he had not been able to sate his appetite of unsatisfied love. He was seventeen years old and lived in the flames of a persistent desire for Zarité. He remembered her tall, abounding, generous, but now she was smaller than he, and her breasts, which then had seemed enormous, fit easily into his hands. Zarité became foam beneath him. In the anguish and voracity of love so long contained he was not quick enough to penetrate her, and in an instant his life escaped in a single burst. He sank into the void, until Zarité's hot breath in his ear brought him back to the madwoman's room. She hummed to him, lightly patting his back, as she did with Maurice to console him, and when she felt he was beginning to return to life she turned him over on the bed, immobilizing him with a hand on his belly as with the other, along with her bitten lips and hungry tongue, she massaged and sucked him, lifting him to the firmament where he was lost among the racing stars of love he had imagined at every instant of repose and in every pause in battle and in every misty dawn in the millenary canyons of the Indian chiefs where he had so many times stood guard. Unable to submit any longer, the boy lifted Tété by the waist and she swung astride him, ramming into herself that burning member she had so longed for, bending down to cover his face with kisses, lick his ears, caress him with her nipples, rock on his hips, squeeze him between her Amazon's thighs, undulating like an eel on the sandy floor of the sea. They romped as if it were the first and the last time, inventing new steps in an ancient dance. The air in the room became saturated with the fragrance of semen and sweat, with the prudent violence of pleasure and the lacerations of love, with smothered moans, silenced laughter, desperate attacks, and nearly moribund panting that in the instant changed into happy kisses.

Exhausted with happiness, they fell into sleep pressed together in a knot of arms and legs, stunned by the heavy heat of that July night. Gambo waked after a few minutes, frightened for having let down his guard, but when he heard the abandoned woman purring in her sleep, he gave himself time to lightly run his hand over her, without waking her, and to take note of the changes in that body that when he left had been misshapen with child. Her breasts still held milk but they were less firm, the nipples distended; her waist seemed very slim, but he did not remember how it had been before her pregnancy; her belly, her hips, her buttocks and thighs, were pure opulence and smoothness. Tété's scent had also changed; she no longer smelled of soap but of milk, and in that moment she was imbued with their blended odors. He sank his nose into her neck, feeling the blood running in her veins, the rhythm of her breathing, the beating of her heart. Tété stretched with a long, satisfied sigh. She was dreaming of Gambo, and it took her an instant to realize that they were actually together and she did not have to imagine him.

"I came to look for you, Zarité. It is time for us to go," Gambo whispered.

He explained that he'd not been able to come earlier because he didn't have anywhere to take her, but now he could not wait any longer. He didn't know if the whites would be able to crush the rebellion but they would have to kill the last Negro before they could proclaim victory. None of the rebels was prepared to be a slave again. Death was on the loose and lying in wait across the island. There was no safe corner, but for them to continue to be apart was worse than fear and war. He told her he did not trust the chiefs, not even Toussaint; he owed them nothing and planned to fight in his own way, changing bands or deserting, according to how things went. For a while they could live together in his camp, he told her; he had built an *ajoupa* with poles and palm leaves, and they would not lack for food. Though she was used to the comforts of this white man's house, all he could offer was a hard life, but she would not be sorry because once you taste freedom you can never turn back. He felt the hot tears on Tété's face.

"I can't leave the children, Gambo," she told him.

"We will take my son with us."

"She is a girl, her name is Rosette, and she isn't your daughter, she is the daughter of the *maître*."

Gambo sat up, surprised. In that year and a half, thinking about his son, the black boy named Honoré, the possibility that "he" was the mulatta girl child of the master had never crossed his mind.

"We can't take Maurice because he's white, nor Rosette, for she is too small to survive hardship," Tété explained.

"You have to come with me, Zarité. And it has to be tonight—tomorrow will be too late. These are the white man's children. Forget them. Think of us and the children we will have. Think of freedom."

"Why do you say tomorrow will be too late?" she asked, wiping away tears with the back of her hand.

"Because the plantation will be attacked. It is the last one left; all the rest have been destroyed."

Then she understood the magnitude of what Gambo was asking; it was much more than her leaving the children, it was to abandon them to a horrible fate. She turned to him with an anger as intense as the passion of minutes before: she would never leave them, not for him and not for freedom. Gambo held her tight against his chest, as if he meant to pick her up and carry her. He told her that Maurice was lost at any rate, but in the camp they would accept Rosette, as long as she was not too light-skinned.

"Neither of them would survive among the rebels, Gambo. The only way to save them is for the *maître* to take them. I am sure he will protect Maurice with his life, but not Rosette."

"There's no time for that, your master is already a corpse, Zarité," he replied.

"If he dies, the children will die too. We have to take all three away from Saint-Lazare before dawn. If you don't want to help me, I will do it alone," Tété decided, pulling on her shift in the darkness.

Her plan was of a childish simplicity, but she presented it with such determination that Gambo finally agreed. He could not force her to go with him, and neither could he leave her. He knew the area, he was used to hiding out, he could move at night, escape danger, and defend himself, but she couldn't.

"Do you think the white man will agree to this?" he asked finally.

"What choice does he have? If he stays, he and Maurice will be disemboweled. Not only will he accept, he will pay a good price. Wait for me here."

Zarité

My body was hot and moist, my face swollen with kisses and tears, and my skin scented with what I'd done with Gambo, but I didn't care. In the corridor I lighted one of the oil lamps, went to the maître's room, and entered without knocking, something I had never done before. I found him limp with liquor, lying on his back, his mouth gaping open with a thread of saliva down his chin; he had a two-day beard, and his pale hair was wild. Suddenly, all the repulsion I felt for him seized me, and I thought I was going to vomit. My presence and the light took an instant to penetrate the fog of the cognac; he waked with a cry and with one quick move pulled out the pistol he kept beneath his pillow. When he recognized me, he lowered the gun but did not put it down. "What is it, Tété?" he said with a tone of rebuke, and jumped out of the bed. "I have come to propose something to you, maître," I told him. My voice did not tremble, nor did the lamp in my hand. He didn't ask me how it had occurred to me to wake him in the middle of the night, sensing that it had to be something very serious. He sat on the edge of the bed with the pistol on his knees as I explained that within hours rebels would attack Saint-Lazare. It was useless to alert Cambray, it would take an army to hold them back. Just as everywhere else, his slaves would join the attackers, there would be a slaughter and a fire, and that was why we had to flee immediately with the children or tomorrow we would be dead. And that would be the good fate—worse would be to die slowly in horrible pain. This is how I told him.

And how did you know? he asked. One of your slaves, who escaped more than a year ago, came back to warn me. And he was going to lead us, because alone we would never reach Le Cap; the region was in the hands of the rebels.

"Who is he?" he asked while he hurriedly threw on some clothes.

"His name is Gambo, and he is my lover—"

He slapped me so hard that I was dazed, but when he started to hit me again, I grabbed his wrist with a strength I didn't know I had. Up to that very moment, I had never looked him in the eye, and I didn't know that he had light-colored eyes, like a cloudy sky.

"We are going to try to save you and Maurice, but the price will be my freedom, and Rosette's," *I told him, enunciating every word very clearly so he would understand.*

He dug his fingers into my arms, and his face was menacingly close to mine. He ground his teeth as he cursed me, his eyes bulging with rage. An eternal moment passed; again I felt nausea, but I did not drop my eyes. At last he sat back down with his head in his hands, defeated.

"You go with that bastard. You don't need for me to free you."

"And Maurice? You can't protect him. I don't want to live always running away, I want to be free."

"Very well, you will have what you ask. Come, hurry, get dressed and get the children ready. Where is that slave?" *he asked.*

"He isn't a slave any longer. I will call him, but first you write me the paper that will free Rosette and me."

Without another word, he sat down at his desk, took a piece of paper and hurriedly wrote, dried the ink with talc, blew on it, then imprinted his ring on sealing wax, as I had always seen him do with important documents. He read it to me aloud, since I couldn't read. My throat clutched and my heart began to pound in my chest: that sheet of paper had the power to change my and my daughter's lives. I folded it four times and put it in the little pouch of Doña Eugenia's rosary I always wore around my neck beneath my blouse. I had to leave the rosary and hope that Doña Eugenia would forgive me.

"Now give me the pistol," *I asked.*

He did not want to let go of the weapon; he explained that he did not mean to use it against Gambo because he was our only means of salvation. I do not remember very well how we got organized, but within a few minutes he was armed with two additional pistols and had collected his gold from the office while I gave the children laudanum from one of Doña Eugenia's blue vials we had kept. They were knocked out, and I was afraid I had given them too much. I didn't worry about the field slaves—tomorrow would be their first day of freedom—but in those attacks the fate of the domestics was usually as atrocious as that of the masters. Gambo decided to warn Tante Mathilde. The cook had provided him an advantage of several hours when he'd run away and had been punished for it; now it was up to him to return the favor. Within a half hour, when we were far enough away, she could gather the domestics and go mix in with the field slaves. I tied Maurice to his father's back, handed two packets of provisions to Gambo, and strapped on Rosette. The master thought it was madness to leave on foot—we could take horses from the stable—but according to Gambo that would attract the vigilantes, and the route we were going to follow was not for horses. We crossed the patio in the shadows of buildings, stayed away from the coconut palm avenue, where there was a guard, and started toward the cane fields. The hideous long-tailed rats that infest the fields scurried ahead of us. The master hesitated; Gambo put his knife to his throat but did not kill him because I held his arm. We needed him to protect the children. This I reminded him.

We plunged into the spine-chilling hiss of the cane blown by the wind, with its whistling and knife-clickings, demons hidden in the tall stalks, snakes, scorpions, a labyrinth in which sounds are distorted and distances curl and twist and a person can get lost forever and even if he yells and yells never be found. For that reason the fields are divided into carrés, *or blocks, and are always cut from the edges toward the center. One of Cambray's punishments consisted of leaving a slave in the fields at night and at dawn loosing the dogs after him. I do not know how Gambo led us through, maybe by instinct or perhaps from experience stealing at other plantations. We walked in a line, close together so as not to get lost, protecting ourselves as we could from the knife-edged leaves, until finally, after quite some time, we left the plantation and entered the jungle. We walked for hours, but made little progress. At dawn we could clearly see the orange sky of the fire at Saint-Lazare and were choked by the biting, sweetish smoke carried on the wind. The sleeping children weighed like stones on our backs. Erzulie, mother loa, come to our aid.*

I have always gone about with bare feet, but I was not accustomed to that terrain, and my feet were bleeding. I was falling with fatigue; in contrast my master, twenty years older than I, walked without stopping, with Maurice's weight on his back. Finally Gambo, the youngest and strongest of our three, said we must rest. He helped us untie the children and we laid them on a pile of leaves after poking it with a stick to frighten off snakes. Gambo wanted the master's pistols, but Valmorain convinced him that they were more useful in his hands since Gambo knew nothing about such weapons. They made a pact that Gambo would carry one and the master two. We were near the swamps, and light barely shone through the leaves. The air was like hot water. The mud could swallow a man in two minutes, but Gambo did not seem disturbed. He found a pool; we drank, wet our clothing and that of the children, who were still sleeping hard; we shared some bread from the provisions, and rested a bit.

Soon Gambo started us out again, and the master, who had never taken orders in his life, obeyed without a word. The swamps were not a quagmire as I had imagined, but dirty, stagnant water and foul-smelling vapors. The ground was mud. I thought about Doña Eugenia, who would rather have fallen into the rebels' hands than pass through that dense fog of mosquitoes; fortunately, she was already in the Christians' heaven. Gambo knew the trail, but it wasn't easy to follow him carrying the weight of the children. Erzulie, loa of water, come to our aid. Gambo undid the tignon around my head, wrapped my feet in leaves, and bound them with the cloth. The master was wearing tall boots, and Gambo believed that the fangs of jungle creatures would not penetrate the soles of his feet. We went on.

Maurice was the first to wake, when we were still in the swamp, and he was frightened. When Rosette woke up, I put her to my breast awhile, still walking on, and she went back to sleep. We walked the entire day and reached Bois Cayman, where there was no danger of sinking into mud, but where we could be attacked. There Gambo had seen the beginning of the rebellion, when my godmother, mounted by Ogoun, sometimes called Ogu-Fer, called for war and named the chiefs. This Gambo told me. Since that time Tante Rose had gone from camp to camp healing people, celebrating services for the loas, and seeing into the future; she was feared and respected by all, fulfilling the destiny marked in her z'étoile. She had counseled Gambo to find a place under Toussaint's wing because he would be king when the war ended. Gambo had asked her if then we would be free, and she assured him we would, but first all the whites would have to be killed, including newborn babies, and there would be so much blood on the earth that ears of corn would grow red.

I gave more drops to the children and made them comfortable among the roots of a large tree. Gambo feared the packs of wild dogs more than humans or spirits, but we did not dare light a fire to keep them at a distance. We left the master with the children and the three loaded pistols, sure that he would not leave Maurice's side, while Gambo and I went a little way away to do what we wanted to do. Hatred deformed the master's face when I got up to follow Gambo, but he said nothing. I was afraid of what would happen to me later because I know the cruelty of whites at the hour of revenge, and that hour would come to me sooner or later. I was exhausted and sore from carrying Rosette, but the only thing I wanted was to put my arms around Gambo. At that moment nothing else mattered. Erzulie, loa of pleasure, allow this night to go on forever. This is how I remember it.

Fugitives

The rebels fell upon Saint-Lazare at that imprecise hour when night begins to recede, moments before the work bell rang to wake the workers. At first the attack was a resplendent comet's tail, points of light moving rapidly: the torches. The cane fields hid the human figures, but when they began to emerge from the thick vegetation it could be seen that they were hundreds. One of the guards was able to get to the bell, but twenty hands brandishing knives reduced him to an unrecognizable pulp. The dry cane burned first, then its heat set fire to the rest, and in less than twenty minutes the conflagration covered all the fields and advanced toward the big house. The flames leaped in all directions, so high and so powerful that the firebreak of the patios could not stop them. To the clamor of the fire was added the deafening shouting of the attackers and the lugubrious howls of the conch shells blowing to announce war. The men ran naked, or barely covered by shreds of clothing, armed with machetes, chains, knives, poles, bayonets, and muskets with no balls, which were held like cudgels. Many were smeared with soot, others were in a trance or drunk, but within the disorder was a single goal: destroy. The field slaves, intermingled with the domestics, who had been warned in time by the cook, abandoned their cabins and participated in that saturnalia of revenge and devastation. At first some hesitated, fearing the uncontainable violence of the rebels and the inevitable retaliation of the master, but they no longer had a choice. If they took one step back they would perish.

The commandeurs fell one by one into the hands of the horde, but Prosper Cambray and another two men ran to the storerooms of the big house with weapons and ammunition to defend themselves for several hours. They were confident that the fire would attract the *maréchaussée* or the soldiers patrolling the region. The Negroes' attack had the fury and speed of a typhoon; it would last a couple of hours and then they would disperse. The overseer found it strange that the house was not occupied; he thought that Valmorain had in anticipation prepared an underground refuge and was crouching down there with his son, Tété, and the little girl. Cambray left his men and went to the office, which was always kept locked, but found it open. He did not know the combination to the safe and was ready to blow it apart—no one would know later who stole the gold—but it was open as well. Then came the first suspicion that Valmorain had fled without telling him. Damned coward! he exclaimed, furious. To save his miserable skin he had abandoned the plantation. With no time to bemoan that, he joined the others just as the uproar of the attack was upon them.

Cambray heard the whinnying of horses and barking of dogs, and could distinguish those of his murderous mastiffs; they were hoarser and fiercer. He knew that before his valiant dogs perished they would do away with several victims. The house was surrounded; the attackers had invaded the patios and were running over the garden; not one of Valmorain's precious orchids was left. The overseer heard them in the gallery, breaking down doors, climbing through windows, and demolishing anything they found before them, gutting the French furniture, ripping down Dutch tapestries, emptying Spanish chests, splintering Chinese screens, shattering porcelain, German clocks, golden cages, Roman statuary, and Venetian mirrors—everything that had been acquired by Violette Boisier. And when they tired of ransacking the house they began to look for the family. Cambray and the two commandeurs had stacked sacks, barrels, and furniture against the door of the storage rooms, and they began shooting between the iron bars that protected the small windows. Only wood boards separated them from the rebels, audacious with freedom and indifferent to bullets. In the early dawn light they saw several of them fall so close by they could smell them despite the fetid smoke of the burned cane. Others fell, and more came, stepping over bodies, before Cambray and his men could reload. They heard the blows against the door, the thudding, the wood shaken by a hurricane of hatred that had been accumulating strength across the Caribbean for a hundred years. Ten minutes later the big house was burning like an enormous bonfire. The rebellious slaves waited on the patio, and when the commandeurs ran out from the flames they caught them alive. They were not, however, able to inflict the torture Prosper Cambray deserved, because he chose to stick the barrel of his pistol into his mouth and blow his head off.

During that same time Gambo and his small group were climbing, clinging to rocks, tree trunks, roots, and vines; they crossed precipices and waded through water up to their waists. Gambo had not exaggerated; it was a route not for horsemen but for monkeys. In that profound greenery there were sudden brushstrokes of color: the yellow and orange beak of a toucan, the iridescent feathers of parrots and macaws, tropical flowers dripping from the branches. There was water everywhere, rivulets, pools, rain, crystalline cascades crossed with rainbows falling from the sky and disappearing into dense masses of gleaming ferns below. Tété wet a kerchief and tied it around her head to bandage the eye turned purple by Valmorain's slap. To prevent a confrontation between the two men, she told Gambo that an insect had bitten her eyelid. Valmorain took off his water-soaked boots because his feet were nothing but raw flesh, and Gambo laughed when he saw them, not understanding how the white man could walk through life on those soft, rosy feet that looked like skinned rabbits. After a few steps Valmorain had to put the boots back on. He could not carry Maurice any longer. The child walked some stretches holding his father's hand, and others on Gambo's shoulders, holding onto the hard clump of his hair.

Several times they had to hide from rebels wandering in the area. Once Gambo left the others in a cave and went alone to meet a small group he knew from having been with them in Boukman's camp. One of the men was wearing a necklace of human ears, some dry as leather, others fresh and pink. They shared their provisions with him, cooked sweet potatoes and a few strips of smoked goat meat, and rested a while, commenting on the vicissitudes of the war and rumors about a new chief, Toussaint. They said that he did not seem human; astute and solitary, he had the heart of a jungle dog. He was indifferent to the temptations of alcohol, women, and medals other chiefs strove for; he didn't sleep, he ate only fruit, and he could spend two days and nights on horseback. He never raised his voice, but people trembled in his presence. He was a *docteur-feuilles*, a leaf doctor, and seer; he knew how to decipher nature's messages, the signs in the stars, and men's most secret intentions; that was how he avoided betrayal and ambushes. At dusk, just as it began to grow cool, the men said good-bye. It took Gambo a while to find his way back because he had gone some distance from the cave, but finally he rejoined the others, who were weak from thirst and heat but had not dared step outside or look for water. Gambo led them to a nearby pool where they could drink their fill but had to ration the sparse provisions.

Valmorain's feet were open sores in his boots; the shooting pain ran up his legs, and he wept with frustration; he was tempted to lie down and die but kept going for Maurice's sake. At dusk of the second day they saw a pair of naked men armed with machetes; they wore no adornment other than a strip of leather around the waist to hold a knife. The party was able to hide among some ferns where they waited for more than an hour, until the men were lost in the luxuriant growth. Gambo went to a palm tree whose crest rose several meters above the vegetation; he climbed the slim trunk, grasping the ridges in the bark, and pulled off a few coconuts that fell noiselessly among the ferns. The children drank the milk and shared the delicate pulp. He told them that he had seen the plain; Le Cap was nearby. They spent the night beneath the trees and saved the rest of their few provisions for the next day. Maurice and Rosette slept curled together, watched by Valmorain, who had aged a thousand years. He felt as if he were bits and pieces—he had lost his honor, his manhood, his soul, and had been reduced to a mere animal, flesh and suffering, a bloody hunk of meat following, like a dog, an accursed black man who was fornicating with his slave a few steps away. He could hear them that night, as on previous nights; they were not discreet out of decency or out of fear of him. He clearly heard their moans of pleasure, their sighs of desire, the invented words, the suffocated laughter. Again and again, they copulated like beasts; such desire and energy were not normal for human beings. The master wept with humiliation. He imagined Tété's familiar body, her walker's legs, her firm rump, her narrow waist, her generous breasts, her smooth skin, soft, sweet, wet with sweat, with desire, with sin, with insolence and provocation. He seemed to see her face at those moments, the half-closed eyes, the soft lips giving and receiving, the daring tongue, the dilated nostrils sniffing the scent of that man. And despite all that, despite the torment of his feet, of his immeasurable fatigue, his trampled pride and fear of dying, Valmorain grew hard.

"Tomorrow we will leave the white man and his son on the plains. From there all he has to do is walk straight ahead," Gambo announced to Tété between kisses in the darkness.

"And what if the rebels run into them before they reach Le Cap?"

"I have done my part, I got them away from the plantation alive. Now let them manage alone. We will be going to Toussaint's camp. His *z'étoile* is the most brilliant in the sky."

"And Rosette?"

"She comes with us, if you want."

"I can't do it, Gambo, I have to go with the white man. Forgive me," she whispered, doubled over with sorrow.

The youth pushed her away, incredulous. She had to repeat it twice for him to comprehend the firmness of that decision, the only possible one, because among the rebels Rosette would be a miserable, light-skinned quadroon, rejected, hungry, exposed to the hazards of the revolution, whereas with Valmorain she would be safer. She explained to Gambo that she could not leave the children but he did not listen to her arguments; all he heard was that Zarité preferred the white man.

"And freedom. Doesn't that matter to you?" He grabbed her shoulders and shook her.

"I am free, Gambo. I have the paper in this little bag, written and sealed. Rosette and I are free. I will keep serving the master for a time, until the war ends, and then I will go with you wherever you want."

They separated on the plain. Gambo took charge of all the pistols, turned his back on them, and disappeared, running toward thick growth, without saying good-bye and without turning to take a last look at them, to prevent succumbing to the powerful temptation to kill Valmorain and his son. He would have done that without hesitation, but he knew that if he harmed Maurice he lost Tété forever.

Valmorain, the woman, and the children reached the road, a strip wide enough for three horses, very exposed should they meet rebel blacks or mulattoes incensed against the whites. Valmorain could not take another step on his raw feet; he dragged along, moaning, followed by Maurice, who was crying with him. Tété found shade beneath some shrubs, gave the last mouthful of the provisions to Maurice, and explained that she would be back to get him but it might be a long time and he must have courage. She kissed him, put him beside his father, and started along the road with Rosette on her back. From then on it was all a matter of luck.

The sun fell like lead on her uncovered head. The terrain, of a depressing monotony, was dotted with stone outcroppings and low shrubs bent by the force of the wind and covered by a heavy, dry grass, short and tough. The soil was arid and grainy. There was no water anywhere. That road, well traveled in normal times, had since the rebellion been used only by the army and the *maréchaussée*. Tété had a vague idea of the distance, but she could not calculate how many hours she would have to walk to reach the fort near Le Cap; she had always made the trip in Valmorain's coach. *Erzulie*, loa *of hope, do not forsake me.* She walked with determination, not thinking about how far she had to go but how far she had come. The landscape was desolate, there were no landmarks, everything was the same, she was nailed in the same spot, as in a nightmare. Rosette was clamoring for water, her lips dry and her eyes glassy. She gave her more drops from the blue vial and rocked her until she fell asleep and they could go on.

She walked three or four hours without pause, her mind a blank. *Water, I can't go on without water.* One step, another step, another. *Erzulie, loa of fresh and salt water, do not kill us with thirst.* Her legs were moving on their own, she heard drums: the call of the *boula*, the counterpoint of the *seconde*, the deep sigh of the *maman* breaking the rhythm, the other drums beginning again, variations, subtleties, leaps, suddenly the happy sound of the maracas and again invisible hands beating the taut skin of the drums. The sound filled her inside, and she began to move with the music. Another hour. She was floating in an incandescent space. Always more unconnected, she no longer felt the battering on her bones or the rattling of stones in her head. One step more, one hour more. *Erzulie, loa of compassion, come to my aid.* Suddenly, as her knees were doubling, a flashing current shook her from her cranium to her feet; fire, ice, wind, silence. And then came the goddess Erzulie like a powerful burst of wind and mounted Zarité, her servant.

Etienne Relais was the first to see her because he was at the head of his squad of cavalry. A dark, slim line on the road, an illusion, a trembling silhouette in the reverberations of that implacable light. He spurred his horse and rode ahead to see who was making such a dangerous journey in these solitudes and in this heat. As he approached he saw a woman with her back to him, erect, proud, her arms held out to fly and swaying like a serpent to the rhythm of a secret, glorious dance. He noticed the bundle on her back and deduced it was a child, perhaps dead. He shouted at her, and she did not respond; she kept floating like a mirage until he cut his horse in front of her. When he saw her rolled back eyes, he realized that she was demented or in a trance. He had seen that exalted expression in the *kalendas*, but had believed that it happened only in the collective hysteria of the drums. As a pragmatic French military man, an atheist, Relais was repelled by such possessions, which he considered a further proof of the Africans' primitive condition. Erzulie rose up before the horseman, seductive, beautiful, her serpent tongue between red lips, her body a single flame. The officer raised his crop, touched her on the shoulder, and immediately the enchantment was broken. Erzulie evaporated, and Tété collapsed without a sigh, a pile of rags in the dust of the road. The other soldiers had caught up to their leader, and their horses surrounded the prostrate woman. Etienne Relais jumped down, bent over her, and began to tug at her improvised carrier until he freed the contents: a sleeping or unconscious little girl. He turned the woman over and saw a mulatta very different from the one dancing along the road, a pitiful young woman covered with filth and sweat, her face contorted, one eye purple, her lips parted with thirst, her feet bleeding through rags. One of the soldiers also dismounted and bent down to pour a stream of water from his canteen into the child's mouth and then another into the woman's. Tété opened her eyes and for several minutes did not remember anything, not the forced march, not her daughter, not the drums, not Erzulie. They helped her sit up and gave her more water, until she had enough and the visions in her head took on some sense. "R-Rosette . . . ," she stammered. "She's alive, but she doesn't respond, and we can't wake her," Relais told her. Then the fear of the last days rushed to the slave's memory: laudanum, the plantation in flames, Gambo, her master, and Maurice waiting for her.

Valmorain saw the dust on the road and shrank behind some shrubs, confused by the visceral fear that had begun as he stood before the skinned corpse of his neighbor Lacroix and grown worse up to that moment, when he had lost his sense of time and space and distances; he did not know why he was buried like a hare among a tangle of plants, nor who that runny-nosed little boy who lay in a faint beside him was. The squad stopped close by, and one of the riders shouted Valmorain's name; then he dared take a look, and he saw the uniforms. A howl of relief burst from his gut. He came crawling out, disheveled, ragged, covered with scratches, scabs, and dry mud, sobbing like a baby, and stayed on his knees before the horses, repeating, "Thank you, thank you, thank you." Blinded by the light and dehydrated as he was, he did not recognize Relais, nor was he aware that all the men in the squad were mulattoes; all he needed to see were the uniforms of the French army to know he was safe. He took off the bag tied at his waist and threw a handful of coins before the soldiers. The gold glittered on the ground. "Thank you, thank you." Revolted by that spectacle, Etienne Relais ordered him to pick up his money; he gestured to his subalterns, and one of them dismounted to give Valmorain water and offer him his horse. Tété, who was riding on the croup of a different mount, got down with difficulty because she was not accustomed to riding and had Rosette on her back, and went to look for Maurice. She found him rolled into a ball among the shrubs, delirious with thirst.

They were close to Le Cap and several hours later rode into the city without suffering new mishaps. During that time Rosette had awakened from the stupor of the laudanum, Maurice was sleeping exhausted in the arms of a soldier, and Toulouse Valmorain had recovered his composure. The images of those three days began to fade and the story to change in his mind. When he had a chance to explain what had happened, his version did not resemble what Relais had heard from Tété: Gambo had disappeared from the scene, it was Valmorain who had foreseen the rebels' attack and, given the impossibility of defending his plantation, fled to protect his son, bringing along the slave who had raised Maurice and her little girl. It was he, only he, who had saved them all. Relais made no comment.

The Paris of the Antilles

Le Cap was filled with refugees who had abandoned their plantations. The smoke from the fires, carried by the wind, floated in the air for weeks. The Paris of the Antilles reeked of garbage and excrement, the corpses of the executed rotting on the gallows, and the mass graves of victims of epidemics and the war. The distribution of supplies was very irregular, and the population depended on ships and fishing boats for food, but the *grands blancs* continued to live in their former luxury, though now it cost them more. Nothing was lacking at their tables, rationing was for others. Parties continued with armed guards at the gates, the theaters didn't close, or bars, and dazzling cocottes still enlivened the night. There was not a single place left in which to take lodging, but Valmorain was counting on the house he'd bought from the Portuguese man before the uprising, and there he installed himself to recover from his fright and tend his physical and moral wounds. Six hired slaves served him, directed by Tété; it did not suit him to buy them just when he planned to change his life. He acquired only a cook trained in France, whom he could later sell without losing money, the price of a good cook was one of the few things that had remained stable. He was sure that he would recover his property; it was not the first insurgency of slaves in the Antilles and they had all been crushed. France was not going to allow black bandits to ruin the colony. At any rate, even if the situation was restored to what it had been in the past, he would leave Saint-Lazare, he had already decided that. He knew about the death of Prosper Cambray because the militia had found his body amid the rubble of the plantation. I could not have rid myself of him any other way, he thought. His property was pure ash but the land was there, no one could take that away. He would get a manager, someone who had experience and was habituated to the climate; it was not a time for managers brought from France, as he explained to his friend Parmentier, who was treating Valmorain's feet with healing herbs he had seen Tante Rose use.

"Will you return to Paris, *mon ami?*" the doctor asked.

"I don't think so. My interests lie in the Caribbean, not in France. I am associated with Sancho García del Solar, the brother of Eugenia, may she rest in peace, and we have acquired some lands in Louisiana. And you, what are your plans, Doctor?"

"If the situation does not improve here, I plan to go to Cuba."

"Do you have family there?"

"Yes," the doctor admitted, blushing.

"Peace in the colony depends on the French government. Those republicans bear all the guilt for what has happened here. The king would never have allowed things to reach these extremes."

"I believe that the French Revolution is irreversible," the doctor replied.

"The republic has no idea how to run this colony, Doctor. The commission called back half of the Régiment Le Cap and replaced it with mulattoes. That is a provocation—no white soldier will agree to follow orders from an officer of color."

"Perhaps it is the moment for whites and *affranchis* to learn to live together, since the common enemy are the Negroes."

"I wonder what those savages are after," said Valmorain.

"Freedom, *mon ami,*" Parmentier replied. "One of the chiefs, Toussaint, I think he's called, maintains that the plantations can function with free laborers."

"Even if paid, the blacks would not work!" Valmorain exclaimed.

"That no one can be sure of, for it has not been tested. Toussaint says that Africans are peasants, they know the earth, growing things is what they know and want to do," Parmentier insisted.

"What they know and want to do is kill and destroy, Doctor! Besides, that Toussaint has gone over to the Spanish side."

"He takes refuge under the Spanish flag because the French colonists refused to deal with the rebels," the doctor reminded him.

"I was there, Doctor. I tried in vain to convince the other planters to accept the terms of peace proposed by the blacks; all they asked was freedom for the chiefs and their secondary officers, some two hundred in all," Valmorain told him.

"Then blame for the war rests not on the incompetence of the government in France but on the pride of the colonists in Saint-Domingue," Parmentier argued.

"I concede that we must be more reasonable, but we cannot negotiate on equal terms with the slaves—that would be a bad precedent."

"You would have to make a deal with Toussaint, who seems to be the most reasonable of the rebel leaders."

Tété paid attention when the subject was Toussaint. She guarded in the depths of her soul her love for Gambo, resigned to the idea she would not see him for a long time, perhaps never, but he was embedded in her heart, and she supposed he could be among the ranks of that Toussaint. She heard Valmorain say that no revolt of slaves in history had triumphed, but she dared dream the opposite, and wonder what life would be like without slavery. She organized the house as she had always done, but Valmorain explained that things could not be as they were in Saint-Lazare, where all that mattered was comfort and it was irrelevant whether meals were served with gloves or without them. In Le Cap he had to live in style. However much the revolt blazed at the gates of the city, he must return the attentions of the families who often invited him and had taken on the mission of finding him a wife.

The master made some inquiries and found a mentor for Tété: the majordomo at the Intendance. It was the same African Adonis who had served in the mansion when Valmorain brought the ill Eugenia to ask for hospitality in 1780, except that he was even more attractive, having matured with extraordinary grace. His name was Zacharie, and he had been born and raised among those walls. His parents had been slaves to previous Intendants, who sold them to his successor when they returned to France; that is how they became part of the inventory. Zacharie's father, as handsome as he, trained him from an early age for the prestigious position of majordomo, seeing that his son had the essential virtues for that post: intelligence, cleverness, dignity, and prudence. Zacharie was careful not to be seduced by white women; he knew the risks, and thus had avoided many problems. Valmorain offered to pay the Intendant for the services of his majordomo, but he did not want to hear anything on the subject. "Give him a tip, that will be enough. Zacharie is saving to buy his freedom, though I don't understand why he wants it. His present situation could not be more advantageous." They agreed that Tété would go every day to the Intendance to be refined.

Zacharie received her coolly, establishing a certain distance from the beginning; after all, he held the most prestigious post among all domestics in Saint-Domingue, and she was a slave with no standing. But soon his eagerness to impart information betrayed him, and he ended by imparting to her the secrets of the office with a generosity that greatly surpassed Valmorain's tip. He was surprised that this young woman did not seem to be impressed by him, he was accustomed to female admiration. He usually had to be very tactful in evading compliments and rejecting women's advances, but with Tété he could relax into a relationship without secondary intentions. They addressed each other formally, Monsieur Zacharie and Mademoiselle Zarité.

Tété got up at dawn, organized the slaves, prepared instructions for the food, washing, and any sewing, left the children under the care of a temporary nursemaid the master had hired, and set out in her best blouse and starched *tignon* to her classes. She never learned how many servants there were in the Intendance; in the kitchen alone there were three cooks and seven assistants, but she figured there were no fewer than fifty. Zacharie supervised the budget and served as liaison between masters and their service; his was the highest authority in that complicated organization. No slave would dare speak to him unless called upon, and for that very reason they resented the visits of Tété, who after a few days ignored the rules and entered the sacred temple, the majordomo's tiny office, directly. Without realizing it, Zacharie began to look forward to seeing her. He liked teaching her. She always showed up at the exact time; they had coffee, and then he imparted knowledge. They would circulate through the various areas of the mansion to observe the service. His student learned quickly, and soon mastered the eight indispensable goblets at a banquet, the difference between the fork for snails and the similar one for lobster, at which side the finger bowl was placed, and the order of precedence among various kinds of cheeses, as well as the most discreet way to dispose of chamber pots during a party, what to do with an intoxicated lady, and the hierarchy of guests at the table. When the lesson ended, Zacharie would invite her to have another coffee and take advantage of the moment to speak to her of politics, a subject he was impassioned about. At the beginning she listened out of courtesy, wondering how quarrels among free people could matter to a slave, until he mentioned the possibility that slavery could be abolished. "Imagine, Mademoiselle Zarité, I have been saving for my freedom for years and it may be given to me before I am able to buy it." Zacharie laughed. He knew everything that was said in the Intendance, even the matters behind closed doors. He knew that in the Assemblée Nationale in Paris the unjustifiable incongruity of maintaining slavery in the colonies after it had been abolished in France was being discussed. "Do you know anything about Toussaint, monsieur?" Tété asked. The majordomo recited his biography, which he had read in a confidential document from the Intendant, and added that Commissioner Sonthonax and the Gouverneur would have to reach an agreement with him, because he commanded a very well organized army and could count on the aid of the Spaniards from the other side of the island.

Nights of Misfortune

Thanks to Zacharie's classes, at the end of a couple of months Valmorain's dwelling was functioning with a refinement he had not enjoyed since his youthful years in Paris. He decided to give a party using the expensive, but prestigious, services of the *grand hôtelier* Monsieur Adrien, a free mulatto Zacharie had recommended. Two days before the party Monsieur Adrien invaded the house with a team of his slaves; he banished the cook and replaced him with five fat, bossy women who prepared a menu of fifteen courses inspired by a banquet at the Intendance. Although the house did not lend itself to social festivities, it looked elegant once the horrid adornments of the Portuguese owner had been removed and it was decorated with potted dwarf palms, Chinese lanterns, and flowers everywhere. On the chosen night the innkeeper arrived with dozens of blue-and-gold-liveried servants who took their places with the discipline of a battalion. The distance between the homes of the *grands blancs* was rarely more than a block or two, but the guests came in coaches, and when the parade of carriages had ended the street was a quagmire of manure, which lackeys cleared away to prevent the stench from impinging upon the ladies' perfumes.

"How do I look?" Valmorain asked Tété. He was wearing a gold-and-silver-embroidered brocade waistcoat, enough lace at the cuff and neck for a tablecloth, pink stockings, and dancing slippers. She did not reply, astounded by the lavender wig. "Those boorish Jacobins intend to do away with wigs, but it is the indispensable touch of elegance for a reception like this. That is what my wig maker says," Valmorain informed her.

Monsieur Adrien had offered the second round of champagne and the orchestra had attacked another minuet when one of the secretaries of the government came running with the incredible news that Louis XVI and Marie Antoinette had been guillotined in France. The royal heads were exhibited in the streets of Paris, just as Boukman's and many others had been in Le Cap. The events, which occurred in January, were learned in Saint-Domingue in March. The news produced a stampede of panic; the guests rushed home, and so ended, before the food was served, Toulouse Valmorain's first and only entertainment in that house.

The same night, after Monsieur Adrien, a fanatic monarchist, retired sobbing with his crew, Tété picked up the lavender wig Valmorain had kicked across the floor, checked to see Maurice was calm, bolted the doors and windows, and went to rest in the small room she occupied with Rosette. Valmorain had ordered that his son be moved from Tété's room; it was his intention that Maurice should sleep alone, but he had become a tangle of nerves, and fearing he would come down with a fever, his father had installed him on a temporary cot in his own chamber. Ever since they had arrived in Le Cap, Valmorain had not mentioned Gambo, and neither had he summoned Tété at night. The shadow of the lover stood between them. It took weeks to heal his feet, and as soon as he could walk he went out every night to forget the bad times. From the cloying floral fragrances that drenched his clothing, Tété assumed he was visiting cocottes, and supposed that at last her master's humiliating embraces had ended. For that reason she was distressed to find him sitting at the foot of her bed clad in bedroom slippers and green velvet dressing gown, while Rosette snored spraddle-legged with the impudence of the innocent. "Come with me!" he ordered, pulling her by the arm in the direction of one of the guest rooms, where he whipped her around, tore off her clothing, and hurriedly raped her in the darkness, clawing at her with an urgency closer to hatred than desire.

The memory of Tété fornicating with Gambo infuriated Valmorain, but it also provoked irresistible visions. That foul man had put his filthy hands on what was *his* property. When he caught him, he would kill him. The woman also deserved a punishment that would be a lesson, but two months had passed and he had not made her pay for her incredible brazenness. Bitch. Hot bitch. He could not demand morality and decency from a slave, but it was his duty to impose his will on her. Why had he not done it? He had no excuse. She had defied him, and he had to rectify that aberration. However, he was also indebted to her. His slave had turned her back on freedom to save him and Maurice. For the first time he wondered what that mulatta felt for him. He could relive every moment of those humbling nights in the jungle when she was rolling about with her lover, the embraces, the kisses, the renewed ardor, even the odor of their bodies when they returned. Tété transformed into a demon, pure desire, licking and sweating and moaning. As he raped her in the guest room he could not tear that scene from his mind. He assaulted her again, penetrating her with fury, surprised by his own energy. She groaned, and he began to hit her with his fist, with the anger of jealousy and pleasure of revenge: "Yellow bitch! I am going to sell you, whore! whore! and I will sell your daughter, too." Tété closed her eyes and gave up, her body loose, not offering resistance or trying to avoid the blows, as her soul flew to a different place. *Erzulie*, loa *of desire, make him finish quickly*. Valmorain collapsed atop her for the second time, wet with sweat. Tété lay long minutes without moving. The breathing of both was growing calm, and she tried to slip off the bed, but he grabbed her.

"You're not leaving yet," he ordered.

"Do you want me to light a candle, monsieur?" she asked in a weak voice; her breath was burning between her bruised ribs.

"No, I prefer it like this."

It was the first time she had addressed him as *monsieur* instead of *maître*. Valmorain noticed, but let it pass. Tété sat up in the bed, wiping the blood from her mouth and nose with the blouse ripped in his attack.

"Beginning tomorrow, you will take Maurice out of my room," said Valmorain. "He must sleep alone. You have pampered him too much."

"He is only five years old."

"At that age I had learned to read; I went hunting on my own horse, and took fencing lessons."

They remained in the same postures a bit longer, and finally she resolved to ask the question she'd had on her lips since they arrived in Le Cap.

"When will I be free, monsieur?" she asked, shrinking back in expectation of further beating, but he got up without touching her.

"You can't be free. How would you live? I support and protect you; with me, you and your daughter are safe. I have always treated you very well. What are you complaining about?

"I'm not complaining—"

"The situation is very dangerous. Have you forgotten the horrors we've been through? The atrocities that have been committed? Answer me!"

"No, monsieur."

"Freedom, you say. So do you want to abandon Maurice?"

"If you wish, I can look after Maurice as I always have, at least until you marry again."

"Marry?" He laughed. "I learned my lesson with Eugenia. That would be the last thing I would ever do. If you are going to continue in my service, why do you want to be freed?"

"We all want to be free."

"Women are never free, Tété. They need a man to look after them. When they are unmarried they belong to their father, and when married, to the husband."

"The paper you gave me ... that is my freedom, isn't it?" she insisted.

"Of course."

"But Zacharie says it must be signed by a judge to be lawful."

"Who is Zacharie?"

"The majordomo at the Intendance."

"He's right. But this is not a good time. We will wait until calm is restored to Saint-Domingue, and we will not discuss this again. I'm tired. You may go now: tomorrow I want to sleep alone and have everything go back to how it was. Do you understand me?"

The new Gouverneur of the island, Général Galbaud, arrived with a mission to resolve the disaster in the colony. He had full military powers, but the authority of the République was represented by Sonthonax and the other two commissioners. It fell to Etienne Relais to give him his first briefing. Production on the island had fallen to nothing, the north was a cloud of smoke, in the south there was no end to the slaughters, and the city of Port-au-Prince had been burned to the ground. There was no transport, no working ports, no security for anyone. The rebel blacks were receiving support from Spain, and the British fleet controlled the Caribbean and would soon take over the costal cities. The French were blockaded; it was nearly impossible to get troops or supplies from France to defend themselves. "Don't worry, Major, we will find a diplomatic solution," was Galbaud's reaction. He was having secret conversations with Toulouse Valmorain and the Patriots, zealous partisans for making the colony independent and placing it under the protection of England. The Gouverneur agreed with the conspirators that the républicains in Paris did not understand anything that was happening on the island and were committing one irreparable stupidity after another. Among the most serious had been the dissolution of the Assemblée Coloniale; Saint-Domingue had lost all autonomy, and now every decision took weeks to arrive from France. Galbaud owned land on the island and was married to a Creole whom he still loved after several years of marriage;

he could understand better than anyone the tensions among races and social classes.

The Patriots found an ideal ally in the general, who was more preoccupied with the struggle between whites and *affranchis* than he was with the Negroes' uprisings. Many *grands blancs* had businesses in the Caribbean and the United States; they did not need the mother country for anything and considered independence their best option, unless things changed and a strong monarchy was restored in France. The execution of the king had been a tragedy, but it was also a stupendous opportunity to get less of a fool as monarch. As for the *affranchis*, by contrast, independence would not bring them anything, since only the republican government in France was willing to accept them as citizens, something that would never happen if Saint-Domingue was placed under the protection of England, the United States, or Spain. Général Galbaud believed that as soon as the problem between whites and mulattoes was resolved, it would be reasonably simple to crush the Negroes, put them in chains again, and impose order, but he said none of this to Etienne Relais.

"Tell me about this Commissaire Sonthonax, Major," he said.

"He carries out the government's orders, Général. The decree of April 4 accorded political rights to free people of color. The Commissaire arrived here with six thousand soldiers to implement that decree."

"Yes, yes . . . I knew that. Tell me, confidentially, of course, what kind of man is this Sonthonax?"

"I scarcely know him, Général, but they say he is very clever and takes with great seriousness the interests of Saint-Domingue."

"Sonthonax has stated that it is not his intention to emancipate the slaves, but I have heard rumors that he might do that," said Galbaud, studying the officer's impassive face. "It is understood that that would be the end of civilization on the island, no? Imagine the chaos: blacks unrestrained, whites driven out, mulattoes doing whatever it is they want to do, and the land abandoned."

"I know nothing about that, Général."

"What would you do in that case?"

"Carry out my orders, as always, Général."

Galbaud needed army officers he could trust to confront the power of France, but he could not count on Etienne Relais. He had found out that he was married to a mulatta, probably sympathized with the cause of the *affranchis*, and apparently admired Sonthonax. He seemed to be a man of no great intelligence, with the mentality of a functionary and without ambition; he would have to be totally lacking in those areas to have married a woman of color. It was notable that despite that he had ascended in his career. But Relais interested Galbaud because he had the loyalty of his soldiers: he was the only officer capable of combining whites, mulattoes, and even Negroes in the ranks without problem. He wondered how much the man was worth—everyone has a price.

That same evening Toulouse Valmorain went to the barracks to speak with Relais as friend to friend, as he put it. He began by thanking him for having saved his life when he had to flee the plantation.

"I am in your debt, Major," he said in a tone that sounded more arrogant than appreciative.

"You are not in my debt, monsieur, but your slave's. I was only passing by; it was she who saved you," Relais replied, uncomfortable.

"You sin from modesty. And tell me, how is your family?"

Relais immediately suspected that Valmorain had come to bribe him, and had mentioned family to remind him that he had given them Jean-Martin. They were even: Valmorain's life for the adopted son. He grew tense, as he did before a battle; he glared at Valmorain with the coldness that made his subalterns tremble, and stood waiting to see exactly what his visitor had in mind. Valmorain ignored the knife-edged stare and the silence.

"No *affranchi* is safe in this city," he said affably. "Your wife is in danger; that is why I have come to offer you my aid. And as for the boy—what is his name?"

"Jean-Martin Relais," the officer answered with clenched jaw.

"Of course, Jean-Martin. Forgive me, with all the problems in my head I had forgotten. I have a rather large house facing the port, in a good quarter where there are no disturbances. I can welcome your lady and your son."

Relais interrupted. "You need not worry about them, monsieur. They are safe in Cuba."

Valmorain was disconcerted; he had lost a trump card in his game, but he quickly recovered.

"Ah! That is where my brother-in-law lives, Don Sancho García del Solar. I shall write him today to look after your family."

"That will not be necessary, monsieur. Thank you."

"Of course it is, Major. A woman alone always needs the protection of a gentleman, especially one as beautiful as yours."

Pale with indignation at the veiled insult, Etienne Relais stood to bring an end to the interview, but Valmorain remained seated, legs crossed, as if the office belonged to him, and proceeded to explain, in courteous but direct terms, that the *grands blancs* were going to take back control of the colony, mobilizing all the resources available, and he, Relais, had to make a decision and do his part. No one, especially a military man of high rank, could remain indifferent or neutral before the terrible happenings that had already been unleashed, as well as those to come that without doubt would be worse. It was up to the army to prevent a civil war. The English had landed in the south, and it would be a matter of days before Saint-Domingue declared its independence and sought refuge beneath the British flag. That could happen in a civilized way or by blood and fire, it would depend on the army. An officer who backed the noble cause of independence would have a lot of power; he would be the right arm of Gouverneur Galbaud, and that post naturally carried with it social and economic position. No one would do any harm to a man married to a woman of color if that man were, for example, the new commander in chief of the island's armed forces.

"In a few words, monsieur, you are inciting me to treason," Relais replied, unable to contain an ironic smile, which Valmorain interpreted as an open door to continue the dialogue.

"It is not a matter of betraying France, Major Relais, but of deciding what is best for Saint-Domingue. We are living in an era of dramatic changes, not only here but also in Europe and America. We must adjust. Tell me you will at least think about what we have discussed," Valmorain said.

"I shall think about it very carefully, monsieur," Relais replied, leading him to the door.

Zarité

It took the master two weeks to succeed in getting Maurice to sleep alone. He accused me of raising him to be a coward, like a woman, and I told him in a fit of anger that we women are not cowards. He lifted his hand but did not strike me. Something had changed. I think he respected me. Once, in Saint-Lazare, one of the guard dogs escaped from the kennel, and it had killed a hen on the patio and was about to attack another when Tante Mathilde's dog, a little bit of a thing, confronted it. That cat-sized canine faced the huge dog, growling, teeth bared, and mouth foaming. I don't know what raced through the big brute's head, but it turned and ran off with its tail between its legs, chased by the much smaller dog. Afterward Prosper Cambray shot the guard dog for its cowardice. The master, accustomed to barking loud and inspiring fear, had shrunk like that hostile bully before the first one to challenge him: Gambo. I think he was concerned about Maurice's courage because he himself didn't have any. As soon as night fell Maurice would begin to get nervous over the idea of being left by himself. I would put him to bed with Rosette until they fell asleep. She always dropped off in two minutes, tucked against her brother, while he lay listening to the sounds in the house and the street. On the central place there were gallows for condemned men, and their cries sifted through the walls and settled into the rooms; we could hear them for hours after death had silenced them. "Do you hear them, Tété?" Maurice would ask, shivering. I heard them too, but what was I going to tell him?

"*I don't hear anything, child, go to sleep,*" *and I would sing to him. When finally he fell asleep, exhausted, I carried Rosette to our room. Maurice mentioned in front of his father that hanged men were walking through the house, and the master locked him in an armoire, put the key in his pocket, and went out. Rosette and I sat together in front of the armoire to talk to Maurice about happy things; we did not leave him alone a minute, but the ghosts got inside, and when the master came back and let him out he had a fever from crying so much. He was burning hot for two days; his father never moved from his bedside, and I tried to cool him with compresses of cool water and healing teas.*

The master adored Maurice, but during that period his heart was twisted, all that mattered to him was politics; that was all he talked about and he neglected his son. Maurice didn't want to eat, and began to wet his bed at night. Dr. Parmentier, who was the master's only true friend, told him that the boy was ill with fright and needed affection, so at last his father softened and let him move back to my room. The doctor stayed with Maurice, waiting for the fever to go down, and we could talk alone. He asked me many questions. Major Relais had told him that I helped the master escape from the plantation, but that version did not coincide with the master's. He wanted to know the details. I had to mention Gambo, but I did not tell him about the love between us. I showed him the paper of my freedom. "Take care of it, Tété, it's as valuable as gold," he told me after he read it. I already knew that.

The master met with other whites at the house. Madame Delphine, my first owner, had taught me to be silent, vigilant, and to anticipate the master's wishes; she always said a slave should be invisible. That was how I learned to spy. I did not understand much of what the master talked about with the Patriots, and in truth I was interested only in news about the rebels, but Zacharie—we had remained friends after my classes at the Intendance—asked me to tell him everything they said. "The whites think that we blacks are deaf and that women are dumb. That works in our favor. Lend an ear and come tell all of it to me, Mademoiselle Zarité." For him I learned that thousands of rebels were camped around Le Cap. The temptation to go look for Gambo kept me from sleeping, but I knew that then I would not come back. How could I abandon my children? I asked Zacharie, who had contacts even on the moon, to find out if Gambo was there among the rebels, but he assured me he knew nothing about such things. I resigned myself to sending messages to Gambo in my thoughts. Sometimes I took my freedom paper from the little pouch, opened its four folds with my fingertips, so I wouldn't harm it, and looked at it as if I could learn it by heart, but I did not know the words.

Civil war broke out in Le Cap. The master explained to me that in a war everyone fights against a common enemy, and in a civil war people are divided—and the army as well—and then they kill one another, as was happening now between whites and affranchis. *The blacks didn't count because they were property, not people. The civil war didn't begin overnight, it took more than a week to start, and then the markets and the blacks'* kalendas *and the whites' social life ended; very few businesses opened their doors, and even the gallows on the* place *was empty. Misfortune was in the air. "Be ready, Tété, because things are about to change," the master announced to me. "How do you want me to be ready?" I asked, but he himself didn't know. I followed the example of Zacharie, who was storing provisions and packing the finest things in case the Intendant and his wife decided to set sail for France.*

One night someone brought in a crate of pistols and muskets by way of the service door; now we have enough munitions for a regiment, the master said. It was getting hotter; in the house we kept the floor tiles wetted down, and the children went around naked. Then one night Général Galbaud arrived unannounced; I almost didn't recognize him, though he had often come to the Patriots' meetings, because he was wearing a dark traveling suit and not his medal-festooned red uniform. I had never liked that white man, he was very arrogant and always in a bad humor. The only time he softened was when his mousy eyes rested on his wife, a young red-haired woman. While I served them wine, cheese, and cold meats, I heard that Commissaire Sonthonax had removed Gouverneur Galbaud, accusing him of plotting against the legitimate government of the colony. Sonthonax planned a massive deportation of political enemies; he already had five hundred in the holds of ships in the port awaiting his order to sail. Galbaud announced that the moment to act had come.

In a short while other Patriots who had been informed began to show up. I heard them say that the white soldiers in the regular army, and nearly three thousand sailors in the port, were ready to fight alongside Galbaud. Sonthonax could count only on the backing of the national guards and mulatto troops. The general promised that the battle would be ended within a few hours and that Saint-Domingue would be independent. Sonthonax would see his last day, the rights of the affranchis *would be revoked, and the slaves would be back on the plantations. They all stood to make a toast. I filled their goblets again, then left discreetly and ran to Zacharie, who made me repeat everything word by word. I have a good memory. He gave me a drink of lemonade for my anxiety and sent me home with instructions to keep my mouth shut and to lock up the house tight. That I did.*

The Civil War

Commissaire Sonthonax, sweating from heat and nerves in his black jacket and tight-necked collar, explained the situation to Etienne Relais in a few words. He neglected, nonetheless, to say that he had learned of Galbaud's conspiracy not through his complex net of spies but from gossip given him by the majordomo at the Intendance. A very tall, handsome black had come to his office dressed like a *grand blanc*, as fresh and perfumed as if he had just come from his bath; he introduced himself as Zacharie and insisted on speaking with him alone. Sonthonax led him to an adjoining room, a suffocating windowless space among four bare walls, with nothing in it but a barracks cot, a chair, a jug of water, and a washbasin on the floor. He had been sleeping there for months. He sat on the bed and gestured that the visitor should take the only chair, but he chose to remain standing. Sonthonax, short of stature and chubby, took note with a certain envy of the tall and distinguished figure of the other man, whose head brushed the ceiling. Zacharie repeated Tété's words.

"Why are you telling me all this?" asked Sonthonax, suspicious. He could not place this man who had introduced himself with a given name and no family name, like a slave, but who had the aplomb of a free man and the manners of the upper class.

"Because I sympathize with the government of the *républicains*," was Zacharie's simple answer.

"How did you obtain this information? Do you have proof?"

"The information comes directly from Général Galbaud. You will have the proof in less than an hour, when you hear the first shots."

Sonthonax wet his handkerchief in the water jug and wiped his face and neck. His stomach hurt, the same persistent pain, a claw in his guts, that tormented him when he was under pressure, that is, from the time he first stepped onto the soil of Saint-Domingue.

"Come back to see me if you learn anything more. I will take the necessary measures," he said, indicating the end of the interview.

"If you need me, you already know I am in the Intendance, Commissaire," and Zacharie took his leave.

Sonthonax immediately summoned Etienne Relais and received him in the same room, because the rest of the building was filled with civil officials and military men. Relais, the highest ranking officer he could count on to confront Galbaud, had always acted with impeccable loyalty to whatever French government was in charge.

"Have any of your white soldiers deserted, Major?" he asked.

"I have just learned that they all deserted this morning at dawn, Commissaire. I can count only on the mulatto troops."

Sonthonax repeated what Zacharie had just told him.

"That is, we will have to combat whites of all types, civil, military, in addition to Galbaud's sailors, a number that adds up to three thousand," he concluded.

"We are at a great disadvantage, Commissaire. We will need reinforcements."

"We do not have them. You remain in charge of the defense, Major. After the victory I shall make certain you are advanced in rank," Sonthonax promised.

Relais accepted the task with his usual serenity, after negotiating with the Commissaire to be granted permission to retire rather than advance in rank. He had spent many years in the service, and frankly, he was exhausted. His wife and his son were waiting for him in Cuba, and he was eager to rejoin them, he said. Sonthonax assured him that would be done, without the least intention of doing so. It was no time to worry about anyone's personal problems.

In the meantime, the port was aswarm with boats filled with armed sailors, who fell upon Le Cap like a horde of pirates. They formed a strange lot of various nationalities, lawless men who had been months at sea and were eagerly awaiting a few days of drinking and wantonness. They did not fight out of conviction, since they were not even sure of the colors of their flag, but from the pleasure of stepping on dry land and abandoning themselves to destruction and sacking. They had not been paid in a long time, and that rich city offered everything from women and rum to gold, if they could find it. Galbaud was counting on his military experience to organize the attack, backed by the regular troops of whites, who immediately joined his band, fed up with the humiliations they had suffered under soldiers of color. The *grands blancs* kept themselves invisible, while the *petits blancs* and the sailors ran through the streets, coming upon bands of slaves who like them had taken advantage of the bedlam to come out and sack. The Negroes had declared themselves loyal to Sonthonax to annoy their masters and enjoy a few hours of reveling, though it was the same to them who won that battle in which they were not included. Both factions of improvised ruffians assaulted the warehouses of the port, where barrels of rum were stored for export, and soon alcohol was flowing down the cobbled streets. Among the drunks ran disoriented rats and dogs staggering around after licking up the liquor. The families of the *affranchis* barricaded themselves in their houses to defend themselves as they could.

Toulouse Valmorain sent his slaves off; they were going to escape anyway, as most others had done. He preferred not to have an enemy inside the gate, as he told Tété. They weren't his, only hired, and the problem of recovering them would belong to their owners. "They will come dragging back when order is restored. There will be busy times in the prison," he commented. In the city, masters preferred not to dirty their hands but sent guilty slaves to prison, where for a modest price state executioners took charge of inflicting punishment. The cook did not want to go, and hid in the patio woodpile. No threat could get him out of the hole he was hiding in; he could not be counted on to prepare soup, and Tété, who since none of her multiple labors had to do with cooking barely knew how to light a fire, gave the children bread, fruit, and cheese. She put them to bed early, pretending to be calm so she wouldn't frighten them, though she was shivering herself. In the following hours, Valmorain taught her to load firearms, a complicated task that a soldier performed in a few seconds and she in several minutes. Valmorain had shared some of his weapons among other Patriots, but he held on to a dozen, preparing his defense. In his heart he was sure he would not need to use them; it was not his role to fight, that was what the soldiers and Galbaud's sailors were for.

Shortly after sunset three young conspirators whom Tété had often seen in the political meetings came to the house, bringing notice that Galbaud had taken the arsenal and freed the prisoners Sonthonax had in the ships to be deported, and naturally all of them had put themselves under the général's orders. They decided to use the house as a barracks because of its privileged location and clear view of the port, where a hundred ships and numerous boats transporting men could be seen. After a light snack they left to take part in the fight, but their enthusiasm lasted only a short time, and within an hour they were back to share bottles of wine and take turns sleeping.

From the windows they watched the horde of attackers passing by, but only once were they forced to use the weapons to protect themselves, and that was not against bands of slaves or against Sonthonax's soldiers but against their own allies: some drunken sailors intending to sack the house. They frightened them by shooting into the air, and Valmorain calmed them by offering them *taffia*. One of the Patriots had to go outside, rolling a barrel of liquor, while the rest kept aim on the band from the windows. The sailors opened the cask right there, and after the first swallows several dropped to the ground in the last stages of intoxication; they'd been drinking since that morning. Finally they went away, shouting that the supposed battle had been a fiasco, they'd had no one to mix it up with. It was true. The greater part of Sonthonax's troops had given up the streets without showing their faces and taken positions on the outskirts of the city.

At mid-morning the following day, Etienne Relais, wounded by a ball in his shoulder but firm in his bloodstained uniform, explained once more to Sonthonax, who'd taken refuge with his staff on a nearby plantation, that without aid of some kind they could not defeat the enemy. The assault no longer had the carnival air of the first day; Galbaud had succeeded in organizing his men and was about to take over the city. The irascible Commissaire had refused to listen to reason the previous day when the overwhelming superiority of the enemy force was already evident, but this time he listened to the end. Zacharie's information was proved to be absolutely accurate.

"We will have to negotiate an honorable way out, Commissaire, because I see no way to acquire reinforcements," Relais concluded, pale and hollow-eyed, his arm bound to his chest in an improvised sling, the sleeve of his jacket hanging empty.

"I do, Major Relais. I have thought about it carefully. There are more than fifteen thousand rebels camped outside Le Cap. They will be the reinforcements we need," Sonthonax replied.

"The Negroes? I do not believe they want to get involved in this," said Relais.

"They will in exchange for emancipation. Freedom for them and their families."

It was not his idea, it had occurred to Zacharie, who had found a way to meet with him a second time. By then Sonthonax knew that Zacharie was a slave and realized that he was betting everything on one play, because if Galbaud was victorious, as seemed inevitable, and if he learned of Zacharie's role as informant, he would be broken on the wheel in the public *place*. As Zacharie had explained to him, the only help Sonthonax could summon were the rebellious blacks. All he had to do was give them sufficient incentive.

"And in addition they will have the right to pillage the city. What do you think, Major?" Sonthonax announced to Relais with an air of triumph.

"Risky."

"There are hundreds of thousand of rebel blacks scattered around the island, and I have a way to get them to join with us."

"Most of them are on the side of the Spaniards," Relais reminded him.

"In exchange for freedom they will put themselves under the French banner, I assure you. I know that Toussaint, among others, wants to return to the bosom of France. Choose a small detachment of black soldiers and come with me to speak with the rebels. They are at an hour's march from here. And look after that arm, *mon ami*, don't let it get infected."

Etienne Relais, who had no faith in the plan, was surprised to see how quickly the rebels accepted the offer. They had been betrayed again and again by whites, but they clung to that frail promise of emancipation. The pillaging was a hook almost as powerful as freedom, because they had been inactive for weeks, and boredom was beginning to sap their spirits.

Blood and Ashes

From the window of his balcony Toulouse Valmorain was the first to see the dark mass advancing from the hill toward the city. It was difficult for him to realize what it was because his sight was not as good as it had been, and there was a light fog; the air vibrated with heat and humidity.

"Tété! Come here and tell me what that is!" he ordered.

"Negroes, monsieur. Thousands of Negroes," she replied, unable to avoid a shudder, a mixture of terror before what was coming toward them and hope that Gambo was among them.

Valmorain waked the Patriots snoring in the drawing room and sent them out to sound the alarm. Soon all the neighbors were inside their houses, bolting doors and windows, while Général Galbaud's men crawled out of their drunken state and readied themselves for a battle that was lost before it was begun. They did not know it yet, but there were five blacks for every white soldier, and they came inflamed by the demented courage Ogoun had instilled in them. The first sounds heard from them were a hair-raising saraband of howls and the clear call of war conchs growing louder and louder. The rebels had a far greater number of combatants, and they were much closer than anyone had suspected. They set upon Le Cap in the midst of a deafening tumult, nearly naked, badly armed, without order or plan, ready to demolish everything in sight. They could avenge themselves and destroy at will, with no threat of punishment. In the blink of an eye thousands of torches were lit and the city became one enormous flame, the wood houses catching fire as if from a contagious illness, one street after another, entire quartiers. The heat was unbearable, the sky and the sea were stained with reds and oranges. Through the crackling flames and the crashing of buildings collapsing amid smoke rose the clear sounds of the blacks' cries of triumph and the visceral terror of their victims. The streets filled with bodies trampled by the attackers, by whites running for their lives, and by hundreds of stampeding horses loosed from stables. No one could offer resistance to such an onslaught. Most of the sailors were massacred in the first hours, while Galbaud's regular troops were attempting to save civilian whites. Thousands trying to escape ran toward the port. Some were trying to haul bundles, but after only a few steps they tossed them aside in their haste to escape.

Valmorain was taking in the situation from a window on the second floor. The fire was already very near, a spark would be enough to turn his house into a bonfire. In the side streets he saw bands of sweat- and blood-soaked blacks unhesitatingly moving toward the weapons of the few soldiers left standing. The attackers were falling by the dozens, but others came right behind them, leaping over the piled-up bodies of their brothers. Valmorain saw a group surround a family trying to reach the docks, two women and several children protected by an older man, surely the father, and a pair of boys. The whites, armed with pistols, were each able to get off a point blank shot, only to be immediately surrounded and erased from view. Several Negroes were carrying decapitated heads by the hair; others had broken down the door of a house, its roof already ablaze, and were yelling as they burst through. A woman whose throat had been slit was thrown out a window; furniture and household goods followed, until the flames forced the assailants outside. Minutes later Valmorain heard the first blows against the main door of his own house. The terror that paralyzed him was not unknown; he had suffered the identical fear when he'd escaped from his plantation following Gambo. He did not understand how things could have turned around so radically, and how the uproarious noise of drunk sailors and white soldiers in the streets, which according to Galbaud would last only a few hours and end in a certain victory, had become this nightmare of enraged Negroes. He was holding his pistols in fingers so stiff that he could not have fired them. He broke out in a sour sweat whose stench he could recognize: the odor of the impotence and terror of the slaves Cambray had martyrized. He felt that his fate was sealed and that like the slaves on his plantation, there was no escape. He struggled against nausea and against the untenable temptation to curl up in a corner, paralyzed in abject cowardice. He felt a warm liquid soaking his breeches.

Tété was in the center of the room with the children hidden among her skirts, holding a pistol in both hands, the barrel pointing upward. She had lost hope of finding Gambo; if he was in the city he would never reach her before the mob arrived. She could not defend Maurice and Rosette alone. When she saw Valmorain wetting himself with fright, she realized that the sacrifice of having left Gambo had been useless. The master was incapable of protecting them; it would have been better had she gone off with the rebels and run the risk of taking the children with her. The vision of what was about to happen to her children gave her the blind courage and terrible calm of those knowing they are going to die. The port was only two blocks away, and though the distance seemed insuperable under the circumstances, there was no other hope for safety. "We are going to go out the back, through the door for the domestics," Tété announced with a firm voice. Blows were thudding on the front door, and she could hear glass breaking in the windows on the first floor, but Valmorain believed they were safer inside, that they might somehow hide somewhere. "They are going to burn the house. I am leaving with the children," she replied, turning her back on him. At that instant Maurice thrust his small face, grimy from tears and runny nose, from behind Tété's skirt, and he ran and threw his arms around his father's legs. A current of love for that boy shook Valmorain, and he became aware of his shameful state. He could not have it that if his son miraculously survived he would remember him as a coward. He took a deep breath, trying to conquer the shivering of his body, stuck one pistol into his waistband, cocked the other, took Maurice by the hand, and almost pulled him off his feet following Tété, who with Rosette in her arms was already running down the narrow spiral stairs that joined the second floor with the slaves' quarters in the cellar.

They looked out the service door onto the back alley, bombarded with debris and ashes from the blazing buildings but empty. Valmorain felt disoriented—he had never used that door or that passageway and did not know where it led—but Tété went ahead without hesitating, straight toward the conflagration of the battle. In that instant, when encounter with the rebels seemed inevitable, they heard firing and saw a small squad of Galbaud's regular troops, no longer trying to defend the city but attempting a retreat to the ships. They were shooting with order, serene, not breaking rank. The rebel blacks occupied part of the street, but the steady fire kept them at a distance. At that point Valmorain, for the first time, could think with a certain clarity, and he saw there was no time to vacillate. "Come! Run!" he yelled. They rushed after the soldiers, taking shelter among them, and thus, hopping among fallen bodies and still burning debris, they ran that two blocks, the longest of their lives, as the firearms opened a way for them. Not knowing how, they found themselves at the port, which was illuminated like broad day by the fires; thousands of refugees had already gathered there, and more were arriving. Several lines of soldiers were protecting them, firing at the Negroes attacking on three sides, as the whites fought among themselves like animals to climb into the available boats. No one was in charge of organizing the retreat; it was a maddened stampede. In desperation, some were jumping into the water and attempting to swim toward the ships, but the sea was boiling with sharks attracted by the scent of blood.

At that moment Général Galbaud appeared on horseback with his wife behind him, surrounded by a small praetorian guard that was defending him and clearing the way, beating back the crowd with their weapons. The attack by the Negroes had taken Galbaud by surprise—it was the last thing he had expected—but he realized immediately that the situation had undergone a complete reversal, and all that was left was to try to find safety. He just had time to rescue his wife, who for several days had been in bed recovering from an attack of malaria and had no suspicion of what was happening outside. A shawl was wrapped over her negligee and she was barefoot, with her hair caught into a braid hanging down her back; her expression was indifferent, as if she had not noticed the battle and the fire. In some way she had remained unmarked; in contrast, her husband's beard and hair were singed and his clothing ripped, stained with blood and soot.

Valmorain ran toward the général, waving his pistol; he was able to pass through the guards, get right up to the officer, and hold on to his leg with his free hand. "A boat! A boat!" he implored a man he thought was his friend, but Galbaud replied by pushing him away with a kick to his chest. A flash of anger and desperation blinded Valmorain. The entire scaffolding of good manners that had sustained him during his forty-three years disintegrated, and he was changed into a cornered beast. With a strength and agility he did not know he had, he leaped up, grabbed the général's wife about the waist, and wrenched her off the horse with a violent tug. Legs flailing, the woman fell to the warm cobbles, and before the guard could react Valmorain had put his pistol to her head. "A boat, or I kill her right here!" he threatened with such determination that no one doubted he would do it. Galbaud stopped his soldiers. "All right, friend, be calm, I will get you a boat," he said in a voice hoarse from smoke and gunpowder. Valmorain seized the woman's hair, pulled her up from the ground, and forced her to walk ahead of him, his pistol at her neck. The shawl was left behind on the ground, and through the cloth of her negligee, transparent in the orange light of that fiendish night, he saw her slim body stumble forward on tiptoe as he held her high in the air by the braid. In that way they reached the boat that was waiting for Galbaud. At the last moment the général tried to negotiate; there was room only for Valmorain and his son, he claimed; they could not give priority to the mulatta while thousands of whites pushed forward to climb in. Valmorain prodded the général's wife to the edge of the dock, where the water reflected fire and blood. Galbaud realized that with the least vacillation that unsettled man would throw her to the sharks, and he yielded. Valmorain climbed with his party into the boat.

Help to Die

One month later, on the smoking remains of Le Cap, which was reduced to rubble and ash, Sonthonax proclaimed the emancipation of the slaves on Saint-Domingue. Without them the French would not have been able to wage a war against their internal enemies and against the English, who now occupied the south. That same day Toussaint also declared emancipation from his encampment in Spanish territory. He signed the document as Toussaint Louverture, the name with which he would enter history. His ranks were growing, he exercised more influence than any of the other rebel leaders, and by then he was already thinking of changing sides; only republican France would recognize the liberation of his people, something no other country was prepared to accept.

Zacharie had been waiting for this opportunity from the time he could think; he had lived obsessed with freedom, although his father had, since Zacharie was in the cradle, driven home the pride of being majordomo at the Intendance, a position normally held by a white man. He took off his opera-admiral's uniform, collected his savings, and set sail on the first ship leaving the port that day, never asking where it was going. He knew that the emancipation was only a political card that could be revoked at any moment, and decided not to be there when that happened. From living so long with whites he had come to know them profoundly, and he imagined that if the monarchies triumphed in the next election of the

Assemblée Nationale in France, Sonthonax would be removed from his post, the vote would go against emancipation, and the Negroes in the colony would have to keep fighting for their freedom. He, however, did not want to sacrifice himself; to him the war seemed a squandering of resources and lives, the least reasonable way to resolve conflicts. In any case, his experience as majordomo had little value on an island torn apart by violence since the times of the Spanish Conquest, and he should take advantage of the opportunity to seek other horizons. He was thirty-eight years old, and he was ready to change his life.

Etienne Relais learned of the double proclamation hours before he died. The wound in his shoulder worsened rapidly during the days Le Cap was being sacked and burned to its foundations, and when finally he could worry about it, gangrene had set in. Dr. Parmentier, who had spent those days without rest, attending to hundreds of wounded with the help of the nuns who had survived being raped, examined him when it was already too late. His clavicle was shattered, and because of the position of the wound there was no possibility of the extreme solution of amputation. The remedies he had learned from Tante Rose, along with other curatives, were futile. Etienne Relais had seen wounds of many types, and by the odor he knew he was dying, and what he most lamented was that he would not be able to protect Violette from the unknowns of the future. Lying on the floorboards of a hospital, without a mattress, he was breathing with difficulty, soaked in the pasty sweat of dying. The pain would have been unbearable for another, but he had been wounded before; he had lived a life of privation, and he had a stoic scorn for the pains of his body. He did not complain. With closed eyes he evoked Violette, her cool hands, her purring laughter, her slippery waist, her translucent ears, her dark nipples, and her smile, feeling himself to be the most fortunate man in this world for having had her for fourteen years. Beloved Violette, beautiful, eternal, his. Parmentier did not try to distract him, he merely offered him the choice of opium, the only available sedative, or a powerful potion that would end his torment in a matter of minutes, an option that as a physician he should not propose, but he had witnessed so much suffering on the island that the oath of preserving life at any cost had lost meaning; more ethical in certain cases was to help someone die. "Poison, as long as it isn't needed by another soldier," was the wounded man's choice. The doctor bent very close to hear him, because his voice was barely a murmur. "Look for Violette, tell her I love her," Etienne Relais added before the doctor emptied a little vial into his mouth.

In Cuba, at that very instant, Violette Boisier banged her right hand against the stone fountain where she had gone to get water, and the opal of the ring she had worn for fourteen years shattered. She dropped down beside the fountain with a piercing scream and pressed her hand to her heart. Adèle, who was with her, thought she had been bitten by a scorpion. "Etienne, Etienne," Violette repeated, tears streaming.

Five blocks from the fountain where Violette knew she had been widowed, Tété was standing under an awning in the best hotel in the city of Havana beside a table where Maurice and Rosette were drinking pineapple juice. It was not permitted for her to sit with guests, nor was it for Rosette, but the girl passed as being Spanish; no one suspected her true status. Maurice contributed to the deceit by treating her like his younger sister. At another table, Toulouse Valmorain was talking with his brother-in-law Sancho and their banker. The flotilla of refugees Général Galbaud had led out of Le Cap that fateful night beneath a rain of ashes was heading at full sail toward Baltimore, but several of those hundred ships had turned toward Cuba carrying *grands blancs* who had family or interests there. Overnight, thousands of French families disembarked on the island to escape the political storm on Saint-Domingue. They were received with generous hospitality by the Cubans and Spanish, who never thought that the frightened visitors would become permanent refugees. Among them were Valmorain, Tété, and the children. Sancho García del Solar took them into his house, which during those years without anyone bothering to care for it had deteriorated even further. Faced with the cockroaches, Valmorain decided to install himself and his party in the best hotel in Havana, where he and Maurice occupied a suite with two balconies overlooking the sea, while Tété and Rosette slept in the lodging for slaves accompanying their masters on those voyages, windowless little rooms with dirt floors.

Sancho lived the comfortable life of a confirmed bachelor; he spent more than was wise on parties, women, horses, and gaming tables, but he kept dreaming, as he had in his youth, of making a fortune and restoring his name to the prestige it had known in his grandparents' time. He was always on the lookout for opportunities to make money, so a couple of years earlier he'd had a chance to buy lands in Louisiana with funds sent him by Valmorain. His contribution was his commercial vision, his social contacts, and work—as long as it wasn't too much, as he always said, laughing—while his brother-in-law furnished the capital. Ever since he'd had the idea he had frequently traveled to New Orleans, and there acquired property on the banks of the Mississippi. At first Valmorain had considered the project a wild adventure, but now it was the only sure thing he had, and he proposed to convert that abandoned land into a great sugar plantation. He had lost a lot in Saint-Domingue but he was not without resources, thanks to his investments, his enterprises with Sancho, and the good judgment of his Jewish agent and Cuban banker. That was the explanation he had offered to Sancho, and to anyone who had the indiscretion to ask. Alone before the mirror, however, he could not avoid the truth that stared back at him from deep within his eyes: the greater part of that capital was not his, it had belonged to Lacroix. He kept telling himself that his conscience was clean, he had never intended to benefit from his friend's tragedy nor to take control of his money; it had simply fallen to him from the sky. When the Lacroix family had been assassinated by the rebels on Saint-Domingue and the receipts Valmorain had signed for money received had burned in the fires, he found himself in possession of an account in gold pesos that he himself had opened in Havana to hide Lacroix's savings and that no one knew existed. On each of his voyages he had deposited the money his neighbor had handed him, and his banker had placed it in an account identified only by a number. The banker never knew about Lacroix and later made no objection when Valmorain transferred the funds to his own account, believing that they were in fact his. Lacroix had heirs in France who had full rights to those assets, but Valmorain analyzed the facts and came to the conclusion that it was not up to him to go look for them, and that it would be stupid to leave the gold buried in a bank vault. It was one of those rare cases when Fortune knocked at the door and only an idiot would let her pass by.

Two weeks later, when news from Saint-Domingue left no doubts about the cruel anarchy reigning in the colony, Valmorain decided he would go to Louisiana with Sancho. Life in Havana was very entertaining for anyone eager to pay for it, but he could not lose more time. He realized that if he followed Sancho from gaming house to gaming house, and from brothel to brothel, he would end up eating away his savings and his health. It would be much better to take his charming brother-in-law away from his great friends and give him a project to the measure of his ambition. A Louisiana plantation could stir in Sancho the live coals of moral fortitude that nearly everyone possesses, he thought. In those years he had acquired an older brother's affection for that man whose defects and virtues he lacked. That was why they got along so well. Sancho was a big talker, an adventurer, imaginative and brave, the kind of man able to rub elbows with either princes or buccaneers, irresistible to women, a rogue with a good heart. Valmorain did not consider Saint-Lazare a complete loss, but until he could recover it, he would concentrate his energies on Sancho's project in Louisiana. Politics no longer interested him, the fiasco with Galbaud had scalded him. The hour had come for him to produce sugar again, the only thing he knew how to do.

The Punishment

*V*almorain notified Tété that they would be leaving on an American schooner in two days' time, and gave her money to buy clothing for the family.

"Is anything the matter with you?" he asked when he saw that she had not made a move to pick up the pouch of money.

"I'm sorry, monsieur, but . . . I do not want to go to that place," she mumbled.

"What did you say, idiot? Obey me and say no more!"

"Is the paper of my freedom good there, too?" Tété dared ask.

"Is that what's worrying you? Of course it's good there, it's good anywhere. It has my signature and my seal; it's legal even in China."

"Louisiana is a long way from Saint-Domingue, isn't it?" Tété persisted.

"We are not going back to Saint-Domingue, if that is what you're thinking. Wasn't what we went through there enough for you? You are more thickheaded than I thought!" Valmorain exclaimed, irritated.

Head hanging low, Tété went to prepare for the journey. The wood doll the slave Honoré had carved for her when she was a girl had been left at Saint-Lazare, and now she missed that good luck fetish. *Will I see Gambo again, Erzulie? We are going farther away, more water between us.* After the siesta she hoped the sea breeze would cool the afternoon, and she took the children shopping with her. By order of the master, who did not want to see Maurice playing with a ragged little girl, she dressed the two of them in clothing of the same quality, and to anyone's eyes they would pass as wealthy children with their nursemaid. As Sancho had planned, they would stay in New Orleans, since the new plantation was only a day's journey from the city. They had land but needed everything else: mills, machines, tools, slaves, slave quarters, and the big house. They had to work the land, and plant, and for a couple of years there would not be any crop, but thanks to Valmorain's reserves they would not want for anything. As Sancho said, money does not buy happiness but it does buy nearly everything else. They did not want to arrive in New Orleans with the look of escaping from somewhere; they were investors, not refugees. They had left Le Cap with only the clothing they had on, and in Cuba had bought the minimum, but before traveling to New Orleans they needed a complete wardrobe, and trunks and cases. "All the best quality, Tété. And a dress or two for you, I don't want to see you looking like a beggar woman. And put on shoes!" the master ordered, but the one pair of high-top shoes she owned were a torment. In the *comptoirs* of the center, Tété bought what was needed, after a lot of bargaining, which was the custom in Saint-Domingue and she assumed would be in Cuba. Everyone in the street spoke Spanish, and although she had learned a little of that language from Eugenia, she did not understand the Cuban accent, slippery and singsong, very different from the hard, sonorous Castilian of her deceased mistress. In the city market she wouldn't have been capable of bargaining, but in commercial establishments French was also spoken.

When she had completed her purchases she asked for them to be sent to the hotel, in accord with her master's instructions. The children were hungry and she was weary, but when they went outdoors they heard drums, and she could not resist the call. From one little street to the next, they came upon a small plaza where a crowd had gathered, people of color dancing unconstrained to the sound of a band. It had been a long time since Tété had felt the volcanic impulse to dance in a *kalenda*; she had spent more than a year of fear on the plantation, she'd been assaulted by the howls of the condemned in Le Cap, then fleeing, saying good-bye, waiting. The rhythm rose in her from the soles of her bare feet to the knot of her *tignon*, the drums possessed her entire body with the same jubilation she had felt making love with Gambo. She let go of the children's hands and joined the joyful throng: the slave that dances is free as he dances, as Honoré had taught her. But she was not a slave any longer, she was free, all she needed was a judge's signature. Free! Free! And we are moving with our feet cleaving to the ground, legs and hips animated, buttocks gyrating provocatively, arms like the wings of the dove, breasts bouncing, heads in a fog. Rosette's African blood also responded to the formidable summons of the music, and that three-year-old child jumped into the center of the dances, swaying with the same pleasure and abandon as her mother. Maurice, on the other hand, retreated until he was stopped by a wall. He had witnessed slave dances at the Habitation Saint-Lazare as a spectator, safe holding his father's hand, but in this unfamiliar plaza he was alone, sucked up in a frenetic mass of humankind, stunned by the drums, forgotten by Tété, his Tété, who had been transformed into a typhoon of skirts and arms, forgotten too by Rosette, who had disappeared among the legs of the dancers, forgotten by all. He burst out crying and wailing. A teasing black, barely covered by a loincloth and three rows of shiny beads, jumped in front of him, leaping and shaking a maraca with the intention of distracting him, but all he did was terrorize him further. Maurice went flying away as fast as his legs would carry him. The drums continued thrumming for hours, and maybe Tété would have danced till the last one went silent at dawn had four powerful hands not grabbed her arms and dragged her out of the music and revelry.

It had been almost three hours since Maurice went running, by instinct, toward the sea, which he had seen from the balconies of his suite. He was undone with fear, he didn't remember the hotel, but a blond, well dressed boy, cowed and weeping in the street, could not pass unnoticed.

Someone stopped to help him, found out his father's name, and asked at various establishments until he found Toulouse Valmorain, who had not had time to worry about his son; with Tété he was safe. When he was able to pull from the sobbing boy what had happened, he whirled off like a waterspout to look for the woman, but before he'd gone a block he realized that he didn't know the city and could not locate her, and turned to the city guard. Two men went out to look for Tété, following Maurice's vague indications, and soon from the noise of the drums found the dance in the plaza. They dragged Tété kicking and screaming to the calaboose, and as Rosette followed them, shrieking at them to let her mother go, they locked her up as well.

In the suffocating darkness of the cell, stinking with urine and excrement, Tété crawled into a corner with Rosette in her arms. She realized that there were other people, but it was a while before she could make out a woman and three men in the shadows, silent and motionless, waiting for their turn to receive the lashing ordered by their masters. One of the men had been several days recovering from the first twenty-five lashes to gain enough strength to endure the remainder of his punishment. The woman asked Tété something in Spanish, which she didn't understand. She had just begun to measure the consequences of what she had done: drawn into the vortex of the dance she had abandoned Maurice. If anything bad had happened to the boy she would pay for it with her life; that is why they had arrested her and why she was in that filthy hole. More than what they would do to her, she worried about the fate of her son. *Erzulie, mother* loa, *have Maurice be safe.* And what would happen to Rosette? She touched the pouch under her bodice. They were not yet free, no judge had signed the paper, her daughter could be sold. They spent the rest of that night in the cell, the longest night Tété could remember. Rosette had tired of crying and asking for water and finally fallen asleep, feverish. The implacable Caribbean sun shone in through the thick bars at dawn, and a crow landed on the stone frame of the one window to peck at insects. The woman began to moan, and Tété didn't know whether it was because of the bad omen of the black bird or because this day would bring her turn. Hours went by, it grew hotter, the air was so thin and fiery that Tété felt as if her head was filled with cotton. She didn't know how to calm her daughter's thirst; she put her to her breast but now she had no milk. Sometime around noon the iron-barred door opened and a large figure blocked the space and called her by name. On the second attempt, Tété managed to get to her feet; her legs were wobbly and her thirst caused her to see visions. Without letting go of Rosette, she staggered toward the opening. Behind her back she heard the woman bid her good-bye with words that were familiar because she had heard them from Eugenia: *Virgen María, madre de Dios, ruega por nosotros pecadores*. Tété answered inside because her voice would not pass her dry lips: *Erzulie, loa of compassion, protect Rosette*. The man took her to a small patio with one door, surrounded with high walls, where there were a gibbet, a post, and a black tree trunk stained with dried blood from amputations. The hangman was a Congo as broad as an armoire, his cheeks crisscrossed with ritual scars, his teeth filed to points, his torso naked except for a leather apron covered with dark stains. Before the man touched her, Tété pushed Rosette aside and told her to stay far away. The child obeyed, sobbing, too weak to ask questions. "*Soy libre!* I'm free!" Tété shouted in the little Spanish she knew, showing the executioner the pouch she wore around her neck, but the man's slashing hand ripped it off along with her blouse and bodice. The second sweep of his ham of a hand tore away her skirt, and she was naked. She made no attempt to cover herself. She told Rosette to turn her face to the wall and not to look around for any reason, then she let herself be led to the post and held out her hands so her wrists could be bound with sisal cord. She heard the terrible hiss of the whip in the air and thought of Gambo.

Toulouse Valmorain was waiting on the other side of the door. Just as he had instructed the hangman; for the usual pay and a tip he was to give this slave an unforgettable fright but not harm her. Nothing serious had happened to Maurice, after all, and within two days they would be leaving on the voyage; he needed Tété more than ever and could not take her along striped by a recent lashing. The whip cracked, making sparks on the paving of the patio, but Tété felt it on her back, her heart, her gut, her soul. Her knees doubled, and she was left hanging by her wrists. From far away she heard the loud laughter of the hangman and a cry from Rosette: "Monsieur! Monsieur!" With a brutal effort she opened her eyes and turned her head. Valmorain was standing a few steps away, and Rosette had her arms around his knees, with her face buried in his legs, choked with sobs. He stroked her head and picked her up, and the child sank against his chest, inert. Without a word to his slave, he made a sign to the hangman and turned toward the door. The Congo untied Tété, picked up her torn clothing, and handed it to her. She, who instants before couldn't move, rushed to follow Valmorain, stumbling with an energy born of terror, naked, holding her rags to her chest. The hangman caught up with her at the door and handed her the leather pouch with her freedom.

Part

Two

LOUISIANA

(1793–1810)

Blue-Blooded Creoles

The house in the heart of New Orleans, the quartier where Creoles of French descent and old family lived, was a find of Sancho García del Solar's. Each of these households formed a patriarchal clan, large and closed, that mixed only with others of their same level. Money did not open those doors, contrary to what Sancho claimed, although he should have been better informed since neither did they open among Spaniards of similar social caste. However, when the refugees from Saint-Domingue began to arrive a crack opened that could be slipped through. At first, before the stream became a human avalanche, some Creole families took in the *grands blancs* who had lost their plantations, feeling compassionate and frightened by the tragic news coming from the island. They could not imagine anything worse than an uprising of Negroes. Valmorain dusted off his title of chevalier to introduce himself to society, and his brother-in-law made sure to mention the château in Paris, unfortunately abandoned since Valmorain's mother had found a home in Italy in order to escape the terror imposed by the Jacobin Robespierre. The tendency to decapitate people for reasons of ideas or titles, as was happening in France, roiled Sancho's gut. He did not sympathize with the nobility, but neither did he admire the mob; the French republic seemed as vulgar to him as American democracy. When he learned that Robespierre had been decapitated some months earlier, on the same guillotine where hundreds of his victims had perished, he celebrated with a two-day drinking spree. That was the last time, for while no one was abstemious among the Creoles, drunkenness was not tolerated; a man who lost his composure because of drink did not deserve to be accepted anywhere. Valmorain, who had for years ignored Dr. Parmentier's warnings about alcohol, also had to be more moderate, and in doing so discovered that he did not drink as a vice, as deep down he had suspected, but as a palliative for loneliness.

As they had proposed, the brothers-in-law did not arrive in New Orleans as mere refugees but as owners of a sugar plantation, the most prestigious rank on the scale of castes. Sancho's vision in having acquired land had turned out to be providential. "Do not forget, Toulouse, the future lies in cotton. Sugar has a bad name," he warned Valmorain. Blood-chilling tales circulated about slavery in the Antilles, and the abolitionists were waging an international campaign to sabotage sugar stained by blood. "Believe me, Sancho, even if the lumps were crimson, consumption would continue to increase. Sweet gold is more addictive than opium," Valmorain replied. No one spoke about that in the closed circle of the Creoles, who affirmed that the atrocities of the islands did not occur in Louisiana. Among those people, united by a complex network of family relationships in which it was impossible to keep secrets— everything was known sooner or later—cruelty was badly viewed and inappropriate as well, since only a fool damaged his property. Besides, the priests, led by the Spanish friar Antonio de Sedella, known as Père Antoine and feared for his reputation as a saint, made it a point to drive home their responsibility before God for the bodies and souls of their slaves.

As he began to acquire laborers for the plantation, Valmorain encountered a reality very different from that in Saint-Domingue: the price of slaves was high. That meant a larger investment than he had calculated, and he had to be prudent about expenses, but he also felt secretly relieved. Now there was a practical reason for taking care of one's slaves, not merely humanitarian scruples that could be interpreted as weakness. The worst of the twenty-three years at Saint-Lazare had been the absolute power he held over other lives, with its burden of temptations and degradation, worse than his wife's madness, the climate that corroded health and dissolved man's most decent principles, the solitude and the hunger for books and conversation. Just as Dr. Parmentier had maintained, the revolution in Saint-Domingue had been the inevitable revenge of slaves against the colonists' brutality. Louisiana offered Valmorain the opportunity to revive the youthful ideals smoldering in the embers of his memory. He began to dream of a model plantation capable of producing as much sugar as Saint-Lazare, but one where slaves lived a human existence. This time he would take much better care in selecting a manager and overseers. He did not want another Prosper Cambray.

Sancho devoted himself to cultivating friendships among the Creoles, without whom they could not prosper, and within a brief time he became the soul of parties, with his guitar and silken voice, his talent for losing at gaming tables, his sleepy eyes and fine humor with the matriarchs on whom he lavished praise—without their approval, after all, no one crossed the threshold of their houses. He played billiards, backgammon, dominos, and cards, he danced gracefully, he was informed on every subject, and he had the art of always being in the right place at the right time. His favorite stroll was along the tree-lined road bordering the dike that protected the city from floods, where everyone mixed together, from distinguished families to noisy sailors, slaves, free people of color, and the ever-present Kaintucks, with their reputation for drunkenness, killings, and whoring. Those men came down the Mississippi from Kentucky and other regions to the north to sell their tobacco, cotton, hides, and wood, encountering hostile Indians and a thousand other dangers along the way, which was why they went around well armed. In New Orleans they sold their rowboats for firewood, caroused a couple of weeks, and then undertook the arduous return.

Sancho, if only to be seen, attended theater and opera just as he went to mass on Sundays. His simple black suit, hair pulled into a ponytail, and waxed mustache contrasted with the brocade and lace attire of the French, giving him a slightly dangerous air that attracted the women. His manners were impeccable, an essential requirement in the upper class, where the proper use of the fork was more important than moral tenets. Such splendid virtues would have served that somewhat eccentric Spaniard for nothing without his relationship to Valmorain, a Frenchman of wealth and good family name, but once he was introduced in those salons, no one thought of dismissing him. Valmorain was a widower, only forty-five years old, not bad looking, though several kilos too heavy, and naturally enterprising patriarchs tried to trap him for a daughter or niece. The brother-in-law with the unpronounceable name was also a candidate; even a Spanish son-in-law was preferable to the embarrassment of an unwed daughter.

There were comments, but no one offered any opposition when that pair of strangers rented one of the mansions in the quartier, or later when the owner sold it to them. It had two floors and a mansard, but lacked a cellar because New Orleans floated on water, and digging only a palm's width was enough to get wet. The mausoleums of the cemetery were raised so that the dead would not sail away with every storm. Like many others, Valmorain's house was wood and brick, Spanish in style, with a wide entry for the coach, a patio cobbled with paving stone, a tile fountain, and cool balconies with iron railings covered with fragrant climbing vines. Valmorain avoided any ostentation in decorating the house, for that was a sign of being nouveau riche. He could not carry a tune, but he invested in musical instruments because at every social event the mademoiselles showed their skill at the piano, the harp, or the clavichord, and the young gentlemen shone on their guitars.

Maurice and Rosette had to take music and dance lessons with private instructors, like any other wealthy children. A refugee from Saint-Domingue gave them music classes, using his corrective rod, and a plump, affected man taught them the dances in vogue, also with a rod.

In the future those lessons would be as useful to Maurice as fencing for fighting a duel and salon games, and for Rosette they would serve for entertaining visitors, though never competing with white girls. She had grace and a good voice, whereas Maurice had inherited his father's tin ear and attended the classes with the resigned attitude of a galley slave. He preferred books, which were not going to do anything for him in New Orleans, where intellect was considered suspicious; much more appreciated was a talent for light conversation, gallantry, and living the good life.

To Valmorain, accustomed to a hermit's life at Saint-Lazare, the hours of banal chatter in the cafés and bars Sancho dragged him to seemed a waste. He had to make an effort to participate in the games and betting; he detested the cockfights that left the attendees spattered with blood as well as the horse and greyhound racing at which he always lost. Every day of the week there was a gathering in a different drawing room, presided over by a matron who kept track of who attended and what gossip they brought. Bachelors went from house to house, always with some gift, usually a monstrous sugar and nut dessert heavy as a cow's head. According to Sancho, these *réunions des amis* were obligatory in that closed society. Dances, soirées, picnics, always the same faces with nothing new to say. Valmorain preferred the plantation, but he realized that in Louisiana his taste for seclusion would be interpreted as arrogance or miserliness.

The dining and drawing rooms of the city house were on the first floor, the bedchambers on the second, and the kitchen and slave quarters off the back patio, in separate buildings. The windows gave access to a small but well tended garden. The most spacious room was the dining hall, as it was in all Creole houses, in which life turned around the dining table and the pride of hospitality. A respectable family owned china for at least twenty-four guests. One of the rooms on the first floor had a separate entrance intended for the bachelor sons; in that way they could come and go without offending the ladies of the family. On the plantations their *garçonnières* were octagonal quarters near the road and separated from the main house. Maurice was twelve years short of qualifying for that privilege; for the moment he slept alone, for the first time, in a room between those of his father and his uncle Sancho.

Tété and Rosette did not have quarters with the other seven slaves—cook, washerwoman, coachman, seamstress, two personal servants, and an errand boy—but slept together in the mansard among the family's trunks. As she always had, Tété managed the house. A little bell on a cord that ran through the rooms allowed Valmorain to summon her at night.

The minute Sancho saw Rosette, he knew his brother-in-law's relationship with the slave, and anticipated the problem. "What are you going to do with Tété when you marry?" was his point blank question to Valmorain, who had never mentioned the subject to anyone and, caught by surprise, mumbled that he was not planning to marry. "If we are to live under the same roof, one of us will have to marry or people will think we're perverts," Sancho concluded.

In the confusion of escaping from Le Cap that fateful night, Valmorain had lost his cook, who had stayed hidden as he fled with Tété and the children, but he did not lament that because in New Orleans he needed someone experienced in *cuisine créole*. His new friends warned him that it was not safe to buy the first cook who turned up in the Maspero Échange, no matter that it was the best slave market in America, nor in the establishments along Chartres, where they disguised the slaves in elegant clothing to impress their customers but offered no guarantee of quality. The best slaves were obtained in private among families or friends. That was how he acquired Célestine, who was about forty, had magical hands for stews and pastries, and had been trained by one of the marquis de Marigny's eminent French cooks and sold because no one could put up with her fits of temper. She had thrown a plate of shrimp gumbo at the feet of the imprudent marquis because he dared ask for more salt.

Valmorain was not frightened by that anecdote; doing battle with her would be Tété's task. Célestine was thin, dry, and jealous by nature. She did not allow anyone to step into her kitchen or her larder; she herself chose the wines and liquors and did not accept suggestions regarding menus. Tété explained that she would have to be moderate with spices because her master had stomach troubles. "He'll have to put up with it. If he wants a sick man's broth, you fix it," had been her answer, but ever since she reigned among the cookpots Valmorain had been healthy. Célestine smelled of cinnamon, and in secret, so no one would suspect her weakness, she prepared beignets light as sighs for the children, tarte tatin with carameled apples, mandarin crêpes with cream, *mousse au chocolat* with little honey biscuits, and other treats, which proved the theory that humankind would never tire of consuming sugar. Maurice and Rosette were the only ones in the house who did not fear the cook.

The life of a Creole monsieur was spent at leisure; work was a vice of Protestants in general and Americans in particular. Valmorain and Sancho had a problem hiding the effort required to start up their plantation, which had been abandoned for more than ten years after the death of the owner and the methodical ruin of the heirs.

The first matter was to acquire slaves, some hundred and fifty to begin with, a lot fewer than Valmorain had had at Saint-Lazare. Valmorain installed himself in one corner of the ruined house as another was built following the plans of a French architect. The slave quarters, eaten by termites and humidity, were torn down and replaced by wood cabins with overhanging roofs to give shade and protect from rain; each had three rooms to house two families, lined up in parallel rows perpendicular to a small central square. The brothers-in-law visited other plantations, like so many who arrived at them uninvited on weekends, taking advantage of the tradition of hospitality. Valmorain concluded that compared with the slaves on Saint-Domingue, those in Louisiana could not complain, but Sancho found out that some masters kept their workers nearly naked, fed with a mush poured into a trough like the ones for animals, from which each slave took his portion with an oyster shell, a chipped tile, or hand, because there was no spoon.

It took two long years to construct the basics: to plant, build a mill, and organize work. Valmorain had grandiose plans, but he had to concentrate on the immediate. There would be time later to turn his fantasies into reality: a garden, terraces, gazebos, a decorative bridge over the river, along with other amenities. He lived obsessed with the details, which he discussed with Sancho and lectured Maurice about.

"Look, son, all this will be yours," he said, pointing to the cane fields from his horse. "Sugar doesn't fall from the sky, it requires a lot of work."

"The Negroes do the work," Maurice observed.

"Don't be deceived. They do the manual labor, because they don't know how to do anything else, but the master is the one responsible. The success of the plantation depends on me and, in a certain measure, your uncle Sancho. Not a single stalk of cane is cut without my knowledge. Pay attention, because one day it will be up to you to make decisions and command your people."

"Why don't they command themselves, Papa?"

"They can't, Maurice. You have to give them orders. They're slaves, son."

"I wouldn't like to be like them."

"You never will be, Maurice." His father smiled. "You are a Valmorain."

He could not have shown Saint-Lazare to his son with the same pride. He was determined to correct the errors, weaknesses, and omissions of the past and secretly atone for the atrocious sins of Lacroix, whose money had been used to buy this land. For each man tortured and each girl stained by Lacroix there would be a healthy, well-treated slave on the Valmorain plantation. That justified his having appropriated his neighbor's money, it could not be better invested.

Sancho was not overly interested in his brother-in-law's plans; they did not carry the same weight in his conscience, and he thought only of entertaining himself. The contents of the slaves' soup or the color of their cabins were nothing to him. Valmorain was set on changing his life, but for the Spaniard this adventure was but one among many undertaken with enthusiasm and abandoned without regret. As he had nothing to lose—his partner was assuming all the risks—he had audacious ideas that tended to give surprising results, such as a refinery that would allow them to sell white sugar, which was much more profitable than other planters' molasses.

Sancho found a manager, an Irishman who advised him on purchases of field labor. His name was Owen Murphy, and he set the rule from the beginning that the slaves must attend mass. They would have to build a chapel and find itinerant priests, he said, to fortify Catholicism before the Americans got to the slaves to preach their heresies and innocent people be condemned to hell. "Morality is more important than anything," he announced. Murphy agreed completely with Valmorain's suggestion not to abuse the whip. That huge man with the look of an elite Turkish guard, heavy black hair on his chest, and hair and beard equally black, had a sweet soul. He moved his large family into a campaign tent while their living quarters were being built. His wife, Leanne, who came to his waist, looked like an undernourished adolescent with the face of a fly, but her fragility was deceptive: she had given birth to six male children and was expecting the seventh. She knew it would be male because God was determined to test her patience. She never raised her voice, but one glance and her children and her husband obeyed. Valmorain thought that finally Maurice would have someone to play with and not cling to Rosette every minute; that herd of Irish boys was from a social class very inferior to his, but they were white and free. He could not have imagined that the six Murphys would also trail around enraptured behind Rosette, who had turned five and possessed the arresting personality her father would have wished for Maurice.

Owen Murphy had worked directing slaves since he was seventeen, and he knew by memory the errors and successes of that unpleasant labor. "You have to treat them like children. Authority and justice, clear rules, punishment, reward, and some free time or they get sick," he told his employer; he added that slaves had the right to come to the master regarding a sentence of more than fifteen lashes. "I trust you, Monsieur Murphy, that will not be necessary," replied Valmorain, little disposed to assume the role of judge. "But for my own peace I would prefer it be done that way, monsieur. Too much power destroys the soul of any Christian, and mine is weak," the Irishman explained to him.

In Louisiana the labor force of a plantation cost a third of the value of the land; they had to be looked after. Production was at the mercy of unforeseen mishaps, hurricanes, drought, floods, plagues, rats, fluctuations in the price of sugar, problems with machinery and animals, loans from the banks, and other uncertainties, say nothing of the bad health or spirits of the slaves, said Murphy. He was so different from Cambray that Valmorain wondered whether he'd made a mistake in hiring him, but he soon observed that he worked untiringly and imposed his will with his presence, not brutality. His overseers watched closely, followed his example, and the result was that the slaves produced more than those under Prosper Cambray's regime of terror. Murphy organized them using a system of turns that gave them rest during the perishing day in the fields. His former employer had dismissed Murphy because when he was ordered to discipline a slave woman, Murphy's whip cracked against the ground without touching her, though she screamed at the top of her lungs. The slave was pregnant, and as was done in such cases, she had been laid on the ground with her belly in a depression. "I promised my wife I would never beat children or pregnant women," was the Irishman's explanation when Valmorain asked.

The slaves were given two days a week rest to cultivate their gardens, care for their animals, and tend to their domestic chores, but on Sunday they had to attend the mass decreed by Murphy. They could play music and dance in their free hours, and even—under the manager's supervision—attend the *bambousses*, modest slave gatherings on the occasion of a wedding, a funeral, or other celebration. In principle, slaves could not visit other properties, but in Louisiana few masters paid attention to that rule. Breakfast on the Valmorain plantation consisted of a soup with meat or bacon—none of the stinking dried fish of Saint-Lazare; lunch was a maize tart, fresh or salted meat, and pudding, and dinner a hearty soup. They fitted out a cabin to be used as a hospital and contracted a doctor who came once a month for prevention and when called for an emergency. They gave more food and rest to pregnant women. Valmorain didn't know—he had never asked—that at Saint-Lazare the slaves gave birth while crouching in the cane fields, that there were more abortions than births, and that most of the children died before they were three months old. On the new plantation, Leanne Murphy acted as midwife and looked after the children.

Zarité

From the boat New Orleans looked like a waning moon floating on the sea, white and luminous. When I saw it I knew I would never return to Saint-Domingue. Sometimes I have these premonitions and I don't forget them, so I will be prepared when they happen. The pain of having lost Gambo was like a lance in my chest. Don Sancho was waiting for us in the port. Doña Eugenia's brother had arrived a few days before us and already had a house where we were going to live. The street smelled of jasmine, not smoke and blood like Le Cap when it was burned by the rebels before they moved on to continue their revolution elsewhere. The first week in New Orleans I did all the work myself, helped at times by a slave lent to us by a family Don Sancho knew, but then the master and his brother-in-law bought servants. Maurice was assigned a tutor, Gaspard Sévérin, who had fled from Saint-Domingue like us, and was poor. Refugees were arriving gradually; first the men to find a place somehow, and then women and children. Some brought along their families of color, and slaves. By then there were already thousands, and the people of Louisiana resented them. The tutor did not approve of slavery; I think he was one of those abolitionists Monsieur Valmorain detested. He was twenty-seven years old, he lived in a rooming house for Negroes, he always wore the same suit, and his hands trembled from the fright he'd suffered on Saint-Domingue. Sometimes, when the master wasn't there, I washed his shirt and removed stains from his jacket, but I was never able to get the smell of fear out of his *clothing. I also gave him food to take with him, subtly, so as not to offend him. He took it as if he were doing me a favor, but he was grateful, and that was why he let Rosette attend his classes. I pleaded with the master to let her study, and in the end he yielded, though it is forbidden to educate slaves. He had plans for her; he wanted her to care for him in his old age and read to him when his vision failed. Had he forgotten that he owed us our freedom? Rosette did not know that the master was her father but she adored him, and I suppose that in his way he loved her too. No one could resist being bewitched by my daughter. From the time she was a child, Rosette was seductive. She liked to admire herself in the mirror, a dangerous habit.*

At that time there were many free people of color in New Orleans, for under the Spanish government it was not difficult to obtain or buy freedom and the Americans had not as yet imposed their laws on us. I spent most of my time in the city looking after the house and Maurice, who had to study, while the master was out at the plantation. On Sundays I never missed the bam-bousses *in the place Congo, drums and dancing, only a few blocks from where we lived. These* bambousses *were like the* kalendas *in Saint-Domingue, but without the services of the* loas *because at that time everyone in Louisiana was Catholic. Now many are Baptist, because there is singing and dancing in their churches, so it is joyful to worship Jesus. Voodoo, brought from Saint-Domingue by the slaves, was just getting started, and it mixed so much with Christian beliefs that now it's difficult for me to recognize it. In the place Congo we danced from midday to night, and the whites came to be scandalized, and to give them bad thoughts our behinds whirled like windmills, and to make them envious we rubbed against each other like lovers.*

In the morning, after buying the water and firewood that was distributed from house to house in a cart, I would go out shopping. The Marché Français had been in existence for a couple of years, but now it covered several blocks and, after the dike, was the preferred place for social life. It still is. They sell everything there from food to jewels, and there you find the stalls of seers, magicians, and docteurs feuilles. *There is no shortage of charlatans who "cure" with red-dye water and a tonic of sarsaparilla for sterility, birth pain, rheumatic fever, bloody vomit, heart fatigue, broken bones, and almost every other misfortune of the human body. I have no faith in that tonic. If it were that miraculous, Tante Rose would have used it, but she was never interested in the sarsaparilla vine, even though it grew around Saint-Lazare.*

In the market I made friends with other slaves and so learned the customs of Louisiana. As it was in Saint-Domingue, many free persons of color are educated, living from their work and professions, and some are owners of plantations. They say they tend to be more cruel with their slaves than the whites, but I haven't seen that. This is what they told me. In the market you see women of color and whites with their maids carrying baskets. They themselves carry nothing in their hands except gloves and a little bead embroidered reticule for their money. By law, the mulattas dress modestly so as not to annoy the whites. They keep their silks and jewels for nighttime. The men wear ties, wool breeches, high boots, kidskin gloves, and rabbit hair hats. According to Don Sancho, the quadroons of New Orleans are the most beautiful women in the world. "You could be like them, Tété. Look how they walk, light on their feet, swishing their hips, head proud, buttocks held high, bosom defiant. They move like fine fillies. No white woman can walk like that," he told me.

I will never be like those women, but Rosette may be. What would become of my daughter? The master asked me the same thing when I mentioned my freedom again. "Do you want your daughter to live in misery? A slave cannot be emancipated before she is thirty. You have six years to go, so don't bother me with this again!" Six years! I didn't know that law. It was an eternity for me, but it would give Rosette time to grow up protected by her father.

Festivities

In 1795 the Valmorain plantation was inaugurated with a country festival that lasted three days, pure extravagance, as Sancho wanted and as was the practice in Louisiana. The house, Greek in inspiration, was rectangular with two floors; it was surrounded by columns, with a gallery below and a roofed balcony overhead that went around the four sides, with bright rooms and mahogany floors. It was painted with pale colors as the French Creoles and Catholics chose to do, unlike the houses of the American Protestants, which were always white. According to Sancho, it looked like a sugar copy of the Acropolis, but the general opinion cataloged it as one of the most beautiful mansions along the Mississippi River. It still lacked adornment, but it wasn't bare because it was filled with flowers and so many lights that the three nights of celebration were as bright as day. Everyone in the family came, including the tutor, Gaspard Sévérin, wearing a new jacket, a gift from Sancho, and a less pathetic air because in the country he ate and took the sun. In the summer months, when he was taken to the country so Maurice could continue his classes, he could send his entire salary to his siblings in Saint-Domingue. Valmorain rented two barges with bright canopies and twelve oarsmen to transport his guests, who arrived with trunks and personal slaves, even their hairdressers. He hired orchestras of free mulattoes, who took turns so there would always be music, and had obtained enough porcelain plates and silver settings for a regiment. There were walks, horseback riding, hunts, salon games, dances, and always the soul of the gaiety was the indefatigable Sancho, much more hospitable than Valmorain, comfortable either on binges with troublemakers in Le Marais or at parties demanding the best etiquette. The women spent the morning resting; they went outdoors after siesta wearing heavy veils and gloves, and at night attired themselves in their finest gowns. In the gentle lamplight they all seemed natural beauties, with dark eyes, shiny hair, and mother-of-pearl skin, none of the brightly painted faces and false beauty spots used in France, but in the intimacy of the *boudoir* they darkened their eyebrows with charcoal, rubbed red rose petals on their cheeks, traced their lips with carmine, and burnished their gray hair—if they had any—with coffee grounds, and half the curls they pinned atop their heads had belonged to a different head. They wore pastel colors and light fabric; not even recent widows dressed in black, a lugubrious color neither becoming or consoling.

At the three balls the women competed in elegance, some followed by little slaves carrying their trains. Maurice and Rosette, eight and five, performed a demonstration of the waltz, the polka, and the cotillion, which justified the dance teacher's thumps with the rod and provoked exclamations of delight among the crowd. Tété heard the comment that the girl must be Spanish, the daughter of the brother-in-law, what is his name? Sancho or something like that. Rosette, dressed in white silk and black slippers, with a pink ribbon in her long hair, danced with aplomb while Maurice perspired with embarrassment in his gala outfit, counting his steps: two hops to the left, one to the right, bow and half turn, back, forward, and deep bow. Repeat. She led him, ready to disguise with a pirouette of her own inspiration her companion's bumbles. "When I grow up, I will go to balls every night, Maurice. If you want to marry me, you had better learn," she warned him in their practices.

Valmorain had acquired a majordomo for the plantation, and Tété performed the same function, impeccably, in New Orleans, thanks to her lessons in Le Cap from the handsome Zacharie. Both respected the limits of their mutual authority, and during the party had collaborated so that service would run as smooth as oil. They chose three slaves just to carry water and remove chamber pots, and a boy to clean up the foul trail left by two little dogs belonging to Mademoiselle Hortense Guizot that had fallen ill. Valmorain hired two cooks, free mulattoes, and assigned several helpers to Célestine, the house cook. Even among all of them they were barely able to prepare all the fish and shrimp, domesticated and wild birds, Creole dishes, and desserts. A calf was slaughtered, and Owen Murphy directed the outdoor roasting. Valmorain showed his guests the sugar factory, the rum distillery, and the stables, but what he exhibited with most pride were the slave quarters. Murphy had given the slaves three free days, clothing, and sweets, and afterward had them sing in honor of the Virgin Mary. Several women were moved to tears by the blacks' religious fervor. All the guests congratulated Valmorain, although more than one commented behind his back that he would be ruined by such idealism.

At first Tété did not distinguish Hortense Guizot from the other ladies, except by the picky little diarrhea plagued dogs; her instinct failed to warn her of the role that woman would play in her life. Hortense had reached twenty-nine and still was not married, not because she was ugly or poor but because the sweetheart she'd had when she was twenty-four had fallen from his horse while prancing and pirouetting to impress her, and broken his neck. It had been a rare courtship of love, not of convenience, as was usual among Creoles of high breeding. Denise, her personal slave, told Tété that Hortense was the first to come running and find him dead. "She had no chance to tell him good-bye," she added. At the end of the official mourning, Hortense's father began to look for another suitor. The young woman's name had gone from mouth to mouth because of her fiancé's premature death, but she had an irreproachable past. She was tall, blond, rosy cheeked, and robust, like so many Louisiana women who ate with gusto and had little exercise. Her bodice lifted her breasts like melons, to the pleasure of masculine glances. Hortense Guizot spent those three days changing clothing every two or three hours, happy that the memory of her fiancé had not followed her to the celebration. She took over the piano, singing with a soprano voice, and danced with brio till dawn, exhausting all her partners except Sancho. The woman capable of outdoing him had not been born, he said, but he admitted that Hortense was a formidable contender.

On the third day, when the barges had left with their cargo of weary visitors, musicians, servants, and lap dogs and the slaves were cleaning up the scattered trash, an agitated Owen Murphy brought the news that a band of Maroons were coming upriver, killing whites and inciting the Negroes to rebel. It was known that American Indians were sheltering runaway slaves, and others were surviving in the swamps, transformed into beings of mud, water, and green water growth, immune to mosquitoes and serpents' poisons, invisible to the eye of their pursuers, armed with rusted knives and machetes and sharpened rocks, wild with hunger and freedom. First it was heard that there were about thirty attackers, but within a few hours that number had risen to a hundred and fifty.

"Will they come here, Murphy? Do you think our blacks will join them?" Valmorain asked.

"I don't know, monsieur. They're nearby, and they can overrun us. As for our people, no one can predict how they will react."

"And why can't that be predicted? They receive every kind of consideration here—they would not be better off anywhere. Go talk with them!" exclaimed Valmorain, pacing around the drawing room, extremely perturbed.

"These things are not arranged by talking, monsieur," Murphy explained.

"This nightmare is following me! It's useless to treat the blacks well! They are all incorrigible."

"Be calm, brother-in-law," Sancho interrupted. "Nothing has happened yet. We are in Louisiana, not Saint-Domingue, where there were a half million up in arms Negroes and a handful of merciless whites."

"I must save Maurice. Get a boat ready, Murphy," Valmorain ordered. "I am going to the city immediately."

"No, not that!" yelled Sancho. "No one moves from here. We are not going to scurry away like rats. Besides, the river isn't safe; the rebelling blacks have boats. Monsieur Murphy, we are going to protect the property. Bring all the weapons you can lay hands on."

They lined up the weapons on the dining table, and Murphy's two older sons, thirteen and eleven, loaded them and then distributed them among the four whites, including Gaspard Séverin, who had never pressed a trigger and could not aim with his trembling hands. Murphy looked to the slaves, locking the men in the stables and the children in the master's house; the women would not move from the cabins without their children. The majordomo and Tété took charge of the domestics, disoriented by the news. All the Louisiana slaves had heard the whites talk about the danger of an uprising, but they thought that happened only in exotic places, and could not imagine it. Tété charged two women with looking after the children, then helped the majordomo bolt the doors and windows. Célestine reacted better than expected, given her character. She had worked frenetically during the festival, quarrelsome and despotic, competing with the cooks from outside: "Lazy and impudent," she muttered, "being paid for what I am doing for free." She was soaking her feet when Tété came to tell her what was happening. "No one will be hungry," she announced, and with her helpers went into action to feed everyone.

They waited that entire day, Valmorain, Sancho, and the terrified Gaspard Séverin with pistols in hand, while Murphy mounted guard in front of the stables and his sons watched the river to raise the alarm should it be necessary. Leanne Murphy calmed the women with the promise that their children were safe in the house, where they had been given cups of chocolate. At ten o'clock that night, when they were so fatigued that no one could keep on their feet, Brandan, the eldest of the Murphy boys, came on horseback with a torch in one hand and a pistol at his waist to announce that a patrol was approaching. Ten minutes later the men dismounted in front of the house. Valmorain, who by that time had relived the horrors of Saint-Lazare and Le Cap, received them with such a show of relief that Sancho was embarrassed for him. He listened to the report from the patrol and ordered bottles of his best liquor uncorked to celebrate. The crisis had passed: nineteen black rebels had been arrested, eleven were dead, and the rest would be hanged at dawn. All the others had dispersed and were probably headed to their refuges in the swamps. One of the militiamen, a redhead about eighteen years old, excited by the night of adventure and the alcohol, assured Gaspard Sévérin that from living so long in mud the men they hanged had feet like frogs, gills like fish, and a caiman's teeth. Several planters in the area had joined the patrols with enthusiasm for the hunt, a sport they rarely had opportunity to practice on a big scale and swearing to crush the insurgent Negroes to the last man. The losses on the white side were minimal: a murdered overseer, a planter, three wounded patrolmen, and a horse with a broken leg. The uprising was suffocated quickly because a domestic slave had given the alarm. Tomorrow, when the rebels are hanging from their nooses, that man will be free, thought Tété.

The Spanish Hidalgo

Sancho García del Solar came and went between the plantation and the city; he spent more time on a boat or on horseback than in either of the two destinations. Tété never knew when he was going to appear, his horse winded, in the house in the city, day or night; he was always smiling, noisy, gluttonous. One early Monday he fought a duel with another Spaniard, a government official, in the Saint Antoine gardens, the usual place for gentlemen to be killed or at least wounded, the only way to avenge honor. It was a favorite pastime, and the gardens, with their leafy trees, offered the needed privacy. In the house no one knew anything about it until time for breakfast, when Sancho arrived wearing a bloody shirt and asking for coffee and cognac. Laughing heartily, he announced to Tété that he had only a scratch on his ribs, whereas his rival was left with a slash across his face. "Why were you dueling?" she asked as she cleaned the path of the sword thrust, so near the heart that had it entered a little deeper she would be dressing him for the cemetery. "Because he looked at me the wrong way," was his explanation. He was happy he didn't have a dead man on his back. Later Tété found out that the duel had been over Adi Soupir, a quadroon with disturbing curves whom both men claimed.

Sancho would wake the children in the middle of the night to teach them card tricks, and if Tété objected he lifted her off her feet, gave her a couple of whirls, and proceeded to explain that no one can survive in this world without a trick or two, and it was best to learn as soon as possible. At six in the morning it would suddenly occur to him that he wanted roast pig, and she had to fly to the market looking for one, or he would announce that he was going to the tailor, disappear for two days, and come home stupefied with whiskey, accompanied by several comrades to whom he had offered hospitality. He dressed with great care, although soberly, scrutinizing each detail of his appearance in the mirror. He trained the slave who ran errands, a fourteen-year-old boy, to wax his mustache and shave his cheeks with the Spanish gold-handled razor that had been in the García del Solar family for three generations. "Are you going to marry me when I grow up, Uncle Sancho?" Rosette would ask. "Tomorrow if you wish, precious," he would answer, and plant a couple of big smacks on her cheek. Tété he treated like a relative fallen on bad times, with a mixture of familiarity and respect, spiced with jokes. Sometimes, when he suspected she had reached the limit of her patience, he brought her a gift and gave it to her with a compliment and a kiss on the hand, which she accepted with embarrassment. "Hurry and grow up, Rosette, before I marry your mother," he would tease.

In the mornings, Sancho went to the Café des Emigrés, where he joined friends to play dominos. His entertaining hidalgo fanfaronades and his inalterable optimism were in sharp contrast to the French refugees, shrunken and impoverished by exile, who passed through life lamenting the loss of their wealth, real or exaggerated, and discussing politics. The bad news was that Saint-Domingue continued to be sunk in violence; the English had invaded several cities along the coast, though they had not been able to occupy the center of the country, and for that reason the possibility of the colony's achieving independence had cooled. Toussaint, what is that bastard named now? Louverture? Now there's a name he invented! Well, that Toussaint, who was on the side of the Spanish, turned coat and is now fighting at the side of the republican French, who without his aid would be nowhere. Before he changed over,

Toussaint massacred the Spanish troops under his command. You judge whether you can trust that kind of rabble! Général Laveaux promoted him to commandeur in the Cordon Occidental, and now that monkey goes around in a plumed hat. Makes me die laughing. What we have come to, my compatriots! France allied with Negroes! What historical humiliation! the refugees exclaimed between games of dominos.

But there was also optimistic news for the émigrés, since in France the influence of the monarchical colonists was growing and the public did not want to hear another word about the rights of the blacks. If the colonists won the necessary votes, the Assemblée Nationale would be obligated to send enough troops to Saint-Domingue to end the revolt. The island was a fly on the map, they said, it could never confront the power of the French army. With victory, the émigrés could return, and everything would be as it was before; there would be no mercy for the blacks, they would kill them all and bring fresh meat from Africa.

As for Tété, she learned the news from gossips in the Marché Français. Toussaint was a wizard and a seer; he could send a curse from afar and kill with his thoughts. Toussaint won battle after battle, and no shot could penetrate him. Toussaint enjoyed the protection of Jesus, who was very powerful. Tété asked Sancho—she didn't dare bring the subject up with Valmorain—whether some day they would return to Saint-Lazare, and he answered that they would have to be insane to go back into such a slaughterhouse. That confirmed her presentiment that she would never see Gambo again, even though she had heard her master making plans to recover his property in the colony.

Valmorain was concentrating on the plantation rising from the ruins of the previous one, and spent a good part of the year there. In the winter season he moved unwillingly to the house in town. Tété and the children lived in New Orleans and went to the plantation only in the months of heat and epidemics, when all the powerful families escaped from the city. Sancho made hurried visits to the country because he still clung to his idea of planting cotton. He had never seen cotton in its primitive state, only in his starched shirts, and he had a poetic vision of the project that did not include his personal effort. He hired an American agronomist, and before the first plant had been put in the ground was already planning to buy a recently invented cotton picker he believed was going to revolutionize the market. The American and Murphy proposed alternate crops, so when the soil grew weary of cane they would plant cotton, and then the reverse.

The one constant affection in the capricious heart of Sancho García del Solar was his nephew. Maurice had been small and fragile when born, but he turned out to be healthier than Dr. Parmentier had predicted, and the only fevers he suffered were from nerves. He made up in good health what he lacked in toughness. He was studious, sensitive, and quick to weep; he would rather sit contemplating an anthill in the garden or reading stories to Rosette than participate in the Murphy boys' rough games. Sancho, whose personality could not be more different, defended him from Valmorain's criticism. To prevent disappointing his father, Maurice swam in cold water, galloped on unbroken horses, spied on slave girls when they were bathing, and rolled in the dust with the Murphys till their noses bled, but he was incapable of shooting hares or cutting open a live frog to see what was inside. There was nothing of the boastful, frivolous, or bully about him, unlike other boys raised with the same indulgence. Valmorain was worried that he was so quiet and soft hearted, always ready to protect the most vulnerable; to him those seemed signs of a weak character.

Maurice found slavery shocking, and no argument had been able to make him change his mind. Where does he get those ideas when he has always lived surrounded with slaves? his father wondered. The boy had a deep and unremitting vocation for justice, but he had learned early not to ask too many questions in that regard; the subject was not welcome, and the answers left him unsatisfied. "That isn't fair!" he would say before any form of abuse. "Who told you that life is fair, Maurice?" his uncle Sancho would reply. It was the same thing Tété said. His father delivered complicated speeches on the categories imposed by nature that separated human beings and are necessary for the equilibrium of society, and how it must be taken into account that commanding is very difficult, it is much easier to obey. Maurice lacked the maturity and vocabulary to debate with him. He had a vague notion that Rosette was not free, as he was, though in practical terms the difference was imperceptible. He did not associate that girl or Tété with the domestic slaves, and much less with those in the field. He had had his mouth washed out with soap so often that he stopped calling Rosette his sister, but not enough to make him stop loving her with that terrible, possessive, absolute love that solitary children give. Rosette returned his love with an affection free of jealousy or anxiety. He could not imagine life without her, without her incessant chatter, her curiosity, her childish caresses, and the blind admiration she showed him. With Rosette he felt strong, protective, and wise, because that was how she saw him. Everything made him jealous. He suffered if she paid attention, even if for an instant, to any of the Murphy boys, if she made a move without consulting him, if she kept a secret from him. He needed to share with her his most intimate thoughts, fears, and desires, to dominate her and at the same time serve her with total abnegation. The three years that separated them in age were not noticeable. She seemed older than she was, and he younger; she was tall, strong, clever, vivacious, daring, and he was small, naive, withdrawn, timid; she intended to swallow the world and he lived crushed by reality. He lamented in advance the mishaps that could separate them, but she was still too young to imagine a future. Both understood instinctively that their complicity was forbidden; it was made of crystal, transparent and fragile, and had to be defended with eternal pretense. In front of adults they maintained a reserve that Tété found suspicious, and for that reason she spied on them. If she caught them in corners hugging each other, she pulled their ears with excessive fury and then, repentant, covered them with kisses. She could not explain to them why those private little games, so common among other children, were with them a sin. During the time the three of them shared a room, the children felt for each other in the dark, and later, when Maurice slept alone, Rosette visited him in his bed. Tété would wake at midnight without Rosette by her side and have to go on tiptoe to look for her in the boy's room. She would find them sleeping, arms around each other, still in childhood, innocent, but not so innocent that she could ignore what they were doing. "If I catch you in Maurice's bed one more time I am going to give you a thrashing you will remember for the rest of your days, do you understand?" Tété threatened her daughter, terrified of the consequences their love could have. "I don't know how I got here, Maman," Rosette would cry with such conviction that her mother came to believe she walked in her sleep.

Valmorain watched the behavior of his son closely, fearing that he might be weak or suffering some mental disturbance, like his mother. Sancho considered his brother-in-law's doubts absurd. He gave his nephew fencing lessons and proposed to teach him his version of boxing, which consisted of punches and kicking without mercy. "He who strikes first strikes twice, Maurice. Don't wait for them to provoke you, get off a first kick right to the balls," he explained while the boy cried, trying to elude blows. Maurice was bad at sports, but did have a taste for reading he'd inherited from his father, the only planter in Louisiana to have included a library in the plans of his house. Valmorain was not opposed to books in principle, as he himself collected them, but he was afraid that after so much reading his son would turn out to be a weakling. "Open your eyes, Maurice! You have to be a man!" he exhorted, and proceeded to inform him that women are born women, but men are formed through bravery and toughness. "Leave him alone, Toulouse. When the moment comes I will take charge of initiating him into men's ways," Sancho jested, but Tété did not find it amusing.

The Stepmother

*H*ortense Guizot became Maurice's stepmother a year after the festival at the plantation. For months she had been planning her strategy with the complicity of a dozen sisters, aunts, and cousins determined to resolve the drama of her spinsterhood, and of her father, enchanted with the prospect of attracting Valmorain to his henhouse. The Guizots had a smothering respectability but were not as rich as they tried to appear, and a union with Valmorain would have many advantages for them. At first Valmorain was not aware of the strategy being used to catch him; he believed that the Guizot family's attentions were directed toward Sancho, much younger and handsomer than he. When Sancho himself pointed out his error, Valmorain wanted to flee to another continent; he was very comfortable in his bachelor routines, and something as irreversible as matrimony frightened him.

"I scarcely know that demoiselle, I have seen her very little," he contended.

"Neither did you know my sister, and you married her," Sancho reminded him.

"And look at the trouble it caused me!"

"Bachelors always arouse suspicion, Toulouse. Hortense is a stupendous woman."

"If you like her so much, you marry her," Valmorain replied.

"The Guizots have already sniffed me over, brother-in-law. They know I am a poor devil with dissolute habits."

"Less dissolute than some others around here, Sancho. In any case, I do not plan to marry."

But the idea was planted, and in the following weeks he began to consider it, first as foolishness and then as a possibility. He was still young enough to have more children—he had always wanted a large family—and Hortense's voluptuousness seemed a good sign; she was a young woman ready for motherhood. He did not know that she shaved off her years; in fact, she was thirty.

Hortense was a Creole of impeccable lineage and good education; the Ursulines had taught her the basics of reading and writing, geography, history, domestic arts, embroidery, and catechism; she danced with grace and had a pleasant voice. No one doubted her virtue and she was generally well-liked; because of a gentleman's inability to sit his horse she was widowed before she was wed. The Guizots were pillars of tradition; the father had inherited a plantation and Hortense's two older brothers had a prestigious legal office, the only acceptable profession for that class. Hortense's family line compensated for her minimal dowry, and Valmorain wanted to be accepted in society, not so much for himself as to smooth the way for Maurice.

Trapped in the strong web woven by the women, Valmorain agreed to let Sancho lead him through the twists and turns of courtship, more subtle in New Orleans than in Saint-Domingue or Cuba, where he'd fallen in love with Eugenia. "For the moment, no gifts or messages for Hortense; concentrate on the mother. Her approval is essential," Sancho warned him. Marriageable girls were seldom seen in public and only a time or two at the opera, accompanied by the family en masse, because if seen out and about too often they would appear to be a little shady and could end up as spinsters looking after their sisters' children; however, Hortense had a little more freedom. She had passed the age of being "ripe"—between sixteen and twenty-four—and entered the category of a little "stale."

Sancho and the marriage arranging harpies saw that Valmorain and Hortense were invited to soirées, as the dinner and dancing events were called, of family and friends in the intimacy of the home, where they could exchange a few words, though never alone. Protocol forced Valmorain to announce his intentions promptly. Sancho went with him to speak with Monsieur Guizot, and in private they worked out the financial terms of the union, cordially but with absolute clarity. Shortly after, the agreement was celebrated with a *déjeuner de fiançailles*, a luncheon at which Valmorain handed a fashionable ring to his fiancée, a ruby surrounded with diamonds set in gold.

Père Antoine, the most notable priest in Louisiana, married them on a Tuesday afternoon in the cathedral, the only witnesses the close Guizot relatives, a total of ninety-two persons. The bride wanted a private wedding. They entered the church escorted by the Gouverneur's guards, as was de rigueur, and Hortense shone in a pearl embroidered silk gown that had been worn by her grandmother, her mother, and several of her sisters. It was a little snug, even after the work of seamstresses. Following the ceremony, the bouquet of orange blossom and jasmine was sent to the nuns to place at the feet of the Virgin in the chapel. The reception took place in the Guizots' house, with an array of sumptuous dishes prepared by the same caterer Valmorain had hired for the festival at his plantation: pheasant stuffed with chestnuts, duck in marinade, crab blazing in liqueur, fresh oysters, fish of various kinds, turtle soup, cheeses brought from France, and more than forty desserts in addition to a wedding cake of French inspiration: an indestructible edifice of marzipan and dried fruit.

After the guests bid them good-bye, Hortense awaited her husband arrayed in a muslin gown, her blond hair loose across her shoulders, in her virginal chamber; her parents had replaced her bed with one with a canopy. In those years a great fuss was made over the bride's canopy:

blue silk imitating a clear sky with a cloudless horizon and a profusion of plump cupids with bows and arrows, bunches of artificial flowers, and lace bows.

The newlyweds spent three days enclosed in that room, as custom demanded, attended by a pair of slaves who brought them food and removed chamber pots. It would have been disgraceful for the bride to appear in public, even in front of her family, as she was being initiated into the secrets of love. Suffocating with heat, bored in the closed space, with a headache from so many youthful capers at his age, and aware that outside the room a dozen relatives had their ears glued to the wall, Valmorain realized that he had married not only Hortense but the entire Guizot tribe. Finally on the fourth day he could emerge from that prison and escape with his wife to the plantation, where they would learn to know each other with more space and air. Just that week the summer season was beginning and everyone was fleeing the city.

Hortense never doubted that she would trap Valmorain. Even before the relentless procuresses swung into action she had ordered the nuns to embroider sheets with her and Valmorain's initials intertwined. The ones with the initials of the previous fiancé, perfumed with lavender and kept for years in a hope chest, were not wasted; she simply had flowers embroidered over the letters and destined those sheets to guest rooms. As part of her dowry, she brought Denise, the slave who had served her since she was fifteen, the only one who knew how to dress her hair and iron her gowns to her pleasure, and another house slave her father gave her as a wedding present when she mentioned doubts about the majordomo on the Valmorain plantation. She wanted someone she could trust absolutely.

Sancho again asked Valmorain what he planned to do with Tété and Rosette, since the situation could not be hidden. Many whites kept their women of color, but always separate from the legal family. The case of a slave concubine was different. When the master married, the relationship was ended, and he had to give up the woman, who was sold or sent to the fields where the wife would not see her; having a lover and her daughter in the same house, as Valmorain intended to do, was unacceptable. The Guizot family, and Hortense herself, would understand that he had consoled himself with a slave during his years as a widower, but now the problem had to be resolved.

Hortense had seen Rosette dancing with Maurice at the country party and perhaps had suspicions, though Valmorain believed that in all the boisterous confusion she had not noticed much. "Don't be naive, brother-in-law, women have an instinct for these things," Sancho told him. On the day Hortense, accompanied by her court of sisters, came to inspect the house, Valmorain ordered Tété to disappear with Rosette until the end of the visit. He did not want to do anything hurried, he explained to Sancho. Faithful to his character, he preferred to postpone the decision and hope that things would work out on their own. He did not broach the subject with Hortense.

For a while the master continued to sleep with Tété when they were beneath the same roof, but he had not thought it necessary to tell her he was planning to marry; she found that out through the gossip circulating like a windstorm. During the plantation festival she had talked with Denise, a woman of loose tongue, whom she saw again from time to time in the Marché Français, and through her learned that her future mistress was of a fiery and jealous nature. Tété knew that any change would be unfavorable, and that she would not be able to protect Rosette. Once again, crushed by anger and fear, she realized how profoundly powerless she was. If her master had given her an opening, she would have prostrated herself at his feet, she would have gratefully submitted to all his caprices, whatever he wished, as long as he kept the situation as it was, but as soon as he announced his courtship with Hortense Guizot he had stopped calling her to his bed. *Erzulie, mother loa, at least protect Rosette.* Pressured by Sancho, Valmorain came up with the temporary solution that from June to November Tété would stay with the little girl and look after the house in the city while he went with the family to the plantation; in that way he would have time to prepare Hortense. That meant six months more of uncertainty for Tété.

Hortense installed herself in a chamber decorated in imperial blue, in which she slept alone; neither she nor her husband had the custom of sleeping with someone, and after their suffocating honeymoon they needed their own space. Her childhood toys, horrid dolls with glass eyes and human hair, adorned her room, and her curly-haired little dogs slept on her bed, a piece of furniture three meters wide, with carved pillars, a canopy, cushions, curtains, fringe, and pompons, plus a petit-point headboard she had embroidered in the Ursulines' school. Above the bed hung the same silk sky and butterball angels her parents had given her for the wedding.

The recent bride arose after lunch and spent two-thirds of her life in bed, from which she managed the destinies of others. Their first night as a married couple, while still in the paternal house, she welcomed her husband in a negligee with swan plumes around the neckline, very becoming, but deadly for him because the feathers produced an uncontrollable attack of sneezing. Such a bad beginning did not prevent the marriage from being consummated, and Valmorain had the agreeable surprise that his wife responded to his desires with more generosity than either Eugenia or Tété had ever demonstrated.

Hortense was a virgin, but barely. In some way she had succeeded in escaping family vigilance and learned things that maidens had no knowledge of. The deceased fiancé had gone to the grave without knowing she had surrendered to him with great ardor in her imagination, and would continue to do so in all the following years in the privacy of her bed, martyrized by unsatisfied desire and frustrated love. Her married sisters had provided basic information. They were not expert, but at least they knew that any man appreciates a certain show of enthusiasm, though not enough to arouse suspicion. Hortense decided on her own that neither she nor her husband were at an age for prudery. Her sisters told her that the best ways to dominate a husband were to play the fool and to please him in bed. The first would prove to be much more difficult than the second, for there was not one ounce of fool in her.

Valmorain accepted his wife's sensuality as a gift, without asking questions whose answers he would rather not know. Hortense's remarkable body, with its hills and dales, reminded him of Eugenia before her madness, when she still overflowed her gown and naked seemed sculpted of almond paste: pale, soft, fragrant, nothing but abundance and sweetness. Later, the poor woman was reduced to a scarecrow figure, and he could embrace her only when desperate or stupefied with drink. In the golden splendor of the candles, Hortense was a delight to the eyes, the opulent nymph of mythological paintings. He felt his virility, which he had considered irreversibly diminished, reborn. His wife excited him as once Violette Boisier had done in her apartment on the place Clugny, and Tété in her voluptuous adolescence. He was amazed by his ardor, renewed every night, and even at times at midday, when he arrived unexpectedly, boots covered with mud, and surprised her embroidering among the pillows of her bed, expelled the dogs with one sweep of his hand, and fell upon her with the jubilation of again feeling eighteen. Once during his bucking and curveting a cupid from the sky of the bed broke loose and fell on the nape of his neck, stunning him for brief moments. He awaked covered in icy sweat because his old friend Lacroix had appeared in the fog of his unconsciousness to reclaim the treasure he'd stolen from him.

Hortense exhibited the best side of her character in bed; she made little jokes, like crocheting a beautiful cone-shaped hat to tie around her husband's bayonet, and others darker, like inserting a chicken gut in her ass and telling him her intestines were falling out. From so much entanglement in the nun-initialed sheets the two ended by falling in love, just as she had forseeen. They were made for the complicity of marriage because they were essentially different; he was fearful, indecisive, and easy to manipulate, and she had the implacable determination he lacked. Together they would move mountains.

Sancho, who had advocated marriage for his brother-in-law so strongly, was the first to understand Hortense's true character and repent. Outside her blue chamber, Hortense was a different person, mean, avaricious, and fastidious. Only music could elevate her, briefly, above her devastating common sense, illuminating her with an angelic brilliance and filling the house with tremulous trills that awed the slaves and provoked howls from the lapdogs. She had spent several years in the unpleasant role of spinster and was tired of being treated with barely hidden disdain; she wanted to be envied, and for that to happen, her husband would need to be highly placed. Valmorain would need a great deal of money to compensate for his lack of roots among old Creole families and the lamentable fact that he came from Saint-Domingue.

Sancho proposed to keep the woman from destroying the brotherly camaraderie between him and his brother-in-law, and dedicated himself to flattering her with his smooth talk, but Hortense was immune to any squandering of charm that did not serve an immediate practical purpose. She did not like Sancho and kept him at a distance, though she treated him with courtesy in order not to wound her husband, whose weakness for his brother-in-law was to her incomprehensible. Why did he need Sancho? The plantation and the house in the city were his; he could rid himself of that partner who brought in nothing. "The plan to come to Louisiana was Sancho's, it occurred to him before the revolution in Saint-Domingue, and it was he who bought the land. I would not be here if it weren't for him," Valmorain explained when she asked. For her, that male loyalty was a useless and onerous sentimentality. The plantation was just getting under way; it would be at least three years before they could declare it a success, and meanwhile her husband was investing capital, working, and saving, while the other man lived like a duke. "Sancho is like my brother," Valmorain said, with an air of putting an end to the matter. "But he isn't," she replied.

Hortense kept everything locked up, assuming that the servants all stole, and she imposed drastic economic measures that paralyzed the house. The little pieces of sugar they chiseled from the rock hard cone hanging from a hook in the ceiling were counted before being put in the sugar bowl, and someone kept count of how many were used. The food left over from the table was no longer shared among the slaves, as it always had been, but transformed into other dishes. Célestine grew more and more angry. "If they want to eat leftovers of leftovers and crumbs of crumbs, they don't need me, any Negro from the cane fields can serve them as cook," she announced. Her mistress could not abide Célestine, but word had spread about her garlic frog legs, roast chicken with orange, pork gumbo, and little *mille-feuille* baskets filled with crawfish, and when a couple of offers came to buy Célestine for an exorbitant price, she decided to leave her in peace and turn her attention to the field slaves. She calculated that they could gradually reduce their food to the degree they increased discipline, without drastically affecting productivity. If they'd had a good result with the mules, it would be worthwhile to try it with the slaves. Valmorain opposed those measures in principle because they did not coincide with his original project, but his wife argued that that was how it was done in Louisiana. Her plan lasted a week, until Owen Murphy erupted in a rage that shook the trees and the mistress grudgingly had to accept that the cane fields, like the kitchen of her house, were not her purview. Murphy won, but the tone of the plantation had changed. The house slaves went around on tiptoes, and the ones in the fields were afraid the mistress would dismiss Murphy.

Hortense replaced and eliminated servants in an unending game of chess; one never knew whom to ask for something, and no one had a clear idea of duties. That irritated her, and she ended by lashing them with a coachman's whip she carried in her hand the way other women

carry a fan. She convinced Valmorain to sell the majordomo and replace
him with the slave she'd brought from her parents' house. That man
ran around with handfuls of keys, spied on the other workers, and kept
Hortense informed. The process of change did not take long because she
had the unconditional approval of her husband, whom she would notify
of her decisions between trapeze swings in bed. "Come over here, my
love, and show me how seminarians ease their stress." Then, once the
house was moving along as she wanted, Hortense got ready to confront
three pending problems: Maurice, Tété, and Rosette.

Zarité

The master got married; he took his wife and Maurice to the plantation, and I was left for several months alone with Rosette in the house in the city. The children kicked and wept when they were separated and afterward went around peevish for weeks, blaming Madame Hortense. My daughter didn't know her but Maurice had described her, making fun of her songs, her little dogs, her dresses, and her ways; she was the witch, the intruder, the stepmother, the fat woman. He refused to call her Maman, and as his father would not allow him to address her in any other way he stopped speaking to her. He was compelled to greet her with a kiss, but always managed to leave traces of saliva or food on her face, until Madame Hortense herself liberated him from that obligation. Maurice wrote notes and collected little gifts for Rosette, which he sent via Don Sancho, and she answered with drawings and what words she knew how to write.

It was a time of uncertainty, but also of freedom because there was no one to give me orders. Don Sancho spent a good part of his time in New Orleans, but he paid no attention to details; it was enough that I attended to the little he asked. He was entrapped by that quadroon for whom he had fought a duel, a certain Adi Soupir, and was with her more than with us. I asked around about her and did not like what I heard. At eighteen she already had the reputation of being frivolous, greedy, and of having plucked the fortunes of several suitors. This is what I was told. I did not dare warn Don Sancho, he would have been furious. In the mornings Rosette and I went to the Marché Français where I mingled with the other slaves and sat in the shade to talk. Some cheated on their masters' change and bought a glass of lemonade, or a dozen fresh oysters with lime to squeeze over them, but there was no one to ask an accounting of me, and I didn't have to steal. That was before Madame Hortense came to live in the master's house. Many people noticed Rosette, who looked like a little girl from a good family in her taffeta dress and black patent high-button shoes. I have always liked the market, with its fruit and vegetable stands, the spicy fried food, the noisy crowd of shoppers, preachers and charlatans, filthy Indians selling baskets, mutilated beggars, tattooed pirates, priests and nuns, street musicians.

One Wednesday I came to the market with my eyes swollen from crying all night from thinking about Rosette's future. My friends asked so often that finally I admitted the fears that had not let me sleep. The slave women advised me to get a gris-gris *for protection, but I already had one of those amulets: a little sack of herbs, bones, my daughter's fingernails and mine, prepared by a voodoo priestess. It had not helped at all. Someone mentioned Père Antoine, a Spanish priest with an enormous heart, who served the gentry and slaves equally. People adored him. "Go confess to him, he has magic," they told me. I had never confessed, because in Saint-Domingue the slaves had ended by paying for their sins in this world and not the next, but I had no one to go to, and for that reason I took Rosette to see him. I waited a good while; I was the last in the line of supplicants, each with her own guilt and petitions. When my turn came I didn't know what to do, I had never been so close to a Catholic* houngan *before. Père Antoine was still young, but he had an old man's face: long nose, dark, kind eyes, beard like a horse's mane, and turtle feet in very worn sandals. He called us in with a gesture, lifted Rosette up, and sat her on his knees. My daughter did not resist, though he smelled of garlic and his dark brown habit was grimy.*

"Look, Maman! He has hairs in his nose and crumbs in his beard," Rosette commented, to my horror.

"I am very ugly," he replied, laughing.

"I am pretty," she said.

"That is true, child, and in your case God forgives the sin of vanity."

His French sounded like Spanish with a cold. After joking with Rosette for a few minutes, he asked how he could help me. I sent my daughter outside to play so she wouldn't hear. Erzulie, friend loa, forgive me, I wasn't planning to go to the Jesus of the whites, but the affectionate voice of Père Antoine disarmed me and I began to cry again, even though I had cried most of the night. Tears never run out. I told him that our fate was hanging by a thread; the new mistress had a hard heart, and as soon as she suspected that Rosette was her husband's daughter she would take revenge not on him, but on us.

"How do you know that, my daughter?" the priest asked.

"Everything is known, mon père."

"No one knows the future, only God. At times what we most fear turns out to be a blessing. The doors of this church are always open, you can come whenever you want. Perhaps God will allow me to help you when the moment comes."

"The god of the whites frightens me, Père Antoine. He is crueler than Prosper Cambray."

"Than who?"

"The overseer of the plantation on Saint-Domingue. I am not a servant of Jesus, mon père. My gods are the loas *that came with my mother from Guinea. I belong to Erzulie."*

"Yes, daughter, I know your Erzulie." The priest smiled. "My God is the same as your Papa Bondye, but with a different name. Your loas *are like my saints. There is room in the human heart for all the divinities."*

"Voodoo is forbidden in Saint-Domingue, mon père."

"Here you may follow your voodoo, my daughter, because no one cares as long as there is no scandal. Sunday is God's day—come to mass in the morning and in the afternoon go the place Congo to dance with your loas. *What is the problem?"*

He handed me a filthy piece of cloth, his handkerchief, to wipe away my tears, but I preferred the hem of my skirt. When we were leaving, he told me about the Ursuline nuns. That same night I spoke with Don Sancho. This is how it was.

A Time of Hurricanes

ortense Guizot was a whirlwind of renovation in Valmorain's life, for she filled him with optimism, the opposite of what the rest of the family and the people on the plantation felt. Some weekends the couple received guests in the country, following the custom of Creole hospitality, but the visits diminished and soon ended; Hortense's annoyance was evident when someone came without being invited. The Valmorains spent their days alone. Officially, Sancho lived with them, like so many other bachelors attached to a family, but they saw little of him. Sancho looked for reasons to avoid them, and Valmorain missed the camaraderie they'd always shared. Now he passed his hours playing cards with his wife, listening to her sing at the piano, or reading while she painted scene after scene of maidens in swings and little cats with balls of yarn. Hortense's crochet hook flew, making doilies to cover all available surfaces. She had delicate, plump, white hands with perfect fingernails, busy hands for labors of crocheting and embroidering, agile on the keys, audacious in love. They spoke very little, but they understood each other through affectionate gazes and kisses blown from one chair to another in the enormous dining hall where they ate alone. Sancho rarely appeared, and Hortense had suggested that Maurice, when he was with them, should have his food with his tutor in the gazebo in the garden, if the weather permitted, or in the everyday dining room, and in that way take advantage of that time to continue his lessons. Maurice was nine years old but he acted like a baby, according to Hortense, who had a dozen nieces and nephews and considered herself an expert in raising children. He needed to be around boys of his social class and not just those Murphys, so common. He was very spoiled, and he acted like a girl; he should be exposed to the rigors of life, she said.

Valmorain, rejuvenated, shaved off his sideburns and lost a little weight between his nocturnal acrobatics and the meager servings given him at table. He had found the conjugal happiness he had never had with Eugenia. Even his fear of a slave uprising, which had pursued him from Saint-Domingue, was pushed to the background. The plantation did not keep him from sleep because Owen Murphy's efficiency was ever to be praised; what he did not get done he turned over to his adolescent son Brandan, who was robust like his father and practical like his mother, and had worked on horseback since he was six.

Leanne Murphy had given birth to a seventh baby, identical to his brothers, robust and black-haired, but she took time to look after the slave hospital, going there every day with her baby in a little cart. She could not bear the sight of her employer. The first time Hortense tried to meddle in Leanne's territory, the Irishwoman planted herself in front of her with her arms crossed and an expression of icy calm on her face. That was how she had dominated the Murphy clan for more than fifteen years, and it also worked with Hortense. If the manager had not been such a good employee Hortense would have sent all of them packing just to crush that Irish insect, but she was more interested in production. Her father, a planter with antiquated ideas, said that sugar had maintained the Guizots for generations and they had no need to experiment, but she had discussed the advantages of cotton with the American agronomist and, like Sancho, was considering the advantages of cultivating that crop. She could not do it without Owen Murphy.

A strong August hurricane flooded a large part of New Orleans— nothing serious, it often happened, and no one was too disturbed when the streets turned into canals and dirty water ran across their patios. Life went on as always, except that it was wet. That year the damages were few; only the destitute dead emerged from their graves to float in a muddy soup, while the wealthy dead in their mausoleums continued to rest in peace without being exposed to the indignity of losing bones to the jaws of vagrant dogs. In some streets water reached up to the knees, and several men found jobs transporting people on their backs from one place to another, while children had fun splashing around in puddles filled with rubbish and horse dung.

Physicians, always alarmists, warned there would be a terrible epidemic, but Père Antoine organized a procession with the Most Holy in the lead and no one dared make fun of that method for dominating the climate because it always had a good result. By then the priest was already thought of as a saint, even though he'd been in the city only three years. He had lived there briefly in 1790 when the Inquisition sent him to New Orleans with the mission of expelling Jews, castigating heretics, and propagating the faith with blood and fire, but he had no tint of fanaticism and was happy when the indignant citizens of Louisiana, little prepared to tolerate an inquisitor, sent him to Spain without further thought. He returned in 1795 as rector of the St. Louis Cathedral, recently constructed after the previous one had burned. He arrived ready to tolerate the Jews, to turn a blind eye to heretics, and to propagate faith with compassion and charity. He treated everyone the same, without distinguishing among free and slaves, criminals and exemplary citizens, virtuous women and others of the merry persuasion, thieves, buccaneers, lawyers, hangmen, usurers, and excommunicants. They all fit elbow to elbow in his church. The bishops detested him for being insubordinate, but the flock of his faithful loyally defended him. This Père Antoine, with his Capuchin habit and apostle's beard, was the spiritual torch of that sinful city. The day after his procession the water receded from the streets, and that year there was no epidemic.

The Valmorains' house was the only one in the center of the city affected by the flood. The water did not come from the street but surged through the floor, bubbling like heavy sweat. The foundations had hero-ically resisted the pernicious humidity for years, but that insidious attack won out. Sancho found a foreman and a team of stonemasons and car-penters who invaded the first floor with their scaffolds, crowbars, and cranes. The furniture was covered over with sheets and moved to the second floor, which piled up with boxes. They had to take up the paving stones in the patio, put in drains, and demolish the quarters of the domes-tic slaves, which had sunk into mud.

Despite inconveniences and the expense, Valmorain was satisfied; all that uproar gave him more time to confront the problem of Tété. During the visits to New Orleans he made with his wife, he for business and she for the social life, they stayed at the Guizots' home, a little crowded but better than a hotel. Hortense did not show any curiosity about seeing the work at their Valmorain house, but demanded that it be ready by Octo-ber so the family could spend the season in the city. It was very healthy to live in the country, but it was also necessary to establish their presence among respectable folk, that is, those of their class. They had been away too long.

Sancho came to the plantation when the repairs to the house had been finished, boisterous as always, but with the contained impatience of one who must resolve a disagreeable matter. Hortense noticed, and knew in-stinctively that it had to do with the slave whose name was in the air, the concubine. Every time Maurice asked about her or Rosette, Valmorain turned purple. Hortense dragged out dinner and the game of dominos afterward so as not to give the men an opportunity to talk alone. She was afraid of the influence of Sancho, whom she considered a threat, and needed time to bolster in bed her husband's fortitude for any eventuality. At eleven o'clock, Valmorain stretched, yawning, and announced that the time had come to go to bed.

"I have to talk with you in private, Toulouse," Sancho announced, getting to his feet.

"In private? I have no secrets from Hortense," Valmorain replied, with good humor.

"Of course not, but this is a matter for men. Let's go to the library. Excuse me, Hortense," said Sancho, defying the woman with his eyes.

The white gloved majordomo awaited them in the library with the excuse of serving cognac, but Sancho ordered him to withdraw and close the door, then he turned to his brother-in-law, and told him that he had to make up his mind about Tété. It would be October in only eleven days, and the house was now ready to receive the family.

"I do not plan any changes. The woman will continue to serve as always, and she will do well to comply," Valmorain explained, cornered.

"You promised her freedom, Toulouse—you even signed a document."

"Yes, but I don't want her to press me. I will do it at the proper time. If the matter comes up, I will tell Hortense everything. I am sure she will understand. Why are you interested in this, Sancho?"

"Because it would be regrettable to affect your marriage."

"That will not happen. No one can say I am the first to have bedded a slave, Sancho, for God's sake!"

"And Rosette? Her presence will be humiliating for Hortense," Sancho insisted. "It's obvious she's your daughter. But I have a way to remove her from the center of things. The Ursulines accept girls of color and educate them as well as they do whites, but separately, of course. Rosette could spend the next years interned with the nuns."

"That doesn't seem necessary, Sancho."

"The document Tété showed me includes Rosette. When she's free she will have to earn a living, and for that a certain education is necessary, Toulouse. Or do you intend to keep supporting her forever?"

About that time it was decreed in Saint-Domingue that colonists residing outside the island, anywhere except France, were considered traitors, and their properties would be confiscated. Some émigrés attempted to reclaim their lands, but Valmorain hesitated; there was no reason to suppose that racial hatreds had diminished. He decided to accept the advice of his longtime agent in Le Cap, who proposed by letter that he temporarily register the Habitation Saint-Lazare in his own name to prevent its being taken. Hortense branded that idea grotesque—it was obvious that the Jew would appropriate the plantation—but Valmorain trusted the old man who had served his family for more than thirty years, and as she could offer no alternative, that is what he did.

Toussaint Louverture had been made the commander in chief of the armed forces; he reported directly to the government in France and had announced that he would reduce his troops by half so the rest could return to the plantations as free workers. That "free" was relative: they would have to complete at least three years of forced labor under military control, and in the eyes of many blacks that seemed a undisguised return to slavery. Valmorain thought of making a quick trip to Saint-Domingue to evaluate the situation himself, but Hortense sent screams of terror to the skies. She was five months pregnant and her husband could not abandon her in that state and risk his life on that accursed island, and even less sailing the high seas in the middle of hurricane season. Valmorain postponed the trip and promised her that if he recovered his property in Saint-Domingue he would put it in the hands of a manager and they would remain in Louisiana. That calmed the woman for a couple of months, but then she got it in her head that they should not have any investments in Saint-Domingue. For once, Sancho agreed with her. He had a terrible opinion of the island he'd visited a couple of times to see his sister Eugenia. He proposed the idea of selling Saint-Lazare to the first bidder, and with Hortense's help he twisted the arm of his brother-in-law, who finally yielded after weeks of indecision. That land was connected with his father, with the family name, with his youth, he said, but his arguments fell apart against the irrefutable reality that the colony was a battlefield of people of all colors mutually massacring each other.

The humble Gaspard Séverin went back to Saint-Domingue, ignoring the warnings of other refugees, who kept arriving in Louisiana in a sad dribble. The news they brought was depressing, but Séverin had not succeeded in adapting, and wanted to rejoin his family even though he had not been relieved of his bloody nightmares and trembling hands. He would have returned as poor as he left had Sancho García del Solar not handed him a discreet sum in way of a loan, which was what he called it though both of them knew it would never be repaid. Séverin carried Valmorain's authorization to sell the land to the agent. He found him at the address where he had always been though the building was new, the former having been reduced to ashes in the Le Cap fire. Among the articles stored for export that had burned in the warehouses was Eugenia García del Solar's walnut and silver coffin. The old man was still conducting business, selling what little the colony produced and importing from America houses of cypress wood that arrived in pieces ready to be assembled like toys. The demand was insatiable because every skirmish among enemies ended in fire. There were no longer buyers for the things that had brought in so much money in the past: cloth, hats, ironwork, furniture, saddles, shackles, and large cauldrons for boiling molasses.

Two months after the tutor's departure, Valmorain received the agent's response: he had found a buyer for Saint-Lazare, a mulatto officer in Toussaint's army. He could pay very little, but he was the only one interested, and the agent recommended that Valmorain accept the offer because ever since the emancipation of the slaves and the civil war, no one gave anything for land. Hortense had to admit that she had been entirely wrong about the agent; he had turned out to be more honest than could be expected in such stormy times when moral compasses were spinning so madly. The agent sold the property, took his commission, and sent the rest of the payment to Valmorain.

Whiplashes

With Séverin's departure, Maurice's private lessons had ended and his calvary begun in an upper-class boys' school in New Orleans, where he learned nothing but had to defend himself from the bullies who cruelly harassed him; it had not made him bolder, as his father and stepmother had hoped, only more cautious, as his uncle Sancho had feared. He started to suffer again his nightmares of the prisoners in Le Cap, and once or twice wet his bed, though no one knew but Tété, who washed the sheets on the sly. He could not even count on the solace of seeing Rosette since his father did not let him visit her in the Ursulines' convent, and forbade him to mention her in front of Hortense.

Toulouse Valmorain had awaited with exaggerated dread Hortense's meeting with Tété; he didn't know that in Louisiana something that banal did not merit a scene. Among the Guizots, as in all Creole families, no one dared question the patriarch's caprices; wives endured their husbands' cavortings as long as they were discreet, and they always were. Only the legitimate wife and children mattered in this world, and in the next; it would be demeaning to waste jealousy on a slave, better to reserve it for the famous New Orleans free quadroons, who could possess a man to his last breath. But even in the case of courtesans, a well born lady feigned ignorance and held her tongue; that was how Hortense had been brought up. Her majordomo, who was left on the plantation in charge of the large domestic staff, had confirmed her suspicions about Tété.

"Monsieur Valmorain bought her when she was about nine and brought her to Saint-Domingue. She is the only concubine he's known to have, *maîtresse*," he told her.

"And the little brat?"

"Before he married, monsieur treated her like a daughter, and young Maurice loves her like a sister."

"My stepson has a lot to learn," Hortense muttered.

It seemed to her a bad sign that her husband had resorted to complex strategies to keep that woman away for months, perhaps she still attracted him, but the day they entered the renovated and refurbished house, Hortense felt reassured. The servants welcomed them in a row, dressed in their best, with Tété at their head. Valmorain made the introductions with nervous cordiality while his wife measured the slave from top to bottom and inside to out, deciding finally that she did not pose a temptation for anyone, and less for the husband she had eating from her hand. That mulatta was three years younger than she, but she was worn by work and lack of care; her feet were callused, her breasts drooping, and her expression somber. She admitted that Tété was slim and dignified, for a slave, and had an interesting face. She lamented that her husband was so weak; the woman had been spoiled and it had gone to her head. In the days to follow, Valmorain overwhelmed Hortense with attentions, which she interpreted as an express desire to humiliate the former concubine. You don't have to bother, she thought, I will take charge of putting her in her place; but Tété gave her no motive for complaint. The house that awaited them was impeccable, with not even a memory of the clamor of hammers, the mire in the patio, the clouds of dust, the sweat of stonemasons. Everything was in its place, the fireplaces clean, the curtains washed, the balconies adorned with flowers, and the rooms well aired.

At first Tété was frightened and mute as she performed her duties, but at the end of a week she began to relax; she had learned the routines and whims of her new mistress and made a great effort not to provoke her. Hortense was demanding and inflexible; once she gave an order, however irrational it might be, it had to be carried out. She noticed Tété's long, elegant hands, and set her to washing clothes, while the washer-woman idled away the day in the patio because Célestine did not want her as helper; the woman was monumentally stupid and smelled of lye. Then Hortense decided that Tété could not go to bed before she did; she was to wait, dressed, until they came home, even though she rose at dawn and had to work the whole day, stumbling from missed sleep. Valmorain argued weakly that it wasn't necessary for Tété to wait for them—the errand boy was responsible for putting out lamps and closing up the house, and she had Denise to help her out of her clothing—but Hortense insisted. She was despotic with the servants, who had to put up with her screams and slaps, but, swollen from her pregnancy and very busy with her social life, soirées, and spectacles, in addition to her health and beauty treatments, she had neither the agility nor the time to have her way with the whip, as she had at the plantation.

After lunch, Hortense filled some hours with her voice exercises and getting dressed and combed. She did not emerge until four or five in the afternoon, when she was adorned for going out and ready to devote her complete attention to Valmorain. The prevailing style in France was be-coming to her: lightweight gowns in pastel colors trimmed with Grecian frets, high waists with pleated full skirts, and the indispensable lace shawl across her shoulders. Hats were solid constructions with ostrich feathers, ribbons, and tulles that she herself transformed. Just as she had tried to redo leftover food, she recycled her hats; she took pom-poms off one to put on another and removed flowers from a second to add to the first; she even dyed the feathers without affecting their shape, so that every day she displayed a different look.

One Saturday at midnight, when she had been in the city for a couple of weeks and was returning from the theater in their coach, Hortense asked her husband about Tété's daughter.

"Where is that little mulatta girl, my dear? I haven't seen her since we arrived, and Maurice never tires of asking about her," she said in an innocent tone.

"Are you r-referring to Rosette?" Valmorain stuttered, loosening the loop at his neck.

"Is that her name? She's about Maurice's age, isn't she?"

"She's almost seven. She is quite tall. I didn't think you would remember her, you saw her only once," Valmorain answered.

"She was charming dancing with Maurice. She's old enough now to be working. We can get a good price for her," Hortense commented, caressing the nape of her husband's neck.

"I have no plans to sell her, Hortense."

"But I already have a buyer! My sister Olivie noticed her at the party and wants to give her to her daughter when she is fifteen—that will be two months from now. How can we deny her?"

"Rosette is not for sale," he repeated.

"I hope you won't have reason to regret that, Toulouse. That little sniveler is no help to us in any way and can create problems."

"I do not want to discuss this any further!" her husband exclaimed.

"Please, don't yell at me . . ." Hortense murmured on the verge of tears, clutching her round belly with gloved hands.

"Forgive me, Hortense. How hot it is in this coach! Later we will make a decision, dear, there's no hurry."

Hortense realized she had made a mistake. She had to do as her mother and her sisters did, who pulled strings in the darkness, cleverly, without confronting their husbands and letting them think they made the decisions. Marriage was like stepping on eggs: you had to walk with great caution.

———

When Hortense's belly was obvious, and she had to stay in—no lady appeared in public showing proof of having copulated—she lay in bed spinning her crocheted webs like a tarantula. Without moving a hair, she knew exactly what was going on in her fiefdom, society gossip, the local news, friends' secrets, and every step taken by a miserable Maurice. Only Sancho escaped her vigilance; he was so disorderly and unpredictable that it was difficult to follow his trail. Attended by New Orleans's most renowned physician, Hortense gave birth on Christmas Day, in a house invaded by Guizot women. Tété and the rest of the domestics did not have enough hands to serve the visitors. Even in winter, the atmosphere was suffocating, and two slaves were assigned to swing the ventilators in the drawing room and madame's room.

Hortense was no longer in the bloom of youth, and the doctor warned that complications might arise, but in less than four hours a little girl was born, as rubicund as all the Guizots. Toulouse Valmorain, on his knees beside his wife's bed, announced that the child would be named Marie-Hortense, as was appropriate for the firstborn female, and everyone applauded emotionally, except Hortense, who wept with rage because she wanted a male child to compete with Maurice for the inheritance.

A wet nurse was installed in the mansard and Tété sent to a cubicle off the patio, which she shared with two other slaves. According to Hortense, that measure should have been taken much sooner to end Maurice's bad habit of going over to where the slave slept.

Marie-Hortense rejected the teat with such determination that the doctor counseled replacing the wet nurse before the little thing died of malnourishment. That coincided with her baptism, which was celebrated with the best of Célestine's repertoire: suckling pig with cherries, marinated duck, spiced shrimp, different kinds of gumbo, a turtle shell filled with oysters, French pastry, and a cake of several layers crowned with a porcelain cradle. By custom the godmother was from the family of the mother—in this case one of her sisters—and the godfather from the father's, but Hortense did not want a man as dissipated as Sancho, her husband's only relative, to be her daughter's moral guardian, so the honor fell to one of her brothers. That day there were silver boxes engraved with the baby's name and filled with caramel almonds for each of the guests, and a few coins for the slaves. While the diners dug into the food, newly baptized Marie-Hortense bawled with hunger; she had also rejected the second wet nurse. The third did not last two days.

Tété tried to ignore that desperate wailing, but her will weakened, and she presented herself before Valmorain to tell him that at Saint-Lazare Tante Rose had treated a similar case with goat milk. While they found a goat, she boiled rice till it dissolved, added a pinch of salt and a small spoonful of sugar, strained it, and gave it to the baby. Four hours later she prepared a similar brew, this time with oats, and thus from pap to pap, and with the goat they milked in the patio, the baby was saved. "Sometimes these blacks know more than we think," the doctor commented, amazed. Then Hortense decided that Tété should return to the mansard to care for her daughter full time. As her mistress was still secluded, Tété no longer had to wait till the cock crowed to go to bed, and as the child was no bother at night, at last she could rest.

The mistress spent nearly three months in bed, her dogs around her, the fireplace burning, and curtains open to let in the winter sun, consoling her boredom with female friends and plates of sweets. She had never appreciated Célestine so highly. When finally she ended her repose, at the insistence of her mother and her sisters, who were worried about that odalisque lethargy, no dress fit her, so she kept wearing the ones she had worn during her pregnancy, with alterations to make them look different. She emerged from her prostration with new airs, ready to take advantage of the pleasures of the city before the season ended and they had to go back to the plantation. She went out in the company of her husband or her women friends to take a turn along the broad dike, well called the longest road in the world, with its shady trees and enchanting nooks and crannies, where there were always coaches and girls with their chaperones and young men on horseback sneaking glances at them out of the corner of their eyes, along with the rabble that were invisible to Hortense. At times she sent a pair of slaves ahead with the dogs and a picnic, while she took a stroll, followed by Tété carrying Marie-Hortense.

About that time the marquis de Marigny offered his splendid hospitality to a member of the French royalty during his prolonged visit to Louisiana. Marigny had inherited an extraordinary fortune when he was barely fifteen, and it was said that he was the richest man in America. If he weren't, he did everything possible to seem so, lighting his cigars with paper bills. His squandering and extravagance was so extreme that even the decadent upper class of New Orleans was shocked. Père Antoine denounced those displays of opulence from his pulpit, reminding the parishioners that a camel would pass through the eye of a needle before a rich man through the gates to heaven, but his message of moderation went right through his congregation's ears. The proudest families crawled to get an invitation from Marigny; no camel, however biblical, would make them miss those parties.

Hortense and Toulouse were invited not because of their names, as they had hoped, but thanks to Sancho, who had become Marigny's companion and between drinks had hinted that his in-laws would like to meet the noble guest. Sancho had a lot in common with the young marquis—the same heroic bent for risking his skin in duels over imaginary offenses, an inexhaustible energy for entertainment, an extreme gusto for gaming, horses, women, good food, and liquor, and the same divine scorn for money. Sancho García del Solar deserved to be treated like a Creole of purest stock, proclaimed Marigny, who prided himself on being able to recognize a true gentleman with his eyes closed.

The day of the ball, the Valmorain house entered a state of emergency. From the break of dawn the servants trotted back and forth, fulfilling Hortense's peremptory orders, up and down stairs with pails of hot water for the bath, massage creams, diuretic teas to evaporate several years of fat in three hours, applications to clear the skin, shoes, gowns, shawls, ribbons, jewels, face paints. The seamstress was exhausted, and the French hairdresser swooned and had to be resuscitated with a vinegar rub. Valmorain, run into a corner by the frenetic agitation, went with Sancho to kill a few hours in the Café des Emigrés, where there was never a shortage of friends to bet on cards. Finally, after the hairdresser and Denise had shored up Hortense's tower of curls, which were adorned with pheasant feathers and a gold and diamond brooch that matched her necklace and earrings, came the solemn moment of putting on the dress from Paris. Denise and the seamstress had her step into it in order not to disturb the hairdo. It was a prodigy of white veils and deep pleats that gave Hortense the disturbing aspect of an enormous Greco-Roman statue. When they attempted to fasten the back, with its thirty-eight minuscule mother-of-pearl buttons, they found that even with all their tugging and pulling it would not close; despite the diuretics she had, suffering nerves, just that week put on another five pounds. Hortense let out a shriek that nearly shattered the lamps and attracted everyone in the house.

Denise and the seamstress retreated to a corner and curled up on the floor, awaiting death, but Tété, who knew less than they about her mistress, had the bad idea of suggesting she fasten the dress with pins hidden beneath the bow of the sash. Hortense answered with another strident screech, picked up the whip, which she always had near, and threw herself upon Tété, spitting out sailors' curses and lashing her with all the resentment she had accumulated against her, the concubine, as well as irritation she had for herself for having gained the five pounds.

Tété fell to her knees, bent over, covering her head with her arms. *Ssssh, crack!* sang the whip, and every moan from the slave inflamed her mistress further. Eight, nine, ten lashes fell, resounding like powder kegs, and Hortense, red and sweating, her tower of hair collapsed into pathetic hanks, showed no signs of being satisfied.

At that instant Maurice charged into the room like a bull, scattering the paralyzed onlookers, and with one great shove, totally unexpected in a boy who had spent the eleven years of his life trying to avoid violence, he pushed his stepmother to the floor. He grabbed the whip and delivered a blow meant to mark her face, but it landed on her neck, cutting off both her breath and the scream in her throat. He lifted his arm to strike again, as beyond himself as a second before she had been, but somehow Tété got to him, caught hold of his breeches, and pulled him back. The second lash fell on the pleats of Hortense's dress.

The Slave Village

aurice was sent to a boarding school in Boston, something his father had so often threatened, where strict American teachers would make him a man using didactic and disciplinary methods of military inspiration. Maurice went off with his few belongings in a trunk, accompanied by a chaperon hired for the purpose, who left him at the doors of the establishment with a pat of consolation. The boy had not been able to say good-bye to Tété, because the morning after the incident of the whip she was sent without discussion to the plantation, with instructions to Owen Murphy to put her immediately to cutting cane. The manager saw her arrive covered with welts, each the width of a rope for driving oxen, but fortunately none on her face, and sent her to his wife's hospital. Leanne, occupied with a complicated birth, pointed to an aloe pomade Tété should apply, as she was concentrating on a screaming girl terrified by the torment that had been shaking her body for many hours.

Leanne, who had quickly and without much ado given birth to seven sons that were spit out from her chicken frame between two Our Fathers, realized she had a calamity on her hands. She took Tété aside and explained in a low voice, so the girl wouldn't hear, that the baby was lying crossways in the womb, and there was no way for it to get out. "I have never lost a woman in birth, this will be the first," she whispered. "Let me see her, madame," Tété replied. She convinced the girl to let her examine her, oiled her hand, and with her fine and expert fingers found that the mother was dilated and that Leanne's diagnosis was accurate. Through the tight skin of the belly she followed the baby's form as well as if she could see it. She had the girl get on her knees with her head on the floor and rear in the air to relieve pressure on the pelvis as she massaged her belly, pressing with both hands to turn the baby from outside. She had never performed that maneuver but she had watched Tante Rose do it and had not forgotten. At that instant Leanne cried out: a tiny fist had appeared from the birth canal. Tété delicately pushed it back inside to keep from dislocating the arm, until it disappeared inside the mother, and then continued her task with patience, talking with the woman to calm her. At the end of a time that seemed very long, she felt the little creature move, slowly turning to finally slip its head into the birth canal. She could not contain a sob of gratitude, and seemed to see Tante Rose smiling at her side.

Leanne and she each took one arm of the mother, who had realized what was happening and was helping instead of madly resisting, and they walked her in circles, talking to her and stroking her. Outdoors the sun had set, and they realized that they were in the dark. Leanne lighted an oil lamp and they continued until the moment came to receive the baby. "*Erzulie, mother* loa, *help it be born*," Tété prayed aloud. "*Saint Raymond Nonatus, pay attention, do not let an African saint get ahead of you*," Leanne answered in the same tone, and they both burst out laughing. They had the mother crouch over a clean cloth, holding her under her armpits, and ten minutes later Tété held a purplish baby in her hands that, as Leanne cut the cord, she forced to breathe with a slap on the backside.

Once the mother was clean and had the baby on her chest, they cleaned up the bloody rags and remnants from the birth and went to sit on a bench at the door, resting beneath a black, star-filled sky. That was how Owen Murphy found them when he arrived swinging a lantern in one hand and a jug of hot coffee in the other.

"How are things going?" the burly man asked, passing them coffee without coming too close—he was intimidated by female mysteries.

"Your employer has another slave and I have a helper," his wife answered, pointing to Tété.

"Don't complicate my life, Leanne. I have an order to put her in a crew in the cane fields," Murphy mumbled.

"Since when do you obey someone else's orders over mine?" She smiled, standing on tiptoes to kiss him on the neck where the black beard ended.

So that is how it was, and no one asked because Valmorain did not want to know and Hortense had dealt with the irritating matter of the concubine and cleared it from her mind.

On the plantation, Tété shared a cabin with three women and two children. She got up like all the rest with the morning bells and spent the day working in the hospital, the kitchen, with domestic animals, the thousand chores assigned to her by the manager and Leanne. The work seemed light compared with Hortense's whims. Tété had always served in a house, and when she'd been ordered to the field, she believed she was sentenced to the slow death she'd seen in Saint-Domingue. She had never imagined she would find anything resembling happiness.

There were nearly two hundred slaves, some from Africa or the Antilles, but most born in Louisiana, all joined together by the need to support each other and the misfortune of belonging to another human. After the evening bell, when the crews returned from the fields, real life in the community began. Families got together and while there was light stayed outdoors, because there was no space or air in the cabins. From the kitchen in the plantation they were sent soup, which was shared from a cart, and people brought vegetables and eggs and, if there was something to celebrate, hens or hares. There were always chores waiting: cooking, sewing, watering the garden, repairing a roof. Unless it was raining or very cold, the women took time to talk and the men to play the banjo or a game with little stones on a design drawn on the ground. The girls combed each other, the children raced around, groups formed to listen to a story. The favorites about Bras Coupé terrorized both children and adults; he was a gigantic man with one arm who wandered the swamps and had escaped death more than a hundred times.

It was a hierarchical society. The most appreciated were the good hunters, whom Murphy sent to look for meat for the soup—deer, birds, and wild boars. At the top of the ranks were those who had a trade, like the blacksmiths or carpenters, and the least valued were newcomers. Grandmothers gave the orders, but the one who had most authority was the preacher, some fifty years old with skin so dark it looked blue; he was in charge of the mules, oxen, and draft horses. He directed religious songs in an irresistible baritone voice, quoted parables from saints of his invention, and served as arbiter in disputes, because no one wanted to air their problems outside the community. The overseers, though they were slaves and lived with the rest, had few friends. The domestics tended to visit their cabins, but no one liked them because they were arrogant, dressed and ate better than the others did, and might be spies for the masters. Tété was welcomed with cautious respect when it became known that she had turned the baby inside its mother. She said it had been a combined miracle of Erzulie and Saint Raymond Nonatus, and her explanation satisfied everyone, even Owen Murphy, who had never heard of Erzulie and confused her with a Catholic saint.

During hours of rest, the overseers left the slaves in peace; there were no patrolling, armed men or constant barking of tracking dogs, nor a Prosper Cambray in the shadows with his rolled whip claiming an eleven-year-old virgin for his hammock. After dinner, Owen Murphy, with his son Brandan, went around for a last look, ensuring order before going to the house where family was waiting for them to eat and pray. He pretended not to notice if at midnight the odor of burned meat told him that someone had gone out to hunt possum in the dark. As long as the man showed up punctually at dawn, no measures were taken.

As happened everywhere, discontented slaves broke tools, started fires, and mistreated the animals, but those were isolated cases. Others got drunk, and there was always someone reporting to the hospital with a feigned illness to get some rest. Those who were truly ill relied on traditional remedies: slices of potato applied to where it hurt, caiman grease for arthritic bones, boiled thorns to wash out intestinal worms, and Indian roots for colic. It was pointless for Tété to try to introduce any of Tante Rose's formulas; no one wanted to experiment with their health.

Tété found that very few of her companions were obsessed with escaping, as had been true in Saint-Domingue, and if they did, they generally were captured by the highway vigilantes or came back on their own after two or three days, tired of wandering through the swamps. They were flogged and rejoined the community humbled; they did not find much sympathy, no one wanted problems. Itinerant priests and Owen Murphy drove in the virtue of resignation, whose reward was in heaven, where all souls enjoyed equal happiness. Tété thought that seemed more rewarding for whites than for blacks—it would be better if happiness were fairly distributed in this world—but she didn't dare tell Leanne that, for the same reason she good-naturedly attended masses: she didn't want to offend her. She had no faith in the religion of her masters. The voodoo she practiced in her way was also fatalistic, but at least she could experience divine power when mounted by the *loas*.

Before she lived with the field people, Tété didn't know how solitary her life had been with only Maurice and Rosette's affection, without anyone with whom to share memories and hope. She quickly settled into that community; all she missed were the two children. She imagined them alone at night, frightened, and her heart broke with the pain.

"The next time Owen goes to New Orleans, he will bring you news of your daughter," Leanne promised.

"When will that be, madame?"

"It will have to be when the master sends him, Tété. It is very expensive to go to the city, and we are saving every centime."

The Murphys dreamed of buying land and working it along with their children, as so many immigrants did, as well as some free mulattoes and Negroes. There were not many plantations as large as Valmorain's. Most were medium size fields or small ones cultivated by modest families, who if they possessed a few slaves gave them almost the same life as their own. Leanne told Tété that she had come to America in the arms of her parents, who had contracted to work on a plantation as indentured servants for ten years to pay the cost of the passage from Ireland, which in practice was no different from slavery.

"Did you know there are white slaves too, Tété? They're worth less than blacks because they aren't as strong. They do pay more for white women, though. And you know what they use them for."

"I have never seen white slaves, madame."

"There are a lot of them in Barbados, and also here."

Leanne's parents did not calculate that their masters would charge them for each piece of bread they threw in their mouths, or that they would discount each day they didn't work, even if the fault of the weather, so that their debt kept growing, not decreasing.

"My father died after twelve years of forced labor, and my mother and I kept serving for several years more, until God sent us Owen, who fell in love with me and spent all his savings to cancel our debt. That was how my mother and I gained our freedom."

"I never imagined that you had been a slave," said Tété, moved.

"My mother was ill and died shortly after, but she lived to see me free. I know what slavery means. You lose everything—hope, dignity, faith," Leanne added.

"M-monsieur Murphy . . ." Tété stammered, not knowing how to put her question.

"My husband is a good man, Tété, he tries to ease the lives of his people. He does not like slavery. When we have our land, we will cultivate it using only our sons. We will go north, it will be easier there."

"I wish you luck, Madame Murphy, but all of us here will be desolate if you go."

Capitaine La Liberté

*D*r. Parmentier arrived in New Orleans at the beginning of the year 1800, three months after Napoleon Bonaparte was proclaimed first consul of France. The physician had left Saint-Domingue in 1794, following the massacre of more than a thousand white civilians executed by the rebels. Among them had been several of his acquaintances, and that, plus the certainty that he could not live without Adèle and their children, had decided him to leave. After sending his family to Cuba, he had continued to work in the Le Cap hospital with the irrational hope that the storm of the revolution would subside and his family would be able to return. Because he was one of the few medical men left, he was safe from roundups, conspiracies, attacks, and killings, and Toussaint Louverture, who respected that profession like no other, extended him his personal protection. More than protection it was a veiled arrest order, which Parmentier was able to contravene only with the secret complicity of one of Toussaint's closest officers, his *homme de confiance*, a Capitaine La Liberté. Despite his youth—he was just twenty—the capitaine had given proof of absolute loyalty; he had been beside his général day and night for several years, and Toussaint pointed him out as an example of the true warrior, courageous and cautious. It would not be the rash heroes who defied death that would win that long war, Toussaint said, but men like La Liberté, who wanted to live. He assigned him his most delicate missions because of his discretion, and his boldest because of his sangfroid. The capitaine was an adolescent when he put himself under Toussaint's command; he came nearly naked and with no capital but swift legs, a razor-sharp knife for cutting cane, and the name his father had given him in Africa. Toussaint elevated him to the rank of capitaine after the youth saved his life for the third time; another rebel leader set an ambush for him near Limbe in which his brother Jean Pierre was killed. Toussaint's revenge was instantaneous and definitive: he leveled the traitor's camp. In a long conversation near dawn, while survivors dug graves and women piled up bodies before the vultures stole them, Toussaint asked the youth why he was fighting.

"For the same reason we all are fighting, Mon Général, for freedom," he had replied.

"We have that already—slavery was abolished. But we can lose it at any moment."

"Only if we betray one another, Général. United we are strong."

"The road of freedom twists and turns, son. At times it will seem that we are retreating, making pacts, losing sight of the principles of the revolution," the général murmured, observing him with his dagger sharp eyes.

"I was there when the leaders offered the whites a pact to send Negroes back to slavery in exchange for liberty for themselves, their families, and some of their officers," the youth countered, aware that his words could be interpreted as a reproach or a provocation.

"In the strategy of war very few things are clear, we move among shadows," Toussaint explained, unaffected. "Sometimes it is necessary to negotiate."

"Yes, Mon Général, but not at that price. None of your soldiers will be a slave again; we would all prefer death."

"I as well, son," said Toussaint.

"I am sorry about the death of your brother Jean-Pierre, Général."

"Jean-Pierre and I loved each other very much, but personal lives must be sacrificed for the common cause. You are a fine soldier, boy. I will promote you to capitaine. Would you like a last name? What, for example?"

"La Liberté, Mon Général," the youth replied without hesitation, snapping to attention with the military discipline Toussaint's troops copied from the whites.

"Very well. From this day you will be Gambo La Liberté," said Toussaint.

Capitaine La Liberté decided to help Dr. Parmentier quietly leave the island after he placed on the balance scales the strict fulfillment of duty Toussaint had taught him and the debt of gratitude he owed the doctor. The gratitude weighed more. Whites left the island as soon as they obtained a passport and arranged their finances. Most of the women and children had gone to other islands or to the United States, but it was very difficult for the men to get a passport since Toussaint needed them to swell his troops and manage the plantations. The colony was nearly paralyzed; it was short of artisans, planters, businessmen, officials, and professionals of every kind; the only oversupply was in bandits and courtesans, who survived under any circumstance. Gambo La Liberté owed the discreet doctor Général Toussaint's hand and his own life. After the nuns emigrated, Parmentier managed the military hospital with a team of nurses he had trained. He was the only doctor and the only white man in the hospital.

In the attack on Fort Belair a cannon ball destroyed Toussaint's fingers, a dirty, complicated wound for which the obvious solution would have been to amputate, but the général believed that should be a last resort. In his experience as a *docteur feuilles*, Toussaint had preferred to keep his patients whole, as long as it was possible. He wrapped his hand in a poultice of leaves, mounted his noble horse, the famous Bel Argent, and with Gambo La Liberté rode at full gallop to the hospital in Le Cap. Parmentier examined the wound, astonished that without treatment and exposed to the dust of the road, it had not become infected. He ordered half a liter of rum to stun his patient and two orderlies to hold him, but Toussaint refused that help. He was abstemious and he did not allow anyone outside his family to touch him. Parmentier cleaned the wounds, inflicting agonizing pain, and reset the bones, one by one, under the attentive eye of the général, whose solace was to bite into a thick piece of leather. When the doctor completed bandaging him and put the arm in a sling, Toussaint spit out the chewed leather, thanked him courteously, and told him to tend to his capitaine. Then Parmentier turned for the first time toward the man who had brought the general to the hospital, and saw him leaning against the wall, standing in a pool of blood, his eyes glassy.

Gambo twice had one foot in the grave during the five weeks Parmentier kept him in the hospital, and each time had come back to life smiling and with the memory intact of what he had seen in the paradise of Guinea; his father was waiting, there was always music, the trees were bent down with fruit, vegetables grew untended, fish leaped from the water and could be caught without effort, and everyone was free: the island beneath the sea. He had lost a lot of blood from the three shots that had perforated his body: two in a thigh and the third in his chest. Parmentier spent whole days and nights by his side, battling tooth and nail without ever yielding, because he had taken a liking to the capitaine. He was an exceptionally brave man, something he himself would have liked to be.

"It seems to me I've seen you somewhere before, Capitaine," he told him during one of his excruciating treatments.

"Ah! I see you are not one of those whites incapable of distinguishing one black from another," Gambo jested.

"In this work, the color of one's skin matters little; we all bleed alike, but I confess that sometimes it's difficult for me to tell one white from another," Parmentier replied.

"You have a good memory, Doctor. You must have seen me on the Saint-Lazare plantation. I was the cook's assistant."

"I don't remember that, but your face seems familiar," said the physician. "During that time I used to visit my friend Valmorain, and Tante Rose, the healer. I think she got away before the rebels attacked the plantation. I have never seen her again, but I think of her always. Before I knew her, I would have started by cutting off your leg, Capitaine, and then tried to heal you with bloodlettings. I would have quickly killed you even with the best intentions. If you come out alive it's because of methods she taught me. Do you have any news of her?"

"She is a *docteur feuilles* and a *mambo*. I have seen her several times because even my Général Toussaint consults her. She goes from camp to camp healing and giving advice. And you, Doctor, do you know anything about Zarité?"

"About whom?"

"A slave of the white man Valmorain. Tété they called her."

"Yes, I knew her. She went with her master after the Le Cap fire, I think to Cuba," said Parmentier.

"She isn't a slave though, Doctor. She has her freedom. Signed and sealed on a paper."

"Tété showed me that paper, but when they left they still had not legalized her emancipation," the doctor clarified.

During those five weeks, Toussaint Louverture often asked about the capitaine, and on each occasion Parmentier's answer was the same: "If you want me to send him back, don't hurry me, Général." The nurses were in love with La Liberté and could scarcely leave him alone; more than one slipped into his bed at night, climbed upon him without crushing him, and administered in measured doses the best remedy for anemia, as he murmured Zarité's name. Parmentier was not unaware, but concluded that if with love the man was getting well, then let them keep loving him. Finally Gambo recovered sufficiently for him to get on his stallion, throw a musket over his shoulder, and go to rejoin his général.

"I thank you, Doctor. I thought I would never know a decent white man," he said in farewell.

"And I thought I would never know a grateful black one," the doctor replied, smiling.

"I never forget a favor or an offense. I hope to be able to repay you for what you have done for me. Count on me."

"You can do that now, Capitaine, if you wish. I need to join my family in Cuba, and you know that leaving here is nearly impossible."

Eleven days later, on a moonless night, Dr. Parmentier was rowed in a fisherman's skiff to a frigate anchored a certain distance from the port. Capitaine Gambo La Liberté had obtained a safe conduct and a passage, one of the few arrangements he made behind Toussaint Louverture's back during his brilliant military career. As a condition, he charged the physician with delivering a message to Tété should he see her again: "Tell her that my life is war and not love; not to wait for me because I have forgotten her." Parmentier smiled at the discrepancy in the message.

Adverse winds pushed the frigate in which Parmentier was traveling with other French refugees to Jamaica, where they were not allowed to debark, but after many changes of course in the treacherous waters of the Caribbean to elude typhoons and buccaneers, they reached Santiago de Cuba. The doctor traveled by land to Havana to look for Adèle. He had not been able to send her money during the time they'd been separated and did not know in what state of poverty he would find his family. He had an address she had sent by mail several months before, so he reached a barrio of modest but well tended buildings on a paving stone street: saddlers, wig makers, cobblers, furniture makers, painters, and cooks who were preparing food on their patios to sell in the street. Large, majestic black women in starched cotton dresses and brightly colored *tignons* were coming out of their houses balancing baskets and trays with delicious fried foods and pastries, surrounded by naked children and dogs. The houses had no numbers but Parmentier had a description, and it was not difficult to find Adèle's; it was painted cobalt blue and had a red tile roof and a door and two windows embellished with pots of begonias. A card hanging on the front of the house announced in large

Spanish letters: "Madame Adèle, *modas de París*." He knocked with his heart racing, heard a bark and some running footsteps; the door opened, and before him was his youngest daughter, a hand's breadth taller than he remembered her. The girl gave a shout and threw her arms around his neck, wild with joy, and within a few seconds the rest of the family was around him, as his knees doubled with fatigue and love. He had often imagined that he would never see them again.

Refugees

Adèle had changed so little that she was wearing the same dress in which she had left Saint-Domingue a year and a half before. She earned her living sewing, as she always had done, and with great difficulty stretched her modest income to pay her rent and feed her children; it was not in her character to complain about what she didn't have but to be grateful for what she did. She and her children adapted among the many free blacks in the city, and soon she acquired a faithful clientele. She knew her needle and thread trade very well but did not understand fashion. For designs she enlisted Violette Boisier. The two women shared that intimacy that tends to unite people in exile who would not have given each other a second glance in their place of origin.

Violette, with Loula, had settled into a modest house in a barrio of whites and mulattoes, several grades above Adèle in the hierarchy of class thanks to her distinction and the money she had saved in Saint-Domingue. She had emancipated Loula against her wishes and put Jean-Martin in a Catholic school to give him the best possible education. She had ambitious plans for him. At eight, the boy, who had the skin of a bronzed mulatto, had such harmonious features and gestures that if he had not worn his hair very short he could have passed for a girl. No one—he least of all—knew he was adopted; that was a secret sealed between Violette and Loula.

Once her son was safe in the hands of the priests, Violette put out her nets to connect with people of the upper classes who could make their life easier in Havana. She moved among the French because the Spanish and Cubans scorned the refugees who had invaded their island in recent years. The *grands blancs* who arrived with money ended up going out to the provinces, where there was land to spare and they could plant coffee or sugarcane, but the rest survived in the cities, some from their savings or from renting out their slaves; others worked or had businesses, not always legitimate, while the newspaper denounced the seditious competition of the foreigners who were threatening Cuba's stability.

Violette did not have to take badly paying work, like so many of her compatriots, but the cost of living was high, and she had to be careful with her savings. She was not of an age, nor did she have the will, to return to her former profession. Loula intended to trap an affluent husband but Violette still loved Etienne Relais and did not want to impose a stepfather on Jean-Martin. She had spent her life cultivating the art of being well liked, and soon she found a group of women friends among whom she sold Adèle's dresses and the beauty lotions Loula prepared and earned a living that way. Violette and Adèle came to be close friends, the sisters neither had. They had coffee together on Sundays, in house slippers, under an awning on the patio, making plans and adding up bills.

"I will have to tell Madame Relais that her husband died," Parmentier told Adèle when he heard that story.

"You won't have to, she knows already."

"How could she know that?"

"Because the opal in her ring broke," Adèle explained, serving him a second helping of rice with fried plantain and chopped meat.

Dr. Parmentier, who had proposed in his solitary nights to make it up to Adèle for the unconditional love, always in the shadows, she had given him for years, took a separate house and re-created in Havana the dual life he had lived in Le Cap, hiding his family from others' eyes. He became one of the most sought after physicians among the refugees, although he did not gain access to high Havana society. He was the only doctor able to cure cholera with water, soup, and tea, the only one sufficiently honest to admit that there is no remedy for syphilis or yellow fever, the only one who could stop infection in a wound or prevent a scorpion bite from ending in a funeral. His one drawback was that he attended people of all colors. His white patients put up with it because in exile differences of nature tend to be erased and they were not in a situation to demand exclusive attention. They would not, however, have forgiven him a wife and children of mixed blood. That is what he told Adèle, though she never asked for explanations.

Parmentier rented a two story house in a barrio for whites and used the first floor as an office and the second for his living quarters. No one knew that he spent his nights several blocks away in a little cobalt blue house. He saw Violette Boisier on Sundays at Adèle's. The woman was a very well preserved thirty-eight and in the community of émigrés had the reputation of being a virtuous widow. If someone thought he recognized in her a famous cocotte of Le Cap, he immediately discarded that idea as an impossibility. Violette always wore the ring with the broken opal, and there was not a single day she didn't think of Etienne Relais.

None of them had been successful in adapting, and now, several years later, they were just as much foreigners as they'd been on the first day, with the added aggravation that the Cubans' resentment of the refugees had become worse as their numbers grew; they were no longer the wealthy *grands blancs* but ruined people who clustered in barrios where crime and illness fermented. No one liked them. The Spanish authorities harassed them and strewed their paths with legal obstacles, hoping they would succeed in sending them off forever.

A governmental decree annulled any professional license that had not been obtained in Spain, and Parmentier found himself practicing medicine illegally. The parchment with the royal seal of France had no value, and under those conditions he could treat only slaves and poor who rarely were able to pay him. Another difficulty was that he had not learned a single word of Spanish, unlike Adèle and his children, who spoke it at top speed with a Cuban accent.

For her part, Violette finally yielded to Loula's pressure and was on the verge of marrying a sixtyish Galician hotel owner, rich and in ill health, perfect according to Loula because he would soon be gone of a natural death, or with a little aid on her part, and leave them well set. The hotel owner, maddened by that late-in-life love, did not try to clarify rumors that Violette wasn't white because it didn't matter to him. He had never loved anyone as he did that voluptuous woman, and when finally he had her in his arms, he discovered that she provoked in him a senseless grandfatherly tenderness that was comfortable to her because it did not compete with the memory of Etienne Relais. The Galician opened his purse, and she could have spent like a sultana, had she wished, but he had forgotten to mention one thing: he was married. His wife had remained in Spain with their only son, a Dominican priest, and neither of them had any interest in that man whom they hadn't seen in twenty-seven years. Mother and son supposed that he was living in mortal sin, pleasuring himself with fat-assed women in the depraved colonies of the Caribbean, but as long as he sent them money regularly they were not concerned with the state of his soul. This suitor believed that if he married the widow Relais his family would never hear of it, and he would have done so had it not been for the intervention of a greedy lawyer who learned about his past and proposed to reap a good harvest. The Galician realized that he could not buy the lawyer's silence, and that the blackmail would be repeated a thousand times. An epistolary battle was begun, and a few months later the son unexpectedly appeared, prepared to save his father from the claws of Satan and the inheritance from the claws of the harlot. Violette, advised by Parmentier, backed out of the marriage, although she continued to visit her lover from time to time so he would not die of sorrow.

That year Jean-Martin turned thirteen, and for five years had been saying that he was going to follow a military career in France, as his father had. Proud and stubborn, as he had always been, he refused to listen to the arguments of Violette, who did not want to be parted from him and who had a horror of the army, where a boy as handsome as he could end up sodomized by a sergeant. Jean-Martin's insistence was so unshakable that finally his mother had to yield. She used her friendship with a ship captain she had known in Le Cap to get him to France. There he was welcomed by a brother of Etienne Relais, also a military man, who took him to the Paris school for cadets in which all the men of his family had been formed. He knew that his brother had married an Antillean woman and so was not surprised by the boy's color; he would not be the only one of mixed blood in the academy.

Considering that the situation in Cuba was continuously growing worse for refugees, Dr. Parmentier decided to test his fortune in New Orleans, and if things went well, he would send for his family later. Then, for the first time in the eighteen years they had been together, Adèle spoke up and stated that they would not be separated again; they would all go together, or no one would go. She was prepared to continue to live a clandestine life, hidden, like the sin of the man she loved, but she would not allow her family to be torn apart. She proposed that they travel on the same ship, she and the children in third class, and that they debark separately, so that no one would see them together. She herself got passports, after bribing the proper authorities, as was the usual custom, and proving that she was free and could support her children with her work. She was not going to New Orleans to ask for charity, she told the consul with her characteristic smoothness, but to be a seamstress.

When Violette Boisier learned that her friends were planning to emigrate for the second time, she exploded in a fit of rage and weeping, something that had often happened when she was young but not in recent years. She felt betrayed by Adèle.

"How can you follow that man who does not recognize you as the mother of his children?" she sobbed.

"He loves me the best he can," Adèle replied, without anger.

"He has taught his children to pretend in public that they don't know him!" Violette exclaimed.

"But he supports them, educates them, and loves them very much. He is a good father. My life is bound to his, Violette, and we are not going to be apart again."

"And me? What's to become of me here alone?" Violette asked her, disconsolate.

"You could come with us," her friend suggested.

That idea seemed splendid to Violette. She had heard that there was a flourishing society of free people of color in New Orleans, where all of them could prosper. Without losing a minute, she consulted with Loula, and they both agreed that nothing was holding them in Cuba. New Orleans would be their last chance to put down roots and make plans for their old age.

Toulouse Valmorain, who had by means of sporadic letters kept in touch with Parmentier during those seven years, offered him his aid and hospitality, but he warned that there were more physicians in New Orleans than bakers, and the competition would be strong. Fortunately Parmentier's French royal license would be good in Louisiana. "And here," he added in his letter, "you won't have to speak Spanish, my most esteemed friend, because the language is French." Parmentier descended from the ship and fell into the embrace of his friend, who was waiting on the dock. They hadn't seen each other since 1793. Valmorain did not remember his friend being so small and fragile, and in turn Parmentier did not remember Valmorain that rotund. Valmorain had a new air of satisfaction; there was no trace of the tormented man with whom he'd had those interminable philosophical and political discussions in Saint-Domingue.

While the rest of the passengers debarked, they waited for the luggage. Valmorain did not notice Adèle at all, a dark mulatta with two boys and a girl, who was attempting to hire a cart to transport her bundles, but he did notice among the crowd a woman wearing a handsome vermilion travel suit with a hat, bag, and gloves of the same color, so beautiful it would have been impossible not to notice her. He recognized her immediately, although that was the last place he expected to see her. He shouted out her name and ran to greet her with a boyish enthusiasm. "Monsieur Valmorain, what a surprise!" Violette Boisier exclaimed, holding out a gloved hand, but he put his hands on her shoulders and planted three kisses on her face, in the French style. He found, enchanted, that Violette had changed very little, and that the years had made her even more desirable. She told him in a few words that she was widowed, and that Jean-Martin was studying in France. Valmorain did not remember who that Jean-Martin was, but when he learned that she'd come alone, he was overcome by his youthful desires. His farewell words, "I hope you will allow me the honor of visiting you," were spoken in the intimate tone he hadn't used with her for a decade. They were interrupted at that instant by Loula, who was cursing at a pair of porters to get them to carry their trunks. "The rules haven't changed," she told him, elbowing him aside; "you will have to get in line if you plan to be received by madame."

Adèle rented a small cottage on Rampart Street, where many free women of color lived, most of them kept by a white protector, according to the traditional system of *plaçage*, or "left-handed marriage," which had started in the early times of the colony when it was not easy to convince a young European woman to follow a man to those savage lands. There were nearly two thousand arrangements of that kind in the city. Adèle's dwelling was similar to others on her street: small, comfortable, well ventilated, with a back patio with walls covered in bougainvillea. Dr. Parmentier had an apartment a few blocks away, where he had also installed his clinic, but he spent his free hours with his family much more openly than he had in Le Cap or Havana. The only thing strange about this situation was the age of the participants, because a *plaçage* was an arrangement between white men and girls about fifteen; Dr. Parmentier was nearly sixty, and Adèle could have been the grandmother of any of her neighbors.

Violette and Loula found a larger house on Chartres. It took them only a few turns around the place d'Armes, the dike at the hour of the afternoon strolls, and Père Antoine's church at midday on Sunday to assess the vanity of the local women. The whites had succeeded in passing a law that forbade women of color to wear a hat, jewels, or showy clothes in public places, under threat of a lashing. The result was that the mulattas adorned themselves in their *tignons* with such charm that they surpassed the finest hat from Paris, and displayed necklines so tempting that any jewel would have been a distraction; they had such elegant bearing that by comparison the white women looked like washerwomen. Violette and Loula immediately calculated the money they could make with their beauty lotions, especially the snail slime crème and pearls dissolved in lemon juice to clear the skin.

The School in Boston

The whiplash Maurice had dealt Hortense Guizot had not prevented her from attending Marigny's celebrated ball; she masked it under a fine veil that draped to the floor and covered the pins that closed the dress at the back, but the blow left an ugly bruise for several weeks. Using that blemish she had convinced Valmorain to send his son to Boston. She also had another point: she had menstruated only once since the birth of Marie-Hortense. She was pregnant again and had to pamper her nerves; it would be better to send the boy away for a while. Her conception was not a marvel, the rumor she attempted to spread among her friends, but due to the fact that two weeks after giving birth she was frolicking with her husband with the same determination as during her honeymoon. This time it would be a son, she was sure, destined to carry on the family name and the family dynasty. No one dared remind her that a Maurice Valmorain already existed.

Maurice detested the school from the moment he crossed the threshold and the heavy wooden double door closed behind his back. His displeasure lasted unrelieved to the third year, when he had an exceptional teacher. He arrived in Boston in winter beneath an icy mist and found an entirely gray world: overcast sky, squares covered with frost, and skeletal trees with ugly, numbed birds on the naked branches. He had never known true cold. The winter went on forever; he went around with pains in his bones, ears blue with cold, and hands red with chilblains; he did not take off his overcoat even to sleep and lived with one eye on the sky, hoping to see a miserable ray of sun. The dormitory had a coal stove at one end that was lighted only two hours in the evening, so the boys could dry their socks. The sheets were always icy, the walls stained with greenish mold, and to wash in the mornings he had to break a skim of ice on the basins.

The boys, noisy and quarrelsome, in uniforms as gray as the landscape, talked a language Maurice could barely decipher—his tutor Gaspard Séverin had had only a smattering of English—and he had to improvise the rest in his classes with the help of a dictionary. Months went by before he could answer his teachers' questions, and a year before he shared in the jokes of his American companions, who called him "the Frenchy" and bedeviled him with ingenious torments. His uncle Sancho's peculiar notions of boxing were useful because they enabled him to defend himself by kicking his enemies' balls, and his practices in dueling served him well to emerge victorious in the tourneys imposed by the school director, who made bets with the teachers and then punished the loser.

The food had the purely didactic purpose of tempering character. Whoever was capable of swallowing boiled liver or chicken necks with bits of feathers still attached, accompanied by cauliflower and burned rice, could confront the hazards of life, including war, for which the Americans were always preparing. Maurice, used to Célestine's refined kitchen, fasted like a fakir for thirteen days without anyone's caring a whit, and finally, when he fainted from hunger, there was no alternative left but to eat what was put on his plate.

Discipline was as iron hard as it was absurd. The unhappy boys had to leap out of bed at dawn, wash off with icy water, run three times around the courtyard, slipping in pools of water, to warm up—if tingling in your hands can be called warm—and study Latin for two hours before a breakfast of hot chocolate, dry bread, and lumpy oatmeal, then endure several hours of classes and sports, at which Maurice was incompetent. At the end of the day, when the victims were swooning with fatigue, they were given a moralizing lecture for one or two hours, depending on the director's inspiration. Their calvary ended in reciting in chorus the Declaration of Independence.

Maurice, who had been spoiled by Tété growing up, submitted to that prison routine without complaint. Following in the footsteps of the other boys and defending himself from the bullies kept him so busy that his nightmares ended, and he did not think anymore of the gallows in Le Cap. He enjoyed learning. At first, he hid his eagerness for books so as not to be perceived as arrogant, but soon he began to help the others with their lessons and that way earned respect. He did not confess to anyone that he knew how to play the piano, dance a quadrille, and write poetry; the other boys would have drawn and quartered him. His companions watched him write letters with the dedication of a medieval monk, but did not openly make fun because he told them they were for his invalid mother. The mother, like the homeland, was not a subject for jokes: she was sacred.

Maurice coughed throughout the winter, but with spring it cleared up. For months he had huddled in his overcoat, with his head sunk between his shoulders, stooping, invisible. When the sun warmed his bones and he could take off his two jackets, his wool underdrawers, the mufflers, the gloves, and the overcoat, and walk erect, he realized his clothing was too tight and too short. He had undergone one of those classic growth spurts typical of pubescent boys, and from being the thinnest in his level had become one of the tallest and strongest. Observing the world from above, with several centimeters' advantage, made him feel safe.

The summer with its warm humidity did not bother Maurice, used to the boiling climate of the Caribbean. The college emptied, the students and most of the teachers left on vacation, and Maurice was left nearly alone, awaiting instructions to return to his family. Those instructions never arrived; instead his father sent Jules Beluche, the same chaperon who had come with him on the long, depressing voyage on the ship from his home in New Orleans, across the waters of the Gulf of Mexico, sailing around the peninsula of Florida, slipping along the Sargasso Sea, and facing the waves of the Atlantic Ocean, to the school in Boston. The chaperon, a remote relative of the Guizot family who'd fallen on bad times, was a middle-aged man who took pity on the boy and tried to make the voyage as agreeable as possible, but in Maurice's memory it would always be associated with his exile from his paternal hearth.

Beluche appeared at the school with a letter from Valmorain, explaining to his son the reasons why he would not go home that year and containing enough money to buy clothing, books, and any whim he might want to indulge. His orders were to take Maurice on a cultural trip to the historical city of Philadelphia, a place every young man of his position should know because it was there that the seed of the American nation had germinated, as Valmorain's letter pompously stated. Maurice left with Beluche, and for those weeks of forced tourism he remained silent and indifferent, trying to disguise the interest the trip aroused in him and to fight off the sympathy he was beginning to feel for that poor devil Beluche.

The next summer the boy was again left waiting two weeks at the school with his trunk all packed, until the same chaperon showed up to take him to Washington and other cities he had no desire to visit.

Harrison Cobb, one of the few teachers who stayed at the college during Christmas week, had noticed Maurice Valmorain because he was the only student who did not have visitors or gifts, and who spent the holidays reading alone in the nearly empty building. Cobb belonged to one of the oldest families in Boston, established in the city since the beginning of the seventeenth century and of noble origin, as everyone knew but he denied. He was a fanatic defender of the American republic and abominated nobility. He was the first abolitionist Maurice met, and he would mark the boy profoundly. In Louisiana abolitionism was considered worse than syphilis, but in the state of Massachusetts the subject of slavery was discussed constantly because the state's constitution, written twenty years before, contained a clause that prohibited it.

Cobb found an avid intellect in Maurice, and a fervent heart in which his humanitarian arguments immediately took root. Among other books, he had him read *The Interesting Narrative of the Life of Olaudah Equiano*, published in 1789 in London with enormous success. This dramatic story of an African slave, written in the first person, had caused a commotion among European and American audiences, but few knew of it in Louisiana, and the boy had never heard it mentioned. The teacher and his student spent evenings studying, analyzing, and discussing; Maurice could at last articulate the uneasiness slavery had always caused him.

"My father has two hundred plus slaves that one day will be mine," Maurice confessed to Cobb.

"Is that what you want, son?"

"Yes, because I will be able to emancipate them."

"Then there will be two hundred plus Negroes abandoned to their fate and an imprudent boy in poverty. What is gained by that?" his teacher rebutted. "The struggle against slavery is not done plantation by plantation, Maurice, the way people think; the laws in this country and the world must be changed. You must study—prepare yourself and get involved in politics."

"I'm no good for that, sir!"

"How do you know? We all have an unsuspected reserve of strength inside that emerges when life puts us to the test."

Zarité

I had stayed on the plantation almost two years, according to my
calculations, before my masters again brought me to serve with the domestics.
In all that time I had not seen Maurice because during his vacations his father
did not let him come home; he always arranged to send him on a trip to other
places, and finally, when his studies were complete, he took him to France to
meet his grandmother. But that came later. The master wanted to keep him far
away from Madame Hortense. Neither was I able to see Rosette, but Monsieur
Murphy brought me news of her every time he went to New Orleans. "What
are you going to do with that pretty girl, Tété? You'll have to lock her up to
keep her from stirring a storm in the street," he would joke with me.

Madame Hortense gave birth to a second daughter, Marie-Louise, who
was born with a tight chest. The climate did not suit her but since no one can
change the weather, except Père Antoine in extreme cases, not much could be
done to make her comfortable. It was because of her that they brought me back
to the house in the heart of the city. That year Dr. Parmentier had arrived in
New Orleans after a long time in Cuba, and he replaced the Guizot family's
physician. The first thing he did was stop the leeches and mustard rubs, which
were killing the child, and the next was to ask about me. I don't know how he
remembered me after so many years. He convinced the master that I was the
best person to look after Marie-Louise because I had learned a lot from Tante
Rose. Then they ordered the manager to send me to the city. It was very sad to

bid farewell to my friends and the Murphys and travel for the first time alone, with a permit to keep from being arrested.

Many things had changed in New Orleans during my absence; more garbage, more coaches and people, and a fervor of constructing houses and extending streets. Even the market had been expanded. Don Sancho no longer lived in the house with the Valmorains, he had moved to an apartment in the same neighborhood. According to Célestine, he had forgotten Adi Soupir and was in love with a Cuban woman whom no one in the house had ever seen. I moved into the mansard room with Marie-Louise, a pale little thing so weak she didn't even cry. It occurred to me to bind her to my body—that had given a good result with Maurice, who was also born sickly—but Madame Hortense said that that might be fine for blacks but not for her daughter. I did not want to put her in a cradle—she would have died—so I opted to always carry her in my arms.

As soon as I had a chance, I spoke with my master to remind him that I would be thirty that year and was due my freedom.

"Who will care for my daughters?" he asked me.

"I will, if that is what you want, monsieur."

"You mean that everything will be the same?"

"Not the same, monsieur; if I am free, I can leave if I want, none of you can beat me, and you will have to pay me a little so I can live."

"Pay you!" he exclaimed with surprise.

"That's how coachmen, cooks, nurses, seamstresses, and other free persons make a living, monsieur."

"I see you are very well informed. Then you know that no one employs a nursemaid; she is always part of the family, like a second mother, and later like a grandmother, Tété."

"I am not a part of your family, monsieur. I am your property."

"I have always treated you as if you were family! Well, then, if that is what you plan, I will need time to convince Madame Hortense, though it is a dangerous precedent and it will cause a lot of gossip. I will do what I can."

He gave me permission to go see Rosette. My daughter had always been *tall and at eleven she looked fifteen. Monsieur Murphy had not lied, she was very pretty. The nuns had succeeded in curbing her impetuousness but had not erased her dimpled smile and seductive gaze. She greeted me with a formal curtsy, and when I hugged her she went rigid. I think she was embarrassed that her mother was a café au lait slave. My daughter was what mattered most to me in the world. We had lived like a single body, a single soul, until my fear that she would be sold, or that her own father would rape her, as he had me, had forced me to separate from her. More than once I had seen the master feeling her, the way men touch girls to know if they're ripe. That was before he married Madame Hortense, when my Rosette was an innocent little girl and he set her on his lap with affection. My daughter's coolness hurt me; to protect her, I might have lost her.*

Nothing was left of Rosette's African roots. She knew about my loas, and Guinea, but in the school she had forgotten all that and become a Catholic; the nuns were nearly as horrified by voodoo as by Protestants, Jews, and Kaintucks. How could I reproach her for wanting a better life than mine? She wanted to be like Valmorain, not me. She talked to me with false courtesy, in a tone I didn't recognize, as if I were a stranger. This is how I remember it. She told me she liked the school, that the nuns were kind and were teaching her music, religion, and to write with a good hand, but no dance because that tempted the devil. I asked about Maurice, and she told me he was fine but that he felt lonely and wanted to come back. She knew about him because they wrote each other, as they'd done ever since they were separated. The letters took a long time to arrive, but they kept sending them without waiting for answers, like a conversation between fools. Rosette told me that sometimes a half dozen came the same day, but then several weeks would go by with no word. Now, five years later, I know that they addressed each other as "brother" or "sister" to throw off the nuns, who opened their students' correspondence. They had a religious code for referring to their feelings: the Holy Spirit meant love, prayers were kisses, Rosette posed as the guardian angel, he could be any saint or martyr from the Catholic calendar, and, logically, the Ursulines were devils. A typical letter from Maurice said that the Holy Spirit visited him at night, when he was dreaming of the guardian angel, and that he waked with a desire to pray and pray. She answered that she prayed for him and had to be careful among the hordes of devils that were always threatening mortals. Now I guard those letters in a box, and though I can't read them, I know what they say because Maurice read me some parts, those that were not too daring.

Rosette thanked me for the gifts of sweets, ribbons, and books that came, though I didn't know who sent them. How could I buy anything for her without money? I thought that Master Valmorain sent them, but she told me he had never visited. It was Don Sancho who gave the gifts in my name. May Papa Bondye bless the good Don Sancho! Erzulie, mother loa, I have nothing to offer my daughter. This is how it was.

A Promise to Be Kept

At the first possible opportunity Tété went to talk with Père Antoine. She had to wait a couple of hours because he was making his rounds at the jail, visiting prisoners. He brought them food and cleansed their wounds and the guards did not dare stop him because word of his holiness had spread everywhere; some claimed that he had been seen in several places at the same time, and that sometimes a luminous plate floated above his head. Finally the Capuchin monk returned to the little stone house that served as his dwelling and office with his basket empty, wanting only to sit down and rest, but other needs awaited him and it was some time before sunset, the hour of prayer, when his bones took their ease as his soul rose to heaven. "I greatly regret, Sister Lucie, that I do not have the energy to pray more and better," he would say to the nun who attended him. "And why do you need to pray more, *mon père*, if you are already a saint?" she invariably replied. He welcomed Tété with open arms, as he did everyone. He hadn't changed; he had the same sweet eyes of a big dog and the smell of garlic, he wore the same filthy robe, his wood cross, and prophet's beard.

"Where have you been, Tété!" he exclaimed.

"You have thousands of parishioners, *mon père*, and you remember my name," she said, moved.

She explained that she had been at the plantation, and showed him for the second time the yellowed and brittle document of her freedom that she had been keeping for years, though it had done nothing for her because her master always found a reason to postpone what he had promised. Père Antoine put on some thick astronomer's spectacles, took the paper over to the one candle in the room, and slowly read.

"Who else knows of this, Tété? I'm referring to anyone who lives in New Orleans."

"Dr. Parmentier saw it when we were in Saint-Domingue, but he lives here now. I also showed it to Don Sancho, my master's brother-in-law."

The priest sat down at a table with wobbly legs and wrote with difficulty, for the things he saw in this world were enveloped in a light fog, though he saw things in the other world with clarity. He handed her two messages spattered with ink stains and gave her instructions to take them herself to the two gentlemen.

"What do these letters say, *mon père?*" Tété wanted to know.

"For them to come speak with me. And you, too, must be here next Sunday after mass. In the meantime I will keep this document," said the priest.

"Forgive me, *mon père*, but I have never been parted from that paper," Tété replied with apprehension.

"Then this will be the first time." The Capuchin smiled and put the paper in a drawer in the table. "Don't worry, child, it is safe here."

That broken down table did not seem the best place for her most valuable possession, but Tété did not dare show misgivings.

On Sunday half the city gathered in the cathedral, among them the Guizot and Valmorain families with several of their domestics. It was the one place in New Orleans, aside from the market, where white people and those of color, free and slaves, mixed together, though the women were seated on one side and the men on the other. A Protestant pastor visiting the city had written in a newspaper that Père Antoine's church was the most tolerant place in Christianity. Tété could not always attend mass—that depended on Marie-Louise's asthma—but that morning the baby waked feeling well, and they could take her out of the house. After the mass, Tété turned over the two girls to Denise and announced to her mistress that she had to stay a while; she needed to talk with the saint.

Hortense did not object, thinking that at last the woman was going to confession. Teté had brought her satanic superstitions from Saint-Domingue, and no one had greater authority than Pére Antoine to save her soul from voodoo. With her sisters she often commented that the Antilleans were introducing that fearsome African cult in Louisiana, as they had seen when, out of healthy curiosity, they went with their husbands and friends to the place Congo to witness the Negroes' orgies. Once it had been nothing more than shaking and twisting and noise, but now there was a witch who danced as if possessed with a long, fat snake coiled round her body, and half of the participants fell into a trance. Sanité Dédé she was called, and she had come from Saint-Domingue with other Negroes and with the devil in her body. It was something to see the grotesque spectacle of men and women foaming at the mouth and with their eyes rolled back, the same ones who later crawled behind the bushes and wallowed like animals. Those people adored a mixture of African gods, Catholic saints, Moses, the planets, and a place named Guinea. Only Père Antoine understood that hodgepodge and, unfortunately, allowed it. If he weren't a saint, she herself would initiate a public campaign to have him removed from the cathedral, Hortense Guizot made clear. People had told her of the voodoo ceremonies in which they drank the blood of sacrificed animals and the devil appeared in person to copulate with women from the front and the men from behind. It would not surprise her if the slave to whom she entrusted nothing less than her innocent daughters participated in those bacchanals.

In the little stone house the Capuchin, Parmentier, Sancho, and Valmorain were already seated in their chairs, intrigued; they did not know why they had been called. The saint knew the strategic value of the surprise attack. The ancient Sister Lucie, who came in shuffling her house slippers and with difficulty balancing a tray, served them an ordinary wine in chipped little clay cups and withdrew. That was the signal that Tété awaited to go in, as the priest had ordered.

"I have called you to this house of God to rectify a misunderstanding, my sons," said Père Antoine, taking the paper from the desk drawer. "This good woman, Tété, should have been emancipated seven years ago, according to this document. Is that not so, Monsieur Valmorain?"

"Seven? But Tété has just turned thirty! I couldn't have liberated her any sooner!" the one addressed replied.

"According to the Code Noir, a slave who saves the life of a family member of the master has an immediate right to freedom, whatever her age. Tété saved the lives of you and your son Maurice."

"That cannot be proved, *mon père*," replied Valmorain with a disdainful sneer.

"Your plantation on Saint-Domingue was burned, your overseers were murdered, all your slaves escaped to join the rebels. Tell me, my son, do you believe you would have survived without the aid of this woman?"

Valmorain took the paper and glanced over it, breathing heavily.

"This has no date, *mon père*."

"Of course, it seems you forgot to write it in your haste and your anxiety to escape. That is easily understood. Fortunately, Dr. Parmentier saw this paper in 1793 in Le Cap, and that is how we can estimate that it dates from that time. But that is not important. We are among Christian gentlemen, men of faith, with good intentions. I am asking you, Monsieur Valmorain, in God's name, to effect what you promised." The sunken eyes of the saint bored into his soul.

Valmorain turned toward Parmentier, whose eyes were fixed on his cup of wine, paralyzed between loyalty to his friend, to whom he owed so much, and his own nobility, to which Père Antoine had appealed in masterly fashion. Sancho, in contrast, could scarcely hide the smile beneath his bristling mustache. The matter pleased him enormously; for years he had been reminding his brother-in-law of the need to resolve the problem of the concubine, but it had taken nothing less than divine intervention for him to pay attention. He did not understand why he kept Tété if he no longer desired her; she was an obvious nuisance to Hortense. The Valmorains could get another nursemaid for their daughters among their many female slaves.

"Don't worry, *mon père*, my brother-in-law will do what is just," he offered after a brief silence. "Dr. Parmentier and I will be his witnesses. Tomorrow we will go to the judge to legalize Tété's emancipation."

"Agreed, my sons. So now, Tété, from tomorrow on you will be free," Père Antoine announced, lifting his cup in a toast.

The men made the gesture of emptying theirs, but none of them could swallow the concoction, and stood to leave. Tété stopped them.

"Just a minute, please. And Rosette? She has the right to be free too. That is what the document says."

Blood rushed to Valmorain's head, and he could not catch his breath. He clutched the head of his walking stick with pale knuckles, scarcely containing himself from lifting it against the insolent slave, but before he could do that the saint intervened.

"Of course, Tété. Monsieur Valmorain knows that Rosette is included. Tomorrow she, too, will be free. Dr. Parmentier and Don Sancho will see that everything is done in accord with the law. May God bless all of you, my sons. . . ."

The three men left, and the priest invited Tété to have a cup of chocolate to celebrate. One hour later, when she returned to the house, her masters were waiting for her in the drawing room, seated side by side in high-backed chairs like two severe magistrates. Hortense was rabid and Valmorain offended; he could not get it in his head that this woman whom he had counted on for twenty years had humiliated him before the priest and his closest friends. Hortense announced that they would take the affair to the courts, the document had been written under duress and was not valid, but Valmorain would not allow her to continue in that direction. He did not want a scandal.

The masters showered the slave with recriminations that she did not hear because merry bells were jingling in her head. "Ingrate! If all you want is to go, then go immediately. Even your clothing belongs to us, but you can take it so you do not leave naked. I will give you half an hour to get out of this house, and I forbid you ever to enter again. We shall see what becomes of you when you are out in the street! Offer yourself to the sailors like any strumpet, that's the only thing you'll be able to do!" roared Hortense, striking the legs of her chair with her whip.

Tété left the room, closed the door carefully, and went to the kitchen, where the rest of the slaves already knew what was happening. At the risk of attracting her mistress's wrath, Denise offered to let Tété sleep with her and leave at dawn so she would not be in the street at night without a safe conduct. Tété wasn't free yet, and if picked up by the guard would end up in prison, but she was impatient to leave. She embraced each of them with the promise to see them at mass, on the place Congo, or in the market; she did not plan to go far. New Orleans was the perfect city for her, she said. "You won't have a master to protect you, Tété, anything can happen to you, it's very dangerous out there. How are you going to make a living?" Célestine asked her. "The way I always have, working."

She did not stop in her room to collect her meager possessions; she took only her document of freedom and a small basket of food, crossed the square almost floating, turned toward the Cathedral, and knocked on the saint's door. Sister Lucie opened it, holding a candle in her hand, and without a question led her down the hall joining the dwelling with the church to a badly lighted room where a dozen indigents were sitting at a table with plates of soup and bread. Père Antoine was eating with them. "Have a chair, daughter, we've been expecting you. For now, Sister Lucie will provide you a corner to sleep in," he told her.

The next day the saint accompanied her to the court. At the exact hour Valmorain, Parmentier, and Sancho appeared to make legal the emancipation of "the woman Zarité, who is called Tété, a thirty-year-old mulatta of good behavior and loyal service. By way of this document her daughter Rosette, a quadroon of eleven, belongs as a slave to the aforementioned Zarité." The judge ordered a public notice hung so that "any person who has a legal objection should present himself before this Court in the maximum period of forty days from this date." When the ceremony, which lasted barely nine minutes, was ended, they all left in good spirits, including Valmorain. During the night, once Hortense slept, weary from rage and lamentation, he had time to think things through and realized that Sancho was right; he should let Tété go. At the door of the building he touched her arm.

"Although you have inflicted a great injury on me, I hold no rancor against you, woman," he said in a paternal tone, satisfied with his own generosity. "I suppose you will end up begging, but at least I shall save Rosette. She will continue with the Ursulines until she completes her education."

"Your daughter will thank you for it, monsieur," she replied, and danced off down the street.

The Saint of New Orleans

The first two weeks Tété earned her food and a straw mat to sleep on by helping Père Antoine in his many charitable tasks. She got up before dawn, when he had already been praying a good while, and accompanied him to the prison, the hospital, the asylum for the mad, the orphanage, and a few private houses to give communion to the old and the sick abed. The whole day, under sun or rain, the frail figure of the priest with his dark brown robe and tangled beard moved around the city; he was seen in the mansions of the wealthy and in miserable huts, in convents and brothels, seeking charity in the market and cafés, offering bread to mutilated beggars and water to slaves in the auctions at the Maspero Échange, always followed by a pack of starving dogs. He never forgot to console the punished in the stocks installed behind the Cabildo, the most unfortunate of his flock, whose wounds he cleaned with such awkwardness, being as nearsighted as he was, that Tété had to take over.

"What angel hands you have, Tété! The Lord has pointed you out to be a nurse. You will have to stay and work with me," the saint suggested.

"I am not a nun, *mon père*. I cannot work for nothing forever, I must look after my daughter."

"Do not give in to greed, daughter; service to one's neighbor has its payment in heaven, as Jesus promised."

"Tell him to pay me better right here, even if only a little."

"I will tell him, daughter, but Jesus has a lot of expenses," the priest replied with a sly laugh.

At dusk they would return to the little stone house, where Sister Lucie would be waiting with soap and water to clean up before eating with the indigents. Tété would soak her feet in a basin of water and cut strips to make bandages while the priest heard confessions, acted as arbiter, resolved quarrels, and dispelled animosities. He did not give advice, which according to his experience was a waste of time; each person commits his own errors and learns from them.

At night the saint covered himself with a moth-eaten mantle and went out with Tété to rub elbows with the most dangerous rabble, equipped with a lantern since none of the eighty lamp posts in the city was placed where it would help him. The lawless troublemakers tolerated him because he responded to their curses with sarcastic blessings, and no one could intimidate him. He did not come with an attitude of condemnation, or a determination to save souls, but to bandage knife wounds, separate the violent, prevent suicides, succor women, collect corpses, and lead children to the nuns' orphanage. If out of ignorance one of the Kaintucks dared touch him, a hundred fists were raised to teach the foreigner who Père Antoine was. He went into Le Marais, the most depraved place along the Mississippi, protected by his inalterable innocence and his indistinct aureole. There oarsmen, pirates, pimps, whores, army deserters, bingeing sailors, thieves, and murderers gathered in gaming dens and whorehouses. Tété, terrified, inched forward through clay, vomit, shit, and rats, clinging to the Capuchin's habit and invoking Erzulie in a loud voice while the priest savored the thrill of danger. "Jesus watches over us, Tété," he assured her happily. "And if his attention wanders, *mon père*?"

By the end of the second week, Tété had battered feet, an aching back, a heart depressed by human misery, and the suspicion that it would be easier to cut cane than distribute charity among the ungrateful. One

Tuesday in the place d'Armes she ran into Sancho García del Solar, dressed in black and so perfumed that not even flies approached him, very happy because he had just won a game of *écarte* from an overly confident American. He greeted her with a flowery bow and kiss on the hand before several astonished gazes, then invited her to have a cup of coffee.

"It will have to be quick, Don Sancho, because I am waiting for *mon père*, who is off healing the sores of a sinner, and I don't believe he will be long."

"Aren't you helping him, Tété?"

"Yes, but this sinner suffers from the Spanish illness, and *mon père* does not let me see the man's private parts. As if that were a novelty for me."

"The saint is completely right, Tété. If I were attacked by that— may God forbid!—I would not want a beautiful woman to offend my modesty."

"Don't make fun, Don Sancho; that misfortune can happen to anyone. Except Père Antoine, of course."

They sat down at a table facing the square. The owner of the café, a free mulatto acquaintance of Sancho's, did not hide his surprise at the contrast presented by the Spaniard and his companion, one with the air of royalty and the other that of a beggar. Sancho also noticed Tété's pathetic appearance, and when she told him what her life had been during those two weeks he burst out laughing.

"Sainthood certainly is a burden, Tété. You have to escape from Père Antoine or you will end up as decrepit as Sister Lucie," he said.

"I cannot abuse Père Antoine's kindness too much longer, Don Sancho. I will leave when the forty days of the notice in the court ends and I have my freedom. Then I will see what I am going to do; I have to find work."

"And Rosette?"

"She is still with the Ursulines. I know you visit her and take gifts in my name. How can I repay you for your goodness to us, Don Sancho?"

"You owe me nothing, Tété."

"I need to save something to support Rosette when she gets out of the school."

"What does Père Antoine say of all this?" Sancho asked, stirring five spoonfuls of sugar and a dash of cognac into his cup of coffee.

"That God will provide."

"I hope that is the case, but perhaps it would be a good idea if you had an alternate plan. I need a housekeeper—my house is a disaster—but if I hire you the Valmorains will never forgive me."

"I understand, monsieur. Someone will hire me, I'm sure."

"The slaves do all the hard work, from tending the fields to raising the children. Did you know there are three thousand slaves in New Orleans?"

"And how many free persons, monsieur?"

"Some five thousand whites and two thousand of color is what they say."

"That is, there are twice as many free persons as slaves," she calculated. "How can I help but find someone who needs me? An abolitionist, for example."

"An abolitionist in Louisiana? If there are any, they are well hidden," Sancho laughed.

"I don't know how to read, write, or cook, monsieur, but I know how to do things in the house, bring babies into the world, sew up wounds, and heal the sick," she insisted.

"It will not be easy, woman, but I am going to try and help you," Sancho told her. "A friend of mine claims that slaves are more expensive than employees. It takes several slaves to grudgingly do the work one free person does with good will. You understand?"

"More or less," she admitted, memorizing every word to repeat to Père Antoine.

"A slave lacks incentives; for him it is better to work slowly and badly, since his effort benefits only the master, but free people work hard to save and get ahead, that is their incentive."

"At Saint-Lazare, Monsieur Cambray's whip was the incentive," she commented.

"And you've seen how that colony ended, Tété. You cannot impose terror indefinitely."

"You must be a disguised abolitionist, Don Sancho; you talk like Monsieur Zacharie and that tutor in Le Cap, Gaspard Séverin."

"Don't repeat that in public, you will cause me problems. Tomorrow I want to see you right here, clean and well dressed. We are going to call on my friend."

The next day Père Antoine left alone to do his tasks, while Tété, wearing her one dress, recently washed, and her starched *tignon*, went with Sancho to apply for her first job. They did not go far, only a few blocks along picturesque Chartres with its shops of hats, laces, buttons, cloth, and everything that exists to nourish female coquetry, and stopped before a small two story house painted yellow, with green iron railing on the balconies.

Sancho rapped at the door with a small knocker in the shape of a toad, and a fat black woman opened. When she saw Sancho, her expression of bad humor was replaced with an enormous smile. Tété thought she had traveled twenty years in circles, to end at the same place she was when she left Madame Delphine's house. It was Loula. The woman did not recognize her—that would have been impossible—but since she was with Sancho she greeted her and led them to the drawing room. "Madame will be right here, Don Sancho. She is expecting you," she said, and disappeared, making the boards of the floor resound with her elephantine tread.

Minutes later Tété, with her heart leaping, saw the same Violette Boisier of Le Cap at the door, as beautiful as then and with the assurance years and memories bestow. Sancho was transformed in the instant. His

Spanish male pomposity disappeared, and it was a timid boy who bent to kiss the beauty's hand, as the tip of his sword caught and turned over a little table. Tété managed to catch on the fly and clutch to her chest a porcelain medieval troubadour as she stared at Violette with awe. "I suppose this is the woman you were telling me about, Sancho," Violette said. Tété noticed the familiarity of her tone and Sancho's shyness; she remembered the gossip and understood that Violette was the Cuban who, according to Célestine, had replaced Adi Soupir in the Spanish lover's heart.

"Madame . . . we met a long time ago. You bought me from Madame Delphine when I was a girl," Tété managed to get out.

"I did? I d-don't remember," Violette stammered.

"In Le Cap. You bought me for Monsieur Valmorain. I am Zarité."

"Of course! Come to the window so I can see you better. How could I recognize you! You were a skinny little girl then, obsessed with running away."

"I am free now. Well, almost free."

"My God, this is the strangest coincidence. Loula! Come see who's here!" Violette shouted.

Loula came, dragging her huge body, and when she realized who it was, grabbed Tété in a gorilla embrace. Two sentimental tears rose in the woman's eyes when she remembered Honoré, associated in her memory with the little child Tété had been. Loula told Tété that before Madame Delphine went back to France, she had tried to sell him, but he wasn't worth anything, he was just a sick old man, and she had to let him go; he would take care of himself begging.

"He went with the rebels before the revolution. He came to tell me good-bye—we were friends. That Honoré was a true gentleman. I don't know if he managed to reach the mountains; the road was steep, and he had twisted bones. If he got there, who knows whether they accepted him. He was in no condition to fight in any war," Loula sighed.

"I am sure they accepted him—he knew how to drum and to cook.

That is more important than carrying a weapon," Tété said to console her.

She told the priest and the ancient Sister Lucie good-bye, promising to help them tend the sick whenever she could, and moved in with Violette and Loula, as she had longed to do when she was nine. To satisfy a leftover curiosity from two decades back, she asked how much Violette had paid Madame Delphine for her and learned it was the cost of a pair of goats, even though her price went up 15 percent when she was turned over to Valmorain. "That was more than you were worth, Tété. You were an ugly, ill mannered kid," Loula assured her with all seriousness.

They gave Tété the only room for slaves in the house, a room without ventilation but clean, and Violette dug among her clothes and found something adequate for her to wear. Her tasks were so many she couldn't list them, but basically consisted of carrying out the orders of Loula, who no longer had the age or breath for domestic chores and spent the day in the kitchen preparing salves for beauty and syrups for sensuality. No sign on the street announced what was offered inside those walls; word of mouth was enough to attract an endless line of women of all ages, most of them of color, though some whites also came wearing heavy veils.

Violette appeared only in the afternoons; she had not lost the habit of devoting the morning hours to her personal care and to leisure. Her skin, rarely touched by direct sunlight, was as delicate as *crème caramel*, and the fine lines around her eyes gave her character; her hands, which had never washed clothing or cooked, were young, and she had added several pounds that softened her without making her appear matronly. Mysterious lotions had preserved the jet black of her hair, which she combed as she always had in a complicated bun, with a few curls hanging loose to delight the imagination. She still provoked desire in men and jealousy in women and that certainty added a swing to her walk and a purr to her laughter. Her clients confided their cares to her, asked her advice in whispers, and bought her potions without haggling, all with the most absolute discretion. Tété went with Violette to buy the ingredients, from pearls to clear the skin, which she obtained from pirates, to painted glass vials a captain brought her from Italy. "The container is worth more than the content. What matters is the look," Violette told Tété. "Père Antoine maintains the opposite," Tété countered, laughing in return.

Once a week they went to a scribe, who wrote a letter Violette dictated for her son in France. The scribe took responsibility for putting her thoughts into florid phrases and handsome calligraphy. The letters took only two months to reach the hands of the young cadet, who punctually replied with four sentences in military jargon to say that his condition was positive and he was studying the language of the enemy, without specifying which enemy in particular, given that France had several. "Jean-Martin is just like his father," Violette sighed when she read those missives written in code. Tété dared asked how it was that maternity had not made her flesh flabby, and Violette attributed it to her Senegalese grandmother. She did not confess that Jean-Martin was adopted, just as she never mentioned to Tété her affair with Valmorain. However, she told her all about her long relationship with Etienne Relais, her lover and husband, to whose memory she had been faithful until Sancho García del Solar came onto the scene; she had not fallen in love with any of the earlier suitors in Cuba, including the Galician who was on the verge of marrying her.

"I have always had company in my widow's bed to keep myself in shape. That's why I have good skin and good humor."

Tété judged that she herself would soon be wrinkled and melancholy from having consoled herself alone for so many years, with no incentive but the memory of Gambo.

"Don Sancho is a very good man, madame. If you love him, why don't you two get married?"

"What world do you live in, Tété? Whites do not marry women of color, it's against the law. Besides, at my age I have no reason to marry, especially an incurable carouser like Sancho."

"You could live together."

"I don't want to maintain him. Sancho will die a poor man, while I intend to die rich and be buried in a mausoleum crowned with a marble archangel."

A day or two before the time for Tété's emancipation was reached, Sancho and Violette went with her to the Ursulines' school to tell Rosette the news. They met in a room for visitors, large and nearly empty, with four rough wooden chairs and a large crucifix hanging from the ceiling. On a table sat cups of warm chocolate, with a coagulated skim floating on the top, and an urn for the alms that helped maintain the beggars that came to the convent. A nun attended the interview and kept watch out of the corner of her eye; the students could not be in the presence of a male, even the bishop, without a chaperone, and all greater reason a man as seductive as that Spaniard.

Tété had rarely mentioned the subject of slavery with her daughter. Rosette knew vaguely that she and her mother belonged to Valmorain and compared it with the situation of Maurice, who depended completely on his father and could not decide anything for himself. It did not seem strange to her. All the women and girls she knew, free or not, belonged to a man: father, husband, or Jesus. That was, however, the persistent subject of her letters from Maurice, who being free was nevertheless more affected than she by the absolute immorality of slavery, as he called it. In childhood, when the differences between them were less apparent, Maurice had tended to sink into tragic states of mind caused by the two subjects that obsessed him: justice and slavery. "When we grow up, you will be my master and I will be your slave, and we will live together very happy," Rosette told him once. Maurice shook her, choked with tears. "I will never have slaves! Never! Never!"

Among all the students of color Rosette had the lightest skin, and no one doubted that she was the daughter of free parents; only the mother superior, who had accepted her because of the donation Valmorain made to the school, along with the promise that she would be emancipated in the near future, knew her true situation. This visit turned out to be lengthier than the previous ones in which Tété had been alone with her daughter with nothing to say, both of them uncomfortable. Rosette and Violette hit it off immediately. Tété thought that in a certain way they were alike, not so much for their features as for their color and attitude. They passed the visiting hour in lively chatter, while she and Sancho mutely looked on.

"What a clever and pretty girl your Rosette is, Tété! She's the daughter I wish I'd had!" Violette exclaimed as they left.

"What will happen to her when she leaves school, madame? She is used to living like a rich girl; she has never worked, and she thinks she is white." Tété sighed.

"That is still a while away, woman. We'll see," Violette replied.

Zarité

*O*n the appointed day I waited for the judge at the door of the court. *The notice was still attached to the wall, as I had seen it every afternoon for those forty days, when I'd gone, with my soul on a thread and a good luck gris-gris in my hand, to find out whether anyone had opposed my emancipation. Madame Hortense could stop it, it was very easy for her—all she had to do was accuse me of debauchery or bad character—but it seems she did not dare defy her husband. Monsieur Valmorain had a horror of gossip. In those days I'd had time to think, and I had many doubts. Célestine's warnings were ringing in my head, as well as Valmorain's threats; freedom meant I had no help I could count on, no protection or security. If I did not find work, or fell ill, I would end up in the line of beggars the Ursulines fed. And Rosette? "Be calm, Tété. Have faith in God, who never abandons us," Père Antoine would reassure me. No one came to the court in opposition, and on November 30, 1800, the judge signed my freedom and turned Rosette over to me. Only Père Antoine was there; both Don Sancho and Dr. Parmentier, who had promised to come, had forgot. The judge asked me what surname I would like to have and the saint gave me permission to use his. Zarité Sedella, thirty years old, mulatta, free. Rosette, eleven, quadroon, slave, property of Zarité Sedella. That is what the paper said; Père Antoine read it to me word by word before giving me his blessing and a tight hug. This is how it was.*

The saint left immediately to tend to his obligations, and I sat down on a little bench in the place d'Armes to weep with relief. I don't know how long I was there, but it was a long weeping because the sun moved across the sky and my face dried in the shade. Then I felt someone touch my shoulder, and a voice I instantly recognized greeted me: "At last a little calm, Mademoiselle Zarité! I thought you were going to dissolve in tears." It was Zacharie, who had been sitting on another bench watching me, in no hurry. He was the most handsome man in the world, but I had never noticed that before because I was blindly in love with Gambo. In his gala livery at the Intendance in Le Cap he cut an imposing figure, and there in the plaza, in a waistcoat bound with moss colored silk, a batiste shirt, boots with tooled buckles, and several gold rings, he looked even better. "Monsieur Zacharie! Is it really you?" He looked a vision, very distinguished, with a few white hairs at his temples and a slim walking stick with an ivory handle.

He sat down by me and suggested we get past any formal treatment and speak like old friends in view of our long relationship. He told me he had hurried away from Saint-Domingue the minute the end of slavery had been announced and set sail on an American clipper that left him in New York, where he did not know a soul, shivering with cold and unable to understand a word of the gibberish those people speak. He knew that most of the refugees from Saint-Domingue had gone to New Orleans, and so managed to come here. He was doing very well. A couple of days before he had by chance seen the notice of my freedom on the wall of the court; he had investigated, and when he was sure it was the same Zarité he had known, the slave of Monsieur Toulouse Valmorain, he had decided to come on the indicated date, since his boat would be anchored in New Orleans anyway. He had seen me go into the court with Père Antoine, had waited for me in the place d'Armes, and then had the delicacy to let me cry myself out before he said hello.

"I have waited thirty years for this moment, and when it comes, instead of dancing with joy I weep," I told him, embarrassed.

"You have time to dance now, Zarité. We will go out and celebrate this very evening," he offered.

"I don't have anything to wear!"

"*I will buy you a dress, it is the least you deserve on this day, the most important one in your life.*"

"*Are you rich, Zacharie?*"

"*I am poor but I live like a rich man. That is wiser than being rich and living like a poor man.*" *He burst out laughing.* "*When I die, my friends will have to take up a collection to bury me, but my epitaph will say in gold letters: 'Here lies Zacharie, the wealthiest black man along the Mississippi.' I already ordered the inscription on the stone, and I keep it under my bed.*"

"*That's the same thing Madame Violette Boisier wants: an impressive tomb.*"

"*It is the only thing that stays on, Zarité. In a hundred years visitors to the cemetery will be able to admire the tombs of Violette and Zacharie and imagine that we had a good life.*"

He went to the house with me. Halfway there we met two white men, almost as well dressed as Zacharie, who looked him up and down with a sardonic expression. One of them spit very close to Zacharie's feet, but he didn't notice, or preferred to ignore it.

He didn't have to buy me a dress; Madame Violette wanted to get me ready for the first evening out of my life. Loula and she bathed me, massaged me with almond cream, polished my nails, and did the best they could with my feet, though of course they couldn't hide the calluses from so many years of going without shoes. Madame painted my face, and in the mirror I didn't see a gaudily colored me but an almost pretty Zarité Sedella. I put on a muslin dress of Violette's with an empire cut and cape of the same peach color, and she knotted on a silk tignon *in her style. She lent me her taffeta shoes and her large golden earrings, her one jewel aside from the ring with the broken opal that she never removed from her finger. I did not have to leave in clogs and carry the slippers in a bag in order not to dirty them in the street, the usual way, because Zacharie came for me in a rented coach. I supposed that Violette, Loula, and several neighbors who came to look out of curiosity wondered why a gentleman like Zacharie would waste his time with someone as insignificant as me.*

Zacharie brought me two gardenias, which Loula pinned onto my décolletage, and we went to the theater at the Opera. That night they were presenting a work by the composer Joseph Bologne, the chevalier de Saint-Georges, the son of a planter from Guadalupe and his African slave. King Louis XVI named him director of the Paris Opéra, but he didn't last long because the divas and tenors refused to perform under his baton. That is what Zacharie told me. Perhaps none of the whites in the audience that applauded so loudly knew that the music had been composed by a mulatto. We had the best seats in the part reserved for people of color, second floor center. The heavy air in the theater smelled of alcohol, sweat, and tobacco, but I smelled only my gardenias. In the galleries were a number of Kaintucks, who interrupted with jeering shouts, until finally they were pulled out and the music could continue. After that we went to the Salon Orléans, where they were playing waltzes, polkas, and quadrilles, the same dances Maurice and Rosette had learned under their tutor's rod. Zacharie led me without stepping on my feet or running into other couples; we had to cut figures on the floor without flapping our arms or sticking out our rears. There were some white men but no white woman, and Zacharie was the blackest Negro aside from the musicians and waiters, and also the handsomest. He surpassed everyone in height and danced as if he were floating, his smile showing his perfect teeth.

We stayed to dance a half hour, but Zacharie realized that I did not fit in there, and we left. The first thing I did when I got into the coach was take off my shoes. We ended up near the river on a discreet little street far from most of the city's residences. I noticed that there were several coaches with their drivers dozing on the seats, as if they had been waiting quite some time. We stopped before an ivy covered wall with a narrow door, the overhanging lantern shedding a pale light. This entry was guarded by a white man armed with two pistols, who saluted Zacharie respectfully. We walked into a courtyard where a dozen saddled horses stood, and heard the chords of an orchestra. The house, which could not be seen from the street, was a good size, unpretentious, and I couldn't see the inside because heavy drapes were pulled across all the windows. "Welcome to Chez Fleur, the most famous place in New Orleans to come for gaming," Zacharie announced with a broad gesture that took in the entire surroundings. Soon we found ourselves in a large room. Through the cigar smoke I saw white men and men of color, some crowded around gaming tables, others drinking, and some dancing with women in deeply cut dresses. Someone put goblets of champagne in our hands. We could not move forward because someone stopped Zacharie at every step to say hello.

Suddenly an argument broke out among several players and Zacharie made a move to intervene, but faster than he was an enormous person with a mat of hair like wire, a cigar clamped between the teeth, and a wood cutter's boots, who delivered a few ringing slaps that dissolved the argument. Two minutes later the men were sitting with cards in their hands, joking, as if they'd never been cuffed. Zacharie introduced me to the person who had restored order. I thought it was a man with breasts, but it turned out to be a woman with hair on her face. She had the name of a delicate flower and bird that did not go with her looks: Fleur Hirondelle.

Zacharie explained to me that with the money he'd saved for years to buy his freedom, which he'd brought with him when he left Saint-Domingue, plus a bank loan obtained by his partner, Fleur Hirondelle, they were able to buy the house, which had been in bad shape, but they repaired it and put in all the necessary comforts, and even touches of opulence. They had no interference from the authorities, since a part of the take was designated for the inevitable bribes. They sold liquor and food, there was merry music from two orchestras, and they offered the most luscious ladies of the night in Louisiana. These were not employed by the house but were independent artists, as the Chez Fleur was not a brothel; there were many of those in the city and there was no need for another. At the tables fortunes were lost and sometimes won, but the largest part stayed with the house. The Chez Fleur was a good business, though they were still paying off the loan and had a lot of expenses.

"My dream is to have several of these gaming houses, Zarité. Of course it would take white partners, like Fleur Hirondelle, to get the money."

"She's white? She looks like an Indian."

"She is pure blooded French, just burned from the sun."

"You had luck to find her, Zacharie. Partners are not easy; it's better to pay someone to lend you a name. That's what Madame Violette does to get around the law. Don Sancho is a front, but she doesn't let him nose into her business."

At Zacharie's gaming house we danced in my style, and the night went flying by. When he took me back to the house it was nearly dawn, and he had to hold me by one arm because my head was spinning from contentment and champagne, which I'd never had before. Erzulie, loa of love, do not allow me to fall in love with this man because I will suffer, I prayed that night, thinking how the women in the Salon Orléans had looked at him, and how the ones at the Chez Fleur had offered themselves to him.

From the window of the carriage we saw Père Antoine returning to the church, his feet dragging after a night of good works. He was exhausted and we stopped to pick him up, though I was ashamed that my breath smelled of alcohol and my dress was cut low. "I see you have celebrated your first day of freedom in grand style, my daughter. Nothing more deserved in your case than a little dissipation," was all he said before he gave me his blessing.

Just as Zacharie had promised, that was a happy day. This is how I remember it.

The Politics of the Day

n Saint-Domingue, Toussaint Louverture maintained precarious control under a military dictatorship, but the seven years of violence had devastated the colony and impoverished France. Napoleon was not going to allow that bow-legged black, as he called him, to impose conditions. Toussaint had proclaimed himself Gouverneur à Vie, for life, inspired by Napoleon's title of Premier Consul à Vie, and treated him as an equal. Bonaparte planned to crush him like a cockroach, put the blacks to work on the plantations, and return the colony to dominion by the whites. In the Café des Emigrés in New Orleans, the clients followed the confused events of the following months with fervent attention; they had not lost hope of going back to the island. Napoleon sent a large expedition under the command of his brother-in-law, Général Leclerc, who brought with him his beautiful wife Pauline Bonaparte. Napoleon's sister traveled with courtesans, musicians, acrobats, artists, furniture, and decorative objects, everything desirable to establish in the colony a court as splendid as the one she had left behind in Paris.

They left Brest at the end of 1801, and two months later Le Cap was bombarded by Leclerc's ships and reduced to ashes for the second time in ten years. Toussaint Louverture did not blink an eye. Unmoved, he awaited at every instant the precise moment to attack or to fall back, and when that happened his troops left the land leveled, not a tree standing.

The whites who were unable to find refuge under Leclerc's protection were massacred. In April, yellow fever fell like another curse upon the French troops, so little accustomed to the climate and defenseless against the epidemic. Of the seventeen thousand men Leclerc had at the beginning of the expedition, seven thousand were left in lamentable condition; of the remainder, five thousand were dying and another five thousand were in the ground. Again Toussaint was grateful for the timely aid of Macandal's winged armies.

Napoleon sent reinforcements, and in June another three thousand soldiers and officers died of the same fever; there was not enough lime to cover the bodies in the mass graves, where vultures and dogs tore the bodies apart. However, that same month, Toussaint's *z'etoile* burned out in the firmament. The général fell into a trap set by the French under the pretext of a parley; he was arrested and deported to France with his family. Napoleon had conquered the "greatest Negro général of history," as he was defined. Leclerc announced that the only way to restore peace would be to kill every black in the mountains and half those in the plains, men and women, and to leave alive only children under twelve, but he was not able to execute his plan because he fell ill.

The white émigrés in New Orleans, including the monarchists, toasted Napoleon, the invincible, as Toussaint Louverture was slowly dying in an icy cell in a fort in the Alps, at two thousand nine hundred meters near the Swiss border. In Saint-Domingue the war continued, inexorable, through 1802, and very few realized that in that brief campaign Leclerc lost nearly thirty thousand men before he himself perished of the same yellow fever in November. The Premier Consul promised to send another thirty thousand soldiers to the island.

One winter afternoon in 1803, Dr. Parmentier and Tété were talking on Adèle's patio, where they often met. Three years before, when the doctor saw Tété in the Valmorains' house, shortly after he'd arrived from Cuba, he had given her Gambo's message. He told her of the circumstances under which they'd met, his horrible wounds, and the long convalescence that had allowed them to get acquainted. He also told her about how the brave capitaine had helped him get away from Saint-Domingue when that was nearly impossible. "He said for you not to wait for him, Tété, because he had forgotten you, but if he sent you that message it is because he hadn't," the doctor had commented on that occasion. He supposed that Tété had freed herself from the ghost of that love. He had met Zacharie, and anyone could discern his feelings for Tété, though the doctor had never glimpsed between them those possessive gestures that signal intimacy. Perhaps the habit of caution and pretense that had served them in slavery had roots too deep. The Chez Fleur kept Zacharie very busy, and from time to time he also made trips to Cuba and other islands to stock up on liquors, cigars, and other necessities for his business. Tété was never prepared when he appeared at the house on the rue Chartres. Parmentier had met him several times when Violette invited him to dinner. He was friendly and formal, and always came with the classic almond tart to end the meal. With Parmentier, Zacharie talked politics, about which he was obsessive; with Sancho, bets, horses, and his fanciful businesses; and with the women, anything that delighted them. From time to time when Zacharie's partner, Fleur Hirondelle, came with him she seemed to have a curious affinity with Violette. She put her weapons down at the front door, sat to have tea in the little drawing room, and then disappeared inside the house, following Violette. The doctor could swear that she emerged without hair on her face, and once had seen her drop a vial into her powder pouch, surely perfume; he had heard Violette say that all women have a smattering of coquetry in their soul, and a few fragrant drops are enough to awaken it. Zacharie pretended to ignore his partner's weaknesses while he was waiting for Tété to get dressed to go out with him.

Once they took the doctor to the Chez Fleur, where he could appreciate Zacharie and Fleur Hirondelle in their normal surroundings and appreciate Tété's happiness dancing barefoot on the small circular floor in the bar. Just as he had imagined when he met her at the Habitation

Saint-Lazare, when she was very young, Tété possessed a great reserve of sensuality, though at that time it had been hidden beneath her severe expression. Watching her dance, the physician concluded that being emancipated had changed not just her legal status but also liberated that aspect of her character.

In New Orleans, Parmentier's relationship with Adèle was not unusual; several of his friends and patients kept families of color. For the first time the doctor did not have to resort to unworthy strategies to visit his wife—none of that sneaking around at dawn, taking a criminal's precautions not to be seen. He had dinner nearly every night with her, slept in her bed, and the next morning tranquilly returned to his consulting office at ten in the morning, deaf to any commentary he might arouse. He had acknowledged his children, who now bore his surname; the two boys were studying in France and the girl was with the Ursulines. Adèle worked on her sewing and, as she always had, saved as much as she could. Two women helped her with Violette Boisier's corsets, armor reinforced with whalebone, which gave curves to the flattest woman and could not be seen, so dresses seemed to float over a naked body. The whites wondered how a style inspired by ancient Greece could look better on Africans than on them. Tété came and went between houses with patterns, measurements, cloth, corsets, and finished dresses, which Violette was then responsible for selling among her clients.

One evening Parmentier sat talking with Tété and Adèle on the patio of the bougainvillea, at that time of year pale bare sticks without flowers or leaves.

"Toussaint Louverture died seven months ago. Another of Napoleon's crimes. They killed him with hunger, cold, and loneliness in the prison, but he will not be forgotten; the général made his way into history," said the doctor.

They were drinking sherry after a meal of catfish and vegetables, since among her many virtues Adèle was a fine cook. The patio was the most agreeable place in the house, even on cool nights like that one.

A faint light shone from a brazier that Adèle had lit to make charcoal for ironing and for keeping the small circle of friends warm.

"Toussaint's death did not mean the end of the revolution. Now Général Dessaline is in command. They say he is unflinching," the physician continued.

"What must have happened to Gambo? He didn't trust anyone, even Toussaint," Tété commented.

"He later changed his opinion of Toussaint. More than once he risked his life to save him; he was the général's *homme de confiance*."

"Then he was with the général when he was arrested," said Tété.

"Toussaint went to a rendezvous with the French to negotiate a political settlement for the war, but he was betrayed. While he was waiting inside the house, they assassinated his guards and the soldiers who accompanied him. I'm afraid that Capitaine La Liberté fell that day defending his général," Parmentier explained sadly.

"Before, Doctor, Gambo used to be with me."

"How was that?"

"In dreams," said Tété vaguely.

She didn't clarify that she used to call to him every night in her thoughts, like a prayer, and sometimes was able to summon him so successfully that she waked beside his heavy, warm, languid body, with the happiness of having slept in her lover's arms. She felt the warmth and smell of Gambo on her skin, and when that happened she didn't wash, to prolong the illusion of having been with him. Those encounters in her dreams were the only solace in the loneliness of her bed, but that had been a long time ago, and now she had accepted Gambo's death; if he were alive he would somehow have communicated with her. Now she had Zacharie. On the nights they shared, when he was available, she rested satisfied and grateful after making love, with Zacharie's large hand on her. Ever since he had been in her life she had not returned to her secret habit of caressing herself as she called to Gambo, because to want another man's kisses, even a ghost's, would have been a betrayal

Zacharie did not deserve. The secure and calm affection they shared filled her life; she did not need more.

"No one came out alive from the ambush they set up for Toussaint. There were no prisoners other than the général, and later his family, whom they also arrested," Parmentier added.

"I know they didn't take Gambo alive, Doctor, he would never have surrendered. So much sacrifice and so much war to have the whites win in the end!"

"They haven't won yet. The revolution is still going on. Général Dessalines has just vanquished Napoleon's troops and the French have begun to evacuate. Soon we will have another wave of refugees here, and this time they'll be Bonapartists. Dessalines has called on the white colonists to take back their plantations; he says they are needed to produce the wealth the colony once enjoyed."

"We've heard that story several times, Doctor, Toussaint did the same thing. Would you go back to Saint-Domingue?" Tété asked him.

"My family is better here. We will stay. And you?"

"Yes, me too. Here I am free, and Rosette will be very soon."

"Isn't she very young to be emancipated?"

"Père Antoine is helping me. He knows half the world up and down the Mississippi, and no judge would dare deny him a favor."

That night Parmentier asked Tété about her relationship with Tante Rose. He knew that besides helping her in births and healings, she also helped prepare her medications, and he was interested in the recipes for them. She remembered most of them and assured him they weren't complicated, they could obtain the ingredients from the *docteurs feuilles* in the Marché Français. They talked about ways to lower fevers and prevent infections, about infusions to cleanse the liver and relieve bladder and kidney stones, about the salts for migraines, herbs to abort and to stop hemorrhages, about diuretics, laxatives, and formulas to build up the blood, all of which Tété knew from memory. Both laughed about the sarsaparilla tonic the Creoles used for all their illnesses, and agreed that

Tante Rose's knowledge was greatly missed. The next day Parmentier called on Violette Boisier to propose that she broaden her beauty lotion business with a list of curative products from the pharmacopeia of Tante Rose, which Tété could prepare in the kitchen and he would agree to buy in their totality. Violette accepted with no hesitation. The arrangement seemed good all the way around: the doctor would get remedies, Tété would collect for her part, and she would be left with the rest without turning a hand.

The Americans

hen New Orleans was shaken by the most unlikely of rumors. In cafés and taverns, on street corners and squares, people stood around commenting, with irritation and exasperation, on the news, still unconfirmed, that Napoleon Bonaparte had sold Louisiana to the Americans. As the days raced by the idea prevailed that it wasn't true, but they kept talking about the accursed Corsican, because remember, monsieurs, that Napoleon is from Corsica; it can't be said that he's French, he has sold us to the Kaintucks. It was the most formidable and cheap land transaction in history, more than 828,000 square miles—by American reckoning—for the sum of fifteen million dollars, that is, a few cents an acre. The greater part of that territory, occupied by scattered indigenous tribes, had never been explored as it should by whites, and no one could imagine it, but when Sancho García del Solar circulated a map of the continent showing the furthermost reaches, it could be calculated that the Americans had doubled the size of their country. And now what will become of us? How did Napoleon get his hand in this business? Are we not a Spanish colony? Three years before, in the secret treaty of San Ildefonso, Spain had handed Louisiana to France, but very few people knew that yet and life had gone on as usual. The change of government hadn't been noticed; the Spanish authorities stayed on in their posts while Napoleon fought against Turks, Austrians, Italians, and anyone else who got in his way, in addition to rebels in Saint-Domingue. He had to fight on too many fronts, even against England, his ancestral enemy, and he needed time, troops, and money; he could not occupy or defend Louisiana and was afraid it would fall into the hands of the British, so he preferred to sell it to the only interested party: President Thomas Jefferson.

In New Orleans everyone, except for the idlers in the Café des Emigrés, who already had one foot on a boat to return to Saint-Domingue, heard the news with fear. They believed that Americans were barbarians in buffalo skins who ate with their boots on the table and had no trace of decency, moderation, or honor. Don't even mention class! All that interested them was betting, drinking, and shooting or knife fights; they were diabolically disorderly and to top it all off, Protestants. And they didn't speak French! Well, they would have to learn—if not, how did they plan to live in New Orleans? The entire city was in agreement that to belong to the United States was the equivalent of the end of family, culture, and the one true religion. Valmorain and Sancho, who dealt with Americans in their businesses, brought a conciliatory note to all that ruction, explaining that the Kaintucks were frontiersmen, more or less like buccaneers, and not all Americans could be judged by them. In fact, said Valmorain, in his travels he had known many Americans, well educated, sedate people; perhaps they could be reproached for being overly moralistic and Spartan in their habits, just the opposite of the Kaintucks. Their most notable defect was that they considered work a virtue, even manual labor. They were materialists, conquerors, and they were infused with a messianic enthusiasm for reforming those who did not think as they did; they did not, however, represent an immediate threat to civilization. No one wanted to hear that view save a pair of madmen: Bernard de Marigny, who could smell the enormous commercial possibilities to be gained by ingratiating himself among the Americans, and Père Antoine, who lived in the clouds.

The first official event was the transfer of power, with three years' delay, from the Spanish colony to French authorities. According to the prefect's hyperbolic address at the ceremony, the residents of Louisiana had "souls inundated with the delirium of extreme felicity." They celebrated with balls, a concert, banquets, and theatrical spectacles in the best Creole tradition, a true competition of courtesy, nobility, and extravagance between the deposed Spanish and new French government. That did not last long, however, because just as the flag of France was being raised a ship from Bordeaux anchored carrying confirmation of the sale of the territory to the Americans. Sold like cattle! Humiliation and fury replaced the festive spirit of the previous day. The second transfer, this time from the French to the Americans, who were camped two miles outside the city, ready to occupy it, took place seventeen days later, on December 20, 1803, and it was no "delirium of extreme felicity" but of collective mourning.

That same month, Dessalines proclaimed the independence of Saint-Domingue under the name of the République Nègre d'Haïti, with a new blue and red flag. Haïti, "land of mountains," was the name the vanished Arawak Indians had given their island. With the intent to erase the racism that had been the island's curse, all citizens, no matter the color of their skin, were designated *nègs*, and all those who weren't were called *blancs*.

"I think that Europe, and even the United States, will try to sink that poor island for fear its example will incite other colonies to fight for independence. Neither will they permit the abolition of slavery to be propagated," Parmentier commented to his friend Valmorain.

"The disaster of Haïti will work to the benefit of those of us in Louisiana because we will sell more sugar, and at a better price," concluded Valmorain, to whom the fate of the island didn't matter since he no longer had investments there.

The Saint-Domingue émigrés in New Orleans were not entirely absorbed by the news of that first black republic, as events in their city claimed all their attention. On a day of brilliant sunshine a multicolored crowd of Creoles, French, Spanish, Indians, and Negroes came together in the place d'Armes to watch the American authorities ride in, followed by a detachment of dragoons, two companies of infantry, and one of riflemen. No one had any sympathy for those men who swaggered as if each one had taken from his own pocket the fifteen million dollars that bought Louisiana.

In a brief official ceremony in the Cabildo, the keys of the city were handed to the new governor, and then the change of flags took place in the square; the tricolor pennant of France was slowly lowered and the starry flag of the United States raised. As they met midway they were stopped for a moment, and a cannon blast gave a signal, immediately answered by a cannonade from the ships in the port. A band of musicians played a popular American song and people listened in silence; many wept, and more than one lady swooned from grief. The new arrivals set about occupying the city in the least aggressive way possible, while the natives set about making their lives difficult. The Guizots had already circulated cards instructing their relations to keep the Americans at a distance; no one must collaborate with them or welcome them in their houses. Even the most pitiful beggar of New Orleans felt himself superior to the Americans.

One of Governor Claiborne's first measures was to declare English the official language, which was received with mocking incredulity by the Creoles. English? They had lived for decades as a French speaking Spanish colony; the Americans must be categorically demented if they expected their guttural jargon would replace the most melodic tongue in the world.

The Ursuline nuns, terrified by the certainty that first the Bonapartists and then the Kaintucks were going to level the city, profane its church, and rape them, hurriedly set sail, en masse, for Cuba, despite the pleas of their pupils, their orphans, and the hundreds of indigents they helped. Only nine of the twenty-five nuns stayed behind, the other sixteen filed in a row to the port, wrapped in veils and weeping, surrounded by a train of friends, acquaintants, and slaves who went with them to the ship.

Valmorain was sent a hastily written message warning him to withdraw his protégée from the school within twenty-four hours. Hortense, who was expecting another child with the hope that this time it was the immensely desired male, gave him to understand that that black girl would not set foot in her house, and that she never wanted anyone to see her with him. People had evil thoughts, and surely rumors would spread—false of course—that Rosette was his daughter.

With the defeat of the Napoleonic troops in Haïti came a second avalanche of refugees to New Orleans, just as Dr. Parmentier had predicted, first hundreds and then thousands. They were Bonapartists, radicals, and atheists, very different from the Catholic monarchists who had come before. A clash between the new refugees and the émigrés was inevitable, and it coincided with the Americans' entrance into the city. Governor Claiborne, a young military man with blue eyes and a short yellow beard, did not speak a word of French and did not understand the mentality of the Creoles, whom he considered lazy and decadent.

Ship after ship came from Saint-Domingue loaded with civilians and soldiers sick with fever, who represented a political danger because of their revolutionary ideas, and a public health threat given the possibility of an epidemic. Claiborne strove to isolate them in distant camps, but that measure was roundly criticized and did not affect the stream of refugees who in some way were able to get into the city. He put the slaves the whites had brought in prison, fearing they would infect the local ones with the germ of rebellion, and soon there was no further space in the cells and the clamor of their indignant owners at the confiscation of their property spread far and wide. They claimed that their Negroes were loyal and of proven good character—they would not have brought them otherwise. In addition, they were badly needed. Even though in Louisiana no one respected the prohibition against importing slaves and the pirates supplied the market, there was still a great demand. Claiborne was not in favor of slavery but he had to yield to public pressure. He decided he would consider each case individually, which could take months, while all New Orleans was on edge.

Violette Boisier was quick to adjust to the impact of the Americans. She sensed that the amiable Creoles, with their culture of leisure, would not resist the push of those enterprising and practical men. "Pay attention to what I tell you, Sancho; in no time at all those parvenus are going to wipe us off the face of the earth," she warned her lover. She had heard of the egalitarian spirit of the Americans, inseparable from democracy, and thought that if once there had been room for free people of color in New Orleans, with greater reason there would be room in the future. "Make no mistake, they're more racist than the English, French, and Spanish put together," Sancho argued, but she didn't believe him.

While others were refusing to mix with the Americans, Violette devoted herself to studying them up close, to see what she could learn from them and how she could keep afloat through the inevitable changes they would bring to New Orleans. She was satisfied with her life; she had her independence and comfort. She was serious when she said she was going to die rich. With her earnings from her creams and advice on fashion and beauty she had in less than three years bought the house on Chartres and was planning to acquire another. "I have to invest in properties, it's the only thing that lasts, everything else blows away on the wind," she kept saying to Sancho, who owned nothing, the plantation belonged to Valmorain. The project of buying land and making it yield had seemed fascinating to Sancho the first year, bearable the second, and from then on torment. His enthusiasm for cotton evaporated as soon as Hortense showed interest in it; he preferred not to have any dealings with that woman. He knew that Hortense was conspiring to get him out of their lives, and recognized that she was not without reason, he was a burden Valmorain carried out of friendship. Violette advised him to resolve his problems by finding a wealthy wife. "Don't you love me?" Sancho replied, offended. "I love you, but not enough to support you. Get married, and we will go on being lovers."

Loula did not share Violette's enthusiasm for property, she maintained that in that city of catastrophes they were subject to the whims of climate and fires; she should invest in gold, and dedicate herself to loaning money, as they'd done before with good results, but Violette was not eager to make enemies for herself by practicing usury. She had reached the age of prudence, and was working on her social position. Her only worry was Jean-Martin, who, to judge by his cryptic missives, was still unmovable in his proposal to follow in the footsteps of his father, whose memory he venerated. She wanted something better for her son, and knew all too well how harsh military life was; just consider the disastrous conditions in which the defeated soldiers arrived from Haïti. She could not dissuade him with the letters she dictated to the scribe; she would have to go to France and convince him to study a money making profession like the law. However incompetent he might be, no lawyer ended up poor. The fact that Jean-Martin had not demonstrated interest in the law was of no importance—very few lawyers did. Afterward she would marry him, in New Orleans, to the whitest girl possible, someone like Rosette but with a fortune and good family. In her experience, light skin and money made almost anything easier. She wanted her grandchildren to come into the world with an advantage.

Rosette

$\mathcal{V}$almorain had seen Tété in the street; it was impossible not to run into her in that city. He hadn't spoken to her, but he knew she was working for Violette Boisier. He had little contact with his beautiful former lover because before he could renew their friendship, as he had planned when he saw her arrive in New Orleans, Sancho had cut him off using his gallantry, his good looks, and the advantage of being a bachelor. Valmorain still did not understand how his brother-in-law could have won the game from him. His relationship with Hortense had lost its luster since she, absorbed in maternity, had grown negligent about her acrobatics in the large matrimonial bed with the carved angels. She was always pregnant; she could not get over only having girls, and she had no time to recover from each birth before she was expecting the next one, surely a boy—each time becoming more weary, fat, and tyrannical.

Valmorain found the months in New Orleans tedious, he suffocated in the female atmosphere of his house and the constant presence of the Guizots; for that reason he escaped to the plantation, leaving Hortense and the girls to the activities in the city. In truth, she too preferred it that way; her husband took up too much space. On the plantation it wasn't as noticeable, but in the city the rooms grew small and the hours very long. He had his own life out of the house, but unlike other men in his situation he did not keep a lover to sweeten a few afternoons a week.

When he'd seen Violette Boisier on the dock he'd thought she would be the ideal lover, beautiful, discreet, and not fertile. The woman wasn't young any longer, but he didn't want a girl whom he would soon tire of. Violette had always been a challenge and with maturity was doubtlessly more so, with her he would never be bored. However, because of a tacit agreement among gentlemen, he had not made a move after Sancho fell in love with her. That day he went to the yellow house, hoping to see her, with the Ursulines' note in his waistcoat. Tété, to whom he'd not spoken a word in three years, opened the door.

"Madame Violette is not in at the moment," she announced at the door.

"It doesn't matter—I came to speak with you."

She led him to the drawing room and offered him a cup of coffee, which he accepted in order to catch his breath, although coffee made his stomach burn. He sat down on an armchair that scarcely accepted his rear, his walking stick between his legs, gasping. It wasn't hot, but recently he frequently felt short of breath. I have to slim down a bit, he said every morning as he was struggling with his belt and the tie with three turns around his neck; even his shoes were tight. Tété returned with a tray, served him coffee the way he liked it, dark and bitter, then another cup for herself with a lot of sugar. Valmorain noticed, between amusement and irritation, a touch of arrogance in his former slave. Although she did not meet his eyes and did not commit the insolence of sitting, she dared drink coffee in his presence without asking his permission, and in her voice he did not hear the former submission. He admitted that she looked better than ever, surely she had learned a few of Violette's tricks. Remembering that woman, her gardenia skin, her black mane, her eyes shadowed by long eyelashes, made his heart flutter. Tété couldn't compare, but now that she didn't belong to him, she seemed desirable.

"To what do I owe your visit, monsieur?" she asked.

"It's about Rosette. Don't be alarmed. Your daughter is fine, but tomorrow she must leave the school, the nuns are going to Cuba because of the Americans. It is an exaggerated reaction, and without doubt they will return, but for now you have to take charge of Rosette."

"How can I do that, monsieur?" said Tété, startled. "I don't know whether Madame Violette would accept her if I brought her here."

"That isn't my concern. Tomorrow early you must go to get her. You can figure out what to do with her."

"Rosette is also your responsibility, monsieur."

"That girl has lived like a mademoiselle and received the best education thanks to me. The hour has come for her to face reality. She will have to work, unless you find a husband for her."

"She's only fourteen years old!"

"More than old enough to marry. Negro girls mature early." With an effort, Valmorain stood to leave.

Indignation burned through Tété like a flame, but years of obeying that man and the fear she had always had of him kept her from saying what was on the tip of her tongue. She had not forgotten the first time she was raped by her master when she was a girl, the hatred, the pain, the shame, nor the later abuses she'd borne for years. Silent, trembling, she handed him his hat and led him to the door. At the threshold he stopped.

"Has your freedom done you any good? You are poorer than you were, you don't even have a roof over your head for your daughter. In my house Rosette always had a place."

"The place of a slave, monsieur. I would rather live in poverty and be free," Tété replied, holding back her tears.

"Your pride will be your damnation, woman. You don't belong anywhere, you don't have a job or skill, and you're not young any longer. What are you going to do? I feel sorry for you, and that's why I'm going to help your daughter. This is for Rosette."

He handed her a pouch with money, went down the five steps to the street, and walked away, satisfied, in the direction of his house. Ten steps more and he'd forgotten the matter; he had other things on his mind.

During that period an idée fixe had begun to stir around in Violette Boisier's head, one that had first taken shape a year before, when the Ursulines put Rosette out on the street. No one knew men's weaknesses better than she, or women's needs; she planned to take advantage of her experience to make money and, in passing, offer a service that was greatly lacking in New Orleans. With that goal in mind, she offered her hospitality to Rosette. The girl came to the house in her school uniform, serious and haughty, followed two steps behind by her mother, who was carrying her bundles and had not stopped blessing Violette for having taken them under her roof.

Rosette had noble bones and eyes with her mother's golden streaks, the almond skin of the women in Spanish paintings, dark lips, wavy hair to the middle of her back, and the soft curves of adolescence. At fourteen she was already fully aware of the fearsome power of her beauty, and unlike Tété, who had worked from childhood, she appeared to have been born to be served. "She's going to have a hard time. She came into this world as a slave and she gives herself the airs of a queen. I will be putting her in her place," Loula observed with a disdainful snort, but Violette made her see the potential of her idea: investment and income, American concepts that Loula had adopted as her own. That convinced her to give her room to Rosette and go sleep with Tété in the servants' cell. The girl would need her rest, Violette said.

"Once you asked me what you were going to do with your daughter when she got out of school. The solution has occurred to me," Violette announced to Tété.

She reminded her that for Rosette the alternatives were scarce. To marry her without a good dowry would be to condemn her to forced labor at the side of a destitute husband. They could not even consider a Negro, it had to be a mulatto—but they tried to marry above them to better their social or financial situation, something Rosette could not offer. Neither did she have the makings of a seamstress, hairdresser, nurse, or any other of the jobs suitable to her situation. For the moment, her only capital was beauty, but there were a lot of beautiful girls in New Orleans.

"We are going to arrange things so that Rosette lives well without having to work," Violette declared.

"How will we do that, madame?" Tété smiled, incredulous.

"*Plaçage*. Rosette needs a white man to keep her."

Violette had analyzed the mentality of the clients who bought her beauty lotions, her whalebone armament, and the airy dresses Adèle sewed. They were as ambitious as she was, and they all wanted their descendants to prosper. They gave a skill or a profession to their sons but they trembled in fear of the future for their daughters. To place them with a white man was usually better than marrying them to a man of color, but there were ten available girls for every white bachelor, and without good connections it was difficult to accomplish. The man chose the girl and then treated her as he wished, a very comfortable arrangement for him but risky for her. Usually the union lasted until the hour came at around thirty for him to marry someone of his own class, but there were also cases when the relationship continued for the rest of the man's life, and some in which a man remained a bachelor out of love for a woman of color. Whichever way it was, her luck depended on her protector. Violette's plan consisted of imposing fairness: the girl *placée* would demand security for herself and her children, since in turn she gave him total devotion and faithfulness. If the young man could not offer guarantees, his father had to do it for him, just as the mother of the girl guaranteed the virtue and good conduct of her daughter.

"W-what will Rosette think of this, madame?" Tété stammered, frightened.

"Her opinion doesn't count. Think about it, woman. This is a long way from prostitution, though some say it is. I can assure you, from personal experience, that protection by a white is indispensable. My life would have been entirely different without Etienne Relais."

"But you married him . . ." Tété contended.

"That is impossible here. Tell me, Tété, what difference is there between a married white woman and a *placée* girl of color? Both are kept, subjected, destined to serve a man and give him children."

"But marriage means security and respect," Tété asserted.

"*Plaçage* should be the same," said Violette emphatically. "It must be advantageous for both parties, not another notch in his hunting knife for the white. I am going to begin with your daughter, who has neither money nor good family but is pretty and already free, thanks to Père Antoine. She will be the best *placée* girl in New Orleans. In a year's time we will present her to society, I just need the right amount of time to prepare her."

"I don't know . . ." And Tété stopped protesting because she had nothing better for her daughter and she trusted Violette Boisier.

They did not consult with Rosette, but the girl turned out to be more willing than they'd expected; she guessed what they were up to and didn't object because she had her own plan.

During the following weeks, Violette visited, one by one, the mothers of adolescent girls in the highest echelon of color, the matriarchs of the Société du Cordon Bleu, and explained her idea to them. Those women commanded in their world; many owned businesses, lands, and slaves, who in some cases were their own relatives. Their grandmothers had been emancipated slaves who had children by their masters for whom they received help and prospered. Family relations, though of different races, were the structure that held up the complex edifice of Creole society. The idea of sharing a man with one or several women was not strange to quadroons whose great-grandmothers came from polygamous families in Africa. Their obligation was to provide well-being for their daughters and grandchildren, even if that came by way of the husband of another woman.

Those formidable, doting mothers, five times more numerous than men of the same class, rarely found an appropriate son-in-law; they knew that the best way to care for their daughters was to place them with someone who could protect them, otherwise they were at the mercy of any predator. Physical violence and rape were not crimes if the victim was a woman of color, even if she were free.

Violette explained to the mothers that her idea was to hold an extravagant ball in the best available hall, financed by their donations. Only young whites with a fortune, and those seriously interested in *plaçage*, would attend, accompanied by their fathers if necessary, no philandering gallants looking for a careless girl for entertainment without commitment. More than one mother suggested that the men should pay to enter, but in Violette's view that would open the door to undesirables, as happened in the carnival balls, or those in Orléans Hall and the Théâtre Français, where for a modest price anyone could go in as long as they weren't black. This would be a ball as selective as those held by white debutantes. There would be time to look into the background of those who were invited, since no one wanted to hand over her daughter to someone with bad behavior or debts. "For once, the whites will have to accept our conditions," said Violette.

To avoid upsetting the mothers, she didn't tell them that in future she planned to add Americans to the list, despite Sancho's having warned her that no Protestant would understand the advantages of *plaçage*. There would be time for all that; for the moment, she had to concentrate on the first ball.

The white man could dance with the girl he chose a couple of times, and if he liked her, he or his father should immediately begin negotiations with the girl's mother; no time to be wasted in pointless courting. The protector had to contribute a house, a yearly pension, and an agreement to educate the couple's children. Once these points were agreed on, the *placée* would be installed in her new house and cohabitation would begin. She would assure him of discretion during the time they were together and the certainty that there would be no drama when the relationship ended, which would depend entirely on him. "The *plaçage* must be a contract of honor; it behooves everyone to respect the rules," said Violette. The whites could not abandon their young lovers to poverty because that would endanger the delicate balance of accepted concubinage. There was no written contract, but if a man violated his given word, the women would make sure his reputation was ruined. The ball would be called Cordon Bleu, and Violette would be responsible for making it the most anticipated event of the year for young people of all colors.

Zarité

I ended by accepting the idea of plaçage, *which the mothers of other girls agreed to quite naturally, but it shocked me. I didn't want that for my daughter, but what else could I offer her? Rosette understood immediately when I dared tell her about it. She had more common sense than I did.*

Madame Violette organized the ball with the help of some French men who produced spectacles. She also created an Academy of Etiquette and Beauty that came to be called the Yellow House, where she prepared the girls who took her classes. She said they would be the most sought after and they could be sure of being selected by a protector; that convinced the mothers, and no one complained about the cost. For the first time in her forty-five years Madame Violette got out of bed early. I waked her with strong black coffee and ran before she threw it at my head. Her bad humor lasted half the morning. Madame accepted only a dozen students, she didn't have room for more but she planned to find a better space next year. She hired instructors for singing and dancing; the girls practiced walking with a cup of water on their heads to improve posture, she taught them to comb their hair and paint their faces, and in their free hours I explained how to run a house, something I knew a lot about. She also designed a wardrobe for each one according to her figure and color, and Madame Adèle and her helpers produced the dresses. Dr. Parmentier suggested that the girls should also have subjects for conversation, but according to Madame Violette no man is interested in what a woman says, and Don Sancho agreed. The doctor, on the other hand, always listens to Adèle's opinions and follows her advice, for he has no head for anything but doctoring. She makes the decisions in their family. They bought the house on Rampart and are educating their sons about work and investments since the doctor's money turns into smoke.

Halfway through the year, the students had progressed so well that Don Sancho made a large bet with his friends at the Café des Emigrés that every one of the girls would be well placed. I watched the classes discreetly, to learn if any of it could help me in pleasing Zacharie. Beside him I look like a servant; I don't have Madame Violette's charm or the intelligence of Adèle, I'm not a coquette, as Don Sancho counseled me to be, nor as entertaining as Dr. Parmentier would wish.

During the day my daughter went around pressed into a bustier, and at night she slept slathered with crème to lighten her skin, with a headband to press back her ears and a girth constricting her waist. Beauty is illusion, madame said; at fifteen all girls are pretty, but to keep being that way requires discipline. Rosette had to read aloud the manifest of the cargo on the ships in port, in that way training herself to bear with a happy expression a boring man; she scarcely ate, she straightened her curls with hot irons, removed hair with caramel, rubbed herself with oats and lemon, spent hours practicing curtsies, dances, and drawing room games. What would it benefit her being free if she had to behave that way? No man deserves that much, I said, but Madame Violette convinced me that it was the only way to ensure her future. My daughter, who had never been docile, submitted without complaint. Something in her had changed; she no longer took pains to please anyone, she had gone silent. Once she had spent her time looking at herself in the mirror, but now she used it only when madame demanded in classes.

Madame taught the way to flatter without servility, to hold back reproaches, to hide jealousy and overcome the temptation to try other kisses. Most important, according to her, was to take advantage of the fire we women have in our belly. That is what men most fear and desire. She advised the girls to know their bodies and to pleasure themselves with their fingers, because *without pleasure there is neither health nor beauty. Tante Rose had tried to teach me the same thing when Master Valmorain began to rape me, but I paid no attention, I was just a child and was afraid of everything. Tante Rose bathed me in herbs and spread a clay dough on my belly and thighs, which at first felt cold and heavy but then got warm and seemed to bubble, as if it were alive. Earth and water heal the body and the soul. I suppose that with Gambo I felt for the first time what madame was talking about, but we were pulled apart too soon. Then for years I felt nothing, until Zacharie came along to waken my body. He loves me, and he is patient. Aside from Tante Rose, he is the only person who has counted the scars in the secret places where sometimes my master put out his cigar. Madame Violette is the only woman I've ever heard use that word:* pleasure. *"How are you going to give it to a man if you don't know what it is?" she asked her students. Pleasure of love, of nursing a baby, of dancing. Pleasure is also waiting for Zacharie, knowing he will come.*

That year I was very busy with my responsibilities in the house besides tending the students, running messages to Madame Adèle, and preparing remedies for Dr. Parmentier. In December, just before the Cordon Bleu ball, I counted and realized it had been three months since I bled. The only surprise was that I hadn't got pregnant before, because I had been with Zacharie for some time without taking the precautions Tante Rose had taught me. He wanted to marry me as soon as I told him, but first I had to place my Rosette.

Maurice

During the vacation time of the fourth year of school, Maurice waited for Jules Beluche as he always did. By then he didn't want to meet his family, and the only reason to go back to New Orleans was Rosette, although the possibility of seeing her would be remote. The Ursulines did not allow spontaneous visits from anyone, much less a boy unable to prove a close relationship. He knew that his father would never give him the necessary authorization, but he never lost hope of going with his uncle Sancho, whom the nuns knew because he had never stopped visiting Rosette. Through his letters Maurice learned that Tété had been relegated to the plantation after the incident with Hortense, and he could only blame himself; he imagined her cutting cane from sunup to sundown and felt a fist in the pit of his stomach. Not only he and Tété had paid dearly for that one crack of the whip, apparently Rosette had fallen into disgrace too. The girl had written several times to Valmorain, asking him to come see her, but she got no answer. "What have I done to lose your father's esteem? Once I was like his daughter, why has he forgotten me?" she repeated in her letters to Maurice, but he could not give her an honest answer. "He hasn't forgotten you, Rosette—Papa loves you the way he always has and he wants you to be doing well, but the plantation and his businesses keep him busy. I haven't seen him myself for more than three years." Why tell her that Valmorain had never thought of her as a daughter? Before he'd been sent to Boston, he had asked his father to take him to visit his sister at the school, and with great anger Valmorain replied that Maurice's only sister was Marie-Hortense.

That summer Jules Beluche did not show up in Boston, instead Sancho García del Solar, in his wide-brimmed hat, thundered up at full gallop with another horse in tow. He jumped down and brushed off the dust with his hat before embracing his nephew. Jules Beluche had been knifed over some gambling debts, and the Guizots intervened to squelch gossip; however distant the relationship that united them, sharp tongues would associate Beluche with the honorable branch of the family. They did what any Creoles of their class did in similar circumstances: they paid his debts, took him in until his wound healed and he could look after himself, gave him pocket money, and put him on a boat with instructions not to get off until he reached Texas, and never to return to New Orleans. Sancho told Maurice all that, doubled over with laughter.

"That could have been me, Maurice. Up till now I've been lucky, but any day they will bring you the news that your favorite uncle has been stitched like a quilt in some hole of a gaming house," he added.

"May God not let that happen, Uncle. Have you come to take me home?" Maurice asked in a voice that shifted from baritone to soprano in the same sentence.

"What makes you think that, boy! Do you want to be buried all summer on the plantation? You and I are going on a trip," Sancho announced.

"That's what I did with Beluche."

"Don't compare me to him, Maurice. I do not intend to contribute to your civic formation by showing you monuments, I mean to pervert you, what do you think of that?"

"How, Uncle?"

"In Cuba, my nephew. No better place for a couple of truants like us. How old are you?"

"Fifteen."

"And your voice hasn't changed yet?"

"It changed, Uncle, but I have a c-cold," the boy stammered.

"By your age I was a hell raiser. You're a little behind, Maurice. Pack your things, because we leave tomorrow," Sancho ordered.

Sancho still had many friends and no few lovers in Cuba, who proposed to shower him with attention during that vacation and put up with his companion, that strange boy who spent his time writing letters and suggested absurd subjects of conversation like slavery and democracy, something none of them had formed an opinion about. It amused them to see Sancho in the role of nursemaid, which he performed with unsuspected dedication. He turned down the best sprees in order not to leave his nephew alone, and stopped going to animal fights—bulls with bears, snakes with weasels, cocks with cocks, dogs with dogs—because they disturbed Maurice. Sancho decided to teach the boy to drink and, halfway through the night ended by cleaning up his vomit. He taught him all his card tricks, but Maurice lacked malice and instead had to pay up after others less principled fleeced him. Soon Sancho had also abandoned the idea of initiating him into the free-for-alls of love, for when he tried it Maurice nearly died of fright. He had arranged the details with a good-hearted woman friend, not young but still attractive, who was willing to act as teacher to the nephew for the pure pleasure of doing the uncle a favor. "This kid is still green behind the ears," Sancho muttered, mortified, when Maurice ran away upon seeing the woman in a provocative negligee reclining on a divan. "No one has ever rebuffed me like that, Sancho." She laughed. "Close the door and come console me." Despite those stumbles, Maurice had an unforgettable summer and returned to school taller, stronger, tanned, and with a definite tenor voice. "Don't study too hard, because it will ruin your sight and your character, get ready for next summer. I'm going to take you to Mexico," Sancho told his nephew as he left. He did as he promised, and from then on Maurice eagerly looked forward to summer.

In 1805, Maurice's last year of school, it was not Sancho who came for him, as he had before, but his father. Maurice deduced that he was there to announce some bad news and was afraid for Tété or Rosette, but it wasn't anything like that, it seemed. Valmorain had organized a trip to France to visit a grandmother and two hypothetical aunts his son had never heard mentioned. "And then we will go home, monsieur?" Maurice had asked, thinking of Rosette, whose letters lined the bottom of his trunk. He had written her one hundred ninety-three letters without a thought for the inevitable changes she had experienced in those nine years they'd been apart; he remembered her as the little girl dressed in ribbons and laces that he'd seen for the last time shortly before his father's marriage to Hortense Guizot. He couldn't imagine her at fifteen, just as she couldn't think of him as eighteen. "Of course we'll go home, son, your mother and sisters are waiting to see you," Valmorain lied.

The journey on a ship that had to skirt summer storms and with difficulty escape an attack by the English, and then a coach to Paris, did not bring the father and son together. Valmorain had conceived the trip in order to postpone for a few months more his wife's displeasure at seeing Maurice again, but he couldn't put it off indefinitely; soon he would have to confront a situation that had not been eased by the years. Hortense never lost a chance to spew venom upon that stepson whom each year she tried vainly to replace with her own son without producing anything but girls. For her, Valmorain had exiled Maurice from the family, and now he repented. A decade had gone by without a serious concern for his son; he was always occupied with his own affairs, first in Saint-Domingue, then in Louisiana, and last with Hortense and the births of the girls. The boy was a stranger who answered his sparse letters in a couple of formal sentences regarding the progress of his studies but he never asked about any member of the family; it was as if he wanted to leave it settled that he had no connection to them. He didn't even react when his father wrote him in a single line that Tété and Rosette had been emancipated and were no longer connected to the Valmorains.

Valmorain was afraid he'd lost his son at some point during those hectic years. This introverted young man, tall and handsome, with his mother's features, did not in any way resemble the rosy-cheeked boy he'd cradled in his arms, praying heaven to protect him from all harm. He loved him as much as he ever had, maybe more, because his emotion was stained with guilt. He tried to convince himself that his fatherly affection was returned by Maurice, even though they were temporarily distanced, but he had his doubts. He had laid out ambitious plans for his son without ever having asked him what he wanted to do with his life. In truth, he knew nothing about his interests or experiences; it was centuries since they had spoken. He wanted to win him back, and had imagined that those months alone together in France would act to establish an adult relationship. He had to prove to him his affection and to make clear that Hortense and her daughters would not change Maurice's situation as his only heir, but every time he tried to broach the subject there was no response. "The tradition of primogeniture is very wise, Maurice; wealth must not be divided among sons because with each division the family's fortune is lessened. Being the firstborn, you will receive my entire estate, and you will have to look after your sisters. When I'm no longer here, you will be the head of the Valmorains. It's time to start preparing you; you will learn to invest money, manage the plantation, and make your way in society," he told him. Silence. Conversations died before they began. Valmorain navigated from one monologue to another.

Maurice took in without comment Napoleonic France, always at war, the museums, palaces, parks, and avenues his father wanted to show him. They visited the ruined château where his grandmother was living out her last years, caring for two unwed daughters more deteriorated by time and loneliness than she. A prideful old woman dressed in Louis XVI style, determined to ignore the changes in the world, she was firmly ensconsed in the epoch prior to the French Revolution, and had erased from her memory the Terror, the guillotine, exile in Italy, and the return to an unrecognizable country. Seeing Toulouse Valmorain, that son absent for more than thirty years, she held out a bony hand with antique rings on each finger for him to kiss, and then ordered her daughters to serve chocolate. Valmorain introduced her grandson to her and tried to summarize his own story from the time he embarked for the Antilles up to the present. She listened without a word while the sisters offered steaming little cups and plates of stale pastries, eyeing Valmorain with caution. They remembered the frivolous young man who told them good-bye with a distracted kiss and left with his valet and several trunks to spend a few weeks with their father in Saint-Domingue, only never to return. They didn't recognize that brother with the scanty hair, double chin, and paunch, who spoke with a strange accent. They knew something of the uprising of slaves in the colony—they'd heard a few sentences here and there about atrocities on that decadent island, but they'd not connected them to a member of their family. They had never been curious to know where the funds that supported them came from. Bloodstained sugar, rebel slaves, burned plantations, exile, and all the rest their brother mentioned was as incomprehensible to them as a conversation in Chinese.

The mother, on the other hand, knew exactly what Valmorain was referring to, but now nothing interested her too much in this world; her heart was too dry for affection and news. She listened to him in an indifferent silence, and at the end, the one question she asked was if she could count on more money because what he regularly sent barely covered things. It was absolutely necessary to repair that house depleted by the years and vicissitudes, she said; she couldn't die leaving her daughters unsheltered. Valmorain and Maurice stayed inside those lugubrious walls for two days that seemed as long as two weeks. "We won't see each other again, better that way," were the elderly dame's words as she told her son and grandson good-bye.

Maurice docilely went everywhere with his father, except the classy brothel where Valmorain planned to fête him with the most expensive cocottes in Paris.

"What is it with you, son? This is normal and necessary. One must discharge the body's humors and clear the mind, that way one can concentrate on other things."

"I have no difficulty concentrating, monsieur."

"I've told you to call me Papa, Maurice. I suppose that in your trips with your Uncle Sancho . . . well, you wouldn't have been lacking for opportunities. . . ."

"That is a private matter," Maurice interrupted.

"I hope that the American school hasn't made you religious or effeminate," his father commented in a jesting tone, but it came out with a growl.

The boy gave no explanations. Thanks to his uncle he wasn't a virgin; in the last vacation time Sancho had succeeded in initiating him, using an ingenious scheme dictated by necessity. He suspected that his nephew suffered the desires and fantasies proper for his age but was a romantic and was repelled by the idea of love reduced to a commercial transaction. It was up to him to help Maurice, he decided. They were in the prosperous port of Savannah, in Georgia, which Sancho wanted to know through the countless diversions it offered, and Maurice as well, because Professor Harrison Cobb had cited it as an example of negotiable morality.

Georgia, founded in 1733, was the thirteenth and last of the colonies founded in the new world and Savannah was its first city. The settlers maintained friendly relations with the indigenous tribes, thus avoiding the violence that was the scourge of other colonies. In the beginning, slavery—along with liquor and lawyers—was forbidden in Georgia, but soon it was realized that the climate and the quality of the soil were ideal for cultivating rice and cotton, and slavery was legalized. After independence, Georgia was converted into another state of the Union, and Savannah flourished as the port of entry for the traffic in Africans that supplied the region's plantations. "This demonstrates, Maurice, that decency quickly succumbs before greed. If it's a matter of getting rich, the majority of men will sacrifice their soul. You cannot imagine how well the planters in Georgia live, thanks to their slaves," Harrison Cobb had declared. The youth did not have to imagine it—he had lived in Saint-Domingue and New Orleans—and he accepted his uncle Sancho's suggestion that they spend their vacation in Savannah so as not to disappoint his teacher. "Love of justice is not enough to defeat slavery, Maurice; you have to see the reality and know in detail the laws and gears of politics," Cobb maintained, who was preparing his student to triumph where he himself had failed. The man knew his limitations; he had neither the temperament nor the health to fight in Congress, as he had dreamed of in his youth, but he was a good teacher; he knew how to recognize the talent of a student and to mold his character.

While Sancho García del Solar fully enjoyed the refinement and hospitality of Savannah, Maurice suffered the guilt of having a good time. What would he tell his teacher when he returned to school? That he had stayed in a charming hotel, attended by an army of solicitous servants, and that there had not been hours enough to indulge his life as an irresponsible bon vivant?

They had scarcely been a day in Savannah when Sancho made friends with a Scots widow who lived two blocks from the hotel. The woman offered to show them the city, with the mansions, monuments, churches, and parks that had been beautifully reconstructed after a devastating fire. Faithful to her word, the widow appeared with her daughter, the delicate Giselle, and the four went out in the afternoon, thus beginning a very convenient friendship for uncle and nephew. They spent many hours together.

While the mother and Sancho played interminable games of cards, and from time to time disappeared from the hotel without explanation, Giselle took charge of showing Maurice around. They went out alone on horseback, far from the vigilance of the Scots widow, which surprised

Maurice, who had never seen a girl have such freedom. Several times Giselle took him to a solitary beach, where they shared a light lunch and bottle of wine. She didn't talk much and what she said was so categorically banal that Maurice didn't feel intimidated, words he normally stored in his chest spilled out in torrents. At last he had a listener who did not yawn at his philosophical thoughts but listened with obvious admiration. From time to time her feminine fingers would carelessly brush him, and from those touches to more daring caresses took only three setting suns. Those outdoor assaults, peppered with insects, entangled in clothing, spiced by the fear of discovery, left Maurice in glory, and Giselle quite bored.

The rest of the vacation went by too quickly, and naturally Maurice fell in love like the teenager he was, love heightened with remorse at having stained Giselle's honor. There was only one gentlemanly way to remedy his fault, as he explained to Sancho as soon as he gathered his courage.

"I am going to ask for Giselle's hand," he announced.

"Have you lost your mind, Maurice? How can you marry her if you don't know how to blow your nose!"

"Have some respect, Uncle. I am a man from head to toe."

"Because you bedded the girl?" and Sancho let out a noisy guffaw.

The uncle barely avoided the punch Maurice aimed at his face. The matter became crystal clear to Maurice shortly after, when the Scots woman told him that the girl was not really her daughter and Giselle confessed that that was her theater name; she wasn't sixteen but twenty-four, and Sancho García del Solar had paid her to entertain his nephew. The uncle admitted that he'd committed a monstrous foolishness, and tried to joke about it, but he had gone too far, and Maurice, devastated, swore he would never speak to him as long as he lived. Nonetheless, when they reached Boston there were two letters from Rosette waiting, and his passion for the beauty of Savannah evaporated, and he was able to forgive his uncle. When they said good-bye, they embraced with their usual camaraderie and the promise to see each other soon.

On the trip to France, Maurice did not tell his father anything about what had happened in Savannah. Valmorain, after softening his son with liquor, insisted twice more that he pleasure himself with ladies of the dawn, but he was not able to make Maurice change his mind, and in the end decided not to mention the subject again until they reached New Orleans, where he would provide him a *garçonnière*, a bachelor apartment like those young Creoles of his social position enjoyed. For the time being, he would not allow his son's suspicious chastity to endanger the tenuous equilibrium of their relationship.

Spies

Jean-Martin Relais turned up in New Orleans three weeks before the first Cordon Bleu ball his mother organized. He came without the military academy uniform he had worn since he was thirteen in the role of secretary to Isidor Morisset, a scientist who was traveling to evaluate the properties of the land in the Antilles and Florida; he had the idea of establishing sugar plantations, given the losses reported by the colony in Saint-Domingue, which seemed definitive. In the new République Nègre d'Haïti, Général Dessalines was massacring, in systematic fashion, all whites, the very ones whom he'd invited to return. If Napoleon was planning to reach a commercial accord with Haïti, since he'd not been able to occupy it with his troops, he desisted after these horrible slaughters, in which even infants ended in common graves.

Isidor Morisset was a man with an impenetrable gaze, a broken nose, and wrestler's shoulders that burst the stitching of his jacket; he was red as a brick from the merciless sun on the crossing and equipped with a monosyllabic vocabulary that made him disagreeable from the minute he opened his mouth. His sentences—always too brief—sounded like sneezes. He wore the suspicious expression of someone who expects the worst from his fellow man, and answered questions with snuffs and snorts. He was immediately welcomed by Governor Claiborne with the attentions due to a stranger owed the respect attested to in the letters of recommendation from a number of scientific societies, delivered by the secretary on a carpet of embossed green leather.

Claiborne, dressed in mourning because of the death of his wife and daughter, victims of the recent epidemic of yellow fever, took note of the secretary's dark skin. From the way Morisset introduced him, he supposed that this mulatto was free and greeted him as such. One never knows what the proper etiquette is with these Mediterranean peoples, the governor thought. He was not a man to appreciate male beauty easily, but he could not help staring at the youth's delicate features—the thick eyelashes, the feminine mouth, the round, dimpled chin—in such contrast to the slim, limber body of undoubted masculine proportions. The youth, cultivated and with impeccable manners, served as interpreter, since Morisset spoke only French. The secretary's command of English left a great deal to be desired, but it was enough, given that Morisset was a man of very few words.

The governor's sharp nose warned him that the visitors were hiding something. The sugar mission seemed as suspicious as the man's muscular physique, which did not correspond to Claiborne's concept of a scientist, but those doubts did not excuse him from greeting him with the hospitality that was de rigueur in New Orleans. After a frugal luncheon, served by free Negroes since he did not own slaves, he offered his guests lodging. The secretary translated that it would not be necessary; they had come for a few days and would stay in a hotel while they awaited the ship that would take them back to France.

As soon as they left, Claiborne had them followed discreetly, and so learned that in the evening the two men left the hotel, the dark young man in the direction of Chartres Street and the muscular Morisset on a rented horse to a modest blacksmith shop at the end of Saint Philip Street.

The governor had been right in his suspicions: of science, Morisset had not a smattering; he was a Bonapartist spy. In December 1804 Napoleon had become the emperor of France; he himself placed the crown on his head, since he did not consider even the pope, especially invited for the occasion, worthy to do it. Napoleon had conquered half of Europe, but he still faced the problem of Great Britain, that tiny nation of horrible climate and homely people, defying him from the other side of the narrow English Channel. On October 21, 1805, those nations met in conflict off Cape Trafalgar, on the southwest coast of Spain, on one side the Franco-Spanish fleet of thirty-three ships and on the other the English twenty-seven, under the command of the celebrated admiral Horatio Nelson, genius of war at sea. Nelson died in the battle, following a spectacular victory in which the enemy fleet was destroyed and the Napoleonic dream of invading England was ended. Just at that time Pauline Bonaparte visited her brother to offer her condolences for the bad news of Trafalgar. Pauline had cut her hair to place in the coffin of her cuckolded husband, Général Leclerc, dead of fever in Saint-Domingue and buried in Paris. The dramatic gesture of the inconsolable widow drew laughter across Europe. Without her long mahogany-colored hair, worn in the style of the Greek goddesses, Pauline looked so young that soon the style became the vogue. That day she arrived adorned with a tiara of famous Borghese diamonds, accompanied by Morisset.

Napoleon suspected that the visitor was another of his sister's lovers, and received him in bad humor, but he was immediately interested when Pauline told him that the ship in which Morisset had sailed across the Caribbean had been attacked by pirates, and that he had been the prisoner of Jean Lafitte for several months, until he could pay his ransom and return to France. During his captivity he had developed a certain friendship with Lafitte based on chess matches. Napoleon interrogated the man about Lafitte's noteworthy organization, which controlled the Caribbean with its ships; no boat was safe except those of the United States, which, because of the pirate's capricious loyalty to the Americans, were never attacked.

The emperor led Morisset into a little room where they spent two hours in private. Perhaps Lafitte was the solution to a dilemma that had tormented him since the disaster at Trafalgar: how to prevent the

English from controlling maritime commerce. As he did not have the naval capacity to stop them, he had thought of allying himself with the Americans, who had been in a dispute with Great Britain since the War of Independence in 1775, but President Jefferson wanted to consolidate his territory and was not thinking of intervening in European conflicts. With a spark of inspiration, like so many that had taken him from a modest rank in the army to the peak of power, Napoleon charged Isidor Morisset with recruiting pirates to harass English ships in the Atlantic. Morisset understood that this was a delicate mission, since the emperor could not appear to be allied with buccaneers, and conjectured that, with his cover as a scientist, he could travel without attracting too much attention. The brothers Jean and Pierre Lafitte had grown untouchably rich over the years from piratical booty and every kind of contraband, but American authorities did not tolerate evasion of taxes, and despite Lafitte's manifest sympathy for the United States' democracy, he was declared an outlaw.

Jean-Martin Relais did not know the man he was going to accompany across the Atlantic. One Monday morning the director of the military academy had called him to his office, handed him money, and ordered him to buy civilian clothing and a trunk; he was going to sail in two days. "Do not say a word of this, Relais, it is a confidential mission," the director instructed. Faithful to his military education, the young man obeyed without asking questions. Later he learned that he'd been selected for being the sharpest in the English course, and because the director thought that since he came from the colonies he would not drop dead at the first bite of a tropical mosquito.

The youth rode at full gallop to Marseille, where Isidor Morisset was waiting with tickets in hand. Jean-Martin silently gave thanks that the man scarcely looked at him; he'd been nervous, thinking they would share a narrow stateroom during the voyage. Nothing injured his monumental pride as much as intimations from other men.

"Don't you want to know where we're going?" Morisset asked when they'd been several days on the high seas without any conversation other than a few words of courtesy.

"I am going wherever France commands me," Relais replied, snapping to attention, on the defensive.

"No military moves, boy. We're civilians, understood?"

"Yes, sir!"

"Speak like normal people do, man, for God's sake!"

"At your orders, sir."

Jean-Martin soon discovered that Morisset, so somber and unpleasant in company, could be fascinating in private. Alcohol loosened his tongue and relaxed him to the point he seemed a different man, amiable, sarcastic, smiling. He played a good game of cards and had a thousand stories that he told without elaboration, in a few sentences. Between glasses of cognac they were coming to know each other, and between them grew the natural intimacy of good comrades.

"Once Pauline Bonaparte invited me to her boudoir," Morisset told him. "An Antillean black, covered only by a loincloth, carried her in and bathed her in front of me. La Bonaparte took pride in being able to seduce anyone, but it didn't work with me."

"Why not?"

"I am annoyed by female stupidity."

"Do you prefer male stupidity?" the youth joked with a touch of a tease; he too had had a few glasses and felt at ease.

"I prefer horses."

But Jean-Martin was more interested in the pirates than in equine virtues or the beautiful Pauline's bath, and again turned the conversation to the subject of the adventure his new friend had lived among them when he was held on Barataria Island. As Morisset knew that not even imperial warships dared approach the Lafitte brothers' island, he had flatly discarded the idea of going there without being invited; their throats would be slit before they stepped onto the beach, not giving them any opportunity to lay out their daring proposition. In addition, he wasn't sure that Napoleon's name would open the Lafittes' door—it might be just the opposite—and that is why he had decided to approach them in New Orleans, a neutral territory.

"The Lafittes are outlaws. I don't know how we're going to find them," he told Jean-Martin.

"It will be very easy, they don't hide," the youth assured him.

"How do you know that?"

"From my mother's letters."

Until that instant it hadn't occurred to Relais to mention that his mother lived in that city; it seemed an insignificant detail, given the magnitude of the mission the emperor had charged them with.

"Your mother knows the Lafittes?"

"Everyone knows them, they are the kings of the Mississippi," Jean-Martin answered.

At six o'clock in the evening, Violette Boisier was resting naked and damp with pleasure in the bed of Sancho García del Solar. Ever since Rosette and Tété had been living with her and her house was invaded by students for the *plaçage*, she had preferred her lover's apartment for making love, or just to have her siesta if the spirit did not move them to more. At first Violette tried to clean and beautify the place, but she hadn't the least inclination to play at being a maid, and it was absurd to lose precious hours of intimacy trying to sort out Sancho's monumental clutter. Sancho's only servant did nothing but brew coffee. Valmorain had lent him to Sancho because it was impossible to sell him; no one would have bought him. He'd fallen from a roof and done something to his brain that caused him to wander around alone, laughing. With good reason, Hortense Guizot could not stand to have him around. Sancho tolerated him and even had a liking for him, for the quality of his coffee and because he didn't steal change when he went shopping in the Marché Français. The man disturbed Violette; she thought that he spied on them when they made love. "That's just your idea, woman. He is so dim-witted he doesn't have the sense to do that," her lover said soothingly.

At that same moment Loula and Tété were sitting in wicker chairs on the street in front of the yellow house, as neighbors did at dusk. The notes of a piano exercise hammered the peace of the autumn evening. Loula was smoking her black cigar with half-closed eyes, savoring the rest her bones demanded, and Tété was sewing a baby's gown. The curve of her belly was not yet noticeable but she had already told her small circle of friends about her pregnancy, and the only one who'd been surprised was Rosette, who went around so self-absorbed that she hadn't noticed the love between her mother and Zacharie. That was where Jean-Martin Relais found them. He hadn't written to announce his voyage because his orders were to keep it secret, and in addition the letter would have arrived after he did.

Loula wasn't expecting him, and as it had been several years since she had seen him she didn't recognize him. When he stopped before her, all she did was take another puff on her cigar. "It's me, Jean-Martin," the boy exclaimed emotionally. It took the huge woman seconds to make him out through the smoke and to be aware it was in fact her boy, her prince, the light of her old eyes. Her shrieks of pleasure shattered the street. She hugged him around the waist, lifted him off the ground, and covered him with kisses and tears while he stood on tiptoe, trying to defend his dignity. "Where is Maman?" Jean-Martin asked as soon as he could free himself and pick up his hat from under their feet. "At church, son, praying for the soul of your departed father. Let's go inside; I'm going to make some coffee while my friend Tété goes to look for her," Loula replied without an instant's hesitation. Tété went running off in the direction of Sancho's apartment.

In the drawing room of the house, Jean-Martin saw a girl dressed in blue playing the piano with a cup on her head. "Rosette! Look who's here! My boy, my Jean-Martin!" Loula screeched in introduction. Rosette interrupted her musical exercises and slowly turned. They greeted each other, he with a stiff nod and click of his heels and she with a fluttering of her giraffe eyelashes. "Welcome, monsieur. Not a day goes by that madame and Loula do not speak of you," said Rosette with the forced courtesy learned from the Ursulines. Nothing could be more true. The memory of the young man floated through the house like a ghost, and from hearing about him so often Rosette already knew him.

Loula took Rosette's cup and went to tend to the coffee, and her exclamations of joy blasted in from the patio. Rosette and Jean-Martin, sitting in silence on the edge of their chairs, cast furtive glances at each other with the feeling they had met before. Twenty minutes later, when Jean-Martin was on his third piece of pastry, Violette came panting in, with Tété close behind. Jean-Martin thought his mother looked more beautiful than he remembered, and did not wonder why she was coming from mass with her hair in a tangle and dress badly buttoned.

From the doorway Tété watched the uncomfortable youth with amusement as Loula pinched his cheeks and his mother kissed and kissed him without letting go of his hand. The salt winds of the crossing had darkened Jean-Martin's skin several tones, and the years of military formation had reinforced the stiffness inspired by the man he thought was his father. He remembered Etienne Relais as strong, stoic, and severe, and for that treasured even more the tenderness he had showered on him in the strict intimacy of the home. His mother and Loula, on the other hand, had always treated him like a baby, and apparently would continue to do so. To compensate for his pretty face, he always kept an exaggerated distance, an icy posture, and that stony expression military men tend to have. In his childhood he'd had to put up with being mistaken for a girl, and in adolescence his schoolmates taunted him or fell in love with him. Those family caresses in front of Rosette and the mulatta, whose name he hadn't caught, embarrassed him, but he did not dare reject them. Tété did not notice that Jean-Martin had the same features as Rosette, she had always thought her daughter resembled Violette Boisier, and that seemed to have been accentuated in the months of training for the *plaçage*, during which the girl imitated her teacher's mannerisms.

In the meantime, Morisset had gone to the blacksmith shop on Saint Philip Street, which he had found out was a screen for illegal transactions; he did not, however, find the person he was looking for. He was tempted to leave a note for Jean Lafitte asking for a meeting and reminding him of the relationship they had developed over a chessboard, but realized that would be a major mistake. He had been spying for three months, posing as a scientist, and still was not used to the caution his mission demanded; at every turn he surprised himself on the verge of being imprudent. Later that same day, when Jean-Martin introduced him to his mother, his precautions seemed ridiculous, she offered quite casually to introduce him to the pirates. They were in the drawing room of the yellow house, which had become a little crowded with the family and those who had come to meet Jean-Martin: Dr. Parmentier, Adèle, Sancho, and some neighbor women.

"I understand that they've put a price on the Lafittes' heads," said the spy.

"That's something the Americans are doing, Monsieur Moriste!" Violette laughed.

"Morisset. Isidor Morisset, madame."

"The Lafittes are highly esteemed because they sell at a good price. It would never occur to any of us to turn them in for the five hundred dollars offered for their heads," intervened Sancho García del Solar.

He added that Pierre had a reputation for being crude, but Jean was a gentleman from head to toe, gallant with the women and courteous with men; he spoke five languages, wrote with impeccable style, and entertained with the most generous hospitality. He was of often tested courage, and his men, who numbered nearly three thousand, would die for him.

"Tomorrow is Saturday, and there will be an auction. Would you like to go to the Temple?" Violette asked.

"The Temple, you say?"

"That is where they have the auctions," Parmentier clarified.

"If everyone knows where they are, why haven't they been arrested?" Jean-Martin put in.

"No one dares. Claiborne has asked for reinforcement because those men are something to be feared; their law is violence, and they are better equipped than the army."

The next day Violette, Morisset, and Jean-Martin went on an outing, provided with a basket containing a lunch and two bottles of wine. Violette arranged to leave Rosette behind using the pretext of piano exercises; she had noticed that Jean-Martin was looking at her rather too frequently, and her duty as mother was to prevent any inconvenient fantasy. Rosette was her best student, perfect for the *plaçage*, but absolutely inadequate for her son, who needed to enter the Société du Cordon Bleu by way of a good marriage. She intended to choose her daughter-in-law with an unswerving sense of reality, without giving Jean-Martin the opportunity to commit sentimental errors. As they left, Tété was added to the party. She climbed into the boat at the last minute with some misgivings because she was suffering the usual nausea of the first months of pregnancy, and she was also afraid of the caimans and snakes that infested the water, and others that sometimes fell from overhead branches of the mangroves. The fragile boat was steered by an oarsman who knew his way with his eyes closed in that labyrinth of canals, islands, and swamps eternally enshrouded in pestilent vapors and clouds of mosquitoes—ideal for illegal traffic and imaginative felons.

The Bastard

The Temple turned out to be an island in the swamps of the delta, a compact mound of shells ground by time, with a forest of oaks that once had been a sacred site of the Indians and still held the remains of one of their altars; the name derived from that. The brothers Lafitte had been there since early morning, as they were every Saturday of the year, unless it fell on Christmas or the Virgin's Ascension. Along the shore were lined up flat bottom skiffs, fishing boats, pirogues, canoes, small private boats with awnings for the ladies and rough barges for transporting products.

The pirates had set up several canvas tents, in which they exhibited their treasures and distributed free lemonade for the ladies, Kentucky whiskey for the men, and sweets for the children. The air smelled of stagnant water and the spicy fried crawfish served on corn husks. There was a spirit of carnival, with musicians, jugglers, and a show with trained dogs. A few slaves were on display on a platform, four adults and a naked little boy about two or three years old. Interested parties were examining their teeth to calculate age, the whites of their eyes to check health, and their anuses to be sure they were not stuffed with tow, the most common trick for hiding diarrhea. A mature woman with a lace parasol was weighing with gloved hand the genitals of one of the males.

Pierre Lafitte had already begun the auction of merchandise, which at first view lacked any logic, as if it had been selected with the single purpose of confusing the shoppers, a mixture of crystal lamps, bags of coffee, women's clothing, weapons, boots, bronze statues, jam, pipes and razors, silver teapots, sacks of pepper and cinnamon, furniture, paintings, vanilla, church goblets and candelabra, crates of wine, a tame monkey, and two parrots. No one left without buying; the Lafittes also acted as bankers and lenders. Every object was exclusive, as Pierre shouted at the top of his lungs, and should be, since it all came from boarding merchant ships on the high seas. "Look what we have here, mesdames and messieurs, see this porcelain vase worthy of a royal palace! And what will you give for this brocade cape bordered in ermine! You won't have a chance like this again!" The public responded with clowning and whistling, but the bids kept rising with an entertaining rivalry, which Pierre knew how to exploit.

In the meantime, Jean, dressed in black, with white lace cuffs and collar and pistols at his waist, was strolling through the crowd, seducing the incautious with his easy smile and the dark, beguiling gaze of a snake charmer. He greeted Violette Boisier with a theatrical bow, and she responded with kisses on both cheeks, like the old friends they'd come to be after several years of deals and mutual favors.

"May I ask what might interest the only woman capable of stealing my heart?" Jean asked.

"Don't waste your gallantries on me, *mon cher ami*, because today I am not here to buy." Violette laughed. She gestured to Morisset, four steps behind her.

Distracted by the explorer garb, the shaved face, and the thick spectacles, it took Lafitte a moment to recognize the man he had known with mustache and side-whiskers.

"Morisset? *C'est vraiment vous!*" he finally exclaimed, slapping him on the back.

The spy, uneasy, looked around and pulled his hat down to his eyebrows; it wouldn't help for news of this effusive show of friendship to reach the ears of Governor Claiborne, but no one was paying attention because at that instant Pierre was auctioning an Arab stallion that all the men coveted. Jean Lafitte led him to one of the tents where they could talk in private and refresh themselves with white wine. The spy told him of Napoleon's offer: a corsair's permit, *une lettre de marque*, which was the same as an official authorization to attack other ships, in exchange for which he would vent his spleen on the English. Lafitte replied amiably that in fact he didn't need permission to keep doing what he had always done, and the *lettre de marque* would be a limitation, since it meant abstaining from attacking French boats, with consequent losses.

"Your activities would be legal. You would not be pirates but corsairs, more acceptable to the Americans," Morisset argued.

"The only thing that would change our situation with the Americans would be to pay taxes, and to be frank, we haven't as yet considered that possibility."

"A corsair's license is valuable—"

"Only if we sail under a French flag."

The somber Morisset explained that the emperor's offer did not include that—they would have to continue flying the Cartagena flag, but they could count on impunity and refuge in French territories. That was more words at a time than he'd spoken in a long while. Lafitte agreed to send Morisset their decision since such matters were decided by a vote among his men.

"But in the end the only votes that count are yours and your brother's," Morisset persisted.

"You're mistaken. We are more democratic than the Americans, and certainly much more so than the French. You will have your answer in two days."

Outside the tent, Pierre Lafitte had begun the slave auction, the most awaited part of the fair, and the noise of bids was rising in volume. The one woman in the lot pressed the boy against her and implored a couple of buyers not to separate them; her son was clever and obedient, she said, as Pierre Lafitte described her as a good breeder who'd had a number of children and was still very fertile. Tété watched with her guts in a knot, and a scream caught in her throat, thinking of the children that pitiful woman had lost and the indignity of being auctioned. At least she had not gone through that, and her Rosette was safe. Someone commented that these slaves came from Haïti, delivered directly to the Lafittes by the agents of Dessalines, who was financing arms that way and in passing getting rich selling the same people with whom he'd fought for freedom. If Gambo could see this, he would explode with rage, Tété thought.

When the sale was nearly over, the unmistakable booming voice of Owen Murphy was heard, offering fifty dollars more for the mother and a hundred for the boy. Pierre waited the required minute, and as no one raised the price, shouted that both now belonged to the customer with the black beard. On the platform the woman half collapsed with relief, never loosing her hold on the child, who was crying with terror. One of Pierre Laffite's helpers took her by the arm and turned her over to Owen Murphy.

The Irishman had started off toward the boats, followed by the slave and her child, when Tété came out of her stupor and ran after them, calling to him. He greeted her without any excessive show of affection, but his expression betrayed the pleasure he felt at seeing her. He told her that Brandan, his oldest son, had married overnight and soon would make them grandparents. He also mentioned the land they'd bought in Canada, where they planned to go very soon, and all the family would begin a new life, including Brandan and his wife.

"I imagine that Monsieur Valmorain will not approve of your leaving," Tété commented.

"For some time now Madame Hortense has wanted to replace me.

We don't have the same ideas," Murphy replied. "It's going to annoy her that I bought this black boy, but I've held to the Code. He's not old enough to be separated from his mother."

"There is no law here worth anything, Monsieur Murphy. The pirates do whatever they please."

"That's why I'd rather not deal with them, but I'm not the one who decides, Tété," the Irishman informed her, pointing to Toulouse Valmorain in the distance.

The master was standing away from the crowd, talking with Violette Boisier under an oak, she protected from the sun by a Japanese parasol and he leaning on his walking stick and wiping away sweat with a handkerchief. Tété stepped back, but it was too late; they had seen her, and she felt obliged to go over to them. She was followed by Jean-Martin, who was waiting for Morisset near the Lafittes' tent, and a moment later they were all together under the faint shade of the oak. Tété greeted her former master without looking him in the eye, but was able to note that he was even fatter and redder. She lamented that Dr. Parmentier was treating Valmorain with remedies she herself prepared to cool the blood. That man could with a single wave of his walking stick demolish Rosette's and her precarious existence. It would be better if he were in the grave.

Valmorain was very attentive as Violette Boisier introduced her son. He looked Jean-Martin over from head to toe, appreciating his slim build, the elegance with which he wore the inexpensive waistcoat, the perfect symmetry of his face. The youth greeted him with a bow, respectful of the difference in class and age, but Valmorain held out a fat, yellow-splotched hand he had to shake. Valmorain kept the youth's hand in his much longer than was acceptable, smiling with an indescribable expression. Jean-Martin felt his cheeks blaze red and brusquely pulled back. It wasn't the first time a man had made an insinuation, and he knew how to manage that kind of mortification without a fuss, but the brazenness of this *inverti* was particularly offensive, and he was shamed that his mother witnessed the scene. The rebuff was so obvious that Valmorain realized he had been misinterpreted. Far from being bothered, he snorted a laugh.

"I see that this slave's son has come out a little touchy!" he exclaimed, amused.

A paralyzing silence fell over them as those words dug in their claws. The air became hotter, the light more blinding, the smells of fear more nauseating, the noise of the crowd more deafening, but Valmorain did not notice the effect he had provoked.

"What did you say?" Jean-Martin managed to spit out, livid, when he recovered his voice.

Violette seized his arm and tried to drag him away, but he broke loose from her to confront Valmorain. From habit, his hand went to his hip, where the haft of his sword would have been were he in uniform.

"You have insulted my mother!" he exclaimed hoarsely.

"Don't tell me, Violette, that this boy doesn't know where he comes from," Valmorain commented, still in a mocking tone.

She didn't answer. She had dropped her parasol, which was rolling over the white shell ground, and covered her mouth with both hands, her eyes wide and staring.

"You owe me an apology, monsieur. I will see you in the Saint Antoine gardens with your seconds within a period of no more than two days, because on the third I leave to return to France," Jean-Martin announced, chewing each syllable.

"Don't be ridiculous, son. I'm not going to engage in a duel with anyone of your class. I've spoken the truth. Ask your mother," Valmorain added, pointing at the women with his cane before turning his back and walking without haste toward the boats, stumbling along on swollen knees, to rejoin Owen Murphy.

Jean-Martin tried to follow him, with the intention of pounding his face to a pulp, but Violette and Tété held on to his clothing. At that point, Isidor Morisset, seeing his secretary struggling with the women, red with fury, immobilized him from behind. Tété was quick enough to invent that there'd been an altercation with a pirate, and they should go immediately. The spy agreed—he did not want to endanger his negotiations with Lafitte—and subduing the youth with his woodsman's hands led him, followed by the women, to the boat, where the oarsman was waiting with the untouched lunch.

Worried, Morisset put an arm about Jean-Martin's shoulders in a paternal gesture and tried to find out what had happened, but the youth pulled away and turned his back to him, with his eyes fixed on the water. No one said a word during the hour and a half it took to make their way through that labyrinth of swamps and reach New Orleans. Morisset went alone to his hotel. His secretary ignored his order to accompany him and followed Violette and Tété to the house on Chartres. Violette went to her room, closed the door, and threw herself on the bed to weep her last tear, as Jean-Martin paced like a lion on the patio, waiting for her to calm down enough to question her. "What do you know about my mother's past, Loula? You have an obligation to tell me!" he demanded of his *nana* Loula, who had no idea what had happened at the Temple; she thought he was referring to the glorious days when Violette had been the most divine *poule* in Le Cap and her name traveled in the mouths of captains on remote seas, something she didn't plan to tell her boy, her prince, however much he yelled at her. Violette had striven to erase every trace of her past in Saint-Domingue, and it would not be she, her loyal Loula, who betrayed the secret.

As night fell, when she did not hear the weeping any longer, Tété took Violette a cup of tea for her headache, helped her take off her clothing, brushed the hen's nest her hair had become, sprinkled her with rosewater, pulled a light nightgown over her head, and sat beside her on the bed. In the shadow of the closed shutters, she dared talk with the confidence cultivated day by day during the years they had lived and worked together.

"It isn't that serious, madame. Pretend that those words were never spoken. No one will repeat them, and you and your son can go right on as you always have," she consoled her.

She supposed that Violette Boisier had not been born free, as she had told her once, but had been a slave in her childhood. She couldn't blame her for having kept it secret. Maybe she'd had Jean-Martin before Major Relais emancipated her and made her his wife.

"But Jean-Martin knows now! He will never forgive me for having deceived him," Violette answered.

"It isn't easy to admit that you've been a slave, madame. What is important is that now you both are free."

"I have never been a slave, Tété. The truth is that I am not his mother. Jean-Martin was born a slave, and my husband bought him. The only one who knows is Loula."

"And how did Monsieur Valmorain know?"

So Violette Boisier told her the circumstances under which they'd taken the baby, how Valmorain had brought the infant wrapped in a blanket to ask them to look after it for a while, and how she and her husband ended up adopting him. They didn't know whose baby he was but imagined he was the son of Valmorain by one of his slaves. Tété was not listening any longer—she knew the rest. She had prepared during a thousand sleepless nights for the moment of that revelation, when finally she would learn about the son who had been taken from her, but now that he was within reach of her hand she felt no flash of happiness, not a sob stuck in her breast, not an irrepressible wave of affection, not an impulse to run and throw her arms around him, but a low rumbling in her ears like the wheels of a cart on a dusty path. She closed her eyes and brought up the image of the youth with curiosity, surprised that she hadn't had the least indication of the truth; her instinct had not advised her, she had not even noted his resemblance to Rosette. She raked through her emotions, searching for the bottomless maternal love she knew so well because she had lavished it on Maurice and Rosette, but found only relief. Her son had been born under a good star, under a radiant *z'étoile*, and for that reason he had fallen into the hands of the Relais couple and Loula, who spoiled and educated him, and for that reason the military man had bequeathed him the legend of his life and Violette had worked untiringly to assure him a good future. Tété was grateful without a trace of jealousy, for she could not have given him any of that.

Tété's rancor against Valmorain, that black, hard rock she had felt forever in her breast, seemed to shrink, and the drive to take revenge on her master dissolved in appreciation of those who had taken such good care of her son. She did not have to think too much about what she would do with the information she had just received, gratitude decided that. What would she gain by announcing to the four winds that she was the mother of Jean-Martin and claiming an affection that with justice belonged to another woman? She chose to confess the truth to Violette Boisier, without wallowing in the suffering that had crushed her in the past, for that had eased in recent years. The youth who at that moment was pacing the patio was a stranger to her.

The two women wept, holding hands, joined by a delicate current of mutual compassion. At last the tears dried, and they concluded that what Valmorain had said could not be erased but they might soften its impact on Jean-Martin. Why tell him that Violette was not his mother, that he was born a slave, the bastard offspring of a white man, and that he was given away? It was better for him to continue to believe what he heard from Valmorain, which in essence was true: that his mother had been a slave. Neither was it necessary for him to know that Violette was a cocotte, nor that Relais had a reputation for being cruel. Jean-Martin would believe that Violette had hidden the stigma of her slavery to protect him, but he could always be proud of being the Relais's son. In a couple of days he would return to France and his army career, where prejudice regarding his origins was less harmful than in America or the colonies, and where Valmorain's words could be relegated to a lost corner of memory.

"We will bury this forever," said Tété.

"And what will we do about Toulouse Valmorain?" Violette asked.

"You go see him, madame. Explain to him that it is not wise to divulge certain secrets, or you will be sure that his wife and the entire city know that he is the father of Jean-Martin and Rosette."

"And also that his children can claim the Valmorain name and a part of the inheritance," Violette added with an impish wink.

"Is that true?"

"No, Tété, but scandal would be fatal for the Valmorains."

Fear of Dying

$\mathcal{V}$iolette Boisier knew that the first Cordon Bleu ball would be the model for all future balls, and that she had to establish from the beginning the difference between it and the other festivities that entertained the city from October to the end of April. The large hall was decorated without thought of expense. Stages were built for the musicians, tables set with embroidered cloths, and felt armchairs for the mothers and chaperones were placed around the dance floor. A carpeted runway was constructed for the triumphal entrance of the girls onto the dance floor. The day of the ball all the drains in the street were cleaned and covered with planks, colored lanterns were lit, and the surroundings were enlivened by musicians and black dancers, just as it was during Carnival. The atmosphere inside the hall, nevertheless, was very sober.

In the Valmorain house not too far away they had heard the distant sound of music, but Hortense Guizot, like all the other white women in the city, pretended not to. She knew what was going on; no one had talked about anything else for several weeks. She had finished dinner and was embroidering in the drawing room, surrounded by her daughters, who were playing with dolls while the youngest slept in her cradle, all as blond and rosy as she once had been. Now, ground down by maternity, she used rouge on her cheeks and relied on a blond switch her slave Denise artfully combed in with her own straw-colored hair. Dinner consisted of soup, two main courses, salad, cheeses, and three desserts; nothing too complicated because she was alone. The girls were not yet eating in the dining hall, nor was her husband, who was following a rigorous diet and preferred not to be tempted. He was in the library, where he'd been sent chicken and rice cooked without salt; he was trying to follow Dr. Parmentier's strict orders. Besides starving, he had to take walks in the fresh air and deny himself alcohol, cigars, and coffee. He would have died of boredom without his brother-in-law Sancho, who visited him every day to bring him up to date on news and gossip, cheer him up with his good humor, and beat him at cards and dominos.

Parmentier, who complained so often about his own heart, was not following the monkish regimen he imposed on his patient because Sanité Dédé, the voodoo priestess at place Congo, had read his fortune in the cowrie shells, and according to her prophecy he was going to live till he was eighty-nine years old. "You, white man, are going to close the eyes of that saintly Père Antoine when he dies in 1829." That soothed him in regard to his health but created the sadness of losing in that long life his dearest beloveds, like Adèle and perhaps even one of his children.

The first alarm that things were not going well with Valmorain had occurred during his trip to France. Following the lugubrious visit with his hundred-year-old mother and unmarried sisters, he left Maurice in France and set sail for New Orleans. On the ship he suffered several attacks of fatigue, which he attributed to the buffeting of the waves, excess of wine, and bad food. When he got home, his friend Parmentier diagnosed high blood pressure, fluttering pulse, bad digestion, abundance of bile, flatulence, festering humors, and palpitations of the heart. He told him with no beating about the bush that he must lose weight and change his life or end up in his mausoleum in Saint Louis Cemetery before the end of a year. Terrified, Valmorain submitted to the doctor's demands and the despotism of his wife, who had become his jailer under the pretext of caring for him. Just in case, he went to *docteurs feuilles* and magi, whom he had always mocked until his fright made him change his mind.

Nothing to lose by trying it, he thought. He had obtained a *gris-gris*, he had a pagan altar in his room, he drank potions impossible to identify that Célestine brought from the market, and he had made two nocturnal excursions to an island in the swamp so Sanité Dédé could cleanse him with her incantations and the smoke of her tobacco. Parmentier did not question the priestess's competence, faithful to his idea that the mind has the power to cure, and if the patient believed in magic, there was no reason to discourage him from it.

Maurice, who was working in a sugar importing agency in France, where Valmorain had placed him to learn that aspect of the family business, took the first available ship when he learned of his father's illness and reached New Orleans at the end of October. He found Valmorain transformed into a voluminous sea lion in a large chair beside the hearth, with a knit cap on his head, a shawl over his legs, and a wood cross and a rag *gris-gris* around his neck, vastly deteriorated in comparison to the haughty, extravagant man who had wanted to introduce his son to the dissolute life in Paris. Maurice knelt beside his father, who clasped him in a trembling embrace. "My son, at last you have come, now I can die in peace," he murmured. "Don't be foolish, Toulouse!" Hortense Guizot interrupted, watching them with disgust. And it was on the tip of her tongue to add that he wasn't going to die yet, unfortunately, but she caught herself in time. She had been looking after her husband for three months and had run out of patience. Valmorain irritated her all day and woke her at night with repeated nightmares about some Lacroix, who came to him in raw flesh, dragging his skin along the ground like a bleeding shirt.

The stepmother welcomed Maurice curtly, and his sisters greeted him with learned curtsies, keeping their distance because they had no idea who this brother was, he was mentioned very rarely in the family. The eldest of the five girls, the one Maurice had known before she could walk, was eight, and the youngest was in the arms of a wet nurse. As the house had become crowded with the family and servants, Maurice took lodging at his uncle Sancho's apartment, an ideal solution for everyone except Toulouse Valmorain, who meant to keep his son by his side to shower him with advice and pass on to him how to manage his wealth. That was the last thing Maurice wanted, but it wasn't the moment to contradict his father.

The night of the ball, Sancho and Maurice did not dine at the Valmorain residence, as they did almost daily, more as obligation than pleasure. Neither of the two was comfortable with Hortense Guizot, who never had wanted the stepson and grudgingly tolerated Sancho, with his dashing mustache, his Spanish accent, and his shamelessness; he had to be brazen to parade around town with that Cuban woman, a mixed-blood vixen directly to blame for the much talked about Cordon Bleu ball. Only her impeccable upbringing kept Hortense from bursting out with insults when she thought about that: no lady ever alluded to the fascination those mulatta courtesans exercised over white men or to the immoral practice of offering them their daughters. She knew that uncle and son were making preparations to attend the ball, but not even in the clutch of death would she mention it to them. Neither could she talk about it with her husband; that would be to admit she spied on their private conversations, just as she went through his correspondence and looked into the secret compartments in his desk where he hid his money. That was how she learned that Sancho had received two invitations from Violette Boisier because Maurice wanted to go to the ball. Sancho had to consult Valmorain because his nephew's inopportune interest in *plaçage* required financial support.

Hortense, who was listening with her ear glued to a hole she had drilled in the wall, heard her husband immediately approve the idea and assumed that Maurice's eagerness had dispelled his doubts regarding his son's virility. She herself had contributed to those doubts, using the word *effeminate* in more than one conversation about her stepson. To Valmorain, *plaçage* seemed appropriate, seeing that Maurice had never shown any appetite for brothels or the family slaves. He was young, and had at least ten years to think about marriage, and in the meantime he needed to unburden himself of his masculine impulses, as Sancho called them. A young girl of color, clean, virtuous, faithful, offered many advantages. Sancho explained to Valmorain the financial considerations, which previously had been left to the protector's goodwill but now, since Violette Boisier had taken charge of things, were stipulated in an oral contract, which if it lacked legal value was nonetheless inviolable. Valmorain had not objected to the cost: Maurice deserved it. On the other side of the wall, Hortense Guizot was close to screaming.

Ball of the Sirens

*J*ean-Martin confessed to Isidor Morisset, with tears of shame, what Valmorain had said, and his mother not denied it, simply refused to speak of it. Morisset listened to what he said with a mocking laugh—What the devil does that matter, son!—but immediately he was moved and pulled him to his ample chest to console him. He was not sentimental and was himself surprised at the emotion the youth aroused in him, desires to protect him and kiss him. He pushed him away gently, picked up his hat, and went to take a long walk along the dike until he cleared his mind. Two days later they sailed for France. Jean-Martin bid his small family farewell with his usual public rigidity, but at the last minute he threw his arms around Violette and whispered that he would write her.

The Cordon Bleu ball turned out to be as magnificent as Violette Boisier had conceived it and others had anticipated. The men arrived in full dress, punctual and correct, and scattered into groups beneath the crystal chandeliers alight with hundreds of candles as an orchestra played and the servants passed light drinks and champagne, no strong liquors. The banquet tables were waiting in the next room, but it would be considered impolite to assault them ahead of time. Violette Boisier, soberly dressed, welcomed the men; soon the mothers and chaperones arrived and took their seats. The orchestra attacked a fanfare, a theater curtain opened at one end of the hall, and the girls made their appearance on the walkway, slowly advancing in single file. There were a few dark mulattas, several *sang-mêlés* who passed as European, including two or three with blue eyes, and a vast array of quadroons of diverse shades, all attractive, reserved, docile, elegant, and educated in the Catholic faith. Some were so timid that they did not lift their gaze from the carpet, but others, more daring, cast sidelong glances at the gallants lined up against the walls. Only one came stiff, serious, wearing a defiant, almost hostile, expression. That was Rosette. The floating dresses in pastel colors had been ordered from France or copied to perfection by Adèle, the simple hairdos emphasized lustrous manes, arms and necks were bare, and faces seemed clean of paint. Only the women knew how much effort and art each innocent face had cost.

A respectful silence welcomed the first girls, but after a few minutes there was spontaneous applause. Never had such a notable collection of sirens been seen, those fortunate enough to have been present reported the next day in cafés and taverns. The candidates for *plaçage* glided like swans around the hall, the orchestra abandoned the trumpet salute to play danceable music, and the white youths began their advances with unusual etiquette, none of the bold familiarity that erupted at the quadroons' parties. After exchanging a few words of courtesy to test the terrain, the young men requested a dance. They were allowed to dance with all the girls, but they had been instructed that the second or third dance with the same girl meant they had a decision to make. The chaperones watched everything with eagle eyes. Not one of those arrogant youths, accustomed to doing whatever they pleased, dared violate the rules. They were intimidated for the first time in their lives.

Maurice did not look at anyone. The mere idea that these girls were being offered to benefit the white men made him ill. He was sweating, and felt a pounding at his temples. He was interested only in Rosette. Ever since he got off the ship in New Orleans several days before, he had looked forward to the ball as the way to meet her, a plan they had agreed to in their secret correspondence; however, since he had not even caught sight of her earlier, he was afraid he wouldn't recognize her. The instinct and nostalgia nourished within the stone walls of the school in Boston nevertheless allowed Maurice to deduce at first glance that the haughty girl dressed in white, the prettiest of all, was his Rosette. By the time he was able to pry his feet from the floor, she was already surrounded by three or four interested young men; she scrutinized each one, trying to discover the person she wanted to see. She, too, had anxiously awaited that moment. From childhood she had protected her love for Maurice with duplicity, disguising it as love for a sibling, but she did not plan to do that any longer. This was the night of truth.

Maurice approached, elbowing his way, tight, rigid, and stopped in front of Rosette with bedazzled eyes. They gazed at each other, searching for the person they remembered: she the crybaby with green eyes who had followed her like a shadow in her childhood, and he the bossy little girl who came at night and slipped into his bed. They met in the embers of memory, and in an instant were again the ones they had been: Maurice, unable to speak, and trembling, waited, and Rosette, tossing aside norms, took his hand and led him to the floor.

Through her white gloves the girl felt the heat of Maurice's skin, which traveled down her spine to her feet, as if she had come close to a fireplace. She felt her knees buckling; she stumbled and had to hold on to him to keep from dropping to her knees. The first waltz went by without their knowing it; they could not say anything, only touch and sum each other up, completely indifferent to the other couples. The music ended, and they went on dancing, engrossed in themselves, moving with the awkwardness of the blind, until the orchestra began again and they picked up the rhythm. By then several persons were watching sneeringly, and Violette Boisier had realized that something was threatening the strict etiquette of the ball.

With the last chord, a youth more daring than the others stepped up to dance with Rosette. She didn't notice the interruption, she was clinging to Maurice's arm with her eyes locked on his, but the man insisted. Then Maurice seemed to wake from a sleepwalker's trance; he turned abruptly and shoved away the intruder with a push so unexpected that his rival stumbled and fell to the floor. A collective *Oooooh!* paralyzed the musicians. Maurice stammered an apology and held out his hand to the fallen rival to help him to his feet, but the insult had been too evident. Two of the youth's friends had already rushed to the floor and confronted Maurice. Before anyone could call for a duel, as happened all too frequently, Violette Boisier intervened, trying to ease the tension with jokes and little taps of her fan, and Sancho García del Solar took a firm grip on his nephew and led him to the dining room, where the older men were already savoring the delicious plates of the best *cuisine créole*.

"What are you doing, Maurice! Don't you know who that girl is?" Sancho asked.

"Rosette—who else would it be? I've waited nine years to see her."

"You can't dance with her. Dance with the other girls, several are very beautiful, and once you choose, I will take care of the rest."

"I came only for Rosette, Uncle."

Sancho took a deep breath, filling his chest with a mouthful of air redolent of cigars and the sweetish fragrance of flowers. He was not prepared for this; he had never imagined that it would be up to him to open Maurice's eyes, and even less that such a melodramatic revelation would happen in this place, and so quickly. He had perceived that passion ever since he first saw Maurice with Rosette in Cuba, in 1793, when they were escaping from Le Cap with torn clothing and the ash from the fire on their skin. At that time they were little children walking along holding hands, frightened by the horror of what they had seen, and it was obvious they were united by a strong and possessive love. Sancho could not understand how the others couldn't help but notice.

"Forget Rosette. She is your father's daughter. Rosette is your sister, Maurice." Sancho sighed, his eyes focused on the tip of his boots.

"I know that, Uncle," the youth replied serenely. "We've always known, but that will not prevent us from marrying."

"You must be demented, son. That's impossible."

"We'll see about that, Uncle."

*H*ortense Guizot had never dared hope that heaven would rid her of Maurice without direct intervention on her part. She satisfied her rancor by conceiving ways to eliminate her stepson, the one dream that practical woman allowed herself, though she had nothing to confess to because those hypothetical crimes were only dreams, and to dream is not a sin. She had tried so hard to separate him from his father and replace him with the son she had not been able to conceive that when Maurice sank himself, leaving the way open for her to manage her husband's estate in her own way, she felt vaguely defrauded. She had spent the night of the ball in her queenly bed beneath the canopy of angels that was transported between the city house and the plantation every season, tossing and turning without being able to sleep, thinking that at that very moment Maurice was selecting a concubine, the definitive sign that he had left adolescence behind and fully entered adult life. Her stepson was a man now, and naturally he would begin to take over the family businesses, at which time her own power would be badly diminished because she did not have the influence over him she did over her husband. The last thing she wanted was to see Maurice digging into the accounts or putting limits on her spending.

Hortense could not sleep until finally at dawn she took a few drops of laudanum and was able to fall into a restless state peopled with disturbing visions. She waked near midday, cross from the bad night and bad omens, and pulled the cord to summon Denise and ask her to bring a clean chamber pot and her cup of chocolate. She thought she heard a muffled conversation that seemed to come from the library on the floor below. She knew that the conduit for the cord to call the slaves, which ran through two floors and the mansard, served to help her hear what was going on in the rest of the house. She put her ear to the hole and heard irate voices, but as she could not distinguish the words, she sneaked out of her room. On the stairway she ran into her slave, who, seeing her slipping along like a thief, barefoot and in her nightclothes, pressed against the wall, invisible and mute.

Sancho had come ahead to explain to Toulouse Valmorain what had happened at the Cordon Bleu ball and to prepare him for what was coming, but had not found a tactful way to tell him about Maurice's mad intention to marry Rosette, so he poured out the news in one sentence. "Marry?" Valmorain repeated, incredulous. It seemed hugely comic to him, and he bellowed with laughter, but as Sancho kept telling him more about his son's determination, his laughter turned into violent indignation. He poured himself a cognac, the third of the morning, despite Parmentier's prohibition, and quaffed it in one swallow, which left him coughing.

Shortly afterward, Maurice arrived. Valmorain met him, gesticulating and beating the table, the same old song but this time yelling: he was Valmorain's only heir, destined to carry the title of chevalier with pride and to increase the family's power and fortune, which had been earned with great effort; he was the last male who could perpetuate the dynasty, that was what Valmorain had trained him for, he had imbued him with his principles and sense of honor, he had offered him everything a father can give a son, he would not permit him to stain the illustrious name of the Valmorains with a youthful impulse. No, no, he corrected, it wasn't an impulse it was a vice, a perversion, it was nothing less than incest. He collapsed into his armchair, breathless. On the other side of the wall, glued to her spy hole, Hortense Guizot choked back an exclamation. She had not expected her husband to admit to his son his paternity of Rosette, which he had so carefully hidden from her.

"Incest, monsieur? You forced me to swallow soap when I called Rosette sister," Maurice argued.

"You know very well what I am referring to!"

"I will marry Rosette even though you are her father," said Maurice, attempting to keep a respectful tone.

"But how can you marry a quadroon!" roared Valmorain.

"Apparently, monsieur, you are bothered more by Rosette's color than by our being related. But if you engender a daughter with a woman of color, you should not be surprised that I love another."

"Insolent pup!"

Sancho tried to pacify them with conciliatory gestures. Valmorain understood that he was not getting anywhere down that path and forced himself to appear calm and reasonable.

"You are a good boy, Maurice, but overly sensitive and dreamy," he said. "It was a mistake to send you to that American school. I don't know what ideas they put in your head, but it seems that you do not know who you are, what your position is, or the responsibilities you have to your family and society."

"The school has given me a broader vision of the world, monsieur, but that has nothing to do with Rosette. My feelings for her are the same now as they were fifteen years ago."

"These impulses are normal at your age, son. There's nothing original about your case," Valmorain assured him. "No one marries at eighteen, Maurice. Choose a lover like any other boy of your position. That will calm you down. If there is anything we have a lot of in this city, it's beautiful women of color—"

"No!" his son interrupted. "Rosette is the only woman for me."

"Incest is very serious, Maurice."

"Much more serious is slavery."

"What does one have to do with the other!"

"A great deal, monsieur. Without slavery, which allowed you to abuse your slave, Rosette would not be my sister," Maurice explained.

"How dare you speak that way to your father!"

"Forgive me, monsieur," Maurice replied with irony. "In truth, the mistakes you have made cannot serve as an excuse for mine."

"What you have, son, is lust," said Valmorain with a theatrical sigh. "Nothing easier to understand. You must do what we all do in such cases."

"What is that, monsieur?"

"I thought I did not have to explain these things to you, Maurice. Bed your girl once and for all, and then forget her. That's how it's done. What else can you do with a Negress?"

"That is what you want for your daughter?" Maurice asked, pale, clenching his teeth. Drops of sweat were streaming down his face, and his shirt was damp.

"She is the daughter of a slave! My children are white!" Valmorain shouted.

A frigid silence fell over the library. Sancho backed away, rubbing the back of his neck, with the sensation that all was lost. His brother-in-law's clumsiness seemed irreparable.

"I shall marry her," Maurice said finally, and strode out of the room, ignoring his father's string of threats.

To the Right of the Moon

It had never crossed Tété's mind to go to the ball, and neither had she been invited. She understood it wasn't for people of her status: the other mothers would have been offended and her daughter would have choked with embarrassment, so she worked out an agreement with Violette to act as Rosette's chaperone. The preparations for that night, which had taken months of patience and work, gave the hoped for results: Rosette looked like an angel in her ethereal gown, with jasmine pinned in her hair. Before her daughter climbed into the rented coach, viewed by neighbors who'd come outside to applaud them, Violette repeated to Tété and Loula that she was going to get the best of the young protectors for Rosette. No one imagined that she would come dragging the girl back an hour later, when neighbors were still in the street chatting.

Rosette burst into the house with the mulish expression that had this year replaced her coquetry. She tore off her dress, and locked herself in her room without a word. Violette was hysterical, screaming that that little troublemaker was going to pay, that she had nearly destroyed the ball, that she had deceived everyone, and that she had made her waste time, effort, and money because she had never intended to be *placée*, the ball had been a vehicle for meeting that wretched Maurice. Violette was certain. Rosette and Maurice had in some inexplicable fashion planned to meet there, because the girl could not go out alone. How she sent and received messages was a mystery she refused to reveal, despite the slapping Violette gave her. That confirmed a suspicion Tété had always had: the *z'etoiles* of those two children were joined in heaven: some nights they were clearly visible to the right of the moon.

After the scene in the library of the house where he had confronted his father, Maurice left determined to cut his ties to his family forever. Sancho was able to soothe Valmorain a little and then follow his nephew to the apartment they shared, where he found Maurice distraught, red with fever and with pain in his gut. With his servant's help, Sancho got Maurice's clothing off and put him in bed, then forced him to drink a glass of warm whiskey with sugar and lemon, an improvised remedy that occurred to him as a palliative for the pangs of love and which also tumbled Maurice into a deep sleep. He told his servant to keep him cool with wet cloths to bring down his temperature, but that did not keep Maurice from raving with delirium the rest of the afternoon and a good part of the night.

The next morning the youth waked with less fever. The room was dark because the drapes had been closed but he did not want to call the servant, although he needed water and a cup of coffee. When he tried to get up to use the chamber pot, all his muscles were sore, as if he had galloped horseback a week, and he chose to go back to bed. Shortly afterward Sancho arrived with Parmentier. The doctor, who had known Maurice since he was a boy, could only repeat the cliché observation that time slips away faster than money. Where had the years gone? Maurice had gone out the door in short pants and returned through another changed into a man. The doctor examined him meticulously without reaching a diagnosis; the picture still was not clear, he said, he would have to wait. He ordered Maurice to stay in bed and see how he got along. He had recently attended two sailors in the nuns' hospital who had typhus. It wasn't an epidemic, he assured them, these were isolated cases, but they should be aware of that possibility. Rats from the ships often spread the illness, and perhaps Maurice had been infected on the voyage.

"I am sure it isn't typhus, Doctor," Maurice mumbled, embarrassed.

"What is it then?" Parmentier smiled.

"Nerves."

"Nerves?" Sancho repeated, highly amused. "The thing old maids suffer?"

"This is something I haven't done since I was a boy, Doctor, but I haven't forgotten, and I suppose you haven't either. Don't you remember Le Cap?"

Parmentier saw the little boy Maurice had been at that time, raging with fever from being harassed by ghosts of the tortured men who walked through his house.

"I hope you're right," said Parmentier. "Your uncle Sancho told me what happened at the ball and the fight you had with your father."

"He insulted Rosette! He spoke of her as if she were a tramp," said Maurice.

"My brother-in-law is very angry, as is logical," Sancho interrupted. "Maurice has it in his head to marry Rosette. He not only means to defy his father but the entire world."

"All we ask is for everyone to leave us in peace, Uncle," said Maurice.

"No one will leave you in peace, because if you go ahead with your plan society will be endangered. Imagine the example you two will set. It would be like a hole in the dike. First a trickle and then a deluge that would destroy everything in its path."

"We would go far away, where no one knows us," Maurice insisted.

"Where? To live with Indians, covered with stinking skins and eating corn? I'd like to know how long love would last under those conditions!"

"You are very young, Maurice, you have your whole life ahead of you," the physician argued weakly.

"My life. Apparently that's the only thing that counts. And Rosette? Maybe her life doesn't count too? I love her, Doctor!"

"I understand you better than anyone, son. My lifetime companion, the mother of my three children, is a mulatta," Parmentier confessed.

"Yes, but she isn't your sister!" Sancho exclaimed.

"That doesn't matter," Maurice replied.

"Explain to him, Doctor, that defective children are born of such unions," Sancho insisted.

"Not always," the doctor murmured, thoughtful.

Maurice's mouth was dry, and again he felt his body burning. He closed his eyes, annoyed with himself for not being able to control his shivers, undoubtedly caused by his accursed imagination. He wasn't listening to his uncle; he had the sound of a roaring waterfall in his ears.

Parmentier interrupted the list of Sancho's arguments. "I think there is a way we can satisfy everyone, and for Maurice and Rosette to be together." He explained that very few people knew they were half siblings, and besides, it would not be the first time that something like that had happened. The masters' promiscuity with their slaves produced every kind of confused relationship, he added. No one knew absolutely what happened in the intimacy of a house, to say nothing of a plantation. The Creoles did not attach too much importance to love affairs among relatives of different races—not only among brother and sister but also father and daughter—as long as it wasn't aired in public. Whites with whites, on the other hand, was intolerable.

"Where are we going with this, Doctor?" asked Maurice.

"*Plaçage*. Think about it, son. You would treat Rosette the way you would a wife, and although you did not live with her openly you could visit her whenever you wanted. Rosette would be respected in her circles. Your position would not change, and that way you could protect her much better than if you were a pariah, and poor in addition, as you would be if you persist in marrying her."

"Brilliant, Doctor!" Sancho burst out before Maurice could open his mouth. "All we need is for Toulouse Valmorain to accept it."

In the following days, while Maurice fought what turned out to be typhus, definitively, Sancho tried to convince his brother-in-law of the advantages of *plaçage* for Maurice and Rosette. If previously Valmorain had been willing to finance the expenses of a girl he didn't know, there was no reason to refuse it to the only girl Maurice desired. Up to that point, Valmorain listened with lowered head, but attentive.

"Besides, she was brought up in the bosom of your family, and you can be sure that she's decent, refined, and well educated," Sancho added, but the minute he said it, he realized the error of reminding Valmorain that Rosette was his daughter: it was as if he had pinched him.

"I would rather see Maurice dead than keeping that strumpet!" he bellowed.

The Spaniard crossed himself automatically: that was tempting the devil.

"Pay no attention to me, Sancho, that slipped out without my thinking," his brother-in-law mumbled, also shaken by superstitious apprehension.

"Calm down, dear friend. Children always rebel, it's normal, but sooner or later they become reasonable," said Sancho, serving himself a cognac. "Your opposition merely strengthens Maurice's stubbornness. All you will do is drive him away."

"The one who's losing is him."

"Think it over. You are losing too. You aren't young anymore, and your health is failing. Who will look after you in your old age? Who will manage the plantation and your businesses when you can no longer do it? Who will look after Hortense and the girls?"

"You."

"Me?" and a happy laugh burst from Sancho. "I'm a rogue, Toulouse! You can see me becoming the pillar of the family? Not even God would wish that!"

"If Maurice betrays me you will have to help me, Sancho. You are my partner and my only friend."

"Please, don't frighten me."

"I think you're right. I must not fight Maurice face to face but be shrewd. The boy needs to cool down, think of his future, enjoy himself as befitting his age, and meet other women. That little cheat needs to disappear."

"How?" Sancho asked.

"There are ways."

"What ways?"

"For example, offer her a good sum to go away and leave my son alone. Money buys everything, Sancho, but if that doesn't work—well, we would take other measures."

"Don't count on me for anything like that!" said Sancho, alarmed. "Maurice would never forgive you."

"He wouldn't have to know."

"I would tell him. Precisely because I love you like a brother, Toulouse, I'm not going to let you do such an evil thing. You would regret it all your life," Sancho replied.

"Don't fret, my friend. I was joking. You know I'm not capable of killing a fly."

Valmorain's laugh sounded like a bark. Sancho left, worried, while his brother-in-law kept thinking about the *plaçage*. It seemed the most logical alternative, but to sponsor such a relationship between brother and sister was very dangerous. If it came to be known, his honor would be irreparably stained, and everyone would turn their backs on the Valmorains. How would they show themselves in public? He had to think about the future of his five daughters, his businesses, and his social position, just as Hortense had pointed out to him. He could not have imagined that Hortense herself had already circulated that news. Put in the position of choosing between saving her family's reputation, every Creole lady's first priority, or ruining her stepson's, Hortense ceded to the temptation of the second. If the matter had been in her hands, she herself would have married Maurice to Rosette, gladly, to destroy him. She didn't like the *plaçage* Sancho proposed because once their spirits cooled, as always happened over time, Maurice could exercise his rights as firstborn son without anyone's remembering his slip. People have bad memories. The only practical solution was for her stepson to be forever repudiated by his father. "Marry a quadroon? Perfect. Let him do it and live among blacks, as he deserves," she had commented to her sisters and friends, who in turn made it their business to repeat it.

In Love

Tété and Rosette had left the yellow house on Chartres the day after the embarrassing episode at the Cordon Bleu ball. Violette Boisier's fit of rage had quickly passed, and she forgave Rosette because she was always moved by thwarted love, but nevertheless she felt relieved when Tété announced that she did not want to abuse her hospitality any longer. It was better to put a little distance between them, she thought. Tété took her daughter to the boardinghouse where years ago the tutor Gaspard Sévérin had lived, while the little house Zacharie had bought two blocks from Adèle was being remodeled. She continued to work with Violette as she always had, and started Rosette sewing with Adèle, it was time for the girl to earn a living. She was powerless before the hurricane that had been unleashed. She inevitably had compassion for her daughter but could not get close enough to try to help her, Rosette had closed up like a mollusk. Rosette was not talking to anyone. She sewed in a hostile silence, waiting for Maurice with granite hardness, blind to the curiosity of others and deaf to the advice of the women around her: her mother, Violette, Loula, Adèle, and a dozen nosy neighbors.

Tété learned of the confrontation between Maurice and Toulouse Valmorain from Adèle, who had been told by Parmentier, and from Sancho, who made a quick visit to the pension to bring her news of Maurice. He told her that the youth was weakened by the typhus, but out of danger, and that he wanted to see Rosette as soon as possible. "He asked me to intercede and ask if you would see him, Tété," he added. "Maurice is my son, Don Sancho, he doesn't need to send me messages. I am waiting to see him," was her response. She could speak with frankness, since Rosette had gone to deliver some sewing. It had been several weeks since they had seen each other; Sancho had disappeared from the neighborhood. He hadn't dared be seen near Violette Boisier since she caught him with Adi Soupir, the same frivolous girl he had been close to earlier. Sancho won nothing by swearing he had run into her in the place d'Armes and invited her to have an innocent glass of sherry, that was all. What was bad about that? But Violette had no interest in competing with any rival for the artichoke heart of that Spaniard, least of all with someone half her age.

According to Sancho, Toulouse Valmorain had demanded that his son come speak with him as soon as he was on his feet. Maurice struggled to dress and went to his father's house, he didn't want to keep putting off a resolution. Until he clarified things with his father he was not free to present himself to Rosette. When he saw his son's yellow skin and the way his clothes hung off him—he had lost several kilos during his brief illness—Valmorain was frightened. The old fear that death was going to carry him off that had so often assaulted him when Maurice was a boy again squeezed his chest. Urged by Hortense Guizot, he was prepared to impose his authority, but he realized that he loved Maurice too much: anything was preferable to fighting with his son. On impulse, he opted for the *plaçage* he previously had opposed out of pride and his wife's advice. He saw lucidly that it was the only possible way out. "I will give you what is suitable, son. You will have enough to buy a bungalow for that girl and keep her as is expected. I will pray that there is no scandal and that God will pardon you both. I ask only that you never speak of her in my presence, or in your mother's," Valmorain told him.

Maurice's reaction was not what had been expected by either his father or Sancho, who was also in the library. He replied that he appreciated his father's offer of help, but that was not the destiny he would choose. He did not intend to continue to submit to society's hypocrisy or to expose Rosette to the injustice of *plaçage*, in which she would be trapped while he enjoyed total freedom. In addition, that would be a stigma for the political career he was planning to follow. He said that he was going to return to Boston and live among more civilized people; he would study law, and then, from Congress and newspapers, he would try to change the Constitution, the laws, and finally the customs not only in the United States but in the world.

His father stopped him, convinced that the delirium of typhus had returned. "What are you talking about, Maurice?"

"Abolition, monsieur. I am going to devote my life to struggling against slavery," Maurice replied firmly.

That was a blow a thousand times more grave to Valmorain than the matter of Rosette: it was a direct attack on the interests of his family. His son was more out of his mind than he had imagined; he intended nothing less than to destroy the foundation of civilization and of the Valmorain fortune. Abolitionists were tarred and feathered and hanged, as deserved. They were fanatic madmen who dared to defy society, history, even the divine word, because slavery appeared in the Bible. An abolitionist in his own family? Unthinkable! He let loose a yelling harangue without taking a breath, and ended by threatening to disinherit his son.

"Do so, monsieur, because if I inherited your estate, the first thing I would do would be to emancipate the slaves and sell the plantation," Maurice replied calmly.

The youth got to his feet, leaning on the back of the chair because he was still a little light-headed, said good-bye with a slight bow, and left the library, trying to hide the trembling in his legs. His father's insults followed him to the street.

Valmorain lost control; his anger turned him into a whirlwind; he cursed his son, he screeched that Maurice was as good as dead to him, and that he would not receive a single coin of his fortune. "I forbid you ever to step inside the house or use the Valmorain name! You are no longer a member of this family!" He could not go on because he collapsed, dragging with him an opaline lamp that shattered against the wall. Hortense and several domestics had come at the sound of his yelling; they found him turned purple with his eyes rolled back in his head, while Sancho, on his knees beside him, was trying to loosen the tie buried in the folds of the double chin.

Blood Ties

An hour later Maurice appeared, without notice, at Tété's pension. She had not seen him for several years, but to her that tall, serious youth with a wild head of hair and round glasses seemed unchanged from the child she had cared for. Maurice had the same intensity and tenderness he'd had as a boy. They hugged for a long while, she repeating his name and he whispering *Maman*, *Maman*, the forbidden word. They were in the small, dusty drawing room of the pension, which was kept in eternal darkness. What little light filtered through the shutters fell upon the rickety furniture, a threadbare carpet, and yellowed paper on the walls.

Rosette, who had so eagerly awaited Maurice, did not speak, stunned with happiness and upset to see him so shrunken, so different from the well-built youth she had danced with two weeks before. Mute, she watched as if the unexpected visit of her beloved had nothing to do with her.

"Rosette and I have loved each other forever, Maman, you know that. Ever since we were children, we have talked about marrying, do you remember," asked Maurice.

"Yes, son, I remember. But that is a sin."

"I never heard you use that word; have you become a Catholic maybe?"

"My *loas* are always with me, Maurice, but now I go to Père Antoine's mass as well."

"How can love be a sin? God put it on us. Before we were born, we already loved each other. We aren't guilty because we have the same father. The sin isn't ours, it's his."

"There are consequences . . ." Tété murmured.

"I know that. Everyone insists on telling me that we can have abnormal children. We are ready to run that risk, aren't we, Rosette?"

The girl didn't answer. Maurice went to her and put an arm around her shoulders in a protective gesture.

"What will become of the two of you?" Tété asked with anguish.

"We are free and young. We will go to Boston, and if things do not go well we will look for another place. America is very large."

"And her color? You will not be accepted anywhere. They say that in the free states the hatred is worse, and that blacks and whites do not live or mix together."

"True, but that is going to change, I promise. There are many people working to abolish slavery: philosophers, politicians, church people, every person with any decency . . ."

"I will not live to see it, Maurice. But I know that even if the slaves are emancipated, there will be no equality."

"Over time there will have to be, Maman. It's like a snowball that when it begins to roll grows larger, faster, and then no one can stop it. That is how the great changes in history take place."

"Who told you that, son?" Tété asked, who was not sure what snow was.

"My teacher, Harrison Cobb."

Tété realized that it was useless to reason; the cards had been thrown fifteen years before, when he leaned over for the first time to kiss the face of the newborn baby Rosette.

"Don't worry, we will work it out," Maurice added. "But we need your blessing, Maman. We don't want to run away like bandits."

"You have my blessings, children, but that isn't enough. We will go and ask Père Antoine's advice; he knows things about this world and the other," Tété concluded.

They went hurrying through the February breeze to the priest's little house. He had just finished his first round of charity and was resting a bit. He welcomed them with no hint of surprise; he had been waiting for them ever since the gossip had reached his ears that the heir to the Valmorain fortune was going to marry a quadroon. As he was always au courant with everything that happened in the city, his faithful believed the Holy Spirit whispered information to him. He offered them his mass wine, harsh as varnish.

"We want to marry, *mon père*," Maurice announced.

"But the small detail of race is there, is that not it?" The priest smiled.

"We know that the law . . ." Maurice continued.

"Have you committed the sin of the flesh?" Père Antoine again interrupted.

"How could you believe that, *mon père*? I give you my word as a gentleman that Rosette's virtue and my honor are intact," Maurice proclaimed, startled.

"What a shame, my children! If Rosette had lost her virginity, and you wanted to repair the harm you perpetrated, I would be obliged to marry you to save your souls," the saint explained.

Then Rosette spoke for the first time since the Cordon Bleu ball.

"That can be arranged this very night, *mon père*. Pretend that it has already happened. And now, please, save our souls," she said, flushed and sounding determined.

The saint possessed an admirable flexibility in getting around rules he considered inconvenient. With the same childish imprudence with which he defied the church, he often chopped a little off the body of the law, and until that moment no religious or civil authority had dared call attention to him. He took a barber's razor out of a box, wet the blade in his glass of wine, and ordered the lovers to roll up their sleeves and hold out an arm. Without hesitation he cut a slit on Maurice's wrist with the dexterity of someone who has performed the operation several times. Maurice grunted and sucked the cut while Rosette pressed her lips together and closed her eyes with her hand still outstretched. The priest joined their arms, rubbing Rosette's blood into Maurice's small wound.

"Blood is always red, as you see, but if anyone asks, now you can say that you have black blood, Maurice. So the wedding will be legal," the priest explained, wiping the knife on his sleeve as Tété tore her kerchief to bandage their wrists.

"Let us go into the church. I will ask Sister Lucie to be witness to this impromptu marriage," said Père Antoine.

"Just a minute, *mon père*." Tété held him back. "We have not resolved the fact that these children are half siblings."

"But what are you saying, daughter?" the saint exclaimed.

"You know Rosette's story, *mon père*; I told you that Monsieur Toulouse Valmorain was the father, and you know he is also the father of Maurice."

"I didn't remember, my memory is bad." Père Antoine dropped into a chair, defeated. "I cannot marry these young ones, Tété. It is one thing to mock human law, which can be absurd, but something different to mock the law of God. . . ."

With lowered heads they left Père Antoine's little house. Rosette was trying to contain her tears, and Maurice, upset, was supporting her, his arm around her waist. "How I wanted to help you, my children! But it is not in my power to do so. No one can marry you in this land," was the saint's sorrowful farewell. As the lovers dragged along, disconsolate, Tété walked two steps behind, thinking of the emphasis Père Antoine had placed on that last word. Perhaps it wasn't emphasis but something she confused with the strong accent of the Spanish priest's French, but to her the sentence didn't seem natural, and she heard it again and again like an echo of her bare feet slapping on the tiles of the square, until from being repeated so often in silence she thought she understood a coded meaning. She changed direction to head toward the Chez Fleur.

They walked almost an hour, and when they came to the modest door of the gaming house they saw a line of porters with boxes of liquors and provisions, overseen by Fleur Hirondelle, who noted down each bundle in her account book. The woman greeted them with affection, as always, but could not pay attention to them and gestured toward the salon. Maurice was aware that this was a place of questionable reputation, and it seemed amusing to him that his *maman*, always so concerned about decency, would behave here as if in her own house. At that hour, in the cruel light of day, with the tables empty, bare of customers, cocottes, and musicians, without the smoke, noise, and smell of perfume and liquor, the salon resembled a tawdry theater.

"What are we doing here?" Maurice asked in a funereal tone.

"Waiting for our luck to change, son," said Tété.

Moments later Zacharie appeared in his work clothes, his hands filthy, surprised by the visit. He was no longer the handsome man he had been; his face was like a Carnival mask. That was how he'd looked since being attacked. It had been night, and he was beaten unmercifully; he had not seen the men who came at him with clubs, but as they did not steal his money or the walking stick with the ivory handle, he knew they were not bandits from Le Marais. Tété had warned him more than once that his overly elegant figure and generosity were offensive to some whites. He was found in time, tossed into a drain, hammered to a pulp, his face destroyed. Doctor Parmentier had treated him with such care that he had been able to set his bones in place and save one eye, and Tété had fed him through a tube until he could chew. The assault had not changed his triumphant attitude, but it had made him more prudent, and now he was always armed.

"What can I do for you? Rum? Fruit juice for the little girl?" Zacharie smiled his new twisted smile.

"A captain is like a king—he can do what he wants on his boat, even hang someone. Isn't that true?" Tété asked.

"Only when on the high seas," Zacharie clarified, cleaning himself with a rag.

"Do you know someone like that?"

"Several. Without going too far, Fleur Hirondelle and I are associated with a man named Romeiro Toledano, a Portugese who owns a small schooner."

"Associated to do what, Zacharie?"

"Let's say importing and transporting. . . ."

"You never mentioned any Toledano to me. Can he be trusted?"

"That depends: for some things yes, for others, no."

"Where can I speak with him?"

"At this moment the schooner is in the port. Surely he will come tonight to have some drinks and play a few hands. What is it you want, woman?"

"I need a captain to marry Maurice and Rosette," Tété announced, to the amazement of the two listening.

"How can you ask that of me, Zarité!"

"Because no one else will do it, Zacharie. And it has to be right now, because Maurice is going to Boston on a ship that leaves the day after tomorrow."

"The schooner is in port. The land authorities are in command here."

"Can you ask your Toledano to lift anchor, move his ship a few miles out to sea, and marry them? Fleur Hirondelle and I will be witnesses."

And so, four hours later, aboard a deplorable schooner flying a Cuban flag, Captain Romeiro Toledano, a small man only a little over a meter and a half tall, who compensated for the indignity of his stature with a black beard that barely left his eyes in view, married Rosette Sedella and Maurice Solar, as the young man had called himself since he broke with his father. Witnesses to the wedding were Zacharie in his gala trappings, but still with dirty fingernails, and Fleur Hirondelle, who for the occasion had put on a long bearskin coat and a necklace of the teeth of the same animal. While Zarité dried her tears, Maurice took off his mother's gold medal he always wore and put it around Rosette's neck. Fleur Hirondelle handed out goblets of champagne, and Zacharie made a toast: "To this symbolic couple of the future, when races will be mixed and all human beings will be free and equal under the law." Maurice, who had often heard the same words from his teacher Cobb, and who had become very sentimental during his typhus attack, let out a long, deep sob.

Two Nights of Love

For lack of a more conventional place, the newlyweds spent their one day and two nights of love in the tight little cabin of Romeiro Toledano's schooner, never suspecting that in a secret compartment below the floor there was a crouched slave who could hear them. This ship was the first step in that fugitive's journey to freedom. Toledano, Zacharie, and Fleur Hirondelle believed that slavery was going to end soon, and in the meantime they helped the most desperate, who could not wait until that time.

That night, Maurice and Rosette made love on a narrow bunk of planks, rocked by the sea in light filtered through the worn red felt that covered the little porthole. At first they touched tentatively, timidly, even though they had grown up exploring one another, and not a single nook of their souls was closed to the other. They had changed, and now they had to learn to know each other again. Before the marvel of having Rosette in his arms, Maurice forgot the little he had learned in his prancing with Giselle, the lying seductress of Savannah. He trembled. "It's from the typhus," he said by way of apology. Moved by that sweet clumsiness, Rosette took the initiative and began slowly to take off her clothes, as Violette Boisier had taught her privately. Thinking about that sent her into such a fit of laughing that Maurice thought she was making fun of him.

"Don't be silly, Maurice, how can I be making fun of you?" she told him, drying the tears of her laughter. "I am remembering the classes on making love that Madame Violette offered to the students of *plaçage*."

"Don't tell me she gave you classes!"

"Of course—did you think that seduction is improvised?"

"Maman knows this?"

"Not the details."

"What was that woman teaching you girls?"

"Not much, because soon madame had to stop the practical classes. Loula convinced her that the mothers would not tolerate it, and the ball would go to the devil. But she got in lessons for me. She used bananas and cucumbers to explain."

"Explain what!" Maurice exclaimed. He was beginning to find it amusing.

"How you men are, and how easy it is to manipulate you because you have everything outside. She had to teach me somehow, don't you see? I have never seen a naked man, Maurice. Well, just you, but you were a little boy then."

"Let's suppose that something has changed since then." He smiled. "But don't be expecting bananas or cucumbers. You'd be committing the sin of optimism."

"Oh? Let me see."

In his hiding place, the slave lamented that there wasn't a hole between the planks of the deck that he could look through. After the laughing followed a silence that seemed too long to him. What could those two be doing, and be so quiet? He couldn't imagine; in his experience love was much noisier. When the bearded captain opened the trapdoor to let him out to eat and stretch his bones, taking advantage of the noise from all the people gambling and drinking and the darkness of night, the runaway was at the point of telling him not to bother, he could wait.

Romeiro Toledano foresaw that the newly married pair, in accord with reigning custom, would not come out of their retreat. And following instuctions given by Zacharie, he took them coffee and pastries and set them discreetly at the door of the cabin. In normal circumstances Maurice and Rosette would have spent at least three days closed in the room, but they did not have that much time. Later the good captain left them a tray with delicious food from the Marché Français Tété had sent: shellfish, cheese, warm bread, fruit, sweets, and a bottle of wine that hands quickly pulled inside.

In the too short hours of the one day and two nights that Rosette and Maurice had together, they made love with the tenderness they had shared in childhood and the passion that now inflamed them, improvising one thing and then another to please each other. They were very young, they had been in love forever, and there was the terrible incentive of parting: they did not need instructions from Violette Boisier. During some intervals they took time to talk, never breaking their embrace, of things unfinished and of their immediate future. The only thing that made it possible for them to endure the separation was the certainty that they would be together as soon as Maurice found work and a place where Rosette would be comfortable.

At dawn on the second day they dressed, kissed for the last time, and cautiously went out to face the world. The schooner was again anchored, and in the port Zacharie and Tété and Sancho were waiting with Maurice's trunk. The uncle also handed his nephew four hundred dollars, which he boasted he had won in a single night of playing cards. The youth had bought his passage using his new name, Maurice Solar, the abbreviated surname of his mother, which he pronounced "Soler" in English. That bothered Sancho a little, who was proud of the sonorous García del Solar, pronounced as it should be, So-lar.

Rosette was left behind on land, brokenhearted inside but feigning the serene attitude of someone who has everything she could want in this world, while Maurice waved to her from the deck of the clipper that would take him to Boston.

Purgatory

$\mathcal{V}$almorain lost his son and his health at a single blow. At the same moment that Maurice left the paternal house, never to return, something broke inside him. When Sancho and the others were able to get him up from the floor, they found that one side of his body was dead. Dr. Parmentier determined that his heart was not damaged, as Valmorain had always feared, but that he had suffered a stroke. He was nearly paralyzed, he was drooling, and he had lost control of his sphincter. "With time and a little luck you can improve a lot, *mon ami*, although you will never be the same as you were," Parmentier told him. He added that he knew patients who had lived many years after a similar attack. By signs, Valmorain indicated that he wanted to talk to him alone, and Hortense Guizot, who was watching him like an owl, had to leave the room and close the door. His sputterings were nearly incomprehensible, but Parmentier was able to understand that he feared his wife more than his illness. There was no doubt that Hortense would rather be left a widow than take care of an invalid who peed on himself, and she might be tempted to precipitate his death. "Do not worry, I will take care of that with only a few words," Parmentier assured him.

The doctor gave Hortense Guizot the medications and necessary instructions for the ill man, and advised her to find a good nurse; the recovery of her husband depended very much on the care he received. They should not contradict him or worry him: calm was fundamental. As they said good-bye, he held the woman's hand in an attitude of paternal consolation. "I want your husband to come out of this difficulty well, madame, because I do not believe that Maurice is prepared to take his place," he said. And he reminded her that Valmorain had not had an opportunity to change his will, and legally Maurice was still the family's single heir.

Two days later, a messenger handed Tété a note from the Valmorains. She did not wait for Rosette to read it for her but went directly to Père Antoine. Everything having to do with her former master had the power to knot her stomach with apprehension. She supposed that by then Valmorain had learned about the hurried wedding and his son's departure, the whole city knew, and his anger would be directed not against Maurice alone, whom gossips had already absolved—as the victim of black witchcraft—but against Rosette. She was guilty of causing the Valmorain dynasty to be cut off, ended without glory. After the patriarch's death, his fortune would pass into the hands of the Guizots, and the surname Valmorain would appear nowhere but on the stone in the mausoleum, since his daughters could not pass it down to their descendents. There were many reasons to fear Valmorain's vengeance, but that idea had not occurred to Tété until Sancho suggested she watch Rosette and not let her go out alone. What did he want to warn her of? Her daughter spent the day with Adèle, sewing her modest new bride's trousseau and writing to Maurice. She was safe there, and Tété herself always went to pick her up at night, but they were forever on edge, always alert: the long arm of her former master could reach very far.

The note she received consisted of two lines from Hortense Guizot, notifying her that her husband needed to speak with her.

"It must have cost that prideful woman a lot to call upon you," the priest commented.

"I would rather not go to that house, *mon père*."

"Nothing will be lost by listening. What is the most generous thing you can do in this case, Tété?"

"That's what you always say," she said, with a sigh of resignation.

Père Antoine knew that the sick man feared the abysmal silence and inconsolable solitude of the tomb. Valmorain had ceased to believe in God when he was thirteen, and since then had boasted of a practical rationalism in which fantasies about the Beyond had no place; however, seeing himself with one foot in the grave, he had reverted to his childhood religion. Answering his call, the good Capuchin took him extreme unction. In his confession, mumbled through the contortions of twisted lips, Valmorain admitted that he had stolen Lacroix's money, the only sin that to him seemed relevant. "But tell me about your slaves," the priest said threateningly. "I accuse myself of weakness, *mon père*, because in Saint-Domingue at times I could not prevent my head overseer from going too far in administering punishments, but I do not accuse myself of cruelty. I have always been a kind master." Père Antoine gave him absolution and promised to pray for his health in exchange for a generous donation for his beggars and orphans; only charity softened God's gaze, he explained. After that first visit, Valmorain endeavored to make confession at every opportunity so death would not catch him unprepared, but the saint did not have time or patience for delayed scruples and sent communion with another priest twice a week.

The Valmorain residence had taken on the unmistakable smell of illness. Tété went in through the service door, and Denise led her to the drawing room, where Hortense Guizot was standing waiting, dark circles under her eyes and hair dirty, more furious than weary. She was thirty-eight years old and looked fifty. Tété caught a glimpse of four of her daughters, all so much alike that she couldn't pick out the ones she knew. In very few words, spit through clenched teeth, Hortense indicated that Tété was to go up to her husband's room. She stayed where she was, seething with frustration at seeing that wretched woman in her house, that abomination who had succeeded in getting her way and defying no less than the Valmorains, the Guizots . . . all society. A slave! She did not understand how she had let things get out of her hands. If her husband had listened to her, she would have sold that vixen Rosette when she was seven, and none of this would ever have happened. Everything was the fault of that stubborn Toulouse, who had not known how to bring up his son and who did not treat slaves as they should be treated. You could tell he was an immigrant. They come here and think they can play around with our customs. Look how he emancipated that Negress, and her daughter as well! Nothing like that would ever have happened among the Guizots, she could swear to that!

Tété found the sick man sunk among his pillows, his face unrecognizable, his hair awry, his skin gray, his eyes weepy, and one constricted hand tight to his chest. With his stroke Valmorain had acquired an intuition so powerful that it was a kind of clairvoyance. He supposed that he had waked a sleeping part of his mind while the other part, the one he had formerly used to calculate income from the sugar in only seconds, or move dominos, now did not function. With that new lucidity he divined other peoples' motives and intentions, especially those of his wife, who could no longer manipulate him as easily as she had. His own, and others', emotions had acquired a crystalline transparency, and in some sublime instants it seemed he was cutting through the dense mist of the present and moving, terrified, into the future. That future was a purgatory where he would pay eternally for errors he had forgotten or perhaps had not committed. "Pray, pray, my son, and do charitable works," Père Antoine had advised, and the other priest, who brought the communion Tuesdays and Saturdays, told him the same thing.

With a grunt the sick man dismissed the slave who was with him. Saliva dribbled from the slit between his lips, but he had enough strength to impose his will. When Tété came closer in order to hear him, because she could not understand, he grabbed her arm with his healthy hand, and forced her to sit beside him on the bed. He was not a powerless old man;

he still made her afraid. "You are going to stay here and take care of me," he demanded. It was the last thing Tété expected to hear, and he had to repeat it. Astounded, she realized that her former master did not have the least idea of how much she detested him; he knew nothing of the black rock she had carried in her heart from the time he raped her when she was eleven, he did not know guilt or remorse—maybe the minds of whites did not even register the suffering they caused others. Her rancor had choked her alone, it had not touched him. Valmorain added that she had taken care of Eugenia for many years, she had learned from Tante Rose, and according to Parmentier there was no better nurse. The silence that ate up those words was so long that Valmorain finally realized that he could not give this woman orders any longer and changed his tone. "I will pay you what is fair. No. What you ask. Do it in the name of everything we have gone through together, and our children," he said, words bubbling through drool and mucus from his runny nose.

Tété remembered Père Antoine's usual counsel and dug very deep into her soul, but could not find the slightest spark of generosity. She wanted to explain to Valmorain that it was for those very reasons she could not help him, because of what they had gone through together, because of what she had suffered when she was a slave, and because of their children. He had taken the first child from her when he was born, and he could destroy the second this minute, unless she was careful. But she was not able to articulate any of that. "I cannot. Forgive me, monsieur," was the only thing she said. She stood, unsteady, shaken by the beating of her own heart, and before going left on Valmorain's bed the useless burden of her hatred, which she did not want to keep dragging with her. She silently left that house by way of the servants' door.

Long Summer

*R*osette was not able to rejoin Maurice as quickly as they had planned; the winter was extremely harsh in the north, and it wasn't possible to make the trip under sail. Spring came late, and in Boston the ice lasted until the end of April. By then she couldn't make the voyage. Her pregnancy was not as yet noticeable, but she was supernaturally beautiful, and the women around her had perceived her state. She was rosy, her hair shone like glass, and her eyes were deeper and sweeter; she radiated warmth and light. According to Loula that was normal: pregnant women have more blood in their bodies. "Where do you think the baby gets its blood?" Loula asked. Tété found that explanation irrefutable; she had seen more than a few births and was always amazed by how generously women gave their blood. But she was not having Rosette's symptoms. Her belly and breasts weighed like stone, she had dark streaks on her face, the veins on her legs stood out, and she couldn't walk more than two blocks because of her swollen feet. She didn't remember having felt that weak and ugly in previous pregnancies. She was embarrassed to find herself in the same condition as Rosette: she was going to be a mother and grandmother at the same time.

One morning in the Marché Français she saw a drummer beating a pair of tin drums with his only hand. He was also missing a foot. She thought that perhaps his master had let him loose to earn his bread however he could, since as a slave he was useless to him. He was still young, with all his teeth and a mischievous expression that contrasted with his miserable condition. He had rhythm in his soul, his skin, his blood. He played and sang with such joy and enthusiasm that a group had gathered around him. The women's hips moved on their own to the beat of those irresistible drums, and children of color chorused words that apparently they'd heard many times as they battled one another with wooden swords. At first Tété found the words incomprehensible, but soon she realized that the song was in the obscure Creole of the Saint-Domingue plantations, and she could mentally translate the refrain into French: *Capitaine La Liberté / protégé de Macandal / s'est battu avec son sabre / pour sauver son général.* Her knees gave way, and she had to sit on a fruit crate, with difficulty balancing her enormous belly, where she waited till the music ended and the hat was passed. It had been a long time since she'd used the Creole she learned in Saint-Lazare, but she was able to communicate with the drummer. The man came from Haïti, which he still called Saint-Domingue, and he told her he had lost his hand in a cane crusher and the foot under the executioner's ax because he had tried to run away. She asked him to repeat the words of the song slowly so she could hear them well, and thus she learned that Gambo was already a legend. According to the song, he had defended Toussaint Louverture like a lion, fighting against Napoleon's soldiers until he finally fell with wounds from so many balls and swords that they couldn't be counted. But the capitaine, like Macandal, did not die: he rose up transformed into a wolf, ready to keep fighting forever for freedom. "Many have seen him, madame. They say that the wolf roams around Dessalines and other généraux because they have betrayed the revolution and are selling people as slaves."

For a long time Tété had accepted the possibility that Gambo had died, and the beggar's song confirmed it. That night she went to Adèle's house to see Dr. Parmentier, the only person with whom she could share her sorrow, and told him what she had heard in the market.

"I know that song, Tété; the Bonapartists sing it when they get drunk in the Café des Emigrés, but they add another verse."

"What is that?"

"Something about a common grave where Negroes and freedom rot while France and Napoleon live on."

"That's horrible, Doctor!"

"Gambo was a hero in life, and will continue to be in death, Tété. As long as that song circulates he will be a model for courage."

Zacharie did not learn of the sorrow his wife was living because she was careful to hide it. Tété kept that first love, the strongest in her life, a secret. She mentioned it only rarely because she could not offer Zacharie a passion of the same intensity; the relationship they shared was gentle and free of urgency. Unaware of any such differences, Zacharie proclaimed his coming fatherhood to the four winds. He was accustomed to standing out and to commanding, including in Le Cap where he'd been a slave, and the beating that nearly killed him and had left his face badly pasted together could not squelch him: he continued to be extravagant and exuberant. He distributed free liquor to the clients of Chez Fleur so they could toast the baby his Tété was expecting, and his partner, Fleur Hirondelle, had to restrain him; these were not times to squander money or provoke envy. Nothing was so annoying to the Americans as a black man who swaggered.

Rosette kept them up to date with news from Maurice, which arrived with a delay of two or three months. After hearing the details of Maurice's story, Professor Harrison Cobb offered him hospitality in his house, where he was living with a widowed sister and his mother, a dotty old woman who ate flowers. Months later, when he learned that Rosette was pregnant and would give birth in November, Cobb asked him not to look for another lodging but to bring his family to live with them. Agatha, his sister, was more enthusiastic than anyone; Rosette could help her look after her mother, and the presence of the baby would cheer them all. That enormous, drafty house, with empty rooms no one had stepped into for many years and ancestors keeping guard from their portraits on the walls, needed a loving couple and a baby, she announced.

Maurice realized that Rosette would not be able to travel in summer either, and resigned himself to a separation that was going to last more than a year, until she had recovered from the birth and the baby could safely make the journey. In the meantime, he nourished love with a river of letters, as he had always done, and concentrated on studying in every free minute. Harrison Cobb hired him as his secretary, paying much more than was fitting to file his papers and help him prepare his classes, a light load that left Maurice time to study law and the only thing Cobb considered important: the abolitionist movement. Together they attended public meetings, edited pamphlets, visited newspapers, businesses, and offices, and spoke in churches, clubs, theaters, and universities. Harrison Cobb found in Maurice the son he had never had and the companion he had dreamed of to join in the struggle. With that youth at his side, the triumph of his ideals seemed within reach. His sister, Agatha, also an abolitionist, like all the Cobbs, even the lady who ate flowers, counted the days until they would go to the port to welcome Rosette and the baby. A family of mixed blood was the best thing that could happen to them; it was the incarnation of the equality they preached, the most convincing proof that races can and must be mixed and live together in peace. What an impact Maurice would have when he appeared in public with his wife of color and his child to defend emancipation! That would be more eloquent than a million pamphlets. To Maurice the fiery speeches of his benefactors seemed a little absurd since he had never thought of Rosette as any different from him.

The summer of 1806 became very long and brought a cholera epidemic and several fires to New Orleans. Toulouse Valmorain, along with the nun who was looking after him, was moved to the plantation, where the family always went to survive the worst heat of the season. Parmentier diagnosed his patient's health as stable and believed that moving him to the country would surely improve it. His medicines, which Hortense dissolved in his soup because he refused to take them, had not improved his nature. He had become quarrelsome, antagonistic, so much so that he could not stand himself. Everything irritated him, from the scratchiness of the diapers to the innocent laughter of his daughters in the garden, but more than anything, Maurice. He had fresh in his memory every stage of his son's life. He remembered every word they'd spoken at the end and had gone over them a thousand times, looking for the explanation of that so painful and definitive rupture. He believed that Maurice had inherited the madness of his maternal family. Through his veins ran the weak blood of Eugenia García del Solar, not the strong blood of the Valmorains. He did not recognize anything of himself in that son. Maurice was like his mother—the same green eyes, the same sick inclination toward fantasy, the same impulse to destroy himself.

Contrary to what Dr. Parmentier believed, his patient did not find rest at the plantation but only further worries, since he could plainly watch the deterioration Sancho had anticipated. Owen Murphy had gone off to the north with all his family to occupy the land they had so laboriously acquired after working thirty years as beasts of burden. In his place was a young manager recommended by Hortense's father. The day after he arrived, Valmorain decided to look for a different man; this one lacked experience in running a plantation of that size. Production had decreased notably and the slaves seemed defiant. The logical thing would have been for Sancho to take charge of those problems, but it became obvious to Valmorain that his partner played only a decorative role. That forced him to lean on Hortense, even knowing that the more power she had the deeper he sank into his invalid's chair.

Sancho had discreetly proposed to reconcile Valmorain and Maurice. He had to do it without raising the suspicions of Hortense Guizot, for whom things were working out better than she had planned now that she had control over her husband and all his wealth. Sancho kept in contact with his nephew through letters, brief, he said, because he did not write well in French; in Spanish he wrote better than Góngora, he told everyone, though no one around him knew who Góngora was. Maurice answered with details of his life in Boston and profuse thanks for the help he was giving his wife. Rosette had told him she often received money from his uncle, though Sancho never mentioned it. Maurice also commented on the ant-size steps the abolitionist movement was taking and the other subject he was obsessed with: the Lewis and Clark expedition sent by President Jefferson to explore the Missouri river. The mission consisted of studying indigenous tribes, the flora and fauna of that region nearly unknown to whites, and, if possible, reaching the Pacific coast. The American ambition to occupy more and more land left Sancho cold. "He who has a lot holds nothing closely," he believed, but the mission inflamed Maurice's imagination, and if it hadn't been for Rosette, the baby, and abolitionism, he would have followed the explorers.

In Jail

Tété had her baby girl in the sultry month of June, attended by Adèle and Rosette, who wanted to see at first hand what awaited her in a few months, while Loula and Violette walked up and down the street, as nervous as Zacharie. When she held the baby in her arms, Tété wept with happiness: she could love her daughter without fear she would be taken from her. This baby girl was hers. She would have to protect her against illness, accidents, and other natural misfortunes, as one did with all children, but not from a master with the right to do with her as he wished.

The father's joy was colossal, and the festivities he organized were so generous that it frightened Tété: it could attract bad luck. As a precaution, she took the newborn to the priestess Sanité Dédé, who charged her fifteen dollars to protect her daughter with a ritual involving her own spit and the blood of a rooster. After the voodoo ceremony they all went to the church for Père Antoine to baptize her with her godmother's name: Violette.

The rest of that humid, blazing summer seemed eternal to Rosette. The larger her belly grew, the more she missed Maurice. She lived with her mother in the small house Zacharie had bought, surrounded by women who never left her alone, but she felt vulnerable. She had always been strong—she had thought herself fortunate in that—but now she had become timid, she had nightmares, and was assaulted with ominous presentiments. *Why didn't I go with Maurice in February? What if something happens to him? What if we never see each other again? We should never have separated!* She cried and cried. "Don't think bad things, Rosette, because thinking makes them happen," Tété told her.

In September, some families who had escaped to the country were already back, among them Hortense Guizot and her daughters. Valmorain stayed at the plantation; he still had not succeeded in replacing the head overseer and he had also had his fill of his wife, and she of him. He could no longer count on Sancho to keep him company for he had gone to Spain. He'd been informed that he could reclaim lands of some value, though abandoned, that belonged to the García del Solar family. For Sancho, that unsuspected inheritance was simply a headache, but he did want to go back and see his country, he hadn't been there for thirty-two years, so he undertook a voyage that was going to last several months.

Valmorain was slowly recovering from the stroke owing to the good care of the nun, a severe German woman who was completely immune to her patient's rages and regularly forced him to take a few steps or to exercise his sick hand by squeezing a ball of wool. In addition, she was curing his incontinence by humiliating him over the matter of diapers. In the meantime, Hortense took her train of nursemaids and other slaves back to the house in the city and prepared to enjoy the social season free of the husband who had hung around her neck like an albatross. Perhaps she could manage to keep him alive, as she needed to do, but nowhere near her.

Scarcely a week after the family returned to New Orleans, Hortense Guizot ran into Rosette on Chartres Street, where Hortense often went with her sister Olivie to buy ribbons and plumes; she had kept her custom of transforming her hats. In recent years she had once or twice seen Rosette from a distance, and she had no difficulty recognizing her. This time Rosette was wearing dark wool, with a woven shawl around her shoulders and her hair caught up in a bun, but the modesty of her attire took nothing away from the haughtiness of her bearing. To Hortense the beauty of that girl had always been a provocation, and more than ever now that she herself was choking in her own fat. She knew that Rosette had not gone to Boston with Maurice, but no one had told her she was pregnant. She immediately heard a little alarm bell: that child, especially if it were male, could threaten the equilibrium of her life. Her husband, so very weak, would use the child to reconcile with Maurice and forgive him for everything.

Rosette did not notice the two women until they were very close. She stepped to the side to let them pass, greeting them with a courteous "Bonjour," but with none of the humility whites expected from people of color. Hortense stopped in front of her, challenging her. "Just look, Olivie, how brazen this one is," she said to her sister, who was as startled as Rosette. "And just look what she's wearing. It's gold! Blacks are not allowed to wear gold in public. She deserves some lashes, don't you think?" she added. Her sister, not understanding what was happening, took her arm to move her along, but Hortense jerked away and with one tug pulled off the medal Maurice had given Rosette. The girl stepped back, protecting her neck, and then Hortense slapped her, very hard.

Rosette had lived her life with all the privileges of a girl who was free, first in the Valmorain's house and later in the Ursulines' school. She had never felt she was a slave, and her beauty gave her a remarkable assurance. Until that moment she had never been abused by a white, and she had no idea of the power they had over her. Instinctively, without realizing what she was doing or imagining its consequences, she returned the slap of the stranger who had attacked her. Hortense Guizot, dumb with surprise, stumbled; she broke a heel and nearly fell. She began to scream as if possessed, and in an instant they were enclosed in a circle of curious onlookers. Rosette saw she was surrounded and tried to slip away, but she was seized from behind, and moments later the guards had arrested her.

Tété learned of all this half an hour later. Many people had witnessed the incident; the news flew from mouth to mouth and reached the ears of Loula and Violette, who lived on the same street, but Tété was not able to see her daughter until that night, when Père Antoine accompanied her. The saint, who knew the jail like his own house, pushed aside the guards and led Tété along a narrow passageway lighted by a pair of lamps. Through the bars she glimpsed the men's cells, and at the end was the single cell where all the women were crowded together. Only one girl with blond hair, possibly a servant, was not a woman of color, and there were two little black children in rags, asleep and pressed tight against one of the prisoners. Another had an infant in her arms. The ground was covered with a thin layer of straw; there were a few filthy blankets, a pail in which to relieve themselves, and a large jug with filthy water for drinking. Added to the overall stench was the unmistakable odor of decomposing flesh. In the pale light filtering in from the passageway, Tété saw Rosette in a corner between two women, wrapped in her shawl, with her hands on her belly and her face swollen from crying. She ran to put her arms around her, terrified, and tripped over the heavy chains around her daughter's ankles.

Père Antoine had come prepared; he knew all too well the conditions the prisoners were kept in. In his basket he brought bread and small lumps of sugar to share among the women, and another blanket for Rosette. "Tomorrow morning we will get you out of here, Rosette, isn't that right, *mon père*?" said Tété, sobbing. The priest said nothing.

*T*he only explanation Tété could imagine for what had happened was that Hortense Guizot wanted to avenge herself for the offense Tété had done the family when she refused to take care of Valmorain. She did not know that her and Rosette's mere existence was an injury to the woman. Bereft, Tété went to the very house she had sworn never to enter again and threw herself on the floor before her former mistress to beg her to free Rosette; in exchange she would look after her husband, do as she asked, everything, have pity, madame. The other woman, poisoned with bitterness, gave herself the pleasure of telling Tété everything that came to her mind and then had her thrown out of her house.

Tété did everything possible with her limited resources to make Rosette comfortable. She left baby Violette with Adèle or with Loula and every day took food to the jail for all the women; she was sure that Rosette would share anything she received, and she could not bear the idea that her daughter would be hungry. She had to leave the provisions with the guards; they only rarely let her go in, and she didn't know how much they gave to the prisoners and how much they appropriated. Violette and Zacharie provided the money, and Tété spent half the night cooking. Since she was also working and taking care of her baby, she was always exhausted. She remembered that Tante Rose prevented contagious illnesses with boiled water and begged the women not to drink from the water in the jug, even if they were dying of thirst, only the tea she brought them. In previous months several women had died of cholera. As it was already cold at night, she got wraps and more blankets for all of them—her daughter could not be the only one with warm clothing— but the damp straw on the ground and the water that seeped through the walls gave Rosette a pain in her chest and a persistent cough. She was not the only one sick; another was much worse from a gangrened wound caused by the shackles. At Tété's insistence, Père Antoine got permission to take the woman to the nuns' hospital. The others did not see her again, but a week later learned her leg had been amputated.

Rosette did not want them to notify Maurice of what had happened; she was sure that she was going to be free before the letter could reach him, but justice lagged along. Six weeks went by before the judge reviewed her case, and he acted with relative speed only because she was a free woman and because of Père Antoine's insistence. The other women could wait years before they even knew why they had been arrested. Hortense Guizot's lawyer brothers had presented the charges against her as "having physically attacked a white woman." The sentence consisted of lashes and two additional years of jail time, but the judge ceded to the saint's insistence and suppressed the lashes in view of the fact that Rosette was pregnant and that Olivie Guizot herself described events as they had happened, and refused to back her sister. The judge was also moved by the dignity of the accused, who appeared in a clean dress and answered the charges without haughtiness but without weakening, despite her difficulty in speaking because of her cough and legs so weak she could barely stand.

When she heard the sentence, a hurricane was unleashed in Tété. Rosette would not survive two years in a filthy cell, even less her baby. *Erzulie, mother* loa, *give me strength*. She was going to free her daughter whatever it took, even if it meant tearing down the walls of the jail with her bare hands. Crazed, she announced to everyone she came across that she was going to kill Hortense and the whole accursed family. At that point Père Antoine decided to intervene before she too landed in jail. Without telling anyone, he went to the plantation to speak with Valmorain. The decision was costly to him, first because he could not abandon the people he helped for several days, and next because he was not accustomed to riding a horse, and crossing the river against the current was expensive and difficult, but he managed to get there.

The saint found Valmorain better than he had expected, though still an invalid and speaking in a tangled tongue. Before he threatened him with hell, he realized that the man had no idea of what his wife had done in New Orleans. When he heard what had happened, Valmorain was more indignant that Hortense had succeeded in hiding the episode from him, just as she hid so many other things, than concerned about Rosette, whom he called "the tramp." However, his attitude changed when the priest informed him that the girl was pregnant. He realized he had no hope of reconciling with Maurice if anything bad happened to Rosette or the baby. With his good hand he rang the cow bell to call the nun, and ordered her to ready the boat for a trip to the city, immediately. Two days later the Guizot lawyers withdrew all charges against Rosette Sedella.

Zarité

Four years have gone by, and we are in 1810. I have lost my fear of being free, although I will never lose my fear of whites. I no longer cry over Rosette, I am almost always happy.

Rosette came out of jail infested with lice, wasted away, sick, and with ulcers on her legs from immobility and chains. I kept her in bed, looking after her day and night, I built up her strength with beef bone marrow soups and the nourishing stews neighbor women brought us, but none of that prevented her from giving birth before the time. The baby was not ready to be born; he was tiny and had skin as translucent as wet paper. The birth was quick but Rosette was weak, and she lost a lot of blood. On the second day the fever started, and on the third she was delirious, calling for Maurice. I understood then, desperate, that she was leaving me. I went through all the treatments Tante Rose had handed down to me, the wisdom of Dr. Parmentier, the prayers of Père Antoine, and invocations to my loas. *I put the new baby on Rosette's chest so that her obligation as a mother would force her to fight for her own life, but I don't think she felt it. I clung to my daughter, trying to keep her with me, begging her to take a sip of water, to open her eyes, to answer me, Rosette, Rosette. At three in the morning, as I held her, rocking her with African ballads, I noticed she was murmuring, and I bent down to her dry lips. I love you, Maman, she told me, and immediately after she sighed and her light went out. I felt her frail body in my arms and saw her spirit gently detach itself like a thread of mist and slip outside through the open window.*

The ripping pain I felt cannot be told, but I don't have to do that: mothers know it, for only a few, the most fortunate, have all their children alive. Adèle came in the early morning to bring us soup, and it was she who took Rosette from my stiff arms and laid her on her bed. For a while I let myself moan, doubled up in grief on the floor, and then Adèle put a large cup of soup in my hands and reminded me of the children. My poor grandson was curled up beside my daughter Violette in the same cradle, so small and abandoned that at any moment he could follow right behind Rosette. So I took off his clothes, placed him on the long cloth of my tignon, tying it like a bandolier across my naked breast, binding him next to my heart, skin against skin, so he would believe he was still inside his mother. That was how I carried him for several weeks. My milk, like my affection, was enough for my daughter and my grandson. When I took Justin from his wrapping he was ready to live in this world.

One day Monsieur Valmorain came to my house. Two slaves took him from his coach and carried him to my door. He looked very old. "Please, Tété, I want to see the boy," he asked me in his rasping voice. I did not have the heart to leave him outside.

"I am very sorry about Rosette. . . . I promise you I had nothing to do with that."

"I know, monsieur."

He stood looking at our grandson for a long while and then asked me his name.

"Justin Solar. His parents chose that name because it means justice. If he had been a girl, they would have called her Justine," I explained.

"Ay! I hope to live long enough for me to correct some of my errors," he said, and I thought he was going to cry.

"We all make mistakes, monsieur."

"This boy is a Valmorain by his father and his mother. He has blue eyes and can pass for being white. He should not be brought up among blacks. I *want to help him, I want him to have a good education and bear my surname, as is right."*

"You will have to speak with Maurice about that, monsieur, not me."

Maurice received in the same letter the news that his son had been born and that Rosette had died. He set sail immediately, although we were in midwinter. When he arrived the baby was three months old and was a tranquil little thing with delicate features and large eyes; he looked like his father and his grandmother, poor Doña Eugenia. I greeted Maurice with a long embrace, but it was as if he wasn't there, dried up inside, with no light in his eyes. "It will be up to you to take care of Justin for a while, Maman," he told me. He stayed less than a month and did not want to talk with Monsieur Valmorain, no matter how much his uncle Sancho, who was back from Spain, asked him. Père Antoine, on the other hand, who was always trying to help, refused to act as intermediary between father and son. Maurice decided that the grandfather could see Justin from time to time, but only in my presence, and he forbade me to accept anything from him, not money, not help of any kind, and least of all his name for the boy. He asked me to tell Justin about Rosette so the boy would always be proud of her and of his mixed blood. He believed that his son, fruit of immeasurable love, had a special destiny and would do great things in his life, the ones he had wanted to do before Rosette's death had broken his will. Last, he ordered me to keep him far away from Hortense Guizot. He did not need to warn me.

Soon my Maurice left, but he did not go back to his friends in Boston; he abandoned his studies and became a tireless traveler, he has blown over more land than the wind. He often writes a few lines, and that way we know he is alive, but in these four years he has come only once to see his son. He arrived dressed in skins, bearded, and dark from the sun; he looked like a Kaintuck. At his age no one dies of a broken heart. Maurice merely needs time to grow weary. Walking and walking across the world he will gradually find consolation, and one day, when he is too fatigued to take another step, he will realize that he cannot escape sorrow, he will have to tame it, so it doesn't harass him. Then he will be able to feel Rosette by his side, accompanying him, as I feel her, and perhaps he will come get his son and again be interested in putting an end to slavery.

Zacharie and I have another child, Honoré, who is just beginning to take his first steps holding onto the hand of Justin, his best friend and also his uncle. We want more children, although this house is getting small for us and we aren't young—my husband is fifty-six and I am forty—for we would like to grow old among many children, grandchildren, and great-grandchildren, all of them free.

My husband and Fleur Hirondelle still have the gaming house and continue to be associated with Captain Romeiro Toledano, who sails the Caribbean transporting contraband and runaway slaves. Credit has not been available to them because laws are very harsh for people of color, even for whites associated with blacks, which is the case for Fleur Hirondelle, so their dream of owning several places to gamble along the river has not worked out. As for me, I am very busy with the children, the house, and remedies for Dr. Parmentier that I now prepare in my own kitchen, but in the evenings I give myself time for a café au lait in Adèle's patio of bougainvillea, where all the neighbor women come to chat. We see Madame Violette less, for now she is most often with the ladies of the Société du Cordon Bleu, all very interested in cultivating her friendship since she presides over the balls and can determine the luck of their daughters in the plaçage. It took more than a year for her to reconcile with Don Sancho; she wanted to punish him for his flirtation with Adi Soupir. She knows the ways of men and doesn't expect them to be faithful, but she insists that her lover at least not humiliate her by strolling along the dike with her rival. Madame has not been able to marry Jean-Martin to a rich quadroon, as she planned, because the boy has stayed in Europe and does not plan to return. Loula, who can barely walk because of her age—she must be over eighty—told me that her prince left the military career and lives with that pervert Isidor Morisset, who was not a scientist but an agent for Napoleon or the Lafittes, a drawing room pirate, she swears among sighs. Madame Violette and I have never again spoken of the past, and having guarded the secret so long, we are convinced that she is Jean-Martin's mother. Only rarely do I think about that, but one day I would like to have all my descendants together: Jean-Martin, Maurice, Violette, Justin, and Honoré, and all the other children and grandchildren I will have. On that day I am going to invite all my friends; I will cook the best Creole gumbo in New Orleans, and we will have music till dawn.

Zacharie and I now have a history; we can look to the past and count the days we've been together, add up our sorrows and joys, that's the way love grows, no hurry at all, day after day. I love him as I always have, but I feel more comfortable with him than I once did. When he was handsome, everyone admired him, especially the women, who boldly offered themselves to him, and I fought against the fear that vanity and temptations would take him away from me, though he never gave me any reason to be jealous. Now you have to know the man inside him, as I do, to realize what he is worth. I don't remember how he was; I like his strange, broken face, the patch over his dead eye, his scars. We have learned not to argue over trivial things, only those that are important, which are many. To save him from restlessness and irritation, I take advantage of his absences to entertain myself in my fashion, that's the advantage of having a hardworking husband. He doesn't like for me to walk barefoot through the street because I am not a slave, or for me to go with Père Antoine to comfort sinners in Le Marais because it's dangerous, or for me to attend the bambousses *in the place Congo, because they are vulgar. I tell him none of that, and he doesn't ask. Just yesterday I was dancing in the square to the magical drums of Sanité Dédé. Dancing and dancing. From time to time Erzulie, loa of motherhood and love, comes and mounts Zarité. Then we go galloping together to visit my dead ones on the island beneath the sea. That is how it is.*

P.S.

Ideas,
interviews
& features ...

Life at a Glance

BORN IN PERU and raised in Chile, Isabel Allende is the author of nine novels, including *Inés of My Soul, Daughter of Fortune,* and *Portrait in Sepia,* all of which were *New York Times* bestsellers. She has also written a collection of stories, four memoirs, and a trilogy of children's novels. Her books have been translated into thirty languages and have sold over fifty-seven million copies. In 2004 she was inducted into the American Academy of Arts and Letters. Isabel Allende lives in California.

A Conversation with Isabel Allende

By Deborah McDermott, *Seacoast Online*

This article was published on April 18, 2010, in Seacoast Online, *and is used by permission of Dow Jones.*

AUTHOR ISABEL ALLENDE could not have known that on one terrible day in February this year, an earthquake would shake the island nation of Haiti to its foundation, leaving devastation and death in its wake and for a brief moment in time focusing the world's attention on its plight.

It is nonetheless prescient that at a time when we are riveted by this modern-day tale, Allende publishes a novel that gives us a deeper understanding of Haiti's roots as, first, a country of wealthy French landowners and then as the first black-led republic in the world.

Like so many of Allende's works, *Island Beneath the Sea* is at once intensely personal and contextually political. While it tells a story of half a dozen people who live in Haiti and later Cuba and French-controlled New Orleans in the twilight of the eighteenth century, the sense of place is just as important. Allende weaves real and fictional characters into a rich tapestry that gives the reader a complete sense of this important time in history.

The novel spans the years 1770 to 1810, beginning at a time when Haiti was the richest French colony in the New World ▶

❝ These are people who came from different places in Africa. They didn't share language. All they had in common were drums, a desire to be free, and voodoo. ❞

◀ because of the immense profits from the sugar, coffee, and indigo industries. It continues through a slave rebellion that resulted in the banishment of whites. And it ends in New Orleans on the brink of the agreement between Thomas Jefferson and Napoleon Bonaparte that would result in the Louisiana Purchase.

"I stumbled upon the Haitian revolution. I didn't have an idea of what had happened there before I started my research. This is the only slave revolt in the world that had succeeded," she said. "These are people who came from different places in Africa. They didn't share language. All they had in common were drums, a desire to be free, and voodoo. And they defeated Napoleon's army. Remarkable."

Allende said she actually backed into the novel, the nexus of which occurred while she visited New Orleans to conduct research for her dark and sensual book *Zorro*.

"I was fascinated by the French flavor. When I was researching why, I found that in 1800, ten thousand white refugees from Haiti had to get out in a matter of days because of the slave revolt. They moved there with their white families and their families of color, of course."

What she discovered, when she began to explore prerevolutionary Haiti, is a system of slaveholding even worse—if slavery can be quantified—than that of the United States. As we learn, many Africans came to the Caribbean first and stayed, bought at extremely low prices because new batches came in constantly to replace the sick or dead who were worked to exhaustion. They were more expensive and thus more cared for in America.

She also discovered a rigid society, composed of petits blancs (poor whites), grands blancs (rich whites), affranchis (free people of color), and, at the bottom, slaves. While she draws characters representing all strata, it's clearly the slaves whom she finds compelling—slaves from so many different regions of Africa who learn to communicate through a religion born and formed in Haiti: voodoo.

"Voodoo was an extraordinarily powerful thing, and how they could fight against the cannons of the whites," she said. "They get in touch with loas, like Christian saints, who act as intermediaries. In ceremonies, they go into a trance. The practitioner becomes the loas and acquires the power of loas.

"These slaves would go into battle with the idea that they were invincible. For them, the spirits of the dead, the souls, had gone to the island beneath the sea, to paradise in Africa. Under the sea, because they came by the sea. They would die and it didn't matter because the soul survived. And when they were summoned to war, they all came back. For each man, there were ten thousand souls fighting for them."

For those who know and appreciate Allende's broad body of work—eighteen novels in all, spanning more than twenty-five years—it will come as no surprise that this newest novel also revolves around those who have long held a place in her heart and her spirit—marginalized girls and women.

Tété, the protagonist, was born a slave and remained with her master despite horrific abuse, rape, and neglect. The reader may often ask why, but that would be a mistake, she said.

"We can't judge her from our mentality of people who have always been free," she said.

Allende also warns her readers not to imagine for a moment that this historical tale has no implications for today.

"Today, there are more slaves in the world than ever before," she said. "The difference is that slaves used to be relatively expensive. Now you can buy a slave for $20, no problem. And there's no code that protects them."

She knows what she's talking about. The Isabel Allende Foundation, which she started in 1996, works to help women achieve social and economic justice, and that includes working with many slaves in countries around the world.

"These are girls who have been sold by their families and kidnapped, in Cambodia, Thailand, India, so many places," she said. "If she could get out and go to the police, then what? She has no papers, no identity, she often doesn't know the language, she's terrified. You can go buy her for $50, but then what? You can't give her back to her family, they'll just sell her again."

Allende, who grew up in Chile in what she describes as a very patriarchal family and a very chauvinistic country, said she's always been drawn to the women.

"My obsession in life is to be independent. I was raised to be someone's wife. But I don't want anyone to order me around," she said. "In all ▶

5

A Conversation with Isabel Allende
(*continued*)

◀ my books, I'm drawn to people— not always women, but often women—who are born limited, marginalized, and have to overcome incredible obstacles to own their own life."

Have You Read?

More from Isabel Allende

The House of the Spirits

Allende's debut was an immediate success on
its publication in 1982, garnering critical
acclaim and a huge international fan base for
the Chilean author. It's a grand sweep of a
novel, following the fortunes of the
charismatic Trueba family as they negotiate
the emotional and political upheavals that
beset their lives. Writing in lush, lyrical prose,
Allende introduces clairvoyants, fortune
tellers, playboys, mystics, gentlemen
landowners and reformers to "the big house
on the corner" and the reader to the
enchantment of "magical realism".

"Nothing short of astonishing ... In *The
House of the Spirits* Isabel Allende has indeed
shown us the relationships between past and
present, family and nation, city and country,
spiritual and political values. She has done so
with enormous imagination, sensitivity, and
compassion"   *San Francisco Chronicle*

Portrait in Sepia

As a young girl Aurora del Valle suffered a
brutal trauma that shaped her character
and erased from her mind all recollection
of the first five years of her life. Raised by
her ambitious grandmother, the regal and
commanding Paulina del Valle, she grows
up in a privileged environment, free of
the limitations that circumscribed the lives of
women at that time, but tormented
by terrible nightmares. When she finds
herself alone at the end of an unhappy love ▶

Have You Read? … *(continued)*

◄ affair, she decides to explore the mystery of her past, to discover what it was, exactly, all those years ago, that had such a devastating effect on her young life. Richly detailed, epic in scope, this engrossing story of the dark power of hidden secrets is intimate in its probing of human character, and thrilling in the way it illuminates the complexity of family ties.

"Ingenious … written with inspired elegance. A feast of a novel"

Sunday Telegraph

Daughter of Fortune
Orphan Eliza Sommers goes on a search for love, but ends up on a journey of self-discovery. Brought up in the British colony of Valparaíso in Chile by the well-intentioned spinster Miss Rose (and her more stuffy brother Jeremy), Eliza falls unsuitably in love with the humble but handsome clerk Joaquín. When he heads to California to take part in the 1849 gold rush, Eliza follows him. But in the rough-and-tumble life of San Francisco our unconventional heroine finds that personal freedom might be a more rewarding choice than the traditional gold band on the wedding finger.

"Memory and imagination and myth weave their spells … Allende creates world upon world in dazzling descriptive prose"

Independent on Sunday

Aphrodite

This book of recipes, sensuous stories, aphrodisiacs, and lovers' spells is an irresistible fusion of Allende's favorite things. This personal guide to all things erotic is an international history of seduction through food, ancient and modern stories and poems about sex and eating, titillating recipes, and advice.

"A delightful book, juicy with affectionately prepared vignettes that turn out well every time like an expert chef's soufflés"
MICHÈLE ROBERTS, *The Times*

·····

The Infinite Plan

The Infinite Plan tells the engrossing story of one man's quest for love and for his soul. Gregory Reeves is the son of Charles, an itinerant preacher. As a boy, Gregory accepts the endless journeying and poverty which is his family's lot, never questioning the validity of his father's homespun philosophy of life – the Infinite Plan. But, as manhood approaches, he finds himself possessed by a yearning to escape. Hankering after worldly wealth, he longs to break away from the barrio, the teeming Hispanic ghetto of downtown Los Angeles where his family has finally settled. Gregory's quest, so different from his father's, takes him first to law school at Berkeley, next to the killing fields of Vietnam, then into a headlong (and hedonistic) pursuit of the American Dream. ▶

Have You Read? ... *(continued)*

◀ "A hopeful, warm-hearted, absorbing novel, affirming life and love but not flinching from exploring the pain that inevitably accompanies both"   *Daily Mail*

My Invented Country: A Memoir

Isabel Allende evokes the magnificent landscapes of her country, a charming, idiosyncratic Chilean people with a violent history and an indomitable spirit, and the politics, religion, myth, and magic of her homeland that she carries with her even today. The book circles around two life-changing moments. The assassination of her uncle Salvador Allende Gossens on September 11, 1973, sent her into exile and transformed her into a literary writer. And the terrorist attacks of September 11, 2001, on her adopted homeland, the United States, brought forth an overdue acknowledgment that Allende had indeed left home. *My Invented Country*, mimicking the workings of memory itself, ranges back and forth across that distance between past and present lives. It speaks compellingly to immigrants and to all of us who try to retain a coherent inner life in a world full of contradictions.

"A wise and powerful book"   *Marie Claire*

Paula: A Memoir

With an enchanting blend of magical realism, politics, and romance reminiscent of her classic bestseller *The House of the Spirits*, Isabel Allende presents a soul-baring memoir that seizes the reader like a novel of suspense.

Written for her daughter Paula when she became ill and slipped into a coma, *Paula* is the colorful story of Allende's life – from her early years in her native Chile, through the turbulent military coup of 1973, to the subsequent dictatorship and her family's years of exile. In the telling, bizarre ancestors reveal themselves, delightful and bitter childhood memories surface, enthralling anecdotes of youthful years are narrated and intimate secrets are softly whispered.

In an exorcism of death and a celebration of life, Isabel Allende explores the past, questions the gods, and creates a magical book that carries the reader from tears to laughter, from terror to sensuality to wisdom. In *Paula*, readers will come to understand that the miraculous world of her novels is the world Isabel Allende inhabits – it is her enchanted reality.

"It is a mark of Allende's inspirational storytelling powers that she can transform this tragedy into something rich, vibrant, and positive"   *Sunday Times*

···

The Sum of Our Days
Sequel to her bestselling memoir *Paula*, *The Sum of Our Days* is Isabel Allende's story of her, and family's, struggle to come to terms with Paula's eventual death, aged just twenty-eight. Isabel surrounds herself with her wild and vibrant relatives, a boisterous 'tribe' whose joys, heartbreaks, passions and ▶

Have You Read? ... *(continued)*

◄ disasters she chronicles with verve and lively wit. The sorrow of Paula's death lingers, but ultimately this is a memoir of quiet triumph– a faithful reflection of grieving and remembering from one of the world's most luminous storytellers.

"A vivacious and inspiring memoir about moving on from tragedy and making life bright again"   *Financial Times*

Zorro

An international bestseller, this is the story of the man behind the legend.

Southern California, late eighteenth century: Diego de la Vega is a child of two worlds, his father an aristocratic Spaniard, his mother a Shoshone warrior. Growing up, he witnesses the brutal injustices dealt to Native Americans. Later, following the example of his fencing master, the young Diego joins a secret movement devoted to helping the powerless. But a great rival will emerge from the ranks of the cruel oppressors. How will Zorro defeat him? And will his secret sweetheart claim the prize she so longs for – his true love?

"Absolutely irresistible ... beautiful and disturbing and profound"   *Guardian*

Inés of My Soul

This is the story of a passionate, powerful woman that history forgot – told through the unique talent of the world's finest storyteller.

In an age of savage expansion in the Americas, Inés Suarez's husband disappears to the New World. Escaping the stifling restrictions of sixteenth-century Spain, Inés follows him into danger. Arriving to discover that her husband has been killed in battle, she is quickly thrown together with Pedro de Valdivia, war hero and field marshal to the famed conquistador Pizarro.

Together they wage a terrible, ruthless war against the indigenous Indians of Chile – a struggle that will change Valdivia and his daring conquistadora forever …

"Lush, passionate … breathtaking in scope and vibrant in pace, this is storytelling at its best"   *Financial Times*

City of the Beasts
City of the Beasts is Isabel Allende's first novel for children – an eco-thriller in which fifteen-year-old Alexander Cold has the chance to take the trip of a lifetime. Parting from his family and ill mother, Alexander joins his fearless grandmother, a magazine reporter for *International Geographic,* on an expedition to the dangerous, remote world of the Amazon. Their mission, along with the others on their team – including a celebrated anthropologist, a local guide and his young daughter Nadia, and a doctor – is to document the legendary Yeti of the Amazon known as the Beast.

Under the dense canopy of the jungle, Alexander is amazed to discover much more than he could have imagined about the hidden worlds of the rain forest. Drawing ▶

Have You Read? ... *(continued)*

◄ on the strength of the jaguar, the totemic animal Alexander finds within himself, and the eagle, Nadia's spirit guide, both young people are led by the invisible People of the Mist on a thrilling and unforgettable journey to the ultimate discovery ...

"Allende's writing is so vivid we hear the sounds, see the bright birds, smell and even taste the soft fruit"   *The Times*